24™

DECLASSIFIED

HEAD SHOT

DAVID JACOBS

Based on the hit FOX series created by Joel Surnow & Robert Cochran

HARPER

An Imprint of HarperCollins*Publishers*

HARPER

An Imprint of HarperCollins*Publishers*
10 East 53rd Street
New York, New York 10022-5299

Copyright © 2009 by Twentieth Century Fox Film Corporation
ISBN 978-0-06-177152-1

First Harper paperback printing: May 2009

HarperCollins ® and Harper ® are registered trademarks of Harper-Collins Publishers.

Printed in the United States of America

Visit Harper paperbacks on the World Wide Web at
www.harpercollins.com

10 9 8 7 6 5 4 3 2 1

He was still in the game

Jack stepped into the open in the moonlight so Neal could see he was in position. Neal shouted, "Freeze!"

The shape started, knocking over some garbage cans, stumbling over them, raising a racket as it tried to get clear of them. It fell, crawling on all fours. Jack and Neal closed in from both ends.

The figure scrambled upright and started to run. Jack and Neal moved to intercept him.

The shaggy man started across the open space toward the fence. Jack double-timed at a tangent to cross his path. The shaggy man's hands were empty. If he had a weapon he hadn't drawn it.

He was big, even running stooped forward as he was, big and thick-bodied. Jack neared him. The other looked like the last of the mountain men, with dark, shoulder-length hair and a full beard. He was clumsy, unsteady on his feet.

Jack plowed into him sideways, slamming his right shoulder, upper arm, and elbow into the shaggy man's left side, knocking him off balance. The shaggy man fell sprawling into the dirt, crying out in terror.

He was still in the game. He rolled and got his legs under him, standing on his knees. His hand darted to his right side, drawing a knife worn there in a belt sheath. A hunting knife with a wickedly curved and gleaming eighteen-inch blade.

24 DECLASSIFIED Books
From Harper

HEAD SHOT
TRINITY
COLLATERAL DAMAGE
STORM FORCE
CHAOS THEORY
VANISHING POINT
CAT'S CLAW
TROJAN HORSE
VETO POWER
OPERATION HELL GATE

After the 1993 World Trade Center attack, a division of the Central Intelligence Agency established a domestic unit tasked with protecting America from the threat of terrorism. Headquartered in Washington, D.C., the Counter Terrorist Unit established field offices in several American cities. From its inception, CTU faced hostility and skepticism from other Federal law enforcement agencies. Despite bureaucratic resistance, within a few years CTU had become a major force in the war against terror. After the events of 9/11, a number of early CTU missions were declassified. The following is one of them.

1 2 3 4 5 6 7 8 9
10 11 12 13 14 15 16 17
18 19 20 21 22 23 24

. . . .

**THE FOLLOWING TAKES PLACE
BETWEEN THE HOURS OF
3 A.M AND 4 A.M.
MOUNTAIN DAYLIGHT TIME**

. . . .

Red Notch, Colorado

The Zealot compound's front gate was chained, padlocked, and wrapped with the police's yellow-and-black POLICE: DO NOT ENTER tape.

The Toyota pickup truck that had driven Jack Bauer here from Denver stood idling about twenty feet from the gate, facing it with its headlights on. Jack said, "The police didn't leave any guards behind?"

Frank Neal said, "Why guard the henhouse when the chickens have already flown the coop?"

Jack countered one old saw with another. "Why not? They locked the barn door after the horses were stolen."

Neal made a sound that was half snort, half

chuckle. Then he got serious. "The forensics teams have already come and gone. Local law enforcement's already shorthanded on account of Sky Mount and don't have any men to spare to station out here in hopes that Prewitt and his strayed lambs will come straggling home. That goes for us, too." By "us" he meant CTU/DENV, the outfit to which he was assigned.

Jack pointed out, "You're here."

Neal said, "Thanks to you." It was not an expression of gratitude. "You're the one who wanted to see the compound as soon as possible. Besides, I'm the in-house expert on Prewitt and his cult, if only by default. Lucky me. Who needs sleep?"

"Sorry to pull you out of bed at this hour. Thanks."

Neal made a dismissive gesture with his hand. "The boss says cooperate, so I'm cooperating." His boss was Orlando Garcia, head of CTU's divisional headquarters in Colorado covering the state's Rocky Mountain corridor. "I was up anyway. This whole business has got everybody working overtime. Sure stirred up a hornet's nest."

He reached into a side pocket of the red-and-black-checked jacket he was wearing, fishing out a key ring. "I've got the keys from Taggart, one of the state cops working the case." Neal cut a sidelong glance at Jack. "He thought it was a waste of time to go poking around here in the dead of night, but he's cooperating, too."

Jack said, "What do you think?"

Neal said, "I think I better go unlock the gate." He got out of the cab on the driver's side.

Jack had his own opinion on the subject. He was

only recently arrived in the state and wanted to see the compound for himself at the first possible opportunity and this was it. He wanted to get a feel for the site and the terrain, and there was no substitute for firsthand knowledge. Call it the hunter's instinct, the need to physically experience the stalking ground.

Prewitt and his Zealot leadership cadre, an inner circle numbering more than two dozen men and women, had pulled their disappearing act at approximately this time last night. They hadn't gone alone. Two agents from the Bureau of Alcohol, Tobacco, and Firearms who'd been keeping the site under surveillance had vanished at the same time.

Either set of disappearances, that of the cultists or of the ATF agents, would have set off alarms among officialdom, especially in light of the heightened security attendant on the Sky Mount Round Table conference set to convene later on Friday, this day. Not far from here, more than two hundred of the richest and most powerful individuals in America, if not the world, were already gathering to meet in conclave from Friday through Sunday.

The vanishment of both the Zealots and the agents had thrown a shock wave into the array of law enforcement and national security personnel assigned to protect the three-day conference.

Jack climbed out of the passenger side, glad for the chance to stretch his legs after the ninety-minute-plus drive out from Denver to this site in the foothills of the eastern slope of the Rocky Mountains.

Here, at early Friday morning in the last week of July, the air was cool and crisp, a far cry from the thick, choking heat of Los Angeles that Jack had left behind no more than twelve hours ago. He was glad he'd thought to wear a light jacket for this late-night trip into the hills of Red Notch.

He was in his mid-thirties, sandy-haired, clean-shaven, athletic. He didn't feel athletic, though; he felt off his feed, with an oncoming headache knotting behind his eyes.

The compound was dark, except where the pickup's headlights shone through the gate, an eight-foot-tall construction of chicken wire stretched across a wooden beam framework. The secluded retreat was ringed by a chain-link, barbed-wire-topped fence. Prewitt was a man who jealously guarded his privacy and that of his followers.

Jack looked around. The area was dark in all directions, as far as he could see. The compound was the only sign of human habitation in these parts, save for a two-lane blacktop road at the foot of the rise. A winding dirt road linked the hilltop site to the paved roadway. The compound was presently uninhabited and the paved road was empty of all other vehicular traffic.

The Zealots' mysterious disappearance was part of the reason that Jack had been detached from his post as Special Agent in Charge of CTU/L.A. and assigned to temporary duty—TDY—here in the Rockies. Part of the reason, a big part, but not the only one.

Keys jingled as Frank Neal went to the gate, moving in front of the headlights, casting a long, weird shadow deep into the compound. Neal, a heavyset, fortyish African American, was an investigative agent assigned to CTU/DENV, the organization's regional field office in this sector.

CTU, the Counter Terrorist Unit, was a component of the Central Intelligence Agency. The Agency's founding charter back in 1947 had restricted its operations to foreign soil, prohibiting it from engaging in domestic activities in the United States. Cold War realities had ensured that that prohibition was honored more in the breach than the observance. The nightmare of 9/11 had finished off what remained of those antiquated laws, brushing them aside like cobwebs.

One result was the creation of CTU, an elite branch of CIA whose proactive mission was to detect, deter, and prevent foreign and domestic terrorists from striking within the borders of the United States.

The rugged natural grandeur of this remote highlands locale seemed an unlikely setting for a plot against the national security, but a combination of events had conspired to flag it with a Priority One alert that currently engaged the interests of local, state, and Federal law enforcement agencies, not least of which was CTU.

CTU/DENV had jurisdiction over the incident, and the Sky Mount conference, too, but an extra added element, a special spin on an already loopy curved ball, had sent Jack Bauer from his L.A. headquarters to liaise with the Mile High City team on their home turf.

Frank Neal stood sideways against the front gate, holding up the chain so that he could see the lock better in the headlights. Jack stood to one side of the beams by habit, to avoid being pinned by their glare and to minimize the loss of his night vision.

Neal fitted a key into the lock, opening it. He

separated the prongs from the chain links they were holding together and cleared the chain from where it wrapped the upright gateposts, freeing them.

He opened the gate, exerting some muscle to tear open the POLICE: DO NOT ENTER tape. The thin plastic strands were tougher than they looked, and he had to dig in his heels and put a broad shoulder to the wooden gate frame, throwing his considerable weight into it to snap the tapes. He looped the chain around a crossbar where it would be out of the way and hung the padlock by its hook on one of the chicken wire loops. The yellow-and-black streamers had a forlorn look, like tattered ribbons left over in the aftermath of a party that had already been held and forgotten.

Neal pocketed the key ring and swung the gate open and out, clearing the way. It made a nerve-rattling groan evocative of the opening of a door to a haunted house in a horror movie.

He trudged back toward the truck and got behind the wheel. Jack went to the passenger side, pausing to look back the way they came. A dirt road switch-backed down a long, gentle slope, meeting at its base, at right angles, the blacktop road. No streetlamps on that road; no lamps anywhere, and no streets, either, except for that paved road.

The dirt road was lighter in color than its surroundings and stood out in the moonlight. The paved road was all hard and shiny, looking like a strip of black water in a long, thin canal. All else on the lower slope and beyond was boulders and rock formations, shot through with stands of scraggly pine and clumps of brush.

A big waxing moon hung halfway between the

zenith and the midpoint of the western sky. It would have been hidden behind the mountains in most places along the eastern slope, but not here, not in Red Notch. The notch was just that, a gap between the mountains, though its upper levels were too steep and hazardous for it to serve as a pass for anything less nimble than a mountain goat.

The lowlands were less forbidding down near the base, where the compound was located. The dark hills bracketing it were mostly granite and basalt, but the notch was a different strata, an outcropping of softer, reddish-brown sandstone.

Here wind, water, and, above all, time, had done their work, eroding the sandstone into a jumble of fantastic shapes, forming needles, spires, arches, pinnacles, domes, and buttresses. It resembled a vest-pocket edition of the similar but infinitely more stupendous Garden of the Gods near Colorado Springs.

Beautiful in its way, but alien. Lonesome.

Jack hopped into the cab, where Neal was using the handheld microphone of the vehicle's scanner/communicator to report in to a temporary command post that CTU/DENV had established in nearby Pike's Ford to be closer to Sky Mount for the duration of the three-day conclave. The post's call sign was designated Central. He reported that his mobile unit was at Red Notch and about to enter the site. The dispatcher at Pike's Ford acknowledged the message.

Neal signed off, then drove the pickup through the gate and into the compound. It was set on a flat-topped rise, an oval whose long axis ran north-south. It was open on the east and rimmed on the other three sides by a gnarly, jagged border of weirdly angular rock formations that resembled a mouth of broken teeth. Barbed-wire fencing enclosed the entire area.

A handful of wooden frame and concrete block buildings, crude but functional, utilitarian, were grouped in an arc along the western edge of the oval. Their peaked roofs were steeply slanted, to resist heavy winter snows. A two-story structure with a veranda and second-floor balcony stood at the center. Long, shedlike buildings alternated with single-room cabins on either side of it, with a few shacks and blockhouses straggling off along the periphery.

The grounds consisted of mostly sandy soil speckled with patches of thin, dry, colorless grass. A maze of tire tracks and footprints crisscrossed the terrain. Neal drove diagonally toward a cubed blockhouse at the north end of the oval. He said, "The lab boys have already done their thing, going over the grounds, photographing tire tracks, taking moulage impressions and all the rest, so there's no worry about spoiling evidence. It's all been documented."

Jack said, "What evidence have they got?"

Neal said, "Too much—but of what? That's the question. Maybe you'll be able to supply the answer." The tone of his voice suggested that he believed the contrary. He went on, "All that's known is that sometime last night over two dozen human beings vanished from Red Notch, departing for points unknown. Since then, no one's seen hide nor hair of them."

"Or of the two ATF agents monitoring them."

"Or their patrol vehicle, either."

"They didn't get off any emergency calls or distress signals?"

"Nope. They radioed in at two A.M. according to schedule, reporting that everything was all quiet. That's the last time anything was heard from them. So whatever happened, happened after then."

After a pause, Neal added, "I knew both men, Dean and O'Hara. They were both pros, not the type to be caught napping."

Jack picked up on Neal's use of the past tense in referring to the missing pair. "Think they're dead?"

Neal shrugged massive shoulders. "If they could report in, they would. I can't see the Zealots taking them without a fight. To be honest, though, I can't see the Zealots taking them at all. They're a bunch of wimps, mostly. Armchair revolutionaries. The only thing violent about them is their rhetoric. Or at least that was the case till last night."

Jack said, "They have guns."

"Everybody in this part of the country has guns, it's part of the lifestyle. There were some weapons stockpiled at the compound, true. That's why the ATF was monitoring them. Ever since Waco, they like to keep an eye on cults with guns. But the weapons were ordinary shotguns, rifles, and handguns, legally bought and registered where registration was required. Prewitt's a stickler for that kind of detail; he wasn't going to leave himself open to an illegal firearms rap."

"What do you think happened last night?"

"Damned if I know. But something happened— something violent. There's some bullet holes and bloodstains around."

Jack said, "The background I got on Prewitt was that he and his group were nonviolent."

Neal said, "So it seemed. He took pains to put up

a legitimate front. He took a fall on a tax evasion rap about ten years back and served eighteen months in a Federal pen. Since then he's been careful to be seen obeying the letter of the law."

"Until now."

"Cults like the Zealots are always basically unstable. That's because they're personality cults and the dominant personality is usually cracked."

"Was Prewitt cracked? He seemed more tightly wrapped than most cult leaders, at least publicly."

"Maybe he was wrapped so tightly that he just plain burst. Or maybe having two hundred of the richest folks in America gathered less than thirty miles away finally pushed him over the edge."

Jack said, "It never has before. The compound's been here during the last four or five annual Round Table meetings without incident."

Neal barked a laugh. "Hell, the reason Prewitt set up here was just so he could irritate the Sky Mount crowd. If he could have moved any closer to them than this, he would have, but the Round Table Trust has all the land locked up for miles around.

"Anyway, there's a first time for everything. Especially with the economy in the toilet the way it is now. Maybe Prewitt saw that as a sign his time has come."

Neal halted the pickup outside a concrete blockhouse with a steep-sided roof. He got out, taking a flashlight with him. Jack followed. The concrete cube had a solid, brown-painted metal door and narrow, horizontal slitted windows set high in the walls.

The door was locked. Neal said, "Can you hold this flash for a second?"

Jack said, "Sure," taking the flashlight and pointing the beam at the doorknob.

Neal held the key ring in the light, flipping through it before finding a likely looking candidate. He tried it on the keyhole in the doorknob but it wouldn't fit. After a couple more tries, he found a key that did, unlocked the door, and opened it.

A heavy gasoline smell came wafting out. Jack and Neal stepped away from the open doorway, letting the reeking fumes dissipate. The dark interior was dominated by heavy, hulking forms. Jack shone the flashlight beam inside, revealing a generator in the foreground whose base was bolted to the cement floor. Gasoline drums were stacked against a rear wall.

Neal said, "Gas-powered generator. We had to leave it locked up so nobody came back later to, er, liberate the fuel. Gas prices being what they are nowadays, even some of our local lawmen might be led into temptation."

Jack had nothing to say to that. He held the flashlight while Neal worked over the generator, trying to start it up. The machine sputtered, coughed, choked, spasmed, raced, shuddered like it was going to shake itself to pieces, and finally caught, turning over steadily. The racket was tremendous, sounding like the biggest leaf blower in all creation. The blockhouse filled with fumes, noxious blue-gray clouds that caused Jack and Neal to beat a hasty retreat outside.

Lights started coming on all over the compound. They winked on inside and outside the buildings, beginning as dim, fuzzy glowing patches and brightening as the generator continued supplying a steady source of power.

Some of the buildings had exterior-mounted floodlights that came on. Some had interior lights that came on, too. Other structures remained dark inside and out.

The lights did little to dispel the darkness that hung over the site. They were islands of brightness on a lake of black shadow.

The inside of the generator room remained dark. Neal reached inside the doorframe, groping around for the light switch. He flicked it on, a ceiling lamp filling the space with burnished brightness. The generator continued yammering noisily.

This was Neal's turf, and protocol dictated that he be the one to communicate directly with Central. He went to the pickup and spoke into the hand mic. "Central, this is Unit Three. Over."

Each mobile unit operating in the area had its own designation; Neal's was Unit Three. The comm system worked on a secure tight-beam band whose frequency was in constant automatic change to thwart electronic eavesdroppers. The reply came back: "Unit Three, this is Central. Over."

Neal said, "We have arrived at Red Notch and will be going temporarily out of service. I'll be switching to handset mode. Over."

"Roger that, Three. Over."

Neal signed off, going over and out. He switched off the dashboard-mounted communicator, its green "on" light fading to darkness. He switched on his portable handset, running a comm check with Central to make sure it was working properly. It checked out okay. Neal fitted the handset into a holster fastened to his belt.

Jack was equipped with a similar handset, which was tuned to Central's frequency. He ran a comm check on it, too, as a routine safeguard. It was functioning properly.

Neal killed the pickup's headlights, a zone of darkness springing into being where the twin beams had been. He turned off the engine, dropping the keys into his right front pants pocket.

Jack gave the scene a quick visual scan. Lighting the compound didn't help much. It added to the air of unreality, making it look like a stage set. Shadows were weird, elongated.

He found himself reaching under his jacket, adjusting the way his gun sat in the speed-rig shoulder harness under his left arm so that it settled the way he liked it.

Neal caught what he was doing and grinned. "Kind of gets to you, doesn't it?"

Jack said feelingly, "It looks like a prison camp on Mars."

Neal said, "Come on, I'll give you the grand tour."

Jack had been in his office in CTU's Los Angeles Domestic Unit headquarters twelve hours earlier on Thursday afternoon, meeting with Ryan Chappelle. Jack was the SAC, the Special Agent in Charge of the site. Chappelle was the Regional Division Director. That made him Jack's boss.

Jack regarded a meeting with Chappelle as something akin to having root canal work done. It was sure to be not only unpleasant but costly. The fact that Chappelle had come there to see Jack rather than summoning Jack to see him was a portent that Chappelle meant to hand him the dirty end of a stick. What remained to be seen was the size and shape of the problem he was about to dump in Jack's lap.

Chappelle began by saying, "What do you know about put options?"

Jack said, "Not much, except that it's the kind of tricky financial manipulation that casual investors like me would do well to steer clear of."

It was typical of Chappelle to come at him sideways, rather than just coming out and saying what it was he wanted. Jack sat back and decided to let Chappelle carry the conversational ball. It was an old interrogator's trick. You find out more when you let the subject tell the story in his own way, while at the same time committing yourself to nothing.

Chappelle looked mildly irked. "I didn't come down here to rope you into some stock deal. This is official CTU business and it could be an important lead."

Jack was all open-faced earnestness. "I know. You're a busy man who doesn't waste time on nonessentials. You wouldn't be here if it weren't important."

Chappelle nodded, accepting the other's remark at face value. He went back into his pitch. "I'll keep it simple. A put option is a financial instrument for short selling. Essentially, the investor is betting that certain stocks are about to experience a sudden drop in price. An extreme drop in price. By selling those stocks in advance of the drop, selling short as the term goes, the investor stands to make a steep profit—a killing.

"That's as long as the investor has guessed right, of course. In most cases, no guesswork is involved. The short seller is acting on the basis of inside information. Which is illegal, but easily gotten around by anybody who knows their stuff."

Jack nodded to show Chappelle he was with him so far. Chappelle continued, "The unit of fiscal analysts which I set up has detected a disturbing pattern of recent shorting on the market."

There was no denying that Chappelle was a wizard with numbers. Today's intelligence professionals tend to specialize in one of two areas: HUMINT and ELINT. HUMINT stands for human intelligence; that is, data collected by human sources. This is the side of the trade that concentrates on cultivating informants with access to data desired in a targeted area, including but not restricted to military personnel, government officials, scientists, technicians, diplomats and consular attachés, and members of other intelligence services—usually, but not always, citizens of other countries. Such informants may be motivated by altruism, greed, or extortionary pressures, depending on the individual. It is, in the words of former CIA counter-intelligence expert James J. Angleton, a "wilderness of mirrors," a shadowy world of spies and counterspies, defectors and double agents.

ELINT—electronic intelligence—is the other side of the coin. Here murky human ambiguities are replaced by hard data acquired by hardware. This is the arena of spy satellites, sonar and radar networks, signal traffic, telephone intercepts, and the myriad communications of cyber sphere and Internet. A vast array of electronic eavesdropping devices are deployed globally to monitor transactions in private and public sectors, vacuuming up mountains of data daily in all areas where information is a commodity. It is a realm of technicians, collectors, analysts, and data miners.

HUMINT and ELINT, the twin-chambered heart of the modern espionage apparatus. A built-in tension exists between practitioners of the two disciplines. The HUMINT crowd tends to view the other half as board operators and number crunchers, overly reliant on technology and tone-deaf to the human element. The ELINT crowd too often regard their counterparts as outdated relics of a bygone cloak and dagger age, trapped in a confusing labyrinth of deceitful and unreliable informants. Yet neither branch can operate successfully without the other.

Jack Bauer was an adept of HUMINT, a superb field operative who was equally skilled at the command level.

Ryan Chappelle was a disciple of ELINT, a technocrat supreme with a gift for selecting out significant data from signal noise, separating the wheat from the chaff. One human element he had not neglected, though, was the art of office politics and bureaucratic infighting. He'd risen far fast, and it was no secret that his goal was to win a berth on the seventh floor of CIA headquarters at Langley, the coveted precinct of the agency's intelligence mandarins.

The Fiduciary Special Investigative Unit was a pet project of Chappelle's. The SIU was a team of specialists who monitored the financial sphere, tracking the fluctuations of the global marketplace to detect patterns, profile motives, and forecast actions of private institutions and foreign governments. It had proved to be particularly useful in charting and deciphering the clandestine money movements and funding of both independent and state-sponsored terrorist groups.

Chappelle went on, "In the last few weeks, several million dollars' worth of put options have been bought in the marketplace. The stocks selected were all those of leading American companies and corporations. We're not talking about any failing, fly-by-night market dogs; these are all solid blue-chippers. Media conglomerates, software titans, genetic engineering, pharmaceuticals, even energy-related combines. Representative of the healthiest sector of the national economy—such as it is nowadays. These stocks have been bucking global recessionary trends by continuing to turn a profit."

Jack said, "But somebody is betting that they'll take a fall. Betting big."

Chappelle said, "Exactly."

"Who?"

"I don't know; not yet, that is. Our mystery shorter has taken great pains to disguise himself. He's covered his tracks by using a variety of shell companies, dummy corporations, and similar cutouts. It's like an onion. Peel back one layer and you find another, peel away that and there's another underneath. He's also been careful to spread out his operations in a variety of exchanges, foreign and domestic."

Chappelle's expression was like a clenched fist as he added, "But we'll get him. We'll peel back that onion to get to the heart of it, no matter how clever he thinks he is. It's just a matter of time."

Jack said, "Where do I come in?"

Chappelle's features relaxed, a crafty look coming

into his eyes. "The catch is we may be running out of time. One pattern stands out: all of the stocks our mystery man is betting against are those of companies whose owners and CEOs are attending the Sky Mount Round Table."

The Round Table was a prestigious annual conclave of the movers and shakers of the U.S. economy. It was held each July in the luxurious and scenic splendor of the Sky Mount estate in the Colorado Rockies. Its invited guests were the elite of American business, members not of the Fortune 500 but of the Fortune 50. They occupied the apex of the national socioeconomic pyramid. It was a domestic counterpart to the periodic Bilderberger meetings of Europe's corporate masters.

Jack's bailiwick was the Los Angeles area, but he and his outfit had been much concerned lately with the imminent Sky Mount gathering. CTU/L.A. had increased its surveillance of local hate groups, militant foreign and domestic anti-American organizations, and the far wider pool of their sympathizers, fellow travelers, and enablers, monitoring them for any credible evidence of a plot aimed at this year's Round Table. Two hundred leading lights of big business gathered in one spot at the same time presented an attractive target to the nation's enemies. Or to any crackpot or group of crackpots who happened to hate rich people and wanted to strike a blow at the corporate empire.

No such plot had been detected by CTU/L.A. Which didn't mean that none existed. Such a conspiracy might have evaded their notice, or could be hatching somewhere in a different jurisdiction.

Chappelle's information certainly put a new and sinister slant to the possibility.

Jack said, "The person or persons betting those stocks will take a sudden and dramatic fall may not be gambling at all. It could be a sure thing. A terror strike or other catastrophic event at Sky Mount could send those stocks tumbling. It could wreck the national economy. What's left of it, that is."

Chappelle said, "A logical conclusion. There was a lot of short selling of airline and insurance stocks in the days before 9/11. Somebody knew in advance that those stocks were going to take a big hit and reaped several billions of dollars due to that inside information. We've never been able to pinpoint the profiteer but there's no doubt about the pattern."

He'd been pacing back and forth in front of Jack's desk. He stopped abruptly, turning to face Jack and point a finger at him. "Now couple that with those Colorado cultists suddenly dropping off the board."

Reports about the disappearance of Abelson Prewitt and two dozen of his most fanatical followers from the Red Notch compound had already come to Jack's attention as part of his daily intelligence summary.

Jack said, "I don't doubt that Prewitt would like to bring a mountain crashing down on the Round Table's guests, but I can't see him playing the market to make a profit off it. That goes against his whole crackbrained ideology, what little I understand of it. His theories are a bit too opaque for me."

Chappelle made a hand gesture like he was shooing away gnats. "Maybe he decided that if you can't beat them, join them. He may be cracked but he knows the financial system inside out. Remember, he used to be an economics professor before he went all political."

"Where would he get a couple of million dollars to invest?"

"Good question. Maybe he's found a sponsor; a hostile foreign power, say. Interests inimical to the United States could be backing him. Using him for a cat's-paw to do their dirty work while they turn a big fat profit at the same time."

"Possibly."

"And I know just the man to find out the answer, too, Jack."

"Who?"

"You."

Jack had seen that one coming but there wasn't much he could do about it. He'd try, though. He said, "That's CTU/DENV's turf."

Chappelle said, "The SIU's findings about the short selling gives us an in."

"I don't think Lando Garcia's going to want us horning in." Garcia headed CTU/DENV.

Chappelle said, "You let me worry about Garcia."

Jack said, "I can't just drop everything here and take off for Colorado—"

"Sure you can. Nina Myers can hold down the fort while you're gone." Nina Myers was the assistant SAC of CTU/L.A. and Jack's chief of staff, fully qualified to take over in Jack's absence.

Chappelle said, "Things are relatively quiet here. Sky Mount is where the action is. You're a top field man, Jack. Garcia hasn't got anybody in your class."

"He's got some good people out there—"

"Not like you. You could make a difference. This is important, Jack. Big. I'm surprised you're not jumping at the chance."

"I've got a full plate here, Ryan. I don't like to leave in the middle of things."

"Nothing that won't keep for a few days. And that's all it'll take, a few days. The Round Table ends on Sunday, and by Monday the guests will all have gone their separate ways."

There was no way out. Jack had to say yes. Chappelle was his superior officer in the chain of command; he could order Jack to take the assignment. It didn't matter that Jack was in charge of CTU/L.A. with its mountainous workload, awesome responsibilities, and important ongoing projects and investigations. It didn't matter that Jack had recently ended a long and painful separation from his wife, Teri, and had moved back home with her and his teenage daughter, Kimberly, a delicate situation that was an emotional minefield of raw sensitivities, resentments, and bruised feelings.

It didn't matter that Garcia and his whole CTU/DENV outfit would see Jack as Chappelle's creature, giving the notoriously ambitious Regional Division Director an opportunity to extend his authority by injecting himself into their operations.

It was a classic Chappelle ploy. The SIU's discovery of the money manipulations gave him the opening wedge he needed to put Jack on temporary duty and strap him on Garcia's CTU/DENV as a consultant. If Jack turned up something at Sky Mount, Chappelle could claim a share of the credit. If things went sour, he could wash his hands of all responsibility and hang it on Jack. And if nothing happened and it all worked out a draw, Chappelle would still have the pleasure of having intruded on the turf of his longtime rival Orlando Garcia.

The hell of it was that Chappelle might just be on to something with the discovery of the suspicious stock manipulations being a warning sign of an anti–Round Table plot. But he couldn't just pass the information along to CTU/DENV for them to handle in their own way. No, he had to use it as a way to get his foot into Garcia's door, like a pushy salesman who won't take no for an answer. He certainly wouldn't take Jack's no for an answer.

Jack accepted the inevitable, stifling the sigh that sought to escape him and keeping a poker face. "When do I leave?"

Chappelle said, "Immediately." He rubbed his palms together, a gesture somehow suggestive of a fly anticipating a choice morsel. "I'm counting on you, Jack. They need you out there. I know you'll make Garcia and his crew look sick."

Jack smiled wanly. Chappelle said, "And stay in close contact with me here. Keep me posted on all developments at all times."

Chappelle had gotten what he wanted. The interview was over.

That was the prelude. Jack was now in the center of things, probing the Red Notch compound. The buildings were grouped close together, within walking distance. Neal indicated the central structure, a white, wooden frame two-story building. He said, "That's the admin building, Prewitt's headquarters."

They crossed toward it. It fronted east, its long axis running north-south. A television satellite receiving dish was mounted on the roof, pointed at a forty-five-degree angle at the sky. Floodlights were mounted at the tops of the building's southeast and northeast corner posts where they met the front ends of the second-floor balcony. The lights on the northeast post were dark. Lights were on inside the first and second floors, shining through the windows.

The northeast corner post floodlight hung at a twisted angle. Broken glass littered the ground below it. Jack stood under it, looking up. Neal said, "It was shot out. The lab crew recovered one of the bullets. It's from a handgun but they haven't typed it yet."

Jack nodded.

Four wide wooden stairs led to a porch, a veranda that fronted the building on three sides, all but the west side. The second-floor balcony was similarly constructed. It was as if the builders had shunned the rear of the building, its west face. Behind the back of the building, behind the entire cluster, rose a jumble of sandstone formations, pillars and needles and boulders, all eroded into angular, distorted shapes.

Jack and Neal climbed the stairs to the porch. The front door hung at a tilted angle, half torn off its hinges. The second-floor balcony roofed over the veranda.

A row of tall windows were set in the walls on either side of the doorway. A window to the right of the doorway was broken, leaving a mostly empty frame. Shards of broken glass were strewn on the porch below it. Dark reddish-brown stains, long-dried, mottled the outside of the windowsill and the wall beneath it. The porch planks under the window were stained, too. The stains were pretty big, the largest being bathmat-sized. White chalk markings had been drawn around the stains by the crime lab team. Each marking was tagged with an identifying letter-number combination written in chalk.

Jack said, "Looks like it was broken from the inside out. Like somebody jumped or was thrown through the window. Whoever it was must've been cut up pretty badly. Bad enough to have bled to death, if all that blood came from one person." He looked at Neal. "No bodies were found?"

Neal said, "None."

Jack took a closer look, while avoiding stepping on the chalked-off bloodstains. The stains went to the front edge of the porch. What looked like bloody handprints showed on the top rail of the waist-high balustrade bordering the edge of the porch.

He switched on his flashlight, shining it down on the ground below the porch. Bloodstains extended out in dribs and drabs for a dozen yards or so before coming to an abrupt halt. He said, "The injured party managed to get that far before dropping. Then what happened?"

Neal said, "Your guess."

Jack edged north along the porch, carefully picking his way through, trying to avoid treading on the broken glass and bloodstains. Neal followed, saying, "The lab crew's already photographed and diagrammed everything, so you don't have to worry about messing up anything or altering the scene." Jack noticed that Neal, too, despite his words made an effort, conscious or not, to avoid stepping on glass or bloodstains.

Jack turned left at the corner, following the north branch of the veranda to its end at the building's northwest corner. He shone the flashlight around, noticing a cluster of propane gas tanks connected by pipes to the building's rear.

An open space about twenty yards wide stretched from the backs of all the buildings in an arc to the foot of the jumbled sandstone formations. It was bordered by an eight-foot-tall chain-link fence topped with three strands of barbed wire. The fence extended in both directions, north and south, enclosing the western edge of the oval before curving eastward on both sides to complete the encirclement of the rest of the space.

Jack said, "The compound is completely fenced in?"

Neal, at his shoulder, said, "Yes."

Jack gestured with the flashlight so its beam played across the jagged rock rim beyond the fence. "Any roads back there?"

"A couple of game trails, maybe. Nothing you could get a vehicle through, not even a dirt bike."

"So the front gate's the only way in or out?"

"I suppose there's places along the fence line that could be hopped, if you were determined and athletic enough. But whoever did it would be walking, not riding. And they'd be in for a hell of a hike. Why?"

"No particular reason, just trying to get the lay of the land."

Jack turned, starting back the way he came, Neal falling into step behind him. Neal said, "The Zealots didn't troop out of here on foot, if that's what you're thinking. We know how they left."

Jack said, "How?"

"They've got an old school bus that they use to get around in. They're always driving in a group to the county seat or down into Denver or wherever to hold protest demonstrations or stage media events. Prewitt's big on that. A natural-born pest. The bus is painted blue, kind of a trademark so people'll know they're coming. They keep it in a garage up here and it's not there now, so we figure that's how they left the scene."

"A blue bus, eh? Sounds like it'd be hard to hide."

Neal said grimly, "You'd think so."

They went to the front of the building and went inside into a long, narrow hall. It ran straight through the building from front to back. There were four rooms on the first floor, two on either side of the hall. A staircase led up to the second floor.

The front room on the right was a kind of communications center. That was the room where the window was broken from the inside out. Not much seemed disturbed, apart from that. A floor lamp was knocked over and lay on its side. A mass of moths flew in circles under an overhead light. A couple of workstations were placed around the space, complete with computers, phone banks, printers, fax machines, and the like. A Styrofoam cup of coffee stood on one of the desks. It gave the impression that the desk's occupant had just stepped away for a minute, except that the cream in the coffee had curdled and the cup's contents were a gray-brown sludge.

Each workstation featured a hardcover book in a prominent position. They were all the same book. Jack picked one up and examined it. The title was: *Whip Them with Scorpions*. It was subtitled, *Driving the Money-Changers from the Temple*.

It was a very thick book, a real doorstopper, with lots of fine print and charts and graphs but no pictures.

Its author was Abelson Prewitt. The back cover displayed a black-and-white photo of Prewitt. A big, double-domed cranium topped a long, bony face. A few thin strands of black hair were plastered across his oversized skull. Dark, intent eyes glared behind thick-lensed black glasses. Thin lips were tightly compressed.

Neal said dryly, "His magnum opus. Ever read it?"

Jack said, "I'm waiting for the movie. You?"

"Part of it. I got farther through it than anybody else in my outfit. That's what makes me the expert."

"What's it like?"

"Let me put it this way: if you think people have some cracked ideas about sex—which they do—that's nothing compared to some of the crazy notions out there about economics."

"That bad, huh?"

"Prewitt's like most philosophers cracked or sane, if there are any of the latter. He comes up with a theory that he claims explains why everything works the way it does better than the theories of all the other thinkers who've done the same thing. They're all just chasing their tails around, as far as I'm concerned."

Jack said, "That makes you a philosopher, too." The book was heavy. Jack set it down. He said, "I take it there's no love lost between Prewitt and the Round Table?"

Neal said, "You can take that to the bank. No, better not. Prewitt's not too happy with the banking system, either."

The left front room was a kind of day room. There was a fireplace, a sofa, and a couple of armchairs.

The mantle over the fireplace was lined with books, every one of them a copy of *Whip Them with Scorpions*. A card table with three opened folding chairs grouped around it stood in a corner. The fourth chair stuck half in and half out of the frame of a big-screen TV it had been pitched through.

The left back room was a storeroom for the cult's publications. One wall had a floor-to-ceiling bookshelf devoted solely to copies of Prewitt's masterwork. Tables were stacked with copies of Zealot newsletters and pamphlets. The subjects reflected such topics as the iniquity of the Federal Reserve banking system, the necessity of returning to the gold standard, the Wall Street/Washington, D.C. plot to repeal the Constitution and turn the United States into a slave state, and various world-historical conspiracies by the Illuminati and Freemasonry to rule the world.

The right back room was a combination kitchen and dining room area.

The second floor was reserved for a double set of private living quarters. Neal said, "It's split in two. One half is Prewitt's, the other belongs to Ingrid Thaler, his second-in-command."

Prewitt's rooms were stark, spare, ascetic, almost monklike in their spartan simplicity. There was a copy of his book on the bedside night table, another on his writing desk and a third on a small bookshelf that also contained copies of Plato's *Republic*, the Bible, a complete edition of Shakespeare's works, a dictionary and thesaurus.

Ingrid Thaler's suite was tastefully decorated, handsomely appointed, and expensively furnished. She certainly didn't lack for any of the creature comforts. One room was filled with nothing but her clothes, shoes, and accessories. The suite was bare of any copies of Prewitt's book. Her boudoir—you couldn't call it a bedroom, it was too luxurious for that—featured a photograph in a silver frame prominently displayed on top of a dresser cabinet. It depicted a glamorous woman in her forties with an upswept blond hairstyle, cool level eyes, a sensuous mouth, and a lot of strong jaw and determined chin.

Jack said, "Is that her?"

Neal nodded. "That's Madame Thaler."

"She doesn't like herself too much, keeping a framed photo of herself on the bureau. Is she Prewitt's mistress?"

Neal shrugged. "Nobody knows. That's one of the cult's best-kept secrets. But it's no secret that she's his lieutenant, his enforcer, chief executive officer, number two in the hierarchy. She sees that the great man's word becomes law among his followers. The compound is for the Zealots' leadership cadre, their inner circle. The outer circle, the rank and file, live in their own private homes. There's hundreds of them, a large part of whom live in this state."

Jack said, "So there's a good potential depth of backfield on short notice if Prewitt needs to call them up."

"Yes."

"Great."

Nothing in the upstairs living quarters showed any signs of violence, chaos, or disorder. It was as if their owners had just stepped out for a minute.

Jack and Neal went downstairs and outside, standing on the front porch. Neal got out a pack of cigarettes. "Smoke?"

Jack said, "No, thanks."

Neal shook loose a cigarette and lit up. He said after a pause, "Anything about the scene speak to you?"

Jack shook his head. "Nothing yet. Weird. Maybe they had some kind of palace coup or something."

Neal said, "That's as good a theory as any. But where did they all go? And why?"

The admin building was bracketed by a pair of identical one-story, cabin-style structures. Neal indicated first the one on the south, then the one to the north. "That's the men's barracks, the other's the women's barracks. Prewitt doesn't just have some funny ideas about economics, he's got some about sex, too."

Jack said, "Do tell."

"To be in the leadership cadre at Red Notch, you've got to dissolve all previous relationships. A married couple can't stay married, at least not to each other. The men bunk in one barracks, the women in another. From time to time Prewitt, or more precisely Ingrid, pairs up a couple to, as they put up, gratify their natural physical urges. There's a couple of smaller bungalow units for their conjugal visitations. That's usually a reward for some meritorious service to the cult. They keep juggling the partners around to keep any permanent relationships from forming. The only permanent relationship that's allowed is to the cause of Zealotry."

"No children in the compound?"

"No, they're too smart for that. With all that partner-swapping going on, they won't risk any charges like child endangerment or contributing to the delinquency of a minor. Prewitt's done time on a tax rap once; since then, he's been damned careful not to give the law any cause to go poking around in the compound."

Jack said, "Until now, on the eve of the Round Table."

Neal said, "Even then, there's not much to go on. The Zealots are free to come and go as they please, there's no law against that. The broken glass and bloodstains and bullet holes are suspicious, but a good lawyer could probably explain them away. Especially with the Zealots cooperating in the cover-up. They could always claim a party got out of hand or somebody had a shooting accident or something. Luckily the Sky Mount conference gives us a loophole to go poking around on national security grounds."

Neal finished his cigarette. He stubbed it out and put the butt in his jacket pocket, explaining, "Force of habit. Even though the criminalistics crew has been over the site, I can't bring myself to litter the scene."

Jack said, "You mentioned bullet holes. You mean the light shot out here?"

Neal said, "There's some more at the men's barracks. Looks like they had a pretty good brawl over there. Want to take a look?"

"Yeah."

Jack and Neal went down the stairs to ground level and started toward the barracks. Jack glanced back over his shoulder at the admin building, all ablaze with electric lights. He said, "I feel funny about not shutting off the lights."

Neal said, "When we're done here I'll shut off the generator. That'll kill all the lights. Personally I'm happy with as much light as we can get."

"You've got a point there."

The men's barracks was a large single room shoebox-shaped cabin with whitewashed wooden walls and a peaked shingled roof. It fronted east, like all the buildings in the compound, as if they were deliberately turning their backs on the alien other-worldliness of the sandstone piles. Its long axis was east-west, so that its short side faced front.

The upper half of the front door consisted of four framed glass panes; they were all broken. A horizontal line of a half-dozen bullet holes pierced the wall to the left of the door below the window cell. On the right side, one of the windowpanes displayed a bullet hole with a corona of spidery cracks. Jack said, "Some party."

He and Neal went inside. An open central aisle was flanked on either side by rows of double-decker bunk beds set at right angles to the center space. Gray metal wardrobe cabinets like gym lockers stood against the far walls between the bunk beds. The floor was uncarpeted wood.

There were bloodstains on the floor and some of the mattresses. A couple of the bunk beds were askew and some of the walls were pocked with bullet holes. Neal said, "Yeah, some party."

He and Jack went back outside. Some bats flitted out from under the eaves, whirling and pinwheeling aloft in seemingly random, zigzag patterns. Jack's hand was under his coat, touching the butt of the gun holstered under his arm. Neal saw it and grinned. Jack grinned, too, a bit sheepishly, bringing his hand out empty and letting it fall to his side.

Neal pointed out the next buildings south of the

barracks. "The near one's the mess hall and the barn next to it is the garage where they kept the blue bus."

They started toward the mess hall. Neal said, "Here's where the Zealots get their chow. Not Prewitt and Ingrid, though. They've got a private chef to rustle up their meals in the kitchen in the admin building."

Jack said, "Rank has its privileges."

The mess hall was a shedlike structure whose long side fronted east. Jack and Neal were closing on it when rattling sounded in back of the building.

The two men froze. Silence reigned for a few heartbeats, only to be broken by a soft metal clangor. Jack whispered, "Don't tell me that was bats."

Furtive rustling and rattling sounds came from behind the mess hall. Jack's semi-automatic pistol, a 9mm Beretta, was in his hand; he didn't even remember drawing it. Neal's gun was drawn, too, a .357 magnum revolver with a shiny metal finish. He said, low-voiced, "It could be a bear."

Jack's face must have reflected his skepticism. Neal said, "No kidding, the mountains are overrun with black and brown bears. Hunts have been curtailed for years because of environmental politics, and the bear population is out of control. Familiarity breeds contempt, and they're not afraid of men."

Jack said, "Let's find out. I'll go the long way around the mess hall, so give me a minute to get in place. If it's a man, we'll take him."

Neal said, "I hope it's a man. If it's a bear, for God's sake don't shoot unless you absolutely have to, if he's charging you. Fire some warning shots, maybe that'll scare him off. Believe me, with all the red tape and paperwork involved, it's less hassle to shoot a man than a bear."

Jack grunted, an acknowledgment that he'd heard what the other had said but that committed him to nothing. He peeled off from Neal, light-footing it at quick time south along the front of the mess hall, down to the southeast corner. Neal rounded the northeast corner, vanishing from sight.

Jack edged along the short south face of the building, keeping close to the wall and crouching low to avoid the oblongs of yellow light shining out through the mess hall windows. More rattling sounded from behind the back of the building.

Maybe it was a bear. Jack's Beretta was armed with cartridges that were made up with a hot hand-loaded powder mix he had on special order. Each round was a potent man-stopper. Would it have the same effect on a charging bear? He'd hate to have to find out. He had no relish for reporting such an encounter to Ryan Chappelle.

Jack halted at the southwest corner of the mess hall, back flat against the wall. He peeked around the corner.

The back of the mess hall wasn't as well-lit as the front. There were fewer windows to let the light shine through. The scarcity of electric light was compensated for by the moonlight. A concrete loading platform jutted out at the midpoint of the building's rear. A Dumpster and a clump of garbage cans stood nearby. A stooped, shaggy figure stood swaying upright among the garbage cans, rummaging around inside them.

Neal stepped out from behind the building's north

face into view, holding his gun leveled at the indistinct shape that stood reeling on two legs.

Jack stepped into the open in the moonlight so Neal could see he was in position. Neal shouted, "Freeze!"

The shape started, knocking over some garbage cans, stumbling over them, raising a racket as it tried to get clear of them. It fell, crawling on all fours. Jack and Neal closed in from both ends.

The figure scrambled upright and started to run. It wasn't a bear, it was a man. A shaggy man. Jack and Neal moved to intercept him.

The shaggy man started across the open space toward the fence. Jack double-timed at a tangent to cross his path. The shaggy man's hands were empty. If he had a weapon he hadn't drawn it.

He was big, even running stooped forward as he was, big and thick-bodied. Jack neared him. The other looked like the last of the mountain men, with dark shoulder-length hair and a full beard. He was clumsy, unsteady on his feet.

Jack plowed into him sideways, slamming his right shoulder, upper arm, and elbow into the shaggy man's left side, knocking him off balance. The shaggy man fell sprawling into the dirt, crying out in terror.

He was still in the game. He rolled and got his legs under him, standing on his knees. His hand darted to his right side, drawing a knife worn there in a belt sheath. A hunting knife with a wickedly curved and gleaming eighteen-inch blade.

Jack's foot lashed out in a front snap kick to the shaggy man's wrist, sending the knife flying from his hand.

Neal came up behind him and laid his gun barrel behind the back of the shaggy man's ear, rapping his skull hard enough to stun him but not so hard as to knock him out. The shaggy man fell forward face-first into the dirt.

Neal's mouth was open, he was breathing hard. Jack said, "Damned funny bears you grow out here!"

Neal said, "That's no bear and no Zealot, either. Who in the hell is he?"

"Let's find out."

• •

THE FOLLOWING TAKES PLACE
BETWEEN THE HOURS OF
4 A.M. AND 5 A.M.
MOUNTAIN DAYLIGHT TIME

• •

Red Notch, Colorado

The shaggy man wore a flannel shirt, overalls, and work boots. He lay facedown in the dirt. Neal stood on one knee beside him, holding the muzzle of the .357 against the back of his skull. He said, "Keep still."

The other grunted something that could have been an affirmative. He remained motionless while Neal's free hand gave him a pat-down frisk, searching him for weapons, finding none.

Jack's gun hand hung along his side. He held the knife that he'd picked up in his free hand. The ball of his foot still throbbed from where he'd delivered the front snap kick to disarm the shaggy man. The knife had deer antler plates inset in the grip, a hilt to keep the hand from slipping, and a long, sharp-pointed blade. He held it up to the moonlight, turning it so that moonbeams glimmered off the steel.

Neal rose, saying, "He's clean. Of weapons, that is. He smells like he hasn't had a bath in a long time. No wallet, keys, or identification of any kind." He nudged the shaggy man in the ribs with the toe of his shoe, none too gently. "Get up. And no tricks. Try anything funny and I'll shoot you in the knee."

He said to Jack, "I don't like guys with knives."

Jack said, "I don't blame you. That's some knife, too. A real pigsticker."

Neal's shoe toe prodded the shaggy man's ribs again, harder. "Come on, get up."

The shaggy man got on his hands and knees, shaking his head to clear it. Neal had him covered with the .357, so Jack holstered his pistol, fitting it into the shoulder sling. He still held the knife.

The shaggy man groaned, rubbing the back of his head where Neal had clipped him with the gun barrel. He rose unsteadily to his feet, swaying. Neal came up alongside him and put the arm on him cop-style, using his free hand, the one not holding his gun, to grip the other firmly just above the elbow, steadying and steering him.

Jack flanked the shaggy man's left side but otherwise let Neal handle the play. He was a visitor, a guest, while this was Neal's home territory. Let Neal have the credit, if any, for bagging a suspect, if the shaggy man should prove to be one. Neal was right about one thing, though; the man was no Zealot. The Zealots' dress code ran to jackets and ties for the men, obedient to their guru Prewitt's admonition that they should always be mindful of making a positive appearance of neatness and cleanliness on the public at large. The shaggy man looked like a tramp, a hobo.

Neal said, "Come into the light and let's see what we've got." He and Jack hustled the shaggy man around the corner of the mess hall, across the north face, and around to the front of the mess hall. The captive lurched forward with a shambling, shuffling gait.

A wooden platform something like a plank sidewalk made a kind of apron along the east face, serving as a kind of unroofed front porch. A lamp mounted over the front door shed a yellow cone of light.

Neal sat the shaggy man down on the platform under the light. The shaggy man rested his elbows on his knees and buried his face in his hands. His long hair fell over the front of his face like a curtain. It was the color and texture of a steel wool scouring pad.

Jack eyed the hunting knife under the light. Its finish was dulled with dark patches, not of dried blood but of rust. He pointed it out to Neal, quietly and out of the hearing of the shaggy man.

Neal nodded. Then he went to work on the captive. "Look up when I'm talking to you."

The shaggy man lifted his head up out of his hands. His raggedy iron-gray beard reached down to his collarbone. It had the texture of a bird's nest. He didn't show much skin between the hair on his head and his face, and what did show was seamed, weathered. Bloodshot watery gray eyes were tucked into baggy pouches between a wide, flat-bridged nose. A threadbare flannel shirt was so grimy that its original red-and-black-checked pattern could barely be made out. A pair of denim bib overalls hung in place by a single shoulder strap; the other was broken.

Neal said, "Who are you? What's your name?"

The shaggy man said, "Lobo . . ."

"Lobo? What kind of a name is that? Lobo what? What Lobo?"

"Just—Lobo. That's what everybody calls me. That's been my name for as long as I can remember." A confused look came over his face. "Which ain't all that long . . ."

Lobo rubbed his face with his hands like he was scrubbing it, trying to rub some feeling into it. Fear stamped his features. He looked up at Jack, Neal, said, "Don't! Don't kill me!"

Jack and Neal exchanged glances. Neal said, "What's all this talk of killing? Nobody mentioned killing but you."

Jack chimed in, "You're the one with the knife."

Lobo said, "I was scared, I didn't know what I was doing!" He rubbed and chafed his right wrist and forearm. "You like to busted my wrist when you kicked it, mister. It hurts awful bad."

Neal was unsympathetic. "You're lucky you didn't get shot pulling a stunt like that. Anyway, the hand's still working. I don't see that anything's broken."

Jack said, "You pulled that knife quick enough."

Lobo said, "To defend myself. I thought you were some of Them." The way he said "Them," you could practically hear it being capitalized.

Jack said, "Them?"

"The devil men!"

Neal scoffed, "That crazy talk won't buy you anything. You're sane enough, so talk sense. And make it quick."

A shift came over Lobo's features, firming them with stubbornness. He looked down, not looking Jack or Neal in the face. He muttered, "I know what I saw . . ."

Jack said, "What did you see?"

Lobo looked up now, staring Jack in the face, studying him. He blinked repeatedly, his watery eyes glimmering. He came to a decision. "Nope. You ain't one of Them."

Jack pressed, "One of who?"

Lobo stared Neal in the face, coming to a quick conclusion. "And I know you ain't one of Them. You got a mean face, but not as mean as they got."

Neal said, "Who's Them? Damn it, man, speak out plain!"

Lobo said, "Them devil men." Tension fled from his face, his expression sliding into slack-jawed relief. "Huh! Maybe you ain't going to kill me after all?"

Jack said, "We're not killers."

Lobo pointed out, "You got guns."

"To defend ourselves. Like you with your knife. You're not a killer. You just wanted to protect yourself. Against the devil men."

Lobo grinned, bobbing his head in agreement. "That's right! Now you got it. So can I have my knife back?"

Neal said, "Don't get ahead of yourself."

Jack said, "You don't need a knife, Lobo. We'll protect you against the devil men."

"So you say. But it's easier said than done. They got Satan's power working for them."

"Remember the Psalm, Lobo: 'I will fear no evil.'"

"You would if you seen what I saw. That's why they want to kill me."

"What did you see?"

Lobo shook his head, sadly. "Can't tell."

"Why not?"

"If I do, they'll have to kill you, too. Nobody is safe who knows the truth."

Neal, fighting down impatience, said, "We'll take our chances."

Jack said, "They'll want to kill us anyway for siding with you, Lobo. So you might as well tell us. The more we know, the better we'll be able to help."

Lobo tilted his head to the side, as if listening to unheard voices. "You may just have something there . . .'Course, bad as they are, the devil men ain't the worst. Oh no." He leaned forward, with an air of one about to impart some great truth. "It's those hog-faced demons you really got to worry about!"

Neal, dangerously calm and soft-spoken, said, "Hog-faced demons, is that right?"

Lobo nodded vigorously. "The gospel truth. The devil men, they look just like us. Like anybody, only more mean-faced. That's how they can walk among us. Two of Them have been dogging me all day, back in the hills. That's where I live, all by myself, in a little hidey-hole I got fixed back up there." He gestured toward the sandstone formations. "Ain't nobody can find me in the rocks if'n' I don't want 'em to, devil men included.

"But I got hungry. I ain't had nothing to eat for two days. There's a hole under the fence that I slip right through sometimes at night. I sneak up in back of the kitchen here and raid them Dumpsters for what I can find. Lawd! The food that these here camp folk throw away would feed an army! Perfectly good food, meat, taters, bread, vegetables, sometimes even cake!" He smacked his lips at the conclusion of the recital.

Jack prompted, "Camp folk? You mean the folks living here in the compound?"

Lobo nodded. "The very same. It's like a church camp, an old-time revival meeting, the way they're always getting together and listening to that ol' preacher of theirs. He'd come on the loudspeaker and jaw to 'em for hours at a time and they'd just be a-setting there in the campground, taking it all in. Hoo-whee, how that man could talk! 'Course, it was way over my head, I couldn't make no never mind of it. But they seemed like decent enough folks, what I seen of them."

His face fell, becoming despondent. "Not that it did 'em any good in the end, though, not when those hog-faced demons came to drag 'em all off to hell last night."

Jack said, "It happened last night, you say?"

"Yes, sir! As I live and breathe. It was only by the purest luck they didn't get me, too! I come sneaking around when the moon was low, like I always do when I plan to do me some Dumpster diving. I was up in the rocks when I seen it, a green fog coming out of nowhere and covering the whole camp."

"Green fog?"

"Green as pea soup, sonny! Damnedest thing I ever seen. Right off I knew it wasn't natural, wasn't nothing that comes from God's good earth. It rose up out of the east and in less time than it takes to tell, it grew into a great big green cloud that rolled right over the whole danged camp and just set on it. Like to froze me in my tracks at the sight of it! I stayed up in the hills to marvel at it and a good thing, too. Else it would have got me, along with the rest of them poor souls."

"The camp folks, the people in the compound."

"None other. They was all sleeping, I reckon, tucked up tight in their bunks when the green cloud come up on 'em. Like a thief in the night, just like the Good Book says. That's when them hog-faced demons showed. Lawd, they must've been vomited up straight out of the gates of hell! You never seen nothing like it, nobody ever did—and pray that you never do!

"Hog faces they had, big ol' long snouts sticking out and big bug eyes a-goggling and staring! Hog faces and the bodies of men! And here's something for you to think on: they didn't come a-riding Satan's lizards or flying in on bat wings, no sir. They drove up in cars! Cars, mind you, just like normal everyday folks out for a moonlight drive! Now, don't that beat all?

"Then all hell broke loose. Them hog-faced demons fell on those poor folks like badgers on a warren of baby rabbits. It was something awful. They just waltzed right into their cabins and houses and carried 'em away. There was screaming and shouting and shooting and all kinds of unholy racket going on. I'm surprised they didn't hear it over to the next county."

Neal said, "You saw all this?"

Lobo's expression was patronizing, almost pitying. "I'm telling it, ain't I? The green cloud covered most of it at first, which was a mercy, but it thinned out and broke up pretty quick, so I seen most of it. The worst of it, sure, when the demons dragged those poor souls out into the open, herding them like cattle to the slaughterhouse. Some they killed straight off, gunned 'em down—seems funny, don't it, Satan's minions using firearms to do the Devil's work here on earth? Guns and cars? Makes sense when you think about it, though. Who better than Lucifer to make use of the modern ways of destruction? No back number him, he's up-to-date!

"The demons loaded every last one of 'em, man and woman, onto that blue bus. A blue bus! Them hog-faces got back in their cars and the blue bus and they all drove off straight to hell! Not before they almost got me, though. Like I said, that green cloud lifted mighty quick and I got antsy to see what was happening. I got a mite careless and showed myself up on the rocks and one of them hog-faces sees me and starts taking potshots at me! Came mighty close, too, but my guardian angel must've been working overtime and the demon missed.

"After that I faded back into the hills and made myself scarce. 'Course, Satan don't give up that easy. That's why he sent two devil men into the hills today to ferret me out. I reckon those hog-faces can't walk around in the daylight. The devil men, though, they look like anybody else, only meaner than most, like I said. That pair was a couple of two-legged rattlesnakes in tandem. Not that it done 'em any good. Trying to track me down in my own hills! Shoot, I seen 'em coming from a country mile away. They were combing the rocks all day until they got tired and went away."

Nobody spoke for a moment. Neal broke the silence at last, saying, "That's some story."

Lobo said, "Every word of it is true. The proof's in the pudding. Look around you. Where'd everybody go? If I'm lying, where'd they all git gone to? Tell me that!"

He looked Neal in the face, then Jack. "No answer, huh? I didn't think so. Well, that's about all of it there is to tell . . . Say, you boys wouldn't happen to have anything to drink on you, would you? I was stone-cold sober last night and I'll swear to it on a stack of Bibles. But I sure could use a drink right about now and I don't mean the nonalcoholic kind, neither. Something with a kick to it. This talking is mighty thirsty work."

Jack said, "Sorry, no."

Lobo said, "Figgers. That's my fool luck working against me." He brightened. "Still, it was working for me pretty good last night, to keep me from getting tooken!"

Neal took a cigarette from the pack and put it between his lips. Lobo looked up hopefully, said, "You wouldn't have a smoke to spare, would you?"

Neal gave him a cigarette. Lobo said, "Thank you kindly." Neal flicked on his lighter, holding the flame to the tip of Lobo's cigarette until it got going, then lighting up his own. Jack instinctively looked away while they were lighting up, to avoid totally canceling out his night vision.

Jack said, "Didn't you see the police searching the compound all day, Lobo?"

"Sure, I seen 'em."

"Why didn't you come down and tell them what you saw?"

"Mister, I make it a practice to keep as much distance between myself and the law as possible. I got no hankering to go back to the state hospital again so the doctors could treat me like I was sick in the head."

Lobo took a long draw on his cigarette, exhaled a cloud of smoke. "Some of them cops had pretty mean faces, too. Could've been devil men for all I know. I sure wasn't going to put myself in their clutches. I laid low until they packed up and went home and I stayed low until that pair that was dogging me in the hills got tired and went away, too.

"Even then I didn't show myself for fear of the hog-faces coming back by night. It was getting late and the moon was low and they still hadn't shown, so I took a chance on breaking cover and coming down into camp to see what I could scrounge up. I was getting powerful hungry, my belly was all twisted into knots. I made my move and that's when you fellows showed up and turned on the lights. I ducked down among all them garbage cans to hide. I was afraid you was gonna search back there and I wanted to get away before you did only I made too much noise and gave myself away."

Lobo smoked his cigarette down to the nub and tossed it away, the bright orange-red tip making a tiny splash of embers when it hit the dirt. He looked up at Neal. "Could I trouble you for another of them smokes?"

Neal gave him a fresh cigarette and held the lighter until Lobo got it going. Lobo said, "Much obliged. You fellows cops?"

Jack said, "No."

Lobo nodded, as if confirming a previously held notion. "Thought not. Cops would've already been whomping on me, beating the piss out of me for drawing my knife, even though I was scared and just trying to defend myself."

Jack said, "We're government men." Neal looked at him sharply, unsure of where Jack was going. Jack went on, "We're part of a top secret outfit set up to investigate satanic crimes."

Lobo cackled, "I knew it! Like the Men in Black."

"We're the Anti-Beast Brigade." Jack was straight-faced, serious. "You're an eyewitness to what happened here, the only eyewitness. We're going to take you to a safe place where the devil men can't get you and you can tell your story. You'll also be able to get cleaned up and get a hot meal."

"I ain't so big for cleaning up but the hot meal sounds all right. You think maybe I could get me a drink or two?"

"I can't make any promises but we'll see when we get there."

"You'll put in a good word for me, won't you? About that drink. After all I seen last night, I sure could use one!"

"I'll see what I can do."

"Let's get out of here then. I don't mind telling you that being bird-dogged by those two devil men day and night kind of got me spooked. I won't mind putting some distance between me and Them."

Lobo rose, standing up. His sudden movement undoubtedly saved Jack's life. Shots cracked; Lobo pitched forward, slamming into Jack, knocking him off his feet.

Jack was still holding Lobo's knife in his right hand and he twisted sideways to keep Lobo from impaling himself on the blade as the other lurched into him. He needn't have bothered because Lobo was already dead, killed by that first shot. But things were happening too fast for Jack to make sense of it all.

They both fell tumbling in a tangle of limbs to the mess hall's wood-planked porch. Jack lay on his left side, with Lobo sprawled half across him.

Jack glanced up in time to see the top of Frank Neal's head explode, spraying blood, bone, and brain matter. It meant instant neural extinguishment, the cessation of all thought and reflex motor action. The body dropped like a stone.

A bullet hole showed in Lobo's upper back between the shoulder blades, marking the shot that had brought him down. His dead weight pinned Jack to the boards. Jack let go of the knife and started wriggling out from under him.

Lobo's body spasmed violently under the impact of a second round thudding into it. The shot had been meant for Jack but hit Lobo instead. Jack clawed out his pistol.

Two figures stood in front of the men's barracks north of the mess hall, barely a stone's throw away. One had a rifle and the other a handgun. A patch of gun smoke like a small, puffy ash-gray cloud hung in mid-air in front of the duo. The rifleman stood with the weapon held at his shoulder, swinging the barrel to get a clear shot at Jack.

Jack fought down the urge to jerk the trigger, squeezing it instead several times to place a couple of rounds into the rifleman's middle. The rifleman went over backward like a tin duck in a shooting gallery.

Jack and the rifleman had had fairly clear firing lines on each other. Jack had been fortunate in that Lobo had been unlucky enough to stand up in time to catch that first bullet that had been meant for

Jack. No such luck for Frank Neal. The rifleman had tagged him with a head shot. Jack and Lobo had gone crashing down to the planks together, and Lobo had caught the rifleman's hasty third shot.

The rifleman had done all the damage; his partner must have been more of a spotter and backup. Now he returned fire with the handgun, loosing a fusillade in Jack's direction. Neither he nor Jack had much in the way of sightlines on each other.

He had a semi-automatic pistol and he must have pumped out a dozen shots. He made a lot of noise, but none of the rounds came close to Jack. He shot out a mess hall window and punched holes in wooden walls, spraying a lot of wood chips, splinters, and sawdust. He was less interested in getting his man than he was in covering his retreat.

He ran north, angling his flight to put the men's barracks building between him and Jack. Jack raised himself up on his elbows, wiping the back of his free hand across his eyes, trying to clear them of the blood that had sprayed his face when Lobo had been tagged. He got his feet under him and hunkered down beside Lobo, feeling his neck for a tremor of a pulse. He knew it for an exercise in futility but went through the motions anyway, confirming what he'd been certain of, that the man was dead. That first shot had done for him, the one that had been meant for Jack.

Neal lay on his back, face upturned to the night sky. It was like the top of his head had been scooped out with a shovel. The rest of his face below the brow line didn't look too bad. Jack knew Neal had put the truck keys in his front pants pocket but he couldn't remember which one so he patted them both down, feeling the keys through his right front pocket.

It's not so easy to pick a dead man's pocket. Jack knelt beside the corpse, twisting his hand at an odd angle to get it inside Neal's pocket. Neal's body was warm with the life that had just been let out of it. Jack's fingers fastened around the keys and fished them out.

A figure darted out from between the women's barracks and the blockhouse holding the generator. The rifleman's partner. He could have done some mischief if he'd thought to disable the Toyota, but the only thing on his mind was escape. He burst out into the open, running east across the oval toward the front gate.

It was a long shot for a pistol, too long, so Jack didn't even bother trying. He started north, double-timing it. Caution and curiosity compelled him to pause to give the rifleman a quick onceover, drawing him to a halt beside the body.

The shooter was middle-aged with a lanky runner's physique. He had short wavy hair, bushy eyebrows, and a mean face. His expression was one of intense irritation, as though he was extremely annoyed at having been shot dead. He wore no flak jacket, no bulletproof vest. Jack's rounds had shattered his chest, one penetrating the heart, negating the need to deliver a coup de grâce to the head.

His weapon was a hunting rifle, a scoped thirty ought-six. A standard telescopic sight, not a night vision rig. Jack snatched up the weapon, shouldering it, but the fleeing gunman was already below the crest of the rise. He put it down and got moving, running to the Toyota.

The triggerman was unknown to Jack, a stranger. No mean feat, since Jack's access to information as

SAC of CTU/L.A. made him cognizant of most of the top pro shooters currently active in the milieu.

He must have been one of Lobo's devil men, part of the team that'd been searching the hills for him. The other half of the duo was fleeing the compound. That much of Lobo's story had been true. And the rest?

Jack reached the pickup truck, jumping behind the wheel and starting it up. He made sure to fasten his seat belt harness, he was going to need it. He drove east, fast, toward the front gate.

Neal knew the area and had said there were no roads into or out of the sandstone piles west of the compound. The two killers couldn't have driven into the compound without having been seen by the CTU agents. Therefore they must have parked their vehicle outside the front gate and entered on foot.

Jack tore across the short axis of the oval, making a beeline for the exit. He paused for an instant at the edge of the top of the slope, scanning the landscape. There weren't too many places where another vehicle could be. It had to be on the access road or the black-top road, or parked somewhere just off either road.

A pair of headlights flashed on behind a clump of brush on the shoulder on the east side of the blacktop road, north of where the access road met it. A dark-colored boxy sedan emerged from behind a screen of foliage. Jack thought it might be a Subaru from the quick glimpse he got of it, but that was only a rough guess. The sedan fishtailed along the shoulder and onto the blacktop, flashing north along it in a big, big hurry.

Jack took off after it. He first had to get to the bottom of the hill. He toyed with the idea of saving time by quitting the road and plowing straight down the hillside but discarded it. A big enough rock could bust a tire or an axle and stop the pursuit before it got started.

The pickup's nose tilted downward as he began descending the dirt switchback road, whipping the steering wheel left and right, standing on the brakes at times, sliding into some of the hairpin turns, whipping through others, laying down fat, feathery plumes of dust as he powered his way down the dirt track.

A couple of heart-stopping instants threatened to see the pickup truck go sailing off the edge, but each time luck or skill or both saw him through, enabling him to thread the twisty course in a speedy blur.

There was a bounce and then a liftoff at the bottom of the slope as all four wheels left the dirt road. Jack felt like a paving stone had been dropped into the bottom of his belly.

A timeless swooping interval came to an abrupt end as all four wheels touched down on the pavement of the two-lane blacktop. The vehicle bottomed out, banging its underside on the roadway with a bone-jarring thud that set Jack's teeth to rattling, but the shocks absorbed the impact and the tires held up without any of them suffering a blowout.

The wheels bit, gaining purchase, squealing as Jack whipped the steering wheel around to make a hard left, then burning rubber as he stomped the gas pedal and the machine bulleted northward, taking up the chase.

• •

THE FOLLOWING TAKES PLACE
BETWEEN THE HOURS OF
5 A.M. AND 6 A.M.
MOUNTAIN DAYLIGHT TIME

• •

Nagaii Drive, Colorado

The road ran north-south, hemmed in by a river on the east and mountains on the west. It ran not in a straight line but in broad, sweeping curves molded to the contours of the river valley.

The pickup truck's engine was well-tuned and possibly customized for speed; there was a lot of power under the hood, as Jack was happy to discover. It handled well on the curves, too.

The sedan ahead knew it was being chased and was doing its best to widen the distance between it and its pursuer. The driver had an advantage over Jack in that he presumably knew the terrain, while to Jack it was all unknown territory.

Jack was a veteran of the Los Angeles Police Department, and while the bulk of his term there had been spent on the SWAT team, he was no stranger to hot pursuit driving. No matter what the locale, a road's a road, and he was a quick study.

The fugitive had been handicapped by having to flee Red Notch on foot, scrambling down the hillside and across the road to reach the place where he'd hidden the sedan. That had cut down considerably on his lead. He was trying to increase it now, while Jack labored to whittle it down.

The scenery shot by in a blur. The river lay east of the road, to the right of Jack's northward course. A thin line of trees stretched along the top of the embankment. Gaps in the tree line afforded glimpses of the river and the terrain beyond it, a long, shallow slope slanting upward for several miles to the ridgeline. The river was about an eighth of a mile wide and flowed southward. It looked fast, frothy and churning with latent power.

The sun was a long way from rising but the sky was lightening in the east, fading from purple-black to royal blue.

This predawn effect was suddenly negated as the pickup truck left Red Notch behind. The notch was just that, a gap between the mountains. The looming bulk of Mount Nagaii appeared to the north of it, a towering rock rampart that rose up and up to dizzying heights. The mountain blocked the low-hanging moon in the west, shutting off the moonlight and throwing the river valley into deep shadow.

A positive result was that the thickened darkness caused the sedan's taillights to stand out more brightly, a pair of hot red dots gliding above the winding roadway.

Jack switched on his high beams, expanding his view of the road ahead. It was a help at the speed he was traveling. There were no crossroads or intersections as far as he could see, no place where the sedan could turn off in another direction.

Events had happened so quickly that Jack hadn't dared risk losing a precious second to the distraction of communicating with Central. He could do something about that now that he was settling into the rhythm of the chase.

The mobile comm unit mounted on the dashboard was a variation of the standard model used by CTU/L.A., so he could work it without too much trouble. He switched it on, its power light brightening to a glowing green bead.

He steered with his left hand, holding the hand mic in his right. He thumbed down the transmit button, said, "Central, this is Unit Three. Over."

Central acknowledged the transmission. Civilian and military police authorities generally use a numerical code system as a kind of verbal shorthand for their radio communications. A "ten-ten," say, means that the unit is going temporarily out of service. Other number codes stand for such things as robbery in progress, shots fired, officer down.

CTU wasn't the police and except for specialized operations, such as those carried out by tactical strike forces, relied on plain speaking and the technological sophistication of their hardware systems to ensure the security and privacy of their communications.

Jack spoke into the hand mic. He had to shout to be heard over the sound of the engine as it ground out the RPMs necessary to keep pace with the sedan. "This is Agent Bauer. This unit was attacked by two shooters at Red Notch. Agent Neal is dead. So is a civilian informant we discovered at the site. One of the shooters is dead, too. His partner is fleeing north in a dark-colored sedan along the road at the foot of Red Notch. I don't know the name of the road but it runs west of a river."

The dispatcher started shouting too, out of excitement. He identified the road as Nagaii Drive. Jack said, "I am in pursuit of the vehicle. The driver is armed with a handgun. He may have other weapons. We're about five miles north of Red Notch and proceeding northward."

The dispatcher had all kinds of questions about the incident that he wanted answered right away. The road started shifting into a series of tricky S-curves that required Jack's undivided attention. The sedan had widened its lead while Jack was talking. He signed off, took hold of the wheel with both hands, and concentrated on driving.

The road snaked around outcroppings and concavities of the mountain, an undulating ribbon unwinding at high velocity. Anxiety gripped Jack each time the sedan's taillights whipped around a curve and out of sight, lessening only when those two red dots came back into view.

Jack drove with one foot on the gas pedal and the other poised above the brake pedal. He put more weight on the accelerator. The engine noise wound up to a higher pitch. He glanced at the temperature gauge on the instrument panel. The needle held steady at the midpoint between the two extremes, right where it was supposed to be. That was good, the engine wasn't running hot.

The chase had been run on the flat with no real

downgrades or slopes to speak of. The road skirted the base of the mountains, avoiding even the foot-hills. That was okay with Jack, he had his hands full keeping up the pace on this course. The road was bare of all but these two vehicles, the sedan and the pickup truck.

Jack sat hunched forward over the steering wheel like a jockey leaning into the saddle. His skull pounded with a splitting headache, the king-sized killer headache of all time.

No mystery about that. It was the altitude. Jack came from Los Angeles, he was a flatlander. But Denver was a mile above sea level and the Red Notch area was higher than that. He wasn't acclimated to the elevation. The experts said that flatlanders should take it easy for their first day or two in the heights to avoid altitude sickness. It wasn't a matter of conditioning, a trained athlete from the lowlands was as likely as an overweight, lazy layabout to suffer ill effects from initial exposure to the rarefied air of the mountains.

Jack's head felt like a railroad spike was being hammered into the center of his skull between the twin cerebral hemispheres. Then he remembered Neal with the top of his head shot off. Jack decided he was damned lucky to have a head to suffer head-aches with. He'd tough it out, let the adrenaline rush of the hunt help power him through it.

The curves started to smooth out, flattening into a long straightaway. Jack floored the gas pedal. The pickup shook from the engine vibration, but it was manageable. The engine roar almost but not quite drowned out the transmissions of the frantic dis-

patcher at Central as he kept firing off demands for
an update on the situation.

The situation was that Jack was closing in on the
sedan. It was only a couple of hundred yards or so
ahead, and the gap was steadily decreasing. Whatever the sedan had under the hood, it lacked the
muscle of the pickup truck, and that lack was inexo-
rably telling.

The sky was lightening. A trestle bridge spanning
the river came into view on the right. A gap opened
opposite it on the left, where Mount Nagaii ended. It
was a crossroad that cut Nagaii Drive at right angles.
A handful of buildings stood at the junction.

The bridge was a railroad bridge, inaccessible to
vehicular traffic. Railroad tracks stretched from the
west end of the bridge, crossing Nagaii Drive and
continuing into the gap between Mount Nagaii and
a mountain to the north of it.

The tracks that crossed the road at right angles
were sunken, the twin rails inset in slotted grooves
in the asphalt. There were no cross ties. A black-and-
white-striped bar and a set of signal lights marked
the crossing. No train was using the line so the signal
lights were dark and the barrier gate was raised to
permit free passage.

A small town was clustered around the crossing.
Town? It wasn't even a village. A hamlet, maybe.
There were a gas station, a diner, a strip lined with
a couple of convenience stores, a post office, and a
handful of houses.

The sedan blew through the crossing with no
slackening of speed. The pickup truck did the same,
flashing over the sunken railroad tracks with noth-

ing but a slight change in pitch in the whirring drone of the racing wheels on the roadway to mark their presence.

Jack glimpsed in the corner of his eye a tiny café fronting the east side of the road. A police car stood parked beside its north wall, facing the road at right angles. Its lights were dark, but he could make out what looked like two figures in the front seat.

He passed them doing about eighty, eighty-five miles per hour. He'd been going faster but had slowed down a hair just to be on the safe side when crossing the railroad tracks. They proved to be no obstacle, so once he'd cleared them he pushed the pickup back up to ninety.

There was a pause while the occupants of the police car woke up or got over their stupefaction at seeing a high-speed chase zip right by them. Then the police car swung out of the lot into the northbound lane, turned on its headlights, switched on the emergency flashers of its rooftop light rack, and took off after the sedan and the pickup truck.

Jack glanced in his rearview mirror, seeing the police car's light rack flickering bright blue and white. They looked bright and happy, like party lights. They were a long way off. The sedan was much closer, the gap between it and the pickup truck closing up.

Telephone poles lining the roadside went by in a blur. Road signs whipped by so fast there was no time to read them.

The road started to slope upward, beginning a long gentle incline that curved slightly to the west, rounding the southernmost limb of Mount Zebulon, the next peak north of the gap beyond Mount Nagaii.

Jack was so close to the sedan that he could make out the outline of the driver's head and shoulders. How to take him? He'd like to take him alive if he could, but at these speeds that would be a tall order. He didn't intend on getting killed himself trying it. The pickup was bigger than the sedan, had more muscle. He could run him off the road, if it came to that. If he came alongside the sedan, he could shoot him. The fugitive had a gun, too, though, and Jack didn't fancy the idea of trading shots with him at ninety miles an hour. No, best to bull him off the road. If the other should survive the crash, so much the better.

The sedan was nearly at the crest of the long incline. A peek in the rearview mirror told Jack that the police car was still a long way behind.

The sedan topped the summit, disappearing down the other side. The hilltop zoomed ahead, and for a split second Jack was looking down at the far side of the slope.

There was a village at the bottom of the hill. There wasn't much to it but it was a metropolis in comparison to the whistle-stop at the railroad crossing. A bridge spanned the river here, too, but this one was for cars and trucks.

A strip of stores lined both sides of Nagaii Drive at the village's center. Jack guessed that was what passed for Main Street, the business district. A dozen or so two- and three-story brick buildings were grouped around both sides of the main drag. A couple of blocks of one-family houses stood on the west side of town.

The intersection of Nagaii Drive and the road to

the bridge formed a square, complete with traffic lights. The lights flashed amber.

A police car came into view in the western arm of the crossroad, rolling eastbound toward the square, its emergency lights flashing.

The sedan got there first, flying through the intersection and continuing north on Nagaii Drive. The police car halted, partially blocking the square.

A second police car appeared, coming from the east branch of the crossroad, rolling west. Its flashers were on, too. It halted in the middle of the square, nose to nose with its twin, the two of them forming a roadblock that walled off Nagaii Drive.

Jack was in a tight spot. He thought about driving up on the sidewalk and swerving around the roadblock, but the sidewalk looked too narrow to accommodate the pickup. It didn't look doable even if the sidewalk had been wide enough, not at the speed he was going. At that speed it looked suicidal. He wasn't sure that even without trying any fancy tricks he could stop in time to avoid crashing into the roadblock.

The cops must have thought so, too, because they jumped out of their cars and hustled to the sides. There were two of them, one per car. One was carrying what looked like a rifle.

Jack's calculations were carried out in split seconds. They weren't so much calculations as reactions. He knew that if he stomped on the brake pedal the brakes were likely to seize up and cause him to lose control of the car. He pumped the brakes instead, manhandling the steering wheel to minimize the inevitable slide.

The tires howled, leaving twin snaky lines of burnt rubber on both sides of the street's painted yellow centerline as the pickup shimmied, fishtailed, and skidded.

The machine slid sideways a good part of the way down the hill, leading with the driver's side. Multiple collisions would have been inevitable if any cars had been parked on either side of the street. Jack needed all the space on both sides of the street to wrestle some kind of control into the pickup.

It was close, very close. The pickup skidded sideways toward the twinned police cars, lurching to a halt less than six feet away from them. The engine stalled out.

The radio still worked, though. Every now and then it squawked out another frantic, near-unintelligible query from the dispatcher at Central.

Jack felt like he'd left his stomach somewhere back on the downgrade, probably at the point where he'd first started working the brakes. The stench of burnt rubber and scorched brake linings was overpowering, stifling. He felt like he could barely draw a breath.

He could see now that what he'd thought had been a rifle in the hands of one of the cops who'd jumped clear of the roadblock was actually a shotgun. It was pointed at his head.

The cop who was wielding it stood on the passenger side of the truck cab. He looked unhappy. He gave off the impression that pulling the trigger might make him happy.

Jack raised his hands in the air, showing they were empty.

A second cop appeared on the driver's side of the

truck, brandishing a long-barreled .44 magnum. Both cops wore Western-style hats that heightened their resemblance to cowboys.

The cop with the handgun was shouting at Jack to get out of the truck. Jack stayed where he was because in order to comply with the command he'd have to use his hands, and he was afraid that if he moved them one or both cops would think he was reaching for something and use that as an excuse to open fire on him.

The cop with the gun used his free hand to open the driver's side door. Pale gray eyes were wide and bulging in a flushed, angry red face. He said, "Get out! Get out of the vehicle!" He pronounced it "vee-hickel."

Jack said, "I can't—the seat belt."

The cop shook his head in seeming disbelief as though this was some new, undreamed-of height of criminal audacity. He stuck the gun muzzle against the underside of Jack's chin and said, "If I see you reaching for anything but that seat belt fastener, I'm gonna see your brains all over the inside of this truck cab."

Jack said, "I'm going to unfasten it now."

"You do just that, mister."

Jack moved very slowly, like he was in a sequence filmed in slow motion. He lowered his arms and worked the seat belt release. It came undone with a click.

The cop grabbed him by the back of his collar and hauled him out of the cab, flinging him out on the street. Jack hit the pavement sprawling, skinning his hands and knees.

The cop with the shotgun circled around the front of the pickup, holding his shouldered weapon so that it pointed down at Jack.

The pale-eyed, red-faced cop said, "Lie facedown on the street and don't you move, boy; don't you even breathe."

Jack did as he was told. He could see that the cop with the .44 wore cowboy boots under his tan pants. The boots had sharp, pointy toes and lots of fancy leatherwork and embossing. They looked expensive.

The cop twisted Jack's arms behind his back, wrenching them as though he'd like to tear them out of the sockets. Steel bracelets encircled Jack's wrists, biting deep, cinching tight.

He grabbed Jack by the back of the neck and hauled him one-handed to his feet. Not by the back of his collar but by the back of his neck. He was strong. Jack stood there with his hands cuffed behind his back.

He looked across the police roadblock, north up Nagaii Drive. There was no sign of the sedan, not even a glimmer of its taillights. It was long gone.

The cop with the shotgun held it pointing muzzle-down. The pale-eyed, red-faced cop was holstering his sidearm. His gun belt was fancy and hand-tooled.

A third police car was on the scene, halted in the middle of the street behind Jack's pickup. It must have been the one that had been beside the café and chased Jack along Nagaii Drive into town.

It yielded two more cops, a male officer and a female one. They both wore Western-style hats. The woman wore her hair pinned up in a bun at the back of her head, below the hat brim.

Her partner was a big, hulking specimen, about six-four with shoulders as wide as an axe handle is long. He was in his mid-twenties, with hair so black it had blue highlights. His hair seemed long for a police officer's. He was clean-shaven, with smooth, bright pink skin. He looked more enraged than the two cops from the roadblock who'd actually made the arrest. That might have been because he had a big, dark patch of wetness staining the crotch and upper thighs of his trousers.

The cop with the shotgun flashed a wolfish grin, showing a lot of teeth and little mirth. He said, "Holy cow, Fisk! What'd you do, piss your pants?"

Fisk said, "Never you mind about that, Cole Taggart! I spilled a cup of coffee on myself when we took off after this lawbreaking son of a bitch!"

"Sure you did."

Fisk indicated the female officer. "It's true! Ask her—"

Taggart said, "Of course Trooper Stallings will cover for you, her being your partner and all." Taggart was the type who obviously liked working the needle, at least on Fisk.

The pale-eyed cop said, "That must've been some hot coffee, Fisk, from the way you're walking around all hunched over and bowlegged, like a little old man."

Fisk said, "Hot? I'll tell the world it was hot! I like to scalded my—"

"Spare me the details. Save it for the medical report."

Taggart chuckled. "That should be some report. Good thing Bryce and me was here to catch this speed demon."

Fisk said, "We'd have caught him. No way he was getting away after causing me to ruin a perfectly good pair of pants!"

Taggart said, "Let's hope that was all that was ruined. Ain't that so, Sharon?"

The female officer said coolly, "You're the one who's interested in what's in his pants, not me, Cole."

Taggart said, "Ouch! That's one on me. Though I guess it's Fisk who's the one who ought to be saying ouch."

The pale-eyed cop, Bryce, said, "All right, can the back chat." The others fell silent. Bryce was in charge.

Jack thought that this was hardly the time or place to try explaining that he was a CTU agent who'd been chasing an accomplice to murder. He said to Bryce, "You'll find my ID in my wallet."

Bryce said, "Shut up." There was no rancor in his tone, which was the same as when he'd told the officers to can the chatter.

Fisk sidled up alongside Jack, peering narrow-eyed at him. "He's got a gun, Lieutenant." He was speaking to Bryce.

Bryce said, "Is that a fact? That's a fine piece of detective work, Fisk. Keep it up and you'll make sergeant in no time." His voice drawled with mild sarcasm. He reached under Jack's coat, freeing the pistol from the shoulder rig. He turned it over in his hands, eyeing it. "Nice piece." He held it under his nose and sniffed it. "Been fired recently, too."

Taggart said, "Looks like we got us a real desperado."

Jack said, "I can explain—"

Bryce said, "That'll take some pretty tall talking, stranger. But you'll get your chance." He handed the pistol to Fisk, saying, "Here, hold this."

Taggart said, "That there's what we call evidence, Trooper."

Fisk took the gun. His heavy-lidded eyes were smoldering, resentful. He called Jack a dirty name and slammed the flat of the gun against the side of Jack's face. Jack went down.

• •

THE FOLLOWING TAKES PLACE
BETWEEN THE HOURS OF
6 A.M. AND 7 A.M.
MOUNTAIN DAYLIGHT TIME

• •

Mountain Lake, Colorado

The pale-eyed cop said, "Is my face red!"

It was just a figure of speech. His face wasn't red, not really, not the way it had been earlier when he'd held a gun to Jack's head. That had been a product of the heat of the moment, the adrenalized rush of apprehending a suspect. His complexion had since reverted to its normal color, the rugged bronze tones of one who spends much time exposed to the elements in the out-of-doors. His eyes were still pale, though, with clear gray irises that accented the prominence of dark pupils.

His name was Bryce Hardin, and he was a lieutenant in the state police, the head of a Mobile Response Team that had been formed as a troubleshooting unit for the Sky Mount Round Table. The MRT consisted of Hardin; his second-in-command, Sergeant Cole Taggart; and troopers Sharon Stallings and Miller Fisk.

They were all state police officers who'd been detached from their regular duties for this special temporary assignment. They operated out of a substation at Mountain Lake, a site on the lower slopes below Sky Mount.

The substation was a tan brick blockhouse, a minimalist single-story structure with a low, peaked roof. It contained a front desk area, a couple of detention cells, a squad room, Hardin's office, and several back rooms. It was only in use during the warm weather months; winter's heavy snows closed all but the main roads for weeks at a time, making it impractical to keep the substation open throughout the icy season.

Hardin's office was a modest-sized rectangle whose entrance was in one of the short sides.

A window in the rear wall opened on a spectacular view of the eastern foothills and the river valley. Hardin sat with his back to it, facing the office door from behind a golden oak desk. A handsome reddish-brown leather couch stood against one of the long walls. The wall space above the couch was decorated with honorary plaques and citations awarded to Hardin for various achievements in law enforcement. A row of gray metal filing cabinets was lined up along the opposite wall. The space above them displayed framed photographs of Hardin posing with important-looking personages, presumably politicians and suchlike dignitaries.

A pair of armchairs stood at tilted angles facing

the front of Hardin's desk. Jack Bauer sat in one of them. It wasn't particularly comfortable, but even if it had been, Jack was in no mood to appreciate it. He noticed that both chairs were short-legged and set close to the floor, forcing those who sat in them to have to look up at Hardin. Hardin's desk was flanked by a pair of flagpoles mounted in floor stands. The flag of the United States stood on the left and the state flag on the right.

Hardin was in his fifties, with wavy dark hair gray at the temples framing a thick-featured, square-shaped face. He was thick-bodied, heavy in the chest and shoulders. His manner expressed sincerity and frankness. It occurred to Jack that Hardin was something of a politician himself.

Hardin said, "As the saying goes, when I make a mistake it's a beaut! I pulled a real boneheaded move when I apprehended you, Agent Bauer. I had no idea that we were both on the same team, you being a Federal officer and all. Quite frankly—I goofed."

Jack sat holding a towel-wrapped ice pack against the left side of his face, where Fisk had smacked him with his own gun. Jack had seen the blow coming and rolled his head with it, deflecting some of the impact. It had knocked him down and stunned him despite his evasive response. He'd never actually lost consciousness but he'd seen stars for a while. Fisk had slapped him with the flat of the gun and Jack had caught most of it on his left cheekbone. Nothing was broken and his teeth on that side were all intact as far as he could tell. The side of his face was numb and swollen with a purple-brown bruise about the size of a man's palm. The altitude headache he'd been suffering from earlier was as nothing compared to the colossal, king-sized headbanger he was experiencing now.

Hardin had picked Jack up off the pavement and half carried, half dragged him to his patrol car and thrown him into the backseat. The first setback to the MRT's certainty that they had snagged a hot one came when they looked inside the pickup truck and saw its sophisticated dashboard-mounted comm system. Sergeant Cole Taggart had explained it away by saying, "He probably stole the vehicle. We'll get it all straightened out at the substation."

The quartet formed a convoy to the substation. Hardin took the lead, with Jack in the back of his car, a wire safety grille separating the lawman in the front seat and the suspect in the back. Taggart drove the pickup truck. Sharon Stallings drove Taggart's car, while Fisk drove the car that had been assigned to him and Stallings.

Jack had been groggy and his ears were still ringing, so he kept his mouth shut during the drive. He learned later that the town where he'd been stopped was named Random. That seemed fitting somehow.

The MRT convoy climbed Rimrock Road to reach the Mountain Lake substation. Rimrock Road was built on a stony ledge; a cliffside loomed on its west, while an ever-increasing drop over an empty void opened on its east. The road leveled off for a mile-long stretch, at the end of which the ledge widened into a large circular outcropping that was a scenic overlook point.

The substation was firmly hunkered down on that outcropping. It presented a spectacular view, but Jack's interest in sightseeing was nil.

Taggart had had time during the drive to work the pickup truck's comm system and make contact with the CTU Central dispatcher at Pike's Ford. It was a tossup as to which of the two was more startled, the dispatcher or Taggart. Central managed to convey something of the reality of the situation before the convoy reached the substation.

Taggart was unable to communicate directly with Hardin through the pickup's comm system without going through Central, something that he was not minded to do in any case now that he realized there had been a screwup of major proportions. Taggart started playing it cagey, his responses to Central becoming vaguer and more evasive before he finally signed off by saying that someone from the MRT would get back to them as soon as the issue had been clarified.

The convoy pulled into the substation parking lot. Taggart was out of the pickup fast, scurrying over to Hardin, who was still in his car. Hardin rolled down his window to allow Taggart to stick his head inside for a hurried urgent consultation. Taggart did most of the talking, or whispering rather, buzzing in Hardin's ear. The more Taggart talked, the redder became Hardin's ears and the back of his neck. Hardin turned around in the driver's seat to look back at Jack, staring at him through the wire mesh grille of the protective barrier. He listened to more of Taggart's whisperings, at one point blurting out, "Impossible!"

Taggart said, "I'm not so sure, Bryce—"

Hardin got out of the car and opened the back door. He said, "Let me give you a hand." He gripped

Jack under the arm, helping him out of the police car. He said, "Careful you don't bump your head." Jack gave him a dirty look.

Hardin held Jack under one of his handcuffed arms and Taggart held him under the other as the two cops walked Jack across the lot and into the station, their manner a lot more solicitous than it had been. They took him to the front desk where a suspect would normally be booked. A phone bank and two-way radio were part of the desk's complement of equipment.

Taggart emptied out Jack's pockets, placing their contents on the countertop. They included a couple of spare clips for his gun, several sets of keys, a notepad and pen, some loose change, a cell phone, and a wallet. His handset transceiver had been in the truck but Taggart had brought it inside.

Taggart went through Jack's wallet. It didn't take him long to find Jack's CTU ID card. It bore a thumbnail photo of Jack. Taggart and Hardin stood side by side, alternately looking at the ID and at Jack. Taggart said, "Jack Bauer, that's the name they gave me over the radio, and believe me, Bryce, they weren't giving much."

Hardin said, "Uh-oh." Stallings and Fisk had been standing off to the side, watching the proceedings. They didn't know what it was all about but they knew that something was up.

Taggart looked at Hardin. Hardin scratched the side of his head, cleared his throat. He said, "Well. Ahem. Er, Mr. Bauer, I'm afraid that we're all the victims of a terrible mistake."

Jack said, "You think?" The numbed side of his face gave him some difficulty in forming the words.

Hardin said, "Cole, take the cuffs off him."

Taggart unlocked Jack's handcuffs. Jack's wrists bore angry red grooves where the tightly fastened cuffs had bitten deep in the skin. Loss of circulation made his hands feel clumsy and oversized, like he was wearing a pair of oven mitts.

Hardin said, "Maybe you'd like to sit down." He indicated a chair in the front desk area. Jack sat down in it, resting his hands on top of his thighs. He flexed them, clenching and unclenching his fists. Electric needles of sensation pierced his hands as feeling began to return. His face was pale, waxen, except for where the bruise had flowered on his left cheek.

One of the front desk phones rang. Taggart answered it. Squalling sounded from the earpiece where he held it to his head. The words were unintelligible but their tenor was unmistakable. Taggart winced, handing the receiver to Hardin. "You better take this, Lieutenant."

Hardin got on the phone. He barely had time to identify himself before receiving an earful. He did a lot of listening and not much talking. His few responses were limited to such phrases as "an honest mistake . . . in the heat of the moment judgments had to be made . . . can't be too careful, with the conference on . . . mistakes were made, yes . . . dreadfully sorry . . . the department regrets . . . I deeply regret . . . you have my full apologies . . ."

He held out the phone to Jack. "They want to speak to you."

Jack rose, took the phone, holding it to the right side of his face. A voice on the other end of the line said, "Hello, Agent Bauer? Anne Armstrong here."

Anne Armstrong was one of Garcia's top staffers at CTU/DENV, one of the special agents overseeing the handling of the Sky Mount assignment out of the Pike's Ford command post.

Their conversation was naturally circumscribed by its being carried on an unsecured phone line and could be conducted in only the most general terms. That didn't prevent her from asking, "What have those idiots gone and done?"

Jack looked at Hardin and Taggart. "Let's call it a case of mistaken identity."

"Are you all right?"

"I've been better, but I'll live."

"I'm on the way. I'll be there in twenty minutes."

"I'll be here. I'm not going anywhere."

The call completed, the connection was broken. Jack handed the phone to Hardin, who placed the receiver back on the hook. Hardin said, "No charges will be filed, of course."

Jack said, "By me or by you?"

"Ha-ha. These things happen, you know. With the Round Table opening today, and those crazy Zealots dropping out of sight to get up to who knows what, I'm sure you can understand that we're all a bit on edge, keyed up as it were, so there may have been a tendency to overreact."

"If you'd acted a bit sooner to catch the guy I was chasing, you would have nabbed a hot lead."

Hardin mustered a sickly smile. "Reckon that makes me the goat. I'll take full responsibility for it. We were just a few seconds off in closing that roadblock. But how were we to know that you were a Federal agent chasing a fugitive? If you or your people had communicated with us in time . . . As it was, though, we didn't know what we were dealing with."

Jack said, "I know the feeling."

"Well, you can see how it is then." Hardin indicated Jack's belongings laid out on the desktop. "You'll be wanting your stuff back."

Jack started picking up items, putting them in his pockets. Hardin said, "When you're done, step into my office and make yourself comfortable."

Jack followed Hardin to a closed office door whose upper half was a translucent pane of pebbled glass. Hardin's title and name were stenciled on it in black letters, along with the legend: "Private."

Hardin opened the door and ushered Jack in, following him and closing the door behind them. He said, "You'll be wanting to clean up. You can use my private washroom."

Jack said, "That's big of you, Lieutenant. Mighty big."

Hardin chose to ignore the sarcasm. "Just a little interagency cooperation. After all, we're all on the same team."

A connecting door in the long wall with the filing cabinets opened on a small bathroom. Jack eyed his reflection in a mirror mounted over the sink. He hoped it was the overhead fluorescent lighting that made him look like death warmed over. The left side of his face was bruised and swollen but not as badly as he'd expected it to be from the way it felt. He ran some cold water and rubbed it on the parts of his face that weren't sore. He soaked a washcloth with hot water and held it against the left side of his face. He patted himself dry with a hand towel and stepped out.

Hardin did his best to make himself agreeable. He offered Jack a cup of coffee. Jack passed on it. He offered Jack a drink from a bottle of whiskey he kept in a desk drawer. That offer was more tempting but Jack declined. He didn't want to meet Anne Armstrong with liquor on his breath.

A discreet knocking sounded on the office door; Hardin said, "Come in." It was Sharon Stallings with a towel-wrapped ice pack. Jack accepted with thanks. She went out. Jack sat in one of the armchairs holding the ice pack against the left side of his face.

Hardin said, "We put out an all-points bulletin on that car you were chasing. Too bad we don't have a license plate number to go on. Maybe something'll come of it. Mind telling me what it's all about?"

Jack said, "The driver's wanted in connection with a shooting."

Hardin showed interest. "You don't tell me! Who got shot?"

"We'll get back to you on that later."

"Top secret stuff, eh? Sure, sure. I understand. Any information you can extend to me will be greatly appreciated. We're both after the same thing, making sure that the Round Table goes off without a hitch." Hardin's chair creaked as he leaned forward in it. "This suspect—he one of Prewitt's crazies?"

Jack shrugged. "That remains to be seen."

"They're a bad bunch, a bad bunch. Them going missing right as the conference kicks off, well, it can't be a coincidence. Or a good thing."

A knock sounded on the door; it opened and Taggart stuck his head in without waiting for Hardin's acknowledgment. He said, "Bauer's people are here, Lieutenant."

Hardin said, "Okay."

Jack got up, placed the towel-wrapped ice pack on top of a filing cabinet, and went out the door. Hardin pushed back his chair and hurried after him. Jack went into the squad room. Fisk and Stallings were talking but fell silent when he entered. Fisk had put on a clean pair of pants since Jack had last seen him. Taggart had regained his seat behind the front desk.

Jack crossed toward the front desk without looking at anyone. His path took him in front of Fisk and Stallings. He stepped on Fisk's foot. That was to pin him in place. Jack pivoted on the spot, driving a left-handed spear thrust at Fisk. The fingers of his hand were held together, the tips slightly curled inward.

He thrust the fingers into the top of Fisk's belly, just below the bottom of the rib cage. He turned in toward Fisk as he struck, leaning into him, putting some weight behind the blow. His body screened Stallings and Hardin from seeing the strike. His curled fingertips went in deep.

Fisk jackknifed, going, "Whoof!"

Jack stepped back, said, "Excuse me."

Fisk folded up, almost doubled over. His eyes bulged and his mouth was a round sucking O, gasping for breath. His pink face whitened, going green at the edges. He hugged his middle with both arms. A trembling right hand drifted toward his right hip where his weapon was holstered.

Jack said, "Reach for that gun and I'll kick your teeth out."

Fisk decided against it and went back to hugging himself with both arms and sucking air, hating eyes glaring out of an anguished face.

Jack said, "Not so much fun when the other guy isn't handcuffed, is it?"

Hardin said, "Here now, what's all this?"

Taggart, elaborately nonchalant, said, "I didn't see anything, Lieutenant."

Hardin got a knowing look on his face. He said to Jack, "Okay, that evens things up. You happy now?"

Jack said, "Happier."

Hardin said, "Fisk, if you're going to be sick, you'd by God better not do it out here."

The station's front door opened and two people walked in, CTU's Anne Armstrong and Ernie Sandoval. Jack nodded to them, said, "I'll be right with you, there's just one more detail I need to get straightened out."

He crossed to Taggart at the front desk. Taggart eyed him warily. Jack held out a hand and said, "My gun."

Taggart opened a drawer in the desk, reached in, and pulled out Jack's pistol and a magazine clip, setting them both down on the desktop. He said, "It's not loaded."

Jack picked up the pistol, examining it, making sure the chamber was empty. It was. He fitted the clip into the slot on the gun butt, slapping it with the heel of his palm to send it on home.

He didn't bother jacking a round into the chamber. He'd already made his point. He fitted the gun into the shoulder holster, letting the flap of his jacket fall to cover it.

He faced the two CTU agents and said, "Let's go."

Anne Armstrong had a primly disapproving look on her face, like a schoolteacher who stepped out into the hall for a minute and found on her return that the pupils were acting up.

Ernie Sandoval indicated Fisk, who stood bent double with one arm extended, clutching the wall for support. He said, "What happened to him?"

Jack said, "Too much coffee."

1 2 3 4 **5** 6 7 8 9
10 11 12 13 14 15 16 17
18 19 20 21 22 23 24

. . . .

THE FOLLOWING TAKES PLACE
BETWEEN THE HOURS OF
7 A.M. AND 8 A.M.
MOUNTAIN DAYLIGHT TIME

. . . .

Sky Mount, Colorado

It was a beautiful morning, and that was part of the problem as far as Jack was concerned. All that bright sunshine pouring out of a cloudless blue sky up here in the heights was dazzling and made his head hurt. He put on a pair of sunglasses. That cut down on the glare, but the pressure of the sunglasses on the bruised left side of his face added to his discomfort.

He sat in the front passenger seat of a car being driven by Anne Armstrong. She was tall, lean, with short blond hair and a long, narrow, high-cheekboned face. She wore a tan blazer, light blue blouse, sand-colored skirt, and brown low-heeled loafers. She also wore a snouty, short-barreled semi-automatic pistol in a clip-on holster attached to her belt over her right hip.

She drove north on Rimrock Road, leaving behind the Mountain Lake substation. Their destination was Sky Mount. Ernie Sandoval had taken the Toyota pickup truck, driving it to the CTU command post at nearby Pike's Ford.

Anne Armstrong said, "Our people found the bodies of Frank Neal and a civilian who fit your description of Lobo at Red Notch, but no dead shooter."

Jack said, "Damn, they work fast."

"Who?"

"The other side, whoever that is."

"The Zealots?"

"I wonder."

Armstrong thought that over for a minute. "No results on finding the Subaru you were chasing."

Jack said, "I'm not surprised. There must be thousands of places to hide a car in these mountains."

"No car of that description has been reported stolen. And with no license plate number . . ."

"Those killers were pros. They wouldn't use their own car. The license plates were probably lifted from another car to further muddy up their tracks."

A mile went by. Anne Armstrong said with a touch of frostiness, "What was the purpose of that macho display at the station?"

Jack said, "Equilibrium."

Her face tightened, a network of fine lines showing around her eyes. "I don't follow."

He said, "Hardin's boy pistol-whipped me when I was handcuffed. Can't let him get away with that kind of thing. This is an aggressive business with a lot of high-testosterone characters who're always testing the limits to see what they can get away with—and that's just the ones who're supposed to be on our side. You don't want the word to get around that a CTU agent can be roughed up without any consequences. Otherwise our guys lose respect with the other agencies we have to work with. It's bad for morale. By paying that thug cop back in kind, proper balance is restored. The word gets out that our guys can't be pushed around without some kind of comeback."

Her pursed lips parted to speak. "I see. So it was all for the benefit of CTU. There wasn't any personal animosity involved." She didn't bother to mask the disbelief in her tone.

Jack said, "Personal feelings aside, I did it for the good of the service."

Anne Armstrong said a dirty word. "You'll be going back to Los Angeles in a few days but the rest of us will be staying here. Try to remember that we have to work with the local authorities."

"Hardin will get the message. I used to be on the LAPD. I know how cops think because I used to be one myself. By the way, what's the story on the MRT?"

"Bryce Hardin is a power in state law enforcement circles. He's a highly decorated officer with numerous commendations for valor and high-profile busts. He's got a lot of pull with the governor's office at the capital. The MRT is his and the governor's way of injecting themselves in Sky Mount doings and increasing their profile and political prestige."

The cliff wall on the west ended, opening into a box canyon whose centerpiece was a lens-shaped lake. The lake was the color of the sky. The picturesque landscape had a gravel parking lot and was dotted with picnic tables scattered among the trees surrounding the lake.

A metal signpost identified the area: MOUNTAIN LAKE STATE PARK. A chain barred the entrance. A printed cardboard sign fixed to it said, TEMPORARILY CLOSED.

Jack said, "So that's Mountain Lake. I was wondering where they were hiding it."

Armstrong said, "It's closed for the duration of the Round Table. The authorities don't want a lot of unauthorized civilians up here during the conference. It's one less variable for them to have to deal with."

They drove past the space and the cliff walls returned. Jack said, "Something else has been bothering me, something that might be a possible lead. It's a long shot but it could be worth following up. The compound at Red Notch should be checked for traces of chemical weapons."

Armstrong's cool demeanor gave way to outright surprise. "Chemical weapons? Where do you get that?"

"Something Lobo said about the compound being covered by a green cloud. It could have been some kind of CW, a toxic gas attack. Or maybe only a smoke bomb."

"Or the demented ravings of a half-mad homeless drunk."

"Somebody was worried about Lobo enough to have him killed by a team of assassins. Cultists and CW isn't so much of a stretch, either. Look at the Aum Shunrikyo doomsday cult that set off sarin nerve gas bombs in the Tokyo subways some years ago."

Anne Armstrong looked worried. "The Zealots and chemical weapons—the idea alone could set off a panic."

Jack said, "There could be traces of residue remaining in the compound. For that matter, it might be worthwhile to have Lobo checked for the same in a postmortem. He might have been exposed to some of the stuff, and it's possible that whatever it is could be retained in organic matter."

Armstrong used her in-car comm system to contact Central. She relayed the message that Red Notch and Lobo should both be examined for possible exposure to airborne chemical weapons. She also noted that this was the suggestion of her colleague, Agent Bauer.

A nice touch, thought Jack. That way she got it on the record that the idea had originated with him. If it failed to pan out, it was his bad idea, not hers. He held no resentment against her for the gambit. That was how the game was played.

Several miles of mountain scenery unrolled in silence. The throbbing in Jack's head worsened as the car continued to climb. He said, "You wouldn't happen to have any aspirin on you, would you?"

She said, "Headache?"

"A little bit."

"You should get checked out by a medic, make sure you're not suffering from a concussion."

"I'm fine. Just a touch of altitude." Jack didn't want to provide any pretext, medical or otherwise, that might result in him getting pulled off this duty. The violent deaths of Frank Neal and that strange hermit Lobo had given him a personal stake in the mission. It wasn't about keeping Chappelle happy, it was about cracking the case, finding the killers, and solving the mystery of the Zealots' disappearance. He now felt that there was a direct and legitimate threat to the Round Table and its array of high-powered, high-finance invitees.

Armstrong said, "Yes, the height can get to you flatlanders, can't it? That's what happens when you're out of your element."

That could have been a veiled crack about his being an outsider who'd been forced on CTU/DENV through power politics. Jack couldn't blame her for feeling that way, but it didn't stop him from saying, "I haven't done too badly so far."

She said, "You're still alive."

A long pause followed, then she said, "I think there's some aspirin in my pocketbook." Her pocketbook was on the transmission hump between their seats. She steered with one hand and opened the pocketbook with the other. She reached inside it, rummaging around.

The road was no longer straight but twisty, winding around a succession of blind curves. Armstrong drove at a quick pace with no reduction in speed, glancing alternately at the road ahead and the interior of her pocketbook. It made Jack a shade anxious, since the road on his side had only a few feet of shoulder and a knee-high metal guardrail standing between him and a thousand-foot drop.

She said, "I know it's in here somewhere . . ."

Jack was on the verge of telling her to forget it, that he could get along fine without the aspirin. The car rounded a curve, coming face to face with a two-and-a-half-ton truck coming in the opposite direction. The truck was a foot or two over the centerline and Armstrong had to swerve to avoid it, the two right-side wheels crunching the loose dirt and stones of the shoulder.

She said, "Jerk!" She passed the truck and swung back into the lane so all four wheels once more gripped solid pavement.

Jack had a hollow feeling in the pit of his stomach. He forced himself to adopt a conversational tone. "That was a catering truck. Must be coming from Sky Mount."

She said, "Oh, there's a regular caravan of suppliers going up and down the mountain for the whole time the conference is on. Nothing but the best for the guests, you know. I wish some of those truckers would learn how to drive."

She went back to rummaging through her pocketbook, finally coming up with a bottle of aspirin. "I knew it was in there." She handed it to Jack.

Jack said, "Thanks." He took his time uncapping the container and shaking out two tablets. His mouth was dry from that recent near miss and he needed to work up some saliva. He popped one pill in the back of his mouth, giving his head a toss to get it started down his gullet, then repeated the process.

Armstrong said, "Swallowing them without any water? My, you are tough."

He said, "Can you spare a few extra for later?"

"Keep the bottle if you like."

"No, that's okay, I just want a couple in reserve." He shook four pills into his palm, dropping them into the breast pocket of his jacket. He capped the bottle, handed it back to her.

A gap opened on the west side, revealing a road sloping up a long incline. Armstrong turned left, entering the road. She said, "Masterman Way. That'll take us up to Sky Mount."

Jack said, "This is the first CTU vehicle I've ever ridden in that was a Mercedes-Benz. How'd you manage to work that with the bean counters?"

"Operational necessity. We needed it for protective coloration to blend in with all the other highline models at Sky Mount. Otherwise we'd have stuck out like a sore thumb."

They climbed the slope. The road split into two branches at the summit. A checkpoint had been established there, manned by two deputies from the county sheriff's department. Their car was parked in the middle of the road. Each branch of the road was blocked by a set of wooden sawhorses.

One of the deputies approached the CTU car on the driver's side. Anne Armstrong presented her credentials, including her ID and a pass to enter Sky Mount. The deputy took the documents to his car and radioed in to Sky Mount to verify them. They must have checked out okay because he returned to the car a moment later and gave Armstrong her paperwork. His partner moved the sawhorse out of the way and waved them through, moving it back to block the road after they had passed.

The road switchbacked up the side of a mountain, unwinding in a series of hairpin curves that topped out on a plateau. High mountain valleys in the Rockies are known locally as parks. This park was a vast circular meadow that was open on the east and ringed the rest of the way around by three mountains: Mount Nagaii, Mount Zebulon, and Thunder Mountain. It created an amphitheaterlike effect, with the park being the floor and the mountains being the semicircular tiers that soared up and up toward the zenith.

An amphitheater of the gods. A fit setting for Sky Mount itself. Sky Mount was the name of both the park estate and the fabulous structure that crowned it. The building was a unique creation, part Gothic castle, part Tudor-style manor house, and part chateau. It was an architectural folly on a grand scale, a magnificent white elephant that could be compared only to such equally monumental efforts as the du Ponts' Winterthur estate, Hearst's San Simeon, and the baroque nineteenth-century castles of Ludwig, the Mad King of Bavaria.

The edifice occupied the flattened top of a rise in the park. It fronted south, its long axis running east-west. Its central portion suggested a medieval keep, with a facade loosely modeled after the church of Notre Dame in Paris. Long, multistoried wings extended east and west from it, garnished with balconies and terraces. The spiky roofline bristled with spires, towers, turrets, and battlements. It had been built in the late 1800s, the Gilded Age, and sought to render the intricate architectural "gingerbread" decor of the period not in woodwork but in stone.

The mansion stood at the center of intricately landscaped grounds, a complex of gardens, fountains, galleries and arcades, patios and pavilions. The rise on which it sat had been cut into stepped terraces that were hanging gardens. The rest of the estate spread out from it in a pastoral vista of gently rolling green fields, woodland groves, and sylvan ponds, honeycombed with winding paths and decorated with statuary.

It was one of the damnedest things Jack Bauer had

ever seen. He said, "Is that really there or is the altitude getting to me?"

Anne Armstrong said, "It is something, isn't it?"

"It makes Neverland look like a country shack."

Cresting the edge of the plateau and suddenly coming upon Sky Mount had created a visceral impact. Now that Jack had had time to process the big picture, he began to pick up on significant details, the telltale signs of modernity.

The mansion's roofline was studded with satellite dishes, looking like white toadstools that had sprouted out of the crevices of a gnarly rock formation. A helicopter landing pad stood on the flat south of the rise, toward the west end of the park. Two helicopters sat there. A large field in the southeast sector had been turned into a parking lot. It was filled with scores of luxury cars, high-end SUVs, and limousines, all arranged in neat, orderly rows. A line of trucks and delivery vans stretched along a driveway that curved around to the rear of the mansion.

Big black limos and shiny new cars followed the main drive up the rise to the front of the building, disgorging passengers and their luggage. Groups of people, guests, swarmed the grounds, wandering among the arcades, galleries, and gardens. The scene was alive with activity, vibrant color, motion.

The site was well covered by a large number of security personnel, some in uniforms, others in civilian clothes. Groups of guards patrolled the estate in golf carts. Jack thought that was a nice touch.

The open, eastern end of the park was ringed by a black iron spear fence ten feet tall. The sections of fence were interspersed with stone pillars. The park had a single entrance, a double-gated portal that controlled access to a two-lane drive into and out of the estate. The guardhouse inside the gates looked like a Tudor mini-mansion. Jack noted with a pang that it was bigger than his own house back home.

Twin guard shacks stood outside the gates, as did a half-dozen uniformed guards all equipped with sidearms. The county sheriff's department and the state police each had several cars in place, standing well off to the edges of the property, away from the front drive and main gate.

Jack said, "Looks like the local law's been shoved over to the sidelines."

Anne Armstrong nodded. "That's about the size of it. The police are good enough for keeping citizens, protestors, reporters, and other pests off the heights, but they're barred from the sacred precincts, too. Sky Mount itself is guarded by the Brand Agency, a private security firm hired by the Masterman Trust, which runs the estate and the Round Tables."

She drove up to the main gate, halted a dozen paces away from it by a guard. The gate was closed.

The guard came around to the driver's side of the car. He wore a gray cruising cap with black patent leather brim, a long-sleeved gray shirt and black tie, and gray trousers with black vertical stripes on the sides. Blazoned on his left breast was a badge-shaped emblem embossed with the words "Brand Agency." He wore a Sam Brown black patent leather belt and hip-holstered sidearm. All the uniformed guards were identically attired.

He said, "Good morning, ma'am."

She said, "Anne Armstrong and Jack Bauer to see Don Bass, please."

"Is Mr. Bass expecting you?"

"We have an appointment."

"May I see your ID, please? Both of you."

Jack and Armstrong handed over their CTU ID cards. The guard studied Anne Armstrong's photo, comparing it with the driver. He did the same thing with Jack but he spent a lot more time doing it. Jack removed his sunglasses to facilitate the identification. The guard's expression was dubious. He walked around the front of the car to take a better look at Jack through the passenger side window. He still seemed unhappy. It occurred to Jack that his misadventures since arriving in Red Notch had left his appearance somewhat disreputable.

The guard returned their ID cards. He said to Armstrong, "I'll have to contact Mr. Bass at the mansion. Please pull over to the side so you're not blocking the gate."

He crossed to the guard shack on the right and went inside.

Jack said, "I don't think he liked my looks. I've got a feeling I might be underdressed for the occasion."

Anne Armstrong said, "You can always say you're working undercover." She put the car in reverse and backed up along the roadside so the Mercedes was out of the way of any incoming traffic.

She said, "Don Bass heads the security for the conference. Dealing directly with him will cut through a lot of red tape. Among other things, we won't have to check our sidearms at the gate.

"I'm sure you'll like that," she added.

Jack just grinned.

Five minutes passed before the guard returned. He

walked briskly to the driver's side of the car, said, "Mr. Bass is unavailable at this time. Mr. Noone will be coming down instead. He's Mr. Bass's assistant."

Armstrong said, "Yes, I know him."

"He'll escort you to the mansion."

"Thank you."

"You're welcome, ma'am. Have a nice day." The guard said nothing to Jack, not even looking at him. He rejoined the other guards outside the gate.

Anne Armstrong said to Jack, "Larry Noone is Bass's number two man. He'll be just as good for facilitating our entry."

Ten minutes later a golf cart rolled down the hill and halted just inside the gate. The driver was a uniformed guard, the passenger a heavyset, bearish man. The latter hopped out of the cart, went through a swinging door to the right of the gatepost, and hurried over to the car.

He was in his mid-fifties, about six feet, two inches and 220 pounds. He wore a canvas duckbilled cap, navy-blue blazer, green open-neck sport shirt and khaki pants. He was balding with a fringe of short blond hair and pale blond eyebrows. Clean-shaven, with a ruddy complexion.

He went to the driver's side and reached in to shake hands with Anne Armstrong. His jacket fell open when he leaned forward, and Jack could see that he wore a short-barreled revolver in a shoulder holster under his left arm. He flashed a big toothy grin like he was glad to see her and said, "Hi, Anne."

She said, "Hello, Larry."

"Don was in conference with Mr. Wright and couldn't get away. Sorry to keep you waiting."

"No problem. Larry, this is Jack Bauer. He's on

loan from our Los Angeles division and will be working with us during the conference. Jack, this is Larry Noone."

Noone came bustling around to the passenger side of the car. He flashed another big grin and thrust out a big right hand. "Pleased to meet you, Agent Bauer."

Jack shook his hand. Noone's grip was solid but he didn't overdo it. "Glad to know you. Call me Jack."

"Okay, Jack. Call me Larry."

Noone climbed into the backseat of the car. "Go ahead, Anne, they'll let you through."

The main gate was already opening. It was powered by an electric motor that caused the gate to slide sideways. One of the guards waved her through, and the car drove into Sky Mount.

. . . .

THE FOLLOWING TAKES PLACE
BETWEEN THE HOURS OF
8 A.M. AND 9 A.M.
MOUNTAIN DAYLIGHT TIME

. . . .

Sky Mount, Colorado

Larry Noone escorted Jack Bauer and Anne Armstrong into a reception area where they were met by Marion Clary. She was a gatekeeper for Cabot Huntington Wright, the man in charge of running the Sky Mount Round Table, among his many other responsibilities. Wright's suite of offices was on the ground floor in the southeast corner of the mansion's east wing.

The reception area, an anteroom to the suite, was itself an imposing space, expansive and high-ceilinged, its wood-paneled walls hung with ornate-framed paintings and tapestries. Jack's wife, Teri, was a graphic artist and designer with an art history background, and Jack had absorbed enough from her through osmosis to recognize the paintings as being in the style of Italian and Northern Renaissance masterworks of landscape and portraiture. He knew that Sky Mount's creator, tycoon H. H. Masterman, had been a celebrated collector of the works of the Old Masters and had no doubt that these were not copies but originals worth several million dollars.

Marion Clary occupied a mahogany desk the size of a compact car. She rose and came around it to meet and greet the newcomers.

She was a handsome woman, sixtyish and well-preserved, with carefully coiffed blondish-white hair, fine features, and dark, bright eyes set in a porcelain-colored complexion.

The porcelain was webbed with a network of fine lines when seen close up. She was slim, straight-backed, with good posture. She wore a tailored jacket and pleated skirt, both charcoal-gray; a white blouse with a thin red and yellow paisley kerchief, and black pumps with chunky three-inch heels.

She was already acquainted with Anne Armstrong and greeted her warmly. Noone introduced her to Jack. They shook hands. Her palm was dry, her grip firm.

Noone's handset radio squawked, prompting him to excuse himself for a moment. He stepped a few paces away and held the transceiver to the side of his head, taking a message and responding to it.

He said to the other three, "I'm needed at the guardhouse to iron out some business. Nice seeing you again, Ms. Clary. I'll see you later, Anne—Jack." He went out.

Marion Clary said, "Mr. Wright's meeting with

some of the event planners is running a little long. Please excuse the delay."

Jack said, "I thought he was meeting with Don Bass."

"He was, but Mr. Bass was called away unexpectedly a few minutes before you arrived and the planners seized the opportunity to see Mr. Wright for a few minutes. He's scheduled to deliver the opening keynote address at ten and there were one or two last-minute details to finalize."

"Mr. Wright is going to speak today?"

"Oh yes, he always delivers the opening address to the conference. It's a tradition and a high point of the Round Table, if I say so myself. Of course, I'm hardly in a position to be objective, knowing him as well as I do. His talk should be especially interesting this year, what with all the turmoil in the global markets."

"I'm sure," Jack said. He was thinking that if Wright and the high-finance attendees knew of the short-selling bets being made against their companies, there'd be some real turmoil right there in the conference room. But that information was being closely held by Chappelle and a handful of others. Chappelle was as tight at disseminating confidential intelligence as a miser would be in handing out dollars. Which was one of his good points as far as Jack was concerned.

The pattern of shorting had of necessity been made known to CTU/DENV head Orlando Garcia, since it was the wedge that had gotten Jack involved in the local operation. Jack didn't know how far down the line Garcia had passed the intel. He didn't know if Anne Armstrong was aware of it. She hadn't mentioned it, and he wasn't about to volunteer anything on the subject until he was sure she had an irrefutable need to know.

Marion Clary said, "While you're waiting, may I offer you some refreshments? Coffee, tea, or some other beverage?"

Jack said, "Coffee would be fine, thanks."

Anne Armstrong said, "Yes, I'd like some, too, please."

The process was nothing so simple as pouring a couple of cups from a coffee urn. Marion Clary spoke into her desk intercom, issuing a summons. A white-coated server appeared within less than two minutes, wheeling in a serving cart. It held silver pitchers, china cups and saucers, and an assortment of muffins, buns, and pastries. One pitcher held coffee, another held decaffeinated coffee. Jack had the full-octane coffee, black.

It was good coffee, rich, aromatic, flavorful. His stomach growled at the sight of the pastries, but the left side of his face still felt too sore for much chewing so he reluctantly passed on them. Anne Armstrong had the decaf coffee with plenty of cream and sugar. Marion Clary had a cup of tea. The server exited, wheeling away the cart.

Jack's eye was caught by a picture that looked out of place among the Old Masters creations. It was a full-length portrait that hung high on the wall behind the mahogany desk. Its subject was a man dressed in the garb of the late nineteenth or early twentieth century. He had a shock of white hair, a hawklike predatory face, and a white walrus mustache that failed to disguise a self-satisfied smirk. His eyes were hard, narrow, and bright, boldly, contemptuously staring out at the viewer with a go-to-hell directness. He stood in a posture of dominance, hands thrust in his jacket pockets with the thumbs hanging out over the edges, narrow feet spread shoulder-length apart.

It was a masterpiece in its own way, the painter certainly having captured the personality of his subject.

Marion Clary noticed Jack's interest in the picture. She said, "That's a portrait of old H. H. Masterman himself, founder of the trust which bears his name, and the builder of Sky Mount."

Jack thought that if the likeness was an accurate one, the H.H. in his name should have stood for "Hard-Hearted." He looked like a money-grubbing skinflint who would have thrown widows and orphans out in the cold if their eviction would have earned him an extra dime. He settled for saying, "He looks like a pretty tough old bird."

Marion Clary said, "He was a self-made man who started with nothing. He struck it rich with a silver mine near Cripple Creek and expanded into banking, railroads, and real estate. And he did it in the days before income tax. Even in an age of robber barons he was considered something of a pirate." She spoke of him with a kind of proprietary pride.

She said, "His financial interests were centered in Denver and in his later years he built Sky Mount as a vacation home and retreat from city living. It was originally planned as a hunting lodge, but as you can see, it developed into a far more grandiose vision."

A faraway look came into her eyes. "'In Xanadu did Kublai Khan a stately pleasure-dome decree'— according to the poet Samuel Taylor Coleridge. But in Sky Mount, H. H. Masterman built his own dream castle. And unlike the poem, which Coleridge never finished, Mr. Masterman finalized his creation, an architectural poem wrought in stone and timber and furnished with some of the greatest masterpieces of the Old World."

Anne Armstrong said, "You certainly know your subject."

Marion Clary said, "I should. Actually I'm the curator of the estate, in charge of overseeing everything from the upkeep and restoration of the art treasures to making sure the lawns get mowed and the garbage collected."

Jack said, "Sounds like a big job."

She said, "I love it. I live here all year round. Sky Mount is open to the public, except when the Round Tables are being held. It's a major tourist attraction and draws thousands of visitors annually."

Anne Armstrong said, "I shouldn't wonder. It's like a fairyland castle come to life."

Marion Clary beamed. "I can say without exaggeration that it's one of the most fantastic realms in all the world."

"No doubt. But you live here? I think I'd find that somewhat overwhelming, making a home in a setting as stupendous as this. Even intimidating."

Marion Clary shook her head. "It's not as if I live here all alone. There's a permanent party of over a dozen staffers who live here full-time, too. That's not including the tour guides, guards, chambermaids, handymen, gardeners, and all the others who are here during working hours. It takes a small army to keep Sky Mount functioning properly.

"I've lived here for over ten years, and even when I think I know every nook and cranny of it, I'm always discovering new and wonderful things about it. To me it's an old friend. I couldn't imagine living anywhere else. There's so much history here, so many art treasures at every turn . . . There's a greatness of spirit here that seems to have gone out of today's modern world. Of course, I'm an antiquarian or I couldn't do my job properly. An antiquarian and something of an antique."

Jack said, "Hardly that, Ms. Clary."

"You're gallant, Mr. Bauer." She smiled piquantly, a bit wryly, as if shaking off her visionary mood and returning to the business at hand. "During the run-up to the Round Tables and the conclaves themselves, my role becomes more that of a personal assistant to Mr. Wright. It's the one time of the year that I do see him. His responsibilities as chairman of the board of trustees take him all over the country—the world, really—and he spends very little time at Sky Mount except during the Round Tables."

A stirring of muffled motion sounded from behind the tall set of double doors accessing Wright's inner sanctum. The doors opened outward, allowing the exit of a handful of staffers, young men and women. Some carried portfolios, others briefcases and oversized loose-leaf binders. They looked sleek, well-groomed, fit, competent, energetic, and enthusiastic. They weren't more than a few years Jack's junior, but they made him feel old by comparison.

They crossed the anteroom and exited. A man, thirty, dark-haired, with tortoiseshell glasses, stood in the doorway. He said to Jack and Anne Armstrong, "Mr. Wright will see you now."

The two CTU agents crossed to the portal and entered the space beyond. The man with the glasses closed the double doors behind them, following. The office space was immense, the walls lofty, the windows tall and arched, the ceiling vaulted. The decor was suggestive of the period of Louis XIV, the Sun King, a mélange of neo-classical formalism and rococo ornamentation. The walls were white with golden trim, the deep-pile wall-to-wall carpeting was royal-blue decorated with white fleur-de-lis, emblem of the Bourbon dynasty. There were paintings by Watteau, Fragonard, even a Poussin.

Alcoves held marble statuary and portrait busts with neo-classical themes, Greek gods and goddesses, nymphs and warriors.

Richly ornamented drapes screened the windows, filtering out the morning sunlight. A crystal chandelier hung down from the ceiling, its radiance augmented by strategically placed floor lamps and indirect wall-mounted pinlights and spotlights.

Glass-fronted cabinets contained shelves lined with rows of volumes handsomely bound in gold-embossed leather bindings. There was an antique desk the size of a pool table. Standing in front of it with his hands held behind his back was Cabot Huntington Wright.

Wright's age was somewhere in his fifties. A leonine head was mounted on a pair of broad shoulders. His square-shaped torso hung straight down from those shoulders, presenting a solid, wall-like front. A superbly tailored summer-weight dark blue suit could not disguise the fact of his spindly legs, giving him a top-heavy appearance. His feet were small and narrow.

Lead-gray hair was brushed straight back from the forehead, giving his sleek hair the aspect of a metallic cap. His face was spade-shaped, with the hint of double chin. His upper lip sported a neatly clipped silver-gray mustache of the type that Jack associated with old-time bank presidents and district attorneys.

Wright was the director of the Masterman Trust, a philanthropic foundation with a billion in assets that were disbursed to a variety of do-good organizations, from cultural centers to soup kitchens. He was president of the executive committee in charge of holding the trust-funded Round Tables, and a multimillionaire in his own right.

He crossed to meet Jack and Armstrong as they entered. He said, "I am Cabot Wright." His voice was deep, resonant—rich. Like him.

Jack said, "I know, I've seen your picture in the papers."

He said, "You must be Agent Bauer. Don Bass told me to expect you."

Anne Armstrong said, "Agent Bauer is on loan to us from the Los Angeles branch."

Wright said, "Glad to have you aboard. We can use all the help we can get."

He and Jack shook hands. Wright's palm was smooth, uncallused, but there was strength in his grip. Wright said, "Good to see you again, Ms. Armstrong." He indicated the man in the tortoise-shell glasses, said, "This is Brad Oliver, my executive assistant."

Brad Oliver had a thicket of oily, wavy black hair parted on the side, pale waxy skin, and a cleft chin. He made no move to shake hands. He said, "Hello."

Wright said, "Please accept my apologies for keeping you waiting. Sky Mount is an absolute madhouse today, buzzing with activity. Everyone on my staff seems unable to do without an urgent last-minute consultation with me and they all want to see me at the same time."

Anne Armstrong said, "That's quite all right, Mr. Wright. We appreciate that you're a busy man."

Wright said, "I'm sure you're busy too, with far greater responsibilities." He gestured toward a group of club chairs facing his desk. "Please sit down and make yourselves comfortable."

Jack and Armstrong seated themselves. Jack's chair was straight-backed and thickly cushioned, so comfortable that he wouldn't have minded having one in his living room at home.

Wright said, "May I offer you some refreshments?"

Jack said, "Thanks, but Ms. Clary has already seen to that."

"Ah, one can always trust Marion to observe the amenities. She's a pearl."

"She certainly seems to know her Sky Mount."

"She's our ultimate authority. I go to her when I need to know any esoterica about the layout." Wright went behind his desk and stood in front of his chair without sitting down. "Well. I understand you've got some updates for me this morning."

Jack said, "Shouldn't we wait for Don Bass? That'll save us from having to do a double briefing."

Wright said, "Quite so. Oliver, go see what's keeping Bass."

"Yes, sir." Oliver turned, exited via the double doors, closing them behind him.

Wright sat down. He picked up what looked like an antique letter opener from the desktop and toyed with it, weighing it in his hand. "Are you a history buff, Agent Bauer?"

"Some."

"Then perhaps this should interest you. This letter opener was once the property of Marshal Fouché. Do you know of him?"

Jack nodded. "He was Napoleon's spymaster."

Wright smiled, pleased. "And before that the spymaster of the French Revolution. One of the greatest intelligence officers of all time. He survived both the Terror and the Empire, living to see Robespierre go to the guillotine and Bonaparte go into exile at St. Helena."

He handed the letter opener to Jack. It was sharp-pointed and slim-bladed, as much dagger as letter opener. Wright said, "Imagine, if you will, the secret correspondences numbering in the hundreds, the thousands, all laid bare to Fouché's inquisitive eye by that instrument; the missives of kings and queens, popes and generals, royalists and revolutionaries."

"It's a real collector's item." Jack handed it back to Wright.

Wright said, "Perhaps you recall Fouché's famous maxim: 'The art of the police is in knowing what not to see.'"

"That might have served him well in the Napoleonic Empire, but it's not so apt for today."

"I'm keenly interested to know what you have seen."

Oliver returned with Don Bass in tow. Bass headed the Brand Agency security presence at Sky Mount. He was middle-aged, beefy, with short, curly brown hair topping a head shaped like a cured ham. He had baggy spaniel eyes and a meatball nose; his face was jowly and his wide mouth turned down at the corners. He wore the standard outfit sported by plainclothes Brand operatives, a blue blazer with the company emblem blazoned on the left breast and khaki pants. Big feet were encased in extra-wide, thick-soled shoes. His blazer was rumpled and his pants needed creasing. He carried a dog-eared brown leather briefcase.

He knew Anne Armstrong; he and Jack were introduced. He pulled a club chair up to Wright's desk and plopped himself down in it.

Brad Oliver hovered around the edges of the scene, notepad and pen in hand. Wright said, "That will be all for now, Oliver; you may go."

"Yes, sir." Oliver went out.

Wright said, "So. What are the latest developments in the Prewitt affair?"

Wright already knew about the abandonment of the Red Notch compound and the disappearance of the Zealots. Jack told of his and Neal's night trip to the site; of the discovery of Lobo; of the shooting deaths of Lobo, Neal, and the rifleman; and of the rifleman's partner's getaway. Those were facts. He said nothing about Lobo's tale of hog-faced demons and the green cloud. That was hearsay, and he didn't want to whip up a storm of excitement and possible hysteria on an as yet unverified account, especially his suspicions that some kind of chemical weapons might have been used on the night of the vanishment. Time enough to open that can of worms if and when CTU forensics turned up actual evidence of such substances. He was keeping quiet until then to avoid stirring up a panic.

That went double for Chappelle's SIU detecting

the sinister short-selling pattern. That would stay secret until events necessitated otherwise, and he saw no sign of that need yet. The intelligence was an ace in the hole, a trump card that might precipitate the final denouement, and he would keep it well hidden up his sleeve in readiness for the showdown.

Jack finished his self-redacted account of the proceedings. That was the time for Anne Armstrong to speak up if she wanted to surface the possible CW involvement but she remained mum on the subject. If she was in on the secret intel about the recent shorting on the market, she kept it to herself.

Don Bass said, "How do you read it, Jack?"

"I think that the Zealots' disappearing act was accompanied by violence. Maybe there was a schism in the sect, some doctrinal or procedural disagreement that led to a falling out between two or more factions."

"Two or more? How do you figure?"

"Notice the timing. It's surely no coincidence that the disappearing act came on the eve of the Round Table. It's possible that one faction of the Zealots was in favor of a violent action against the conference, another was against it, and a third was neutral, just sitting on the fence not wanting to take sides. Things came to a head and the disputants settled it with a Night of the Long Knives. It doesn't necessarily follow that the pro-violence group took the initiative against the dissidents, but that's the way to bet it. It's not likely that the anti-violence bunch took action against the pro-violence crowd to forestall them. It's possible, but not probable."

Jack went on, "The violent ones did in some of the

opposition, maybe all. That would have cowed the faint hearts and the fence-sitters. They all loaded up in the blue bus and whatever other vehicles they had, abandoned Red Notch, and went underground."

Bass said, "What about the ATF agents, Dean and O'Hara?"

Jack said, "They were outside the compound keeping it under surveillance. They had to go to keep from spoiling the Zealots' getaway. It's possible that Zealot assassins took them by surprise and did them in. Dean and O'Hara were monitoring the cult, but nothing on the record shows they were expecting any rough stuff. Up to now, the only thing the Zealots have shot off are their mouths. The killers drove away with the ATF agents' dead bodies in their own car and hid it wherever they hid the rest of the cadre, living or dead, and their blue bus."

Don Bass nodded. "Makes sense."

Cabot Wright said, "Where does this Lobo character fit in?"

Jack said, "Near as I can figure it, he was a homeless guy, a derelict who was living in the sandstone hills above the compound. He saw something on the night of the disappearance. What's more, somebody saw him and sent a kill team to silence him. They didn't know what if anything he told Neal and me so they decided to make a clean sweep."

"They being from the violent faction of the Zealots."

"Possibly." Jack wasn't so sure that that was the case, he had his doubts that the killers were Zealots at all. He even had an alternate theory of the case but for now he was keeping it to himself.

Anne Armstrong said, "We're running a trace on Lobo to determine his true identity. When we know that some more pieces of the puzzle might fit."

Cabot Wright said, "But this is astounding! Where could the Zealots be hiding?"

Jack said, "This isn't my home turf but from what little I've seen of the terrain around here, there's a lot of places where two dozen people and a couple of vehicles could find a hole to hide in. Canyons, gorges, abandoned railway tunnels, ski lodges that've closed for the summer or gone out of business. The cult might not all be hiding in the same spot, either. They could have split up into cells and be hiding in a half-dozen spots, waiting for the go signal to greenlight whatever action they're planning."

Armstrong said, "Search planes and helicopters would be a big help. We could get county and state police pilots to start combing the region."

Wright said flatly, "I can light a fire under them to make that happen."

"But it's got to be done discreetly. A mass panic is the last thing we want."

Wright blanched. "My God, no! That would ruin the Round Table!"

Jack said, "We don't know what the Zealots are up to. Whatever it is, it's vital that they not get into Sky Mount to carry it out."

Don Bass said, "That's something we can do something about! Sky Mount's greatest strength is its defensibility. It's protected by concentric rings of security cordons. The only viable approach is from the east. The mountains provide a natural defense barrier on the other three sides. We've got shooters posted on the high ledges just in case any strike force is mountain goat enough to scale those peaks.

"That leaves us open on the east. We've got the county and state cops controlling all access roads to the park. From there Brand takes over and our cordon is even tighter. Nobody can get in or out of the main gate without proper ID. Between our men on the gate and the police auxiliaries outside, we've got the firepower to repel any mass attack."

Jack said, "Suppose they get close enough to crash the gate with a truck loaded with explosives?"

"The inside of the drive is rigged with a bed of concealed spikes a dozen yards long. If the gate goes down the spikes come up and they'll rip to pieces the tires of any vehicle before it gets more than a couple of feet inside."

"How about if they skip the gate and crash through a section of the fence?"

"The reinforced stone fence pillar posts are strong enough and too close for any truck to get through."

"What about cars?"

Don Bass stroked his chin. "You might have something there. We'll post some extra snipers and run roving patrols of crash cars along the inside of the fence line to harden the targets. We'll pay a double bonus to the crash car drivers—I don't think we'll lack for volunteers."

Jack said, "Sounds good. What about an air assault, a private plane that's a flying bomb designed to crash into the building?"

Anne Armstrong said, "We're ahead of you there, Jack. You came into the middle of the movie on that score. We've got the Air Force and the Air National

Guard posted to forestall just such an attempt. The air space for a several hundred square miles around has been declared a restricted no-fly zone for the conference. Any unauthorized aircraft entering the zone will be forced down or shot down. Besides which, it would take a hell of a pilot to be able to fly through these peaks to make the approach."

Don Bass added, "But in case some hotshot should get through, confidentially, we've got an anti-aircraft nest set up in the heights armed with a couple of Stinger missiles as a last resort."

Jack said, "Glad to hear it."

Cabot Wright shook his head sadly. "Lord! The precautions that must be taken merely to hold a peaceful and positive gathering whose purpose is the betterment of society and the national—and global— economy! It's enough to drive one to despair . . ."

Jack said, "That's the way we have to live today."

The double doors opened and Larry Noone entered, purposeful, grim-faced.

Don Bass said, "What is it, Larry?"

Noone said, "Those ATF agents have just been found."

· ·

THE FOLLOWING TAKES PLACE
BETWEEN THE HOURS OF
9 A.M. AND 10 A.M.
MOUNTAIN DAYLIGHT TIME

· ·

Lone Pine Gorge, Colorado

The car was at the bottom of Lone Pine Gorge. The gorge was a narrow, rocky, V-shaped cleft in the foothills of Mount Nagaii.

Jack and Anne Armstrong had to approach it by a dirt road that turned west off Nagaii Drive, traversing several miles of woodlands before curving north to run along the bottom of the slope. The rutted road was in bad shape, and it was a rough ride for the Mercedes.

The road skirted the gorge, bypassing it. The mouth of the cleft was obscured by a lot of brush and would have been easy to miss had it not been for the cars and emergency vehicles parked outside it.

A woodland path branched off the dirt road, leading into the gorge. The path was too tough for the Mercedes. The two agents had to get out and walk. They were challenged by a county sheriff's department deputy posted at the foot of the path to keep out civilians and other unauthorized personnel. They showed their CTU ID cards and were allowed to proceed.

Trees grew on both sides of the gorge entrance, meeting overhead to form a canopy of foliage. The path was little more than a trail, accessible only to heavy-duty SUVs rigged for off-road running. The overhanging trees formed a tunnel through a hundred feet or so of greenery. It was cool and dim under the trees except where sunbeams slanted through gaps between the boughs.

The tunnel ended, opening into a steep-sided ravine bright with sunlight. A thin trickling creek ran through the middle of the bottom of the gorge. Tufts of dry, weedy grass sprouted in clumps along its length.

The rocky terrain otherwise supported little in the way of vegetation. The north side featured a projecting ledge about two hundred feet above the ground on which stood a single tree. A long-dead tree weathered silver-gray, its twisted branches bare of any foliage. Jack guessed that this was the lone pine that had given the gorge its name, although as far as he could see there was nothing about it to identify it as a pine.

Jack was feeling better, his headache had lessened, possibly because of the aspirins or being at a lower attitude or a combination of the two. The left side of his face where he'd been struck still felt stiff and swollen, though.

A few vehicles—a tow truck and two police SUVs—had managed to bull their way up the trail path and into the gorge. A knot of people was centered around a wreck at the bottom of the ravine.

The wreck had been a dark green sedan; now it looked like a piece of metal that had been wadded up into a ball and thrown away. Jack looked up to see where the car had gone off the edge of Rimrock Road some eight hundred feet above. He had to tilt his head far back to see it, so that he was looking almost straight up.

Police and emergency personnel were clustered around the wreck. A few paramedics stood off to one side, waiting; there wasn't much for them to do until the two occupants were freed from the wreck. They'd have little more to do when that time came than to declare them DOA, dead on arrival.

Some mechanics from the tow truck were wrestling with a Jaws of Life device to pry open the collapsed metal, but the wreck was so crumpled up that they were unsure of where to begin applying the pressure and had already gotten off to a few false starts.

Jack stood at the edge of the group, craning to see inside the wreck. A pulpy mass of flesh and tangled limbs was sandwiched inside the collapsed heap, in such a condition that it was impossible to tell if it comprised one body or two.

A man in a pair of gray twill coveralls who'd been laboring in vain to pry open a compressed metal flange looked up and said, "This ain't working. We'll probably have to cut 'em out with a torch."

A county deputy said, "Can't do that here, too much risk of fire."

The mechanic said, "No gas in the tank. It busted

on the way down and spilled the contents all over the gorge. Lucky it didn't catch fire and burn."

"Yeah, lucky."

"You don't want to start fooling around with a torch with all that spilled gas around here. Might start off a real blaze."

"Best tow it into town then."

"How? Got to have at least two working wheels on it to give it a tow and there ain't none of them. Nothing to tow."

A man in a short-brimmed hat and a dark suit who'd been listening to the conversation put himself forward. "You can't just leave them out here, for God's sake."

Anne Armstrong told Jack, "That's Inspector Cullen of the Denver branch of the ATF." She spoke in a low voice so that only he could hear it.

The mechanic said, "My advice is to hook it up to the tow truck winch and drag it out of here to the dirt road. Get a flatbed truck out there. Flatbed couldn't get into here but it should be able to handle the access road. Hoist the wreck on the flatbed and take it to town where we can open it properly with the right tools."

Cullen said, "Do it, then."

The mechanic looked him up and down. "And who might you be, mister?"

"Cullen of the ATF. Those are my men in there."

"Oh. Sorry. You'll sign the authorization? I got to know who to bill for it, the county or the state or whoever—"

"The Federal government'll pay for it. Give me the paperwork and I'll sign it and you can get the show on the road."

"Coming right up, mister. Again, sorry about them fellows of yours. These mountain roads are a tricky proposition in even the best of weather." The mechanic went to the tow truck to get the paperwork.

Jack and Anne Armstrong went over to Cullen. She and Cullen were professionally acquainted, having worked joint operations in the past. Cullen had a wedge-shaped face with narrow slitted eyes, a knife-blade nose, and a thin horizontal slit of a mouth. Armstrong and Jack expressed their condolences.

Cullen said, "Mountain road my eye! Dean and O'Hara have been working this territory for years. They were both expert drivers. If that is them in the wreck."

Jack said, "Do you have any reason to doubt it?"

"The condition they're in, their own mothers wouldn't recognize them. But I'm sure it'll turn out to be them, worse luck. It was no driving mishap that did them in, though."

"I'd say that's a sure bet."

Cullen turned his narrow-eyed gaze full on Jack. "You know that or are you just guessing?"

"We lost a man at Red Notch last night and it was no accident. He was shot dead."

"Who was it?"

"Frank Neal."

"Too bad. He was a good man. So were O'Hara and Dean. And it happened last night?"

"Yes."

"Dean and O'Hara went missing the night before, Wednesday. I figure that that's when whatever happened to them happened. The car wasn't found until today. Somebody reported a gap in the guardrail up top yesterday, but the wreck couldn't be seen from up there so it wasn't followed up on. A Boy Scout troop hiking in the area found it early this morning.

"Neal was killed last night, eh? That compound's a death trap even after it's been abandoned. Who did it? Zealots?"

Jack shrugged. "No proof on that either way yet."

Cullen shook his head. "They were always a screwball outfit, but nothing compared to some of the other groups on our list. No history of any real violence apart from minor scuffles at demonstrations, breaking windows, resisting arrest, that sort of thing. We monitored them more as a preventive measure than anything else, to make sure they kept out of trouble.

"Well, they're in it now, right up to their necks. Too bad killers don't hang anymore. Lethal injection is a whole lot less satisfying somehow. But I'll settle for it when we get the bastards."

Anne Armstrong said, "Were your men working on anything specific on Wednesday night?"

Cullen shook his head. "Routine monitoring, maybe stepped up a notch on account of this Round Table meeting. What about your man?"

"Just doing a follow-up, checking out the compound."

"The Zealots must've gone kill-crazy. Maybe Prewitt had a divine revelation that the time had come for him to take up the sword."

"He's not the type for divine revelations. More likely he reasoned that events required him to seize the world-historical moment."

"We'll ask him before he's wheeled into the death chamber on a gurney."

Jack said, "Got to find him first."

Cullen said, "We'll find him."

The mechanic approached with a clipboard with a stack of papers attached. Cullen said, "Excuse me, I've got to take care of this."

Anne Armstrong said, "We've got to be going, too. I'm sorry about your men."

Cullen said, "That goes for me, too. I liked Neal."

"I'd appreciate it if you could send me a copy of the autopsy reports on O'Hara and Dean."

"Will do. Keep me posted on anything you get."

"Of course."

Cullen went into a huddle with the mechanic, scowling as he scanned the estimate of charges. The CTU pair drifted away.

Jack said, "I'm sure a postmortem will show that Dean and O'Hara were dead before they went over that cliff. I'd also like to have them tested for traces of CWs in their bloodstream."

Anne Armstrong said, "It can be arranged, but this wasn't the time and place to bring it up. That aspect will have to be handled with extreme delicacy."

"But quickly. The Round Table is already in session."

"You don't need to remind me of that," she said. "I think we've seen all there is to see here."

Jack nodded. They went back down the ravine and through the arcade of overhanging trees to where their car was parked. Jack said, "There's a familiar face."

He was referring to the MRT's Cole Taggart. Taggart and a county deputy were having words with two bikers. The bikers looked like the real thing, hard-core outlaw motorcyclists. "One-percenters," as they were called, their own mocking self-description

to distinguish themselves from the "ninety-nine per-
cent of respectable, law-abiding motorcyclists" that
industry spokesmen and proponents for responsible
biking enthusiasts routinely invoked to polish up the
public image that in their view had been tarnished
by the fringe outlaw element.

Not so unusual a sight in the West, where biker
gangs were more numerous and firmly established
than in the more urbanized areas east of the Mis-
sissippi. Denver and its surroundings had more than
their fair share of renegade motorcycle clubs.

These two specimens were emblematic of the type.
Each sat astride a heavy-duty Harley customized
with extended front forks and all the trimmings.
The duo were down and dirty in greasy, well-worn
denims, but their machines were in top shape, their
gleaming streamlined shapes marred only by a coating of dust picked up while cruising the dirt road.
The machines weren't dirt bikes built for off-roading
but rather muscular cycles designed for high-speed
highway long hauls. One thing outlaw bikers can do
is ride, handling their machines with the facility of a
Cossack on horseback, taking them to the streets or
the back trails as they pleased.

Jack's activities in the past had caused him to work
undercover operations among outlaw motorcycle
clubs with a penchant for gunrunning and operating
meth labs, so he eyed these two with a professional
interest.

One of them was medium-sized, with long, greasy
black hair slicked back and a hipster goatee. His eyes
were banded with oversized sunglasses that looked
like the kind worn by patients recovering from
cataract operations. Jack figured there was nothing

wrong with the cyclist's eyesight and that he sported the shades because they provided a kind of effective half mask, obscuring his features. His face above and below the dark glasses was wizened, sharp-featured, and weasely.

The other was big, hulking, pumped up with that comic book superhero physique that comes from steroid use. Reddish-gold hair was combed up in a pompadour and hung down the back of his neck in a classic mullet. His nose was crooked from having been broken several times, and he had a wide, jack-o'-lantern mouth.

The smaller of the two was saying, "We saw that some joker must've gone off the high side but we couldn't see nothing from up there so we came down for a better look."

The deputy said, "There's nothing to see so you can go back the way you came."

The big biker said, "That's some drop. How many people got killed?"

Taggart said, "You can read about it in the papers."

The big biker snickered. "Reading? What's that, man?"

His buddy laughed, said, "That's telling him, Rowdy."

The deputy said, "You can practice by reading a few traffic summonses if you like."

Rowdy said, "Hey man, what're you picking on us for? We ain't doing nothing."

Taggart said, "Go do it somewhere else."

The deputy said, "We don't rightly care for your kind hereabouts. Make yourself scarce, unless you'd like to spend ninety days as a guest of the county."

Rowdy turned to his buddy, said, "You heard the

man, Griff. No point hanging around where we're not wanted."

Griff said, "I can take a hint."

The dirt road was narrow and the bikers had to maneuver their machines to turn around. Their backs were to Jack and for the first time he could see their colors, the emblem of their club that was sewn to the backs of their sleeveless denim vests.

Their insignia depicted a demonic, quasi-humanoid Gila monster straddling a souped-up cycle on two stumpy legs. It bore the legend: "Hellbenders M.C."

Hellbenders Motorcycle Club. Jack had heard of them. A tough outfit, very tough. They'd been in the headlines about six months ago when some of their leaders had been swooped up in a high-profile gun-running bust.

One area of equipment where their bikes came up short was in the muffler department. The choppers took off with an earsplitting crack of iron thunder. The machines churned up dust clouds as they vroomed east on the dirt road, heading for Nagaii Drive.

The deputy and Taggart watched them go. The deputy muttered, "A-holes. You know if you search them bikers you'd find a half-dozen violations easy. And you know what'd happen if I did that?"

Taggart said, "No, what?"

"The sheriff'd have me on the carpet for a royal ass-chewing, for diverting precious departmental resources on them hog-riding fools when we're already stretched thin providing security for the Round Table."

Taggart laughed. "That's why he's sheriff. He's got his priorities right. Nothing's more important than making sure that nobody crashes that private party for Richie Riches."

The deputy said, "Soon as they haul that wreck with those two stiffs in it out of here, I got to go back to patrolling Sky Mount."

"You and me both, brother."

"I don't know what the big deal is. It ain't like that heap was going anyplace."

"It had a couple of ATF guys in it, so that makes it Federal."

"Big deal."

Taggart joked, "Maybe they were drunk when they went over the edge."

That got a laugh out of the deputy. "That's what I'm going to do when the conference is done—get drunk. And not before then. They've got us all pulling double shifts while it's on. All leaves and days off canceled for the duration."

Taggart said, "Times are tough all over."

Jack and Anne Armstrong had to cross the road to get to where their car was parked. Their path crossed that of Taggart and the deputy. The deputy had seen their credentials when they first arrived so he let them pass without comment.

Jack and Taggart made eye contact. Jack said, "Small world."

Taggart smiled. "Miller Fisk is mad at you."

"He can have a rematch anytime he wants."

"He ain't that mad. Anyhow, Hardin's got him pulling roadblock duty way up in the hills right now. He's so teed off at Fisk that Fisk is lucky he's not cleaning latrines at the station instead."

"Is Hardin mad at him for abusing a prisoner or for getting chopped down to size?"

"There's a question. You'll have to ask Bryce the answer to that one."

"And you?"

"Far as I'm concerned, that overgrown plowboy got what's been coming to him for a long time. 'Course, I ain't related to him, like Bryce is."

"Is that right?"

"Fisk is Hardin's nephew. You don't think Fisk made the MRT because he's a regular Sherlock Holmes, do you?"

Jack said, "I'm going to try to not think about it at all."

Taggart said, "Not a bad idea. See you around."

Jack nodded to him. Anne Armstrong was already in the car, waiting for him. She looked pleased. She said, "I just finished talking with Central. Good news for a change."

Jack said, "What've you got?"

"A lead, maybe. They've turned up somebody who's seen the blue bus."

1 2 3 4 5 6 7 **8** 9
10 11 12 13 14 15 16 17
18 19 20 21 22 23 24

· ·

THE FOLLOWING TAKES PLACE
BETWEEN THE HOURS OF
10 A.M. AND 11 A.M.
MOUNTAIN DAYLIGHT TIME

· ·

Dixon Cutoff, Colorado

Cletus Skeets said, "Is there going to be any reward money in this?" He pronounced it "ree-ward." He was of medium height, reedy, with muddy eyes, a three-day beard, and a prominent Adam's apple.

Anne Armstrong said, "It's possible, Mr. Skeets."

Skeets indicated Ernie Sandoval. "Because that's what he told Mabel. That there was a reward."

Ernie Sandoval, a CTU/DENV investigative agent in his mid-thirties, was short, chunky, moon-faced, with close-cropped dark hair, dark brown eyes, and a thick mustache. He'd been doing some good old-fashioned legwork all morning, canvassing stops along some of the back roads in the Red Notch area. He'd found a possible lead at the Pup Tent, a greasy-spoon diner located on the Dixon Cutoff, a pass between Mount Nagaii and Mount Zebulon that was used by local drivers and long-haul truckers.

Jack Bauer, Armstrong, Sandoval, and Skeets were standing in the parking lot of the Pup Tent, a roadside eatery on the north side of the east-west running Dixon Cutoff. The diner was a white wooden-frame building that looked like what it was, an overgrown hot dog stand. A hand-painted marquee on the roof depicted a cartoonish hot dog in a ten-gallon hat and cowboy boots firing off a pair of six-guns. The legend beneath it read: "Ask about our famous footlong Texas Wieners!"

The structure sat in the middle of an elongated gravel parking lot, extra-sized to accommodate big-rig trucks whose drivers wanted to grab a bite on this side of the mountains. There were no big rigs in the lot now, just Armstrong's Mercedes, the Toyota pickup that Sandoval had been making his rounds in, and a couple of cars belonging to diner patrons and personnel.

Sandoval had warm brown eyes and an engaging smile. He said, "That's not entirely accurate, Mr. Skeets. What I told your employer was that we are prepared to pay a modest sum in the event that the information you supply helps us to locate the people we're looking for."

Skeets said, "That's a reward, ain't it?"

"Call it what you like. The information has to be verified and significantly useful in discovering the whereabouts of the persons of interest. In other words, if your tip pays off, we pay off."

Skeets licked his lips. "How much?"

"That depends on how useful the information is.

We won't be able to assess that until it's been properly evaluated and followed up on."

"A couple of thousand bucks?"

"A couple of hundred bucks, maybe." Sandoval was starting to get irritated. "We're not exactly buying the plans for an atomic bomb here, we're just trying to find some missing persons."

Skeets got a shifty look in his eyes. "Well, I don't know about that. I had to come down here on my time off. I work nights and I ain't had my proper sleep. Could throw off my recollection, that is if I did see anything at all."

Jack, impatient, decided to play bad cop to Sandoval's good cop. He said, "Maybe a stretch in jail will improve your memory."

Skeets tried to tough it out. "You got no call to arrest me. I ain't done nothing. I got my rights!"

"You're a possible material witness who's impeding a Federal investigation. That's grounds for holding you in custody for forty-eight hours. For starters."

Skeets's eyes bulged and his Adam's apple bobbed. "Now hold on a danged minute—"

Jack had an inspiration. "Maybe you know a state cop named Miller Fisk?"

"Who don't? Everybody around here knows him. They ought to, he throws his weight around enough. He's a real mean SOB."

"A session with Fisk might help you get your mind right. Why don't we give him a call and tell him to come on down?"

Skeets held up both hands palms-out in a gesture of surrender. "You don't have to do that! It's all coming back to me now."

"Okay—give."

Skeets said, "I'll tell you what I told Pedro."

"Who's he?"

"The dishwasher on the night shift. We was both working on Wednesday night. Thursday morning, actually. Mabel, she goes home at midnight, so there's just me and Pedro holding down the fort. I do the cooking and he does the cleaning and we get by. Don't get many customers between midnight and dawn, 'cept for some long-haul truckers and night owls with a load on who want to get something in their bellies to help them sober up. So the two of us is plenty.

"Anyhow, pretty late in the shift, it was dead quiet so I went out for a smoke. Mabel used to be a heavy smoker but she quit and now she don't allow no smoking inside nohow. Not the customers or nobody. She knows if anybody's been smoking in the diner when she ain't there, she's got a nose on her. I tried it once or twice and sure enough, as soon as she comes in, first thing at six o'clock in the morning, she wrinkles up her nose and sniffs around and says, 'Cletus, you been smoking.' She told me off but good both times and after you've been told off by Mabel, you've been told. So when I want a smoke I go outside, which is what I done that night."

Jack said, "What time was that, Mr. Skeets?"

"Well, I went out a couple of times, but the time we're talking about was four-thirty in the ay emm. I remember that 'cause I looked at the clock and said to myself, Just another hour and a half to go and I'm out of here. I went outside and sat down on the front stairs and lit up.

"No sooner do I fire up a smoke than I seen a pair of headlights coming. There ain't much traffic at that hour and I said, Dang, don't that beat all? Soon as I take a break, a customer rolls along. Figured it was a customer because there ain't hardly no traffic at all at that hour."

"Which direction was the vehicle coming from, Mr. Skeets?"

"East, from the east. Only it wasn't no vehicle, it was a bunch of them. A regular convoy. A pickup truck, a couple of cars, and a bus, all riding together in a line. They didn't stop, neither, but kept right on going."

"They went west?"

Skeets nodded. "Yep. West, toward the pass. I wouldn't have thought nothing much about it, 'cept for the bus."

"Why is that?"

"It was a school bus. Just struck me funny some-how. I mean, here it is the middle of summer. Ain't no school in session. Summer school, maybe, but they don't need no bus for that and even if they did, they don't run at four-thirty in the morning. Ain't even no schools around here, for that matter. Sure ain't none west of the pass. So I said to myself, What-all do they need a school bus for in July?"

Skeets went on, "Another thing that struck me about it was the color. It was a funny color. Every school bus I ever seen was yellow. Not this one, though."

"What color was it?"

"Blue. It was blue. The diner's all lit up at night so truckers can see it from a long way off and they'll have plenty of time to slow down their rigs and pull in. So I could see the bus nice and clear and sure enough, it was blue."

"Did you notice anything else unusual about it?"

"Nope."

"Were there any people inside it?"

Skeets shrugged. "Danged if I know. It was dark—the bus, I mean. I couldn't see inside it."

"What happened then?"

"It drove by, along with the rest of the convoy. They was heading west, toward the pass. That's all I know. I finished my smoke and went inside. I told Pedro what I saw. It's funny to see a school bus in summer, a blue one at that. Shoot, you can't get these no-account kids today to go to school even when it's in session. They'd rather be going off skylarking and cutting up capers . . . I went back to work and didn't think no more about it. Not till today, when I got roused out of a sound sleep by a phone call from Mabel telling me to get my butt down here to talk to you folks. Which I have now done."

Sandoval said, "And we appreciate it, Mr. Skeets."

"Any chance you could show that appreciation with some folding green?"

"If your information proves to be instrumental in locating the missing persons, there may be some financial remuneration forthcoming."

"I don't suppose you could let me have a couple of twenties now, just on account, say?"

Sandoval shook his head. "It doesn't work that way, Mr. Skeets. Sorry."

Skeets looked glum but resigned. "Reckon I got to trust you folks then."

Sandoval reached for his wallet. Skeets's eyes brightened for an instant, only to dim again when Sandoval took out a card and handed it to him. Sandoval said, "If you should think of anything else in connection with the sighting, you can reach me at that number any time of the day or night."

Skeets dropped the card into the left breast pocket of his T-shirt. He assumed a conspiratorial manner and said, "Hey, who's missing anyhow? You can trust me to keep my mouth shut."

Sandoval said, "We're not authorized to release that information at this time."

Skeets nodded, not surprised. "You done? I can go?"

"Yes, sir. Thank you for your cooperation."

"Reckon I'll go inside. Mabel can't begrudge me a cup of coffee, after getting me out of bed on my time off to come down here. She will, though."

Skeets started toward the diner, halting after a few paces. He turned and looked at Jack, said, "You won't say nothing to Fisk about me calling him a mean SOB? I'd hate to get on his bad side. Not that he's got a good one.

"Er, forget that I said that, too," he added.

Jack said, "You can rely on our discretion, Mr. Skeets. Just like I'm sure we can rely on you not to discuss this conversation with anyone else."

Skeets said, "I'm a closed book. I won't crack to nobody about nothing."

"Fine."

Skeets took a few more steps, paused, looked over his shoulder. "If there is any reward . . ."

"We know where to find you."

"I won't have to split it with Mabel and Pedro, will I? After all, I done the seeing, not them."

Sandoval said, "We'll be in touch."

Skeets crossed to the diner, entered it, the front screen door banging shut behind him. Jack said, "There goes a public-spirited citizen."

Sandoval said, "You forgot something, Jack."

"What?"

Sandoval indicated the sign on the roof. "You didn't ask about their famous Texas wieners."

"Yeah, I missed that one."

"I didn't. I had one while I was waiting for you and Anne."

"How was it?"

Sandoval held his stomach with both hands, looking slightly bilious. "Don't ask."

Anne Armstrong said, "Never mind about that. What do you make of Skeets's story?"

Jack said, "He knew about the blue bus without being told. The Zealots' disappearance has been withheld from the media so he didn't pick it up there."

Sandoval said, "I doubt friend Skeets knows the difference between the Zealots and a basketball team."

Jack said, "The time of the sighting works, too."

Sandoval said, "It's also significant that he didn't come to us. If he were a walk-in I'd be suspicious that he was a plant because the public doesn't know CTU is looking for the Zealots. No, he told Pedro the dishwasher, who told Mabel, who told me when I came in two hours ago. I was canvassing the area, asking around if anybody'd seen anything unusual early on Thursday morning. She volunteered the information, and when I expressed interest she phoned Skeets and told him to come on down."

He added, "Skeets was right about that, too. When Mabel tells you to do something, you get told."

Jack looked westward, where a ribbon of road stretched across the flat before disappearing in a gap between Mount Nagaii and Mount Zebulon. "Where does that pass lead?"

Sandoval said, "Straight through to the western slopes of the mountains."

Anne Armstrong, thoughtful, said, "Shadow Valley is in the pass."

Sandoval said, "That's right!"

Jack looked from one to the other. They both looked intrigued. He said, "What's Shadow Valley?"

Armstrong said, "A canyon complete with its own ghost town, Silvertop. There used to be a big silver mine there before the lode played out. It's been abandoned for years—decades."

Jack said, "You can hide a lot of things in an old mine."

• •

THE FOLLOWING TAKES PLACE
BETWEEN THE HOURS OF
11 A.M. AND 12 P.M.
MOUNTAIN DAYLIGHT TIME

• •

Shadow Valley, Colorado

Shadow Valley is a canyon that cuts deep into the foothills of the southern slopes of Mount Zebulon. The canyon's main trunk runs north-south, with numerous side canyons branching off to the east and west.

A Toyota pickup truck and an Explorer SUV turned right off Dixon Cutoff, entering the canyon. The pickup held Anne Armstrong and Jack Bauer; the SUV held four well-armed members of a CTU/DENV tactical squad.

Jack, Armstrong, and Sandoval had earlier gone from the Pup Tent to the CTU mobile command post at Pike's Ford, located at the foot of Sky Mount. Various bits of business had to be taken care of at the CP.

Armstrong had changed clothes, shedding skirt and loafers for khaki pants and hiking shoes in preparation for probing the canyon ghost town. Jack had taken the opportunity to check his pistol, making sure that it worked properly. It had been out of his hands from the time he'd been busted in Random until it was returned to him at the Mountain Lake substation. It was basic tradecraft: he needed to make sure that it hadn't been tampered with during the time it had been out of his possession. He didn't think it had been but he wasn't going to stake his life on an assumption by going back out in the field with a potentially defective weapon. He'd examined it before going to Sky Mount and everything had seemed to be in order, but he hadn't been able to give it the acid test by firing off some rounds.

He did so at Pike's Ford at a crude but effective firing range that had been set up well away from the group of mobile home trailers that comprised the temporary command post. One of the pluses of this mountain locale was that there was plenty of empty land and no neighbors to kick about guns being discharged in the vicinity. The weapon fired effectively and accurately with the original ammunition that had been in the magazines, which had also been confiscated by the MRT during his arrest. He also fired off some rounds from the Pike's Ford ammo, with equally positive results. He would have liked to break down the weapon and clean it but there wasn't time for it now. He armed himself with a half-dozen magazines of fresh ammo and a couple of handfuls of loose rounds that he put in the side pockets of his jacket.

He checked his cell phone for voice mail. A number of messages had been left for him by Ryan

Chappelle, offering no new information but instead first requesting and then demanding updates and progress reports on the Sky Mount situation. Jack left them unanswered for the time being. He was covered; he was in the middle of an investigation and had no time to spare answering Chappelle's queries. Chappelle could stew in his own juices for a while longer, while Jack prowled Shadow Valley to see what if anything could be found. Jack grinned to himself at the image of Chappelle on the boil waiting for a response back in L.A.

He spent the time more productively by grabbing a few sandwiches from a vending machine in an area of one of the trailers that served as a galley. He heated them in a microwave and wolfed them down with a couple of cups of coffee. They tasted like cardboard, and the coffee was no prize, either, but it felt good to have some food in his belly to restore his strength and energy.

CTU/DENV head Orlando Garcia was off-site but was represented here by his assistant SAC, Dirk Vanaheim. Vanaheim conveyed Garcia's directive that the searchers would be outfitted in protective gear and escorted by a four-person tac squad. This precautionary measure was a result of the attack last night at Red Notch.

Ernie Sandoval had some inquiries he needed to follow up on so he remained behind at the CP. Jack, Armstrong, and the tac squad mounted up in their two vehicles and headed out. The Explorer was a regular battle wagon, with bulletproof glass, armor plating, solid rubber tires, and a souped-up engine with big muscle to propel the machine at high speeds. The pickup truck was customized with some extras but wasn't bulletproof. The Explorer took the lead, the pickup following. Armstrong drove, Jack riding in the cab's passenger seat.

Twenty minutes' motoring put the two-vehicle convoy at the mouth of Shadow Valley canyon. The canyon's floor of hard-packed dirt was crisscrossed with countless tire tracks. Anne Armstrong said, "Off-road enthusiasts use it for dirt biking and ATVs, and teens come out here to park and get drunk and generally party."

Jack said, "Might not hurt to see if any of the locals have been reported missing in the time from early Thursday morning to now. Someone might have seen something that somebody else didn't want seen and been disappeared for it."

Armstrong radioed in to Central requesting information on that score. Central replied they'd look into it and get back to her.

The canyon was seemingly unoccupied today with no other humans in sight. Arroyos, gullies, and gorges branched off to the east and west of the main trunk. A couple of miles deeper into the ravine brought the CTU team in view of a sugarloaf-shaped bluff on the western side of the passage. Its slope was honeycombed with vertical and horizontal trails and speckled with bits and pieces of old weathered wooden structures: here a half-collapsed platform supported by a framework of trestles and cross-braced timbers, there a section of diagonal sluice spillway leading to nowhere, and scattered throughout, the ruins of shacks and sheds.

This was the one area of the canyon where an attempt, however feeble, had been made to restrict public access. The base of the slope was bordered by a chain-link fence; a gate barred the way to a dirt road stretching to the summit.

Armstrong said, "That's Silvertop. The bluff held a rich lode of silver ore and was mined extensively in the 1890s. It gave rise to a boom town, but when the deposit played out, the town did, too."

The SUV and the pickup halted at the gate at the foot of the road that climbed the hill. The long, gentle rise was stepped with terraces that had been carved out so that different veins of the lode could be mined.

The occupants dismounted from the vehicles. The tac squad consisted of four men, Frith, Bailey, Holtz, and Sanchez. All were fit, well-conditioned, clear-eyed, and cool-nerved. They were action men—trigger pullers. Frith and Holtz were armed with M–16s, Bailey and Sanchez with M–4 carbines. They were all equipped with sidearms, too, semi-automatic pistols in hip holsters.

CTU wanted to minimize its footprint in Sky Mount and environs so the squad members wore civilian clothes, utility vests, and T-shirts, baggy cargo-pocketed pants, and hiking boots. They, like Jack and Armstrong, were all outfitted in flak jackets. The squad men openly carried their weapons. Clandestinity only went so far before being superseded by the demands of security.

Frith, long-faced and lanky, was in command of the squad but subordinate to Jack and Armstrong. There was a sensitive issue of protocol here. Jack expected to be obeyed when he gave an order but he was the outsider here, an unknown quantity to the others. He would let Armstrong take the lead, couching his commands where possible in the form of suggestions. The key phrase: where possible.

It was hot out here in the open, hotter still because of the flak jackets. Jack consoled himself with the thought that it was nothing compared to how hot things could get without the protection of the Kevlar vest if trouble happened. Shooting trouble.

Shadows were short under a midday sun that stood almost directly overhead, pouring its rays straight down into the canyon. Sun-baked flats and rock walls threw back the heat. The CTU team all wore headgear. Frith and Sanchez wore baseball caps, Holtz and Bailey wore soft, shapeless fabric hats. Armstrong and Jack wore unmarked baseball caps that had been supplied from tac squad stores at Pike's Ford. Jack's headache had subsided in recent hours but the pounding heat made his temples throb, a portent of returning discomfort.

The fence enclosing the bottom of the hill was old, rusted. It was hung with a number of NO TRESPASS-ING signs, all of which were nearly illegible due to being bullet-riddled by high-spirited sportsmen. Gaps opened in the barrier where whole sections had been trampled flat by dirt bikers and ATV riders, the tracks of whose vehicles had worn clearly marked trails up the sides of the bluff.

The gate blocking the main access road was made of stronger stuff and stood solid and intact. It was secured by a length of padlocked chain. Both chain and lock were shiny and bright. Jack said, "They look brand-new, like they were put here yesterday."

Anne Armstrong said, "Maybe they were."

"But by whom?"

The Explorer's rear hatch was opened, revealing a variety of gear. There were hard hats and flash-lights, coils of rope, picks and shovels and other tools. Bailey pulled on a pair of work gloves, picked up a pair of bolt cutters, and went to the gate. He snugged the open pincers against one section of a link of shiny new chain and squeezed the handles. He had to put some muscle into it, his face reddening and veins standing out on his forehead.

The section parted. He did the same thing to the other half of the link until it parted, too. The chain fell away from the gate. Holtz opened the gate all the way. Bailey stowed the bolt cutters and the work gloves in the rear of the SUV and closed the hatch.

Jack and Armstrong got back into their vehicle, the squad men into theirs. The SUV climbed the main road up the long, low-angled slope, the pickup following. They crested the summit, rolling to a halt on a spacious, flat-topped expanse.

Anne Armstrong radioed Central, informing them that the team vehicles would now be going out of service. Central acknowledged, their response scratchy with static. Armstrong said, "Radio reception is spotty here due to interference from the canyon walls and the mountains, Jack. Our portable handsets lack the power to send or receive messages to Central. The truck radio is stronger because it works off the vehicle's battery, but even it's barely adequate for communication purposes. The same goes for the SUV. So when we go out of service here, our outside comm is really closed down."

Jack nodded. They got out of the pickup. The tac squad piled out of the Explorer. The squad men shared one trait in common: ever-alert eyes that were constantly scanning the surroundings, always in motion, never lingering for too long on any one fixed point. The eyes of hunters. Jack recognized the behavior pattern because he was the same way.

The top of the bluff was a rough oblong the size of several football fields put together, its long axis running north-south. Its western edge bordered the foot of a long, low ridge beyond which could be seen lines of wooded hills, rising in tiers to southern spurs of Mount Zebulon.

The flat-topped mound was littered with remnants of what had once been a thriving mining town at the end of the nineteenth century. It didn't fit in with Jack's notions about a western ghost town. It looked more like a war ruin. Some of the buildings were made of brick or stone and might have been factories or warehouses. Others were rows of wooden frame buildings that had collapsed into heaps. Not a single structure was fully intact. One consisted of fragments of two stone walls that met to form a corner, another was a heap of plank board rubble with part of a stone chimney remaining. That was the pattern.

The weed-grown site had been plucked, pillaged, and otherwise deconstructed by generations of vandals, looters, and troublemakers. No standing section of wall or foundation was without layers of spray-painted graffiti, no pane of glass was unbroken. Mounds of ashes and charred timbers marked the spot where houses had been burned down.

It was a popular site with the locals, judging by the remains of bonfires and the profusion of broken bottles and empty beer cans. Tire tracks from two-, three-, and four-wheeled vehicles overlaid the ground. The raggedy fence and gate below had proved no deterrent to the many who'd driven their machines up and down the sides of the bluff.

Jack and Anne Armstrong each had a set of field

glasses. The entire CTU team was equipped with headset communicators, miniaturized transceivers consisting of an ear bud with a flexible plastic frame that fitted around one ear, extending into a curving plastic tube the width of a pipe cleaner that terminated near the wearer's mouth in a condenser microphone. They all now donned the transceivers, running a comm check to make sure each unit was properly sending and receiving.

The receiver bud buzzed in Jack's ear as he and the others sounded off. Audio quality was good, the signal strong and clear now that they were all grouped together. Whether it would remain so once they were scattered around the mound and no longer in one another's line of sight had yet to be determined.

Anne Armstrong addressed the group. "Watch your step. The town was built on top of the mine and is shot through with vertical air shafts. Some are boarded over and posted with warning signs, others are open holes in the ground that go down a hundred feet or more."

She had accessed the maps and diagrams of Silvertop's inner workings that were archived in the computers at the Pike's Ford CP and printed them out, bringing them along in a folder. They were crude and incomplete but workable as a rough guide to the sugarloaf butte's underground world. They would be of little use, however, unless a starting point was first found.

Sanchez said, "What exactly are we looking for?"

Jack said, "Anything that might indicate the presence of some or all of Prewitt's two dozen Zealots in the recent past or right now. For all we know, they could be holed up in some nest up here or nearby. Or down below, in one of the abandoned tunnels. Some of them could be watching us right now."

A ripple went through the others, causing the squad members to spread out so they wouldn't be bunched up in one tight target group. Bailey said, "That's a happy thought."

Holtz scanned the landscape and shook his head doubtfully. "It sure looks deserted."

"So did Red Notch last night but there were two killers there, and now a CTU agent is dead." Jack paused to let that sink in before continuing. "Zealots might be using this as a base, a rendezvous, or a staging area. They might have stored hardware or vehicles here. They might have left a cell behind for security while the others moved on. They might have come here for some unknown purpose on Wednesday night and moved on."

Holtz said, "They might not have come here at all."

"It's possible. But even then this won't be wasted effort. If Silvertop comes up clean, that's one possibility we can cross off the list and narrow the search perimeters in the hunt for Prewitt and his crew."

Anne Armstrong said, "A final word of caution. Silvertop is what's called an attractive nuisance. It's a hangout for high school kids and might also harbor squatters and hoboes. So if you see someone suspicious, make sure you know who you're shooting at before opening fire. We don't want to accidentally shoot some teens who came up here to get high or make out."

The team split up into two search groups, one consisting of Jack and Frith, the other of Armstrong, Holtz, and Sanchez. Bailey stayed behind to guard the vehicles and keep watch on the canyon below.

Jack and Frith would start at the southern end of

the hilltop and work their way north, Armstrong's group would begin at the northern end and work south. Jack and the squad leader crossed on a diagonal toward the southwest, a path that skirted the southernmost of the ruins.

The air was still, with barely the breath of a breeze. The sun was moving toward its zenith. Jack hadn't gone very far before breaking out into a sweat. His face was slick with wetness, and beads of perspiration trickled between his shoulder blades and down his back.

Frith said, "What do you reckon our chances are of finding something?"

Jack said, "I think it's worth a look or we wouldn't be out here. We've got a witness who saw Prewitt's blue bus and some other vehicles heading for this vicinity around the time of the disappearance early on Thursday. There've been no reported sightings of the convoy west of Dixon Cutoff. The Zealots may not be here now but they might have been here and left evidence that'll point toward where they went."

"The area was covered yesterday by search planes. They didn't turn up anything."

"As an old GI ground-pounder, I believe there's no substitute for on-site recon to see things the flyboys might have missed."

Frith grinned. "I've got to agree with you there. I'm ex-infantry myself."

Jack said, "I'm also a firm believer in taking the high ground." He pointed to the ridge at the western edge of the bluff. "That should be a good spot for surveying the terrain."

Bare dirt gave way to weeds that soon reached mid-calf height. Frith said, "Watch out for snakes."

Jack looked to see if he was kidding. Frith was

dead serious. He said, "Rattlesnakes like to prowl the tall grass for field mice and other varmints."

Jack was careful from then on to keep an even warier eye on the ground he trod. Ten minutes' hiking put him and Frith at the foot of the western ridge. It was a short walk to its low, rounded summit. The far side of the ridge dropped steeply into a deep hollow with a thin trickle of a creek running along the bottom. A higher, more heavily wooded slope rose on the other side.

Jack and Frith stood on the near side of the ridge, below the ridgetop to avoid skylining that would more readily reveal their presence. They faced east toward the ruins on the bluff. Jack took off his sunglasses and slipped them in the left breast pocket of his jacket. The jacket was thin but it still added to the oppressiveness of the heat. He would have liked to have shucked it off but it held his spare clips and loose rounds, and it was worth putting up with a little additional discomfort to have the extra ammo ready to hand. He reminded himself that compared to summer in Baghdad or the Sudan—he'd gone on missions in both—this was brisk, crisp weather.

Sweat stung his eyes and he wiped them against his sleeve in the crook of his arm. The field glasses hung from a strap around his neck. He tilted back the lid of his cap, raised the binoculars to his eyes, peered at a row of ruins, and adjusted the focus, sharpening it to clarity.

He mentally divided the landscape into grid squares and methodically scanned them one by one, working his way along the line of structures from south to north. He saw empty window frames with weeds growing behind them, blackened timbers that were the skeletal remains of a house's framework, ash heaps, and piles of rubble. He saw nothing out of the ordinary, no deviation from the pattern of abandonment and neglect.

Jack said, "Nothing." He removed his cap, freed the binocular strap from around his neck, and handed the field glasses to Frith. "Maybe you'll spot something."

Frith scanned the scene, studying it long and hard. "Nope."

"Let's try it a little further to the north."

They went north along the ridge. Jack contacted Anne Armstrong via his transceiver headset. She reported that so far her results were negative, too.

Jack and Frith halted some fifty yards north of their first position. Jack pointed the optics at a new section of the scene and resumed his methodical grid square survey of the ghost town.

More of the same unrolled itself through the twin lenses until he came to the shell of a long, shedlike structure whose long axis ran east-west. Its short, western wall was mostly intact but slanted inward at a forty-five-degree angle. The part of its north wall he could see was also tilted inward at an acute angle. The southern side was no wall at all but a heaped-up woodpile that was holding up a section of the collapsed roof.

There was something vaguely off and out of place about the ruin's outline that caught his attention, prompting him to give it a closer study. The roof, what there was of it, which wasn't much, was broken into sections that stuck out of the heap at odd angles.

There was a hole in the south side of the roof. It was covered with what looked like a canvas tarp.

The fabric was a tan, sandy-gray color. It would have been hard to see from ground level on the bluff, and even from the elevated vantage point of the ridge, he had to look twice to make sure what he was seeing.

He looked a third time and still saw it. He handed the field glasses to Frith. "Take a look at the roofline on the south side and tell me what you see."

Frith peered at the shed, the lower half of his face impassive below the binoculars. He fiddled with the focus knob and looked some more. "There's a covering on the roof . . . a tarpaulin of some sort."

Jack said, "Who puts a tarp on an old ruin? Somebody who wants to hide something inside, maybe."

Frith lowered the field glasses and looked at Jack. Jack said, "Let's go see."

He took the field glasses and slipped the strap on around his neck. He and Frith started downhill, angling toward the shed. Jack said, "Let's make sure it's not a false alarm before alerting the others."

Frith nodded, said, "Right." He'd been carrying his M–16 so that its barrel pointed at the ground; now he held it level but off to the side. Jack reached inside his jacket to give his gun butt a little nudge, adjusting it in the holster so it would come free easier if he needed it in a hurry.

They came down on the flat and made for the shed's southwest corner. Each step closer made it more evident that a tarp was fixed to part of the roof. Its tan, sandy color was much like the terrain at the top of the bluff—surely no coincidence. The ground around the shed was churned up with a lot of tire tracks, ruts, and broken earth.

Frith suddenly made a wide detour around a patch of ground. Jack froze, said, "Snake?"

Frith shook his head, showed a toothy grin. "Bear scat."

Jack took a closer look. The ground was littered with animal droppings. A sizable pile, not human. He said, "You can tell they're bear?"

Frith said, "Hell, yeah. I grew up in these parts and I live here now. The bear population has been allowed to grow until now they're a real nuisance. They're not afraid of humans and they like the taste of people's garbage better than the food they can forage in the woods."

Jack joked, "I'm warning you in advance. Zealots and killers are one thing but if I see a bear, I'm running."

"Won't do you any good. Bears're fast. They can run faster than you can." Frith eyed the pile with an outdoorsman's discernment. "The spoor's at least a day old so we're probably in the clear."

Jack noticed that they were both talking in low, hushed voices. He said, "I'll tell you this: it wasn't a bear that put that tarp on the roof."

They continued onward, closing on the shed. Planks in the tilted west wall were cracked and splintered at about midbody height and bore fresh gouges and scrapings. The ground on the west side of the shed was noticeably torn up.

The south wall was a massed rubble of broken boards and beams. The edges of the canvas tarp hung down over the top of the pile. Football-sized rocks had been placed along the rim to hold it down and pin it in place.

Jack said, "I want to see what that tarp is covering up." The heaped rubble on the south was too unsteady to climb. The east side, the building's front, was in similar condition, a junk pile.

The long north wall looked more promising. The northwest corner of the shed was its most intact section. Part of the roof there was solid. Much of the wall was broken into slablike sections. There were a couple of empty window frames but the roof had fallen in, blocking a view inside.

Jack tackled the northwest corner. He took off the field glasses and set them down. He pulled his hat down tight on his head. A beam end protruded from the wall at about chest height. Jack hung on to it with both hands, testing it with his weight. It seemed solid enough.

Frith gave him a boost, allowing Jack to scramble up the side of the tilted wall and stand on the beam end. Jack reached up, grabbing the overhang of the roof with both hands, steadying himself. He chinned himself up to the top of the wall, booted feet scrabbling against the boards. He grunted and panted as he heaved his upper body onto the roof.

The wood creaked and groaned under him, giving him a bad moment, but it stayed in place. He got his feet under him and rose into a half crouch, ready to jump clear at the first sign of an imminent collapse.

He could see where a line of nails the size of railroad spikes had been hammered into the wood along the edge where the roof had broken off and fallen in. They anchored the near end of the tarp in place. They looked new. He really wanted to see what was underneath that tarp.

He dropped to his knees and lay prone on the roof. It seemed solid underneath him. He thought that if it had held the weight of whoever drove the nails it could hold his weight. He bellied his way to the edge.

The tarp was tough and nailed down tight. If he only had a knife . . . But the tarp wasn't nailed down on the south side of the shed, it was held in place by rocks. He clawed at the canvas, trying for a handhold. The tarp sagged in the middle, there was some play in it. He grabbed a double handful of a fold in the fabric and started pulling it toward him.

The tarp was heavy and didn't want to move. He tugged the fold over the edge of the roof. Now he could rest his arms on the roof and pull the canvas down toward him. He had the advantage of gravity and his weight working for him. He heaved and pulled.

The tarp yielded, folding toward him. There was the sound of rocks falling down the other side of the shed. Jack kept pouring it on. More rocks fell until there weren't enough of them to hold the tarp in place.

The tarp fell through the hole in the roof, except where it was nailed down on Jack's side. It didn't fall far. Something underneath was holding it up.

Jack stuck his head over the edge and looked down. The tarp was draped over a whalelike shape that filled the collapsed shed, nearly reaching what was left of the roof beams. He reached inside the hole, heaving the tarp toward him with both hands, slowly uncovering what lay beneath.

He said, "Huh!" He was too out of breath to say anything else. He sounded part surprised, part triumphant.

Frith stood with his head tilted back, looking up, but he couldn't see what Jack saw. He called, "What is it?"

Jack said, "The blue bus."

. . . .

**THE FOLLOWING TAKES PLACE
BETWEEN THE HOURS OF
12 P.M. AND 1 P.M.
MOUNTAIN DAYLIGHT TIME**

. . . .

Silvertop, Colorado

There was no stopping Jack, he had to see the thing through. Now that he knew what lay within the collapsed shed, he had a better idea of how to proceed and the tolerances of the structure he was scrambling around on. He was avid for clues but not at the cost of breaking his neck.

The bus was fitted into the shell of the shed so that its front was at the east end. Jack toed the edge of the roof and jumped down through the gap to the top of the bus. It was a short drop, only a few feet; the shed was low and the bus was tall. He came down toward the rear of the vehicle, the impact of his landing making a hollow booming sound. He landed on his feet, knees bent to absorb the shock.

The shed had been knocked down around the bus. Debris hemmed it in on all sides. He kicked the rest of the tarp off the roof; it hung down like a curtain from where it was nailed to the roof. Sunlight streamed in through the hole in the top of the shed.

The roof of the bus was slightly curved but provided solid footing. He knelt facing the right side, thinking to hang over the edge so he could look through the windows. But there was nothing to hang on to and he didn't want to risk sliding off the edge headfirst.

He walked across the roof to the front of the bus. Rubble was piled up to the top of the hood but no higher. The right front door was blocked by too much debris to allow him to open it. He stepped down on to the hood and hunkered down there, facing the windshield. It was opaque with a coating of dust. He rubbed his sleeve against it to clean it and peered through the pane.

The interior was dark, thick with shadows. Jack put his face up close to the glass, holding a hand against the side of his face to screen out the glare.

The bus was empty.

That surprised him. He couldn't see much through the gloom, but as far as he could tell the bus contained no bodies. As far as he could tell.

He had to know for sure. He sat down on the hood. He was able to reach down and pick up a rock from the top of the pile of debris crowding the vehicle. He picked up a big one and brought it down hard on the center of the windshield. The glass puckered where the leading edge of the rock hit it, a spiderweb of cracks radiating out from the point of impact.

He struck again, harder. The spiderweb expanded,

the pane becoming translucent as if frosted in the center. He bashed it a few more times, turning his head away from it to protect his eyes in case of flying glass shards.

The windshield was made of safety glass. It held until it reached its breaking point and then it came apart all at once, disintegrating into a mass of crystal cubes that looked like several shovelfuls of miniature ice cubes. They went crashing into the bus, clearing out the windshield frame.

A wave of heat and stink came pouring out through the opening. The bus had been shut up tight, all windows closed, causing massive heat to build up inside. The stink was the smell of decay. Jack caught a whiff of it. He felt his gorge rise and he had to fight to keep from gagging.

The gloom inside the bus was not static but dynamic, flowing, pulsing—buzzing. Its source was a horde of flies, much of which came pouring out of the hole. Jack climbed on top of the bus's roof and walked to the rear of it, filling his lungs with fresh air.

He waited a few minutes for the worst of it to clear before returning to the front of the bus and squatting on the hood. The smell was still pretty rough. He'd have covered his mouth and nose with a handkerchief or piece of cloth if he'd had one but he didn't, so he had to make do. He held his breath and stuck his head through the windshield frame.

The stench came from masses of dried blood on the inside of the bus. The central aisle was smeared with it. So were the three steps leading down to the front door. The bus had seemed sealed tight but the flies had gotten inside. They always do, somehow.

The safety glass had come apart in cubes that

looked like rock salt. There were no jagged, razor-edged shards. Jack brushed aside the fragments on the hood. He crouched almost double, sticking a foot through the frame and stepping down to the driver's seat. The driver's area was free of blood.

Jack eased himself through the frame into the bus. It was like stepping into a baker's oven. Sweat sprang out from every pore. He breathed through his nose as shallowly as possible. A cloud of flies buzzed around him. He waved his hand in front of his face, batting them away, but they kept coming back.

He took out a small flashlight from one of his pockets and switched it on to dispel some of the murky shadows. He made his way down the aisle toward the rear of the bus, the flashlight beam gliding over rows of seats, the floor and walls. Some seats were blood-stained but most were not. A few side windows were cracked but none had been broken. No bodies were in view. He ducked down to shine the light under the seats but there were no bodies there, either.

He worked his way to the back of the bus. It lacked an emergency rear door. A mass of dried blood stained the floor and back panel. It was reddish-brown and several inches thick. The evidence seemed to indicate that there had been a number of bleeding bodies at the back of the bus, that they had been dragged to the front and out the door.

Jack figured he had seen all there was to see for now. The forensics team could take it from here. He wanted out.

He went to the front of the bus, using the driver's seat as a stepping stone to climb through the windshield frame and out on to the hood. He hopped up on the vehicle's roof and went to the rear. He boosted himself onto the top of the shed and jumped off. He landed on the ground with knees bent, rolling on his shoulder to absorb the impact.

Anne Armstrong, Holtz, and Sanchez had joined Frith and they were all waiting for him. Bailey was still back at the vehicles keeping watch. Sanchez said to Jack, "You look pretty shook, man."

Jack took some deep breaths, filling his lungs with clean air. He could still taste the blood reek in his nostrils and at the back of his throat. Holtz had a canteen. Jack took a mouthful of warm water, swished it around in his mouth, and spat it out. He drank some more before returning the canteen.

Anne Armstrong said, "What did you find?"

Jack told them. Armstrong said, "What do you make of it?"

Jack said, "I'm only guessing based on what I saw. The Zealots didn't just pull a disappearing act on Thursday morning. There was a purge, too. One faction cleaning up on a dissident element, say. The victims were killed or wounded at Red Notch. Maybe some were killed and some only wounded. The entire compound cadre cleared out in the blue bus and some other vehicles. Our witness Skeets said there was a convoy of a couple cars and trucks along with the bus. The victims were in the bus.

"Somewhere along the way but most likely here at Silvertop the bodies were disposed of. The bus was backed into this shed, which was a wreck already. The killers finished the job, probably by battering it down with one or more of their other vehicles. It wouldn't take much to bring the walls down considering the age and state of disrepair of the shed. You could do it with a pickup truck or SUV. The west wall is broken in at just about the right height for a truck bumper and there are fresh scrapes and gouges on the boards.

"What the collapsed shed didn't hide was concealed under the tarp. It's the same color as the surroundings and would blend right in with the scenery. Especially to any air searches doing a flyover."

Sanchez said, "I don't get it. Why go to all that trouble?"

Jack said, "The blue bus was a liability. Too big, too obvious, and too well-known. And one more reason: the surviving Zealots didn't need it anymore. They were able to leave in the other vehicles that made up the convoy. Which tells you another thing—there couldn't have been too many Zealots left out of the original two dozen or so."

Frith said, "That must've been some purge."

Jack nodded. "A real Night of the Long Knives."

Armstrong said, "It sounds plausible but one aspect puzzles me. After taking such pains to hide the bus, why not leave the bodies inside?"

Jack said, "I picked up on that, too. It's a key question. Why *not* leave the bodies inside? It suggests that discovery of the bus by the authorities is less important than the discovery of the bodies. For some reason, the bodies must not be found. Why not?

"One answer comes to mind. Whose bodies are they? What if Prewitt himself was one of the ones purged? Suppose the cult leader and his loyalists were eliminated by an upstart faction. That development would electrify the rest of his crowd, namely the hundreds of rank-and-file members outside the inner circle. Many of whom are known to reside in this state to be close to their guru.

"The usurpers could be the ones planning a strike against the Round Table. Prewitt and his loyalists opposed it so they had to go. But the plotters still require the assistance of Zealots outside the Red Notch cadre to carry out their plan. True believers who'd jump to obey the commands of their grand exalted leader Prewitt would balk if the orders came from someone else, some upstart who's trying to take over the whole works."

Armstrong frowned, stroking her chin. "Prewitt's death—murder—would have the members scrambling like an overturned anthill if it were known."

Jack went on, "Or it could work the other way. Maybe Prewitt's in favor of a strike and liquidated all those who opposed him. That would split the cult, too, at a critical time when unity is required for a Sky Mount action."

He smacked a fist against his palm. "All of which makes it vital that those bodies be found—and quick!"

Armstrong said, "Yes, but how?"

Jack said, "I think I've got a lead. A clue. If I'm right we won't have to look very far." He indicated a gaping hole in the ground about a hundred feet east of the shed. "See that ventilator shaft?"

The others turned to look at where he was pointing. He went on, "There's something different about it from the other holes in the ground on top of the bluff. I noticed it when I was up on the roof of the shed. It stands out when you see it from above. What it is, is that the soil around the hole is a different color from the rest of the terrain. It's darker. Like maybe somebody raked it up to cover their tracks."

Armstrong said, "It's worth a look."

The group crossed toward the shaft. The sun was a bit past the zenith, and the team members cast blobs of shadow that slanted slightly east.

The mouth of the shaft was an unnaturally regular circle of blackness gaping in the middle of the ground. It was not boarded over or fenced in. It was about thirty feet in diameter and was ringed by a brown band of soil. Beyond the ring the ground was light brown streaked with tans and grays.

Sanchez said, "It is a different color."

Jack said, "There's no tracks running through it, either."

Holtz said, "That doesn't mean anything. Nobody's going to ride a dirt bike or off-road vehicle too close to the edge."

Jack said, "Not many weeds or bushes, either. And no trash, bottles, beer cans, and the like."

The group fanned out in an arc bordering a section of the dark band. There was a clear line of demarcation between it and the surrounding lighter-colored soil. Jack dug his heel into the light-colored soil, gouging out a patch several inches deep. The soil that he uncovered was the same dark color as the ring bordering the shaft. He said, "How close can you get to the edge here anyway?"

Anne Armstrong said, "I wouldn't get too close."

Jack stepped into the ring of dark soil and moved toward the rim of the shaft. He moved slowly, carefully, halting about four feet away from the edge. He could see the edge of the rim opposite him on the other side of the shaft. The shaft was a hole bored straight down through the ground.

He took off his baseball cap, folded it in two, and stuck it in his back pocket. He got down on his knees and lay flat on the ground, feeling the warmth of the earth beneath him. Frith and Sanchez crouched behind him, each holding one of Jack's ankles— a safety precaution in case the ground at the rim should give way.

Jack stuck his head over the edge and looked down. The shaft plunged more than a hundred feet straight down. The sun was almost directly overhead, allowing him to see most of the bottom of the hole, except where a fingernail sliver of shadow edged the western rim. A mound of loose dirt and rubble lay at the bottom of the pit. He couldn't tell what color it was.

He eased back from the edge and had Frith hand him the field glasses that the latter had been holding. Jack took another look, this time through the binoculars. He could see now that the bottom of the pit was a junction point with four tunnel mouths opening on it. The tunnels were set ninety degrees apart. The dirt mound covered most of the tunnels so that only their arched tops showed above it.

The binoculars brought the dirt mound into clearer focus but he was still unable to draw any conclusions from it. It looked the same color as its surroundings. Maybe it was a trick of the light, maybe not.

Something sticking out of the dirt mound might have been a tree branch or it could have been a half-buried body part, an arm or a leg. Maybe it, too, was a trick of the light, maybe not. He couldn't tell from up here.

Jack withdrew from the edge and once more felt the relief of having his feet planted on solid ground. He said, "I want to see what's at the bottom of that pit."

* * *

The maps that Anne Armstrong had printed out earlier indicated the location of the tunnel leading to the shaft in question. Guesswork and a degree of uncertainty were involved because the original maps were old and not definitive. But the tunnel she and Jack selected seemed to fit the bill.

Silvertop's north, east, and south faces had had so many tunnels drilled into them that they looked like Swiss cheese. The entrances had all been sealed up a long time ago. It would be necessary to break into the desired tunnel, but the team had come well prepared for such contingencies.

The tunnel mouth was located on the southern slope about a hundred and twenty-five feet below the summit and a hundred yards or so east of that face's western edge where it met at right angles a ridge running north-south, a lower section of the same ridge that Jack and Frith had climbed earlier to survey the top of the bluff.

The pickup truck and SUV were moved close to the southern edge of the hilltop overlooking the tunnel. Hard hats, flashlights, pry bars, crowbars, a pair of bolt cutters, and other tools were unloaded from the rear of the Explorer and distributed among the team members, except for Holtz. Holtz would remain behind to guard the vehicles and keep watch on the canyon as Bailey had done earlier.

Frith and Holtz had the two M–16s, and Frith wanted someone armed with that weapon to stand sentry duty. The M–16 was better suited for long-distance shooting than the M–4s wielded by Bailey and Sanchez. The squad leader had not thought it necessary earlier for the posted sentry to be so armed, but that had been before the blue bus had been found. That finding upped the potential threat level. Frith was going down to the tunnel so Holtz would stay up top.

Armstrong radioed the news of the discovery to Central at Pike's Ford. Central replied that it would be sending a forensics team out to the site. The lab crew had to come out from headquarters in Denver and would reach Silvertop in roughly two and a half hours. Armstrong informed Central that her team would now attempt to access the shaft through the tunnel. Central acknowledged and Armstrong signed off.

Jack, Armstrong, Frith, Sanchez, and Bailey climbed down the slope to the tunnel. The face's low grade made for an easy descent.

The south face, like those of the east and north, was terraced. The tunnel accessing the shaft was aproned by a fifteen-foot-wide ledge. The entrance was a rounded arch ten feet high with a base of about the same width. It was boarded over. A metal sign nailed to the planks warned that trespassing was a Federal offense and that violators would be prosecuted to the full extent of the law. It bore the seal of the U.S. Bureau of Mines.

Jack and Bailey went to work on the barrier with crowbar and pry bar. The boards were old and flimsy and came apart with little trouble. There was a squeal of rusty nails giving way and the splintering of planks. A few minutes' hard work was all it took to open up a man-sized gap in the wooden wall. One of the last boards to give way had the sign on it; it hit the dirt with a thud.

Sanchez said, "Now you've done it. Wait till the Bureau of Mines hears of this."

Bailey said, "I'll never tell. It's top secret."

Frith said, "Let's widen that hole for easier access and exits." He and Sanchez took their turn with the tools and soon doubled the size of the gap.

Jack, Armstrong, and Bailey were going inside, Frith and Sanchez would remain behind at the entrance. The three would-be tunnel probers donned hard hats and equipped themselves with flashlights. Jack hefted a pry bar. It was five feet long with a pointed tip and a wedge at the opposite end. He said, "Might come in handy for poking into that mound at the bottom of the shaft."

Bailey said, "So will this." He picked up an entrenching tool. It had a three-foot-long shaft with a fold-out sharp-pointed spade at one end.

Frith said, "Leave your weapon here, you won't be needing it underground."

Bailey handed him his M–4. "I hate to be without Baby."

Frith said, "I'll take good care of it."

"Here's the ammo pouch." Bailey unslung an olive drab canvas pouch that he wore suspended over one shoulder by a strap. It bulged with loaded clips for the M–4. He gave that to Frith, too.

Sanchez said. "Hey, I hope none of you have claustrophobia."

Bailey said, "This's a hell of a time to be asking but no, not me."

Armstrong smiled and said, "I'm fine."

Jack said, "I'm used to being in tight spots."

Frith saluted them with a half wave. "Have a nice trip."

Jack stepped through the gap in the boards and into the tunnel, Armstrong and Bailey following. It

felt noticeably cooler once he was out of direct sunlight. Light flooded through the hole in the barrier,
shining about a dozen feet into the interior. Beyond
that the tunnel got dark in a hurry.

The tunnel had been carved out of living rock and
was shored up on the walls and roof at regular intervals by timbers and crossbeams that were thick with
dust and dark with age. The floor was covered by a
layer of dirt. No human footprints marred it but it
was marked by tracks made by small varmints, most
likely marmots and field mice. There was a flinty
smell in the air underlaid with a trace of dampness
and moisture; otherwise it seemed fresh and cool.

The hard hats had built-in flashlights above the
center of their rounded brims. Jack reached up and
switched his on, the others doing the same. He said,
"The air seems pretty breathable."

Anne Armstrong said, "That's those air shafts
working, providing natural ventilation. There's a
slight draft blowing from deeper in the tunnel."

Jack said, "Yes, I can feel it."

She said, "Silvertop has no history of methane pockets or other gases, so we won't need respirators."

She went a dozen paces into the tunnel, blackness
engulfing her except for the beam from her hard hat's
built-in light. She took a spray can from one of her
pockets, removed the cap, and turned to face the wall
on her left. She thumbed down the nozzle, spraying
an arrow on the rock at shoulder height. The arrow,
pale green and glowing in the dark, pointed back
toward the tunnel mouth. She said, "Luminous paint
for trail markers. Just in case."

Jack said, "Good idea."

She switched on her handheld baton flashlight,

sending a beam deep into the tunnel's interior. Jack and Bailey did the same.

Bailey said, "Before we get started—I'm the most expendable so I should go first." He looked Armstrong in the face, then Jack. He grinned. "What, no arguments?"

Jack would have liked to take the point but what Bailey said made sense. Armstrong must have felt the same; she nodded in agreement.

Jack said to Bailey, "You take the pry bar, it'll be useful if you need to probe any doubtful footing." He swapped Bailey the bar for the entrenching tool.

They fell into a file with Bailey at the head, Armstrong in the middle, and Jack bringing up the rear. Bailey gripped the bar at mid-shaft with his right hand, holding it horizontally at his side. He said, "Here goes nothing," and started off, the others following.

The tunnel drove north deep into the guts of Silvertop bluff. The trio came to the first branching at fifty yards in and halted. Mouths for side pocket excavations opened to the left and right of the main tunnel.

Jack looked back. The exit was a dot of brightness a long way off. Armstrong sprayed a green arrow on the main tunnel wall. Jack ran a comm check on his headset transceiver. Frith's reply was mushy with interference but intelligible.

They continued onward along the main tunnel. It was much cooler here, sending a chill along Jack's spine. He hoped it was from the coolness. There was something primal about venturing deep into the bowels of the earth, an instinctual aversion to having all those thousands of tons of solid rock between oneself and the open air. A nagging anxiety that poked up from somewhere deep in the psychic basement and sought to override logic and cool-nerved competency.

Jack was mission-oriented, though, and the fear of failing to carry out his duty was far greater than any emotional dreads or apprehension could ever be. The confidence born of hard training and self-mastery asserted itself, narrowing his mental focus to the job at hand. He had to admit, though, that being a miner must be a hell of a way to make a living.

The trio kept on moving forward. There was blackness ahead, beyond the reach of their electric torches and hard hat lights; and blackness behind, the point of light that was the exit having long since been swallowed up by darkness. The three of them were encapsulated in a glare of artificial brightness from their electric lights that glided through the tunnel like a glowworm inching along a sunless pipeline.

Jack reminded himself that the more distant the exit, the closer they were to their objective. Twice more they came to junctions where side passages branched out from the main tunnel. Armstrong marked the rock wall with a green glowing arrow each time. The comm check at the first such junction found Frith's reply breaking up into a garbled word jumble of meaninglessness. The next comm check reduced Frith's transmission to a crackling burst of static. They were out of communication with the outside world.

Walls remained upright, the ceiling unrolled seamlessly, and the tunnel floor continued rock-solid. Bailey had no need of the pry bar to probe doubtful patches of footing; there were none.

There was a change in the air now, a taint of rottenness that rode the current of cool air coming from deep within. It evoked another primal response, raising the hairs on the back of Jack's neck. He knew that smell: it was the scent of death.

Bailey halted, causing the duo in his wake to also fall still. He said, "Whew! Get that?"

Armstrong's nostrils crinkled with distaste. "And how!"

Jack said, "It won't be long now."

They started forward. The darkness must have heightened their other senses because it was some time before they could make out a fuzzy patch of grayness far ahead. The reek of rot and decay had grown with every step and was quite strong now.

It was the herald of the vertical shaft and the mound that lay at its bottom. The trio hurried forward toward the light, drawn to it.

Bailey started coughing, deep hacking coughs that he managed to suppress with difficulty as they neared the end of their quest. Armstrong fastened the hook at the end of her flashlight to her belt, freeing her hands so she could tie a handkerchief over her nose and mouth.

Jack envied her the handkerchief; he wished he had one so he could follow her example. He breathed through his mouth as much as possible, panting as though he were on the final lap of a marathon.

Daylight loomed ahead, not much of it, but what little there was seemed neon-bright after the blackness of darkness through which they had come. The glare was minimized because the mound at the bottom of the pit reached almost to the top of the tunnel's rounded archway where it met the vertical shaft. The dirt and rocks at the top of the heap could be glimpsed through the narrow space left unfilled.

Bailey stopped short so suddenly that if Armstrong's reflexes had been any slower she would have bumped into him. The pry bar slipped from his hand, striking a hollow rattling sound against the tunnel's rock floor.

Rage battled revulsion with rage winning, allowing Bailey to overcome a fit of gagging in order to choke out an obscenity. Armstrong reeled as if from a physical blow.

Jack knew what was coming, had known for a long time, having first guessed the truth up on the hilltop in what now seemed an eternity ago. He was taken aback by the extent of the devastation, though. The slaughter.

The mound was nothing more nor less than a mass grave, a heap of bodies piled high. Many bodies, male and female. The mound would have been higher except that some of the bodies had rolled into the tunnel. No doubt the same thing had happened at the other three tunnel mouths at the junction of the shaft. The overflow had lowered the pile's height.

The corpses had been thrown into the shaft and a mass of loose dirt and rocks and rubble thrown on top of them to cover them up. Enough dirt and debris had been shoveled into the pit to mask the atrocity when seen from the surface but not nearly enough to hide the pathetic remains when seen from below.

Armstrong said, "My God! How many of them?"

Jack said, "Twenty? More? Most of the Zealots, if not all. They're not missing anymore." He took a certain pride that his voice was able to maintain a steady, even tone.

Something fell with a thud on top of the mound. It had fallen a long way and hit the dirt pile with a loud, thwacking slap. It sat there emanating a sizzling sound like bacon frying on a griddle.

It was a bundle of dynamite, sticks of dynamite held together by several loops of tape. The sizzle came from the length of fuse cord that curled out of one end of the bundle. A short length that grew shorter with every eye blink.

Jack grabbed Armstrong by the shoulders, picked her up bodily, and turned her around, giving her a shove that propelled her a half-dozen paces deeper into the tunnel. He shouted, "Run!"

Bailey was already in motion, spinning and leaping forward away from the shaft.

Armstrong ran, Jack close at her heels. She broke into a sprint, arms and legs pumping, rising on the balls of her feet, accelerating with a burst of speed.

Jack and Bailey were right behind her, running neck and neck. The tunnel was wide enough to accommodate both of them.

There was a chaos of pounding footfalls and their resounding echoes, a blur of hard hat lights and flashlight beams flickering over rock walls as the trio fled, racing to put some distance between themselves and the bomb in the pit.

The dynamite exploded.

. . . .

THE FOLLOWING TAKES PLACE
BETWEEN THE HOURS OF
1 P.M. AND 2 P.M.
MOUNTAIN DAYLIGHT TIME

. . . .

Shadow Valley, Colorado

Out of the frying pan, into the fire. Out of the bomb
blast and into a firefight. Jack Bauer, already bru-
talized by the effects of the explosion, now found
himself in a raging gun battle with a ruthless strike
force.

It was a blessing in a way. It meant that he was
alive and now faced a foe he could come to grips
with.

The wraithlike nature of the opposition, up to now
as hard to get hold of as a fistful of smoke, had resolved itself into flesh-and-blood attackers who were
trying to kill him and what remained of the CTU
team. Flesh could be made to bleed, and Jack ached
for a reckoning with the enemy.

He ached, period. But he knew it could have been worse. To ache is to be alive, and to live offers the prospect of a righteous revenge.

It had been a lucky break that the bundle of dynamite had landed on top of the pile instead of rolling down its side to fall into the tunnel. That had been the second lucky break, actually. The first had been that the bundle survived the long fall without detonating the blasting caps and triggering off the sticks of TNT on impact. Dynamite is relatively stable; it's the blasting caps that are fluky, fickle, and chancy. It was blind fate that had caused the bundle to hit the mound in such a way as to avoid touching off the caps. The soft dirt at the top of the heap must have cushioned the fall to prevent premature detonation.

The fuse had been short but long enough to give the trio precious time for a good running start. Time? Time had seemed to stand still during that nightmare interval of mad flight away from the shaft.

More luck: the shaft and the pile of bodies at its bottom had absorbed most of the force of the explosion. What got through was devastating enough.

The blast came like the Trump of Doom at the End of Days, rocking all creation with a shock wave that mingled light, heat, and noise in a rush of pure force. Jack was lifted up and catapulted bodily by a senses-shattering pressure that wiped everything blank.

He came to in a howling torrent of darkness. The darkness was incomplete, lacking the utter black of totality. He saw as much as sensed a whirlwind of smoke and dirt streaming over him. That he could distinguish gradations in the murk meant that at least one light was still working.

It wasn't his. His hard hat lamp had gone dark

and the flashlight had fallen from his hand. He was unsure whether he even still wore a hard hat. He felt around the top of his head but numbed fingers and stunned senses were unable to feel the difference between his skull and the protective headgear.

Some of the murk thinned as reality returned with each heartbeat. He was on his hands and knees and a light dangled back and forth, swinging pendulum-like in front of his face. Was it the sun? The moon?

Hands were tugging at him, hooked under his arms and urging him to his feet. The chaos was strangely silent, drowned out by the ringing in his ears. The picture came into tighter focus. The shining globe waving before his eyes resolved itself into the lens of a blazing flashlight. The lens was cracked but the beam still shone.

The flashlight hung from where it was hooked to Anne Armstrong's belt, hanging down from the side of her hip. She was crouching over him, trying to help him stand up. He knelt on the tunnel's rocky floor, smoke and dust roiling all around him.

It was hard to breathe in the murk-laden air. Mouth and nostrils seemed filled with dirt. He coughed, choked, spat, managing to clear his throat. It helped him draw a breath, then another.

Armstrong's face was close to his, weirdly under-lit by the flashlight's glow, her eyes wide and staring, her features harsh and angular. Her mouth was moving but Jack was unable to hear what she was saying due to the roaring in his ears. More impera-tive than words was the pull of her hands urging him upward.

He said, "I'm all right!" He mouthed the words but couldn't hear them. He reached out with his right hand, touching the tunnel wall. He braced himself and rose to his feet, lurching into a half crouch. A wave of dizziness overswept him and he stumbled sideways, bumping his head against the wall. A chin-strap throttled him; that's how he realized he was still wearing his hard hat.

He got his back against the wall and stood there with legs bent at the knees until the dizziness passed. Armstrong tilted the flashlight at her hip so that it shone at a forty-five-degree angle. It was pointed at something to Jack's left and behind him. His gaze followed the direction of the beam.

It shone on Bailey, crawling forward head-down on his hands and knees. He was bareheaded, having lost his hard hat in the blast. The view wavered as banks of dust and smoke rolled by. Bailey raised his head, looking up when the light hit him. The whites of his eyes stood out in a dirt-smeared face. Blood trickled from his nose and the corners of his mouth. He lowered his head and continued crawling forward.

Jack staggered to one side of Bailey and Armstrong the other. They each took hold of an arm and tried to lift Bailey to his feet. Jack could barely stay on his own. He tottered, almost falling before managing to right himself. A fall would be disastrous; he was unsure whether he'd be able to get back up. He spread his feet wider for balance; it helped stabilize him.

He and Armstrong somehow managed to get Bailey up and standing. Bailey got his arms across their shoulders as they propped him upright. Armstrong tilted the baton flashlight level so that it shone forward, pointing the way ahead.

The dust and smoke clouds were drifting away and ahead of them, seeking an exit at the far end of the tunnel, wherever that might be. They must be going in the direction opposite that from which the blast had come. That was the way the trio must go, too.

That was good. Jack's sense of direction was scrambled and he would have been just as likely to go the wrong way as not. The streaming airborne debris was a signpost showing the way out.

The three agents started forward. Jack and Armstrong had to half carry, half drag Bailey at the start. Each lurching pace forward was a win. Jack's thoughts flashed back to Army days, to forced marches with full field battle gear where trainees were pushed to the limits of endurance and beyond, to prepare them for combat conditions that would demand that one must march or die. There had been times later during his term of service when that became literally true and survival depended on the ability to put one foot forward and then the other, slogging along until you were all used up and continuing to keep on going after that.

Now as then he concentrated all his thoughts and energies on forward motion. The passage became a torturous nightmare, a seeming treadmill to oblivion. But he kept on going, reaching down deep somewhere to find something to pick up those feet and put them down.

Bailey began carrying more of his own weight. That helped. Jack was in top condition, and his tremendous endurance began to reassert itself. That helped more.

Armstrong kept the flashlight hooked to her belt. That was smart, keeping it safely tethered so as to avoid having it slip free from a betraying hand to fall and shatter, blacking out their sole source of light. Jack had his pocket flash but he didn't know if it still worked. It took all the energy he had to continue moving ahead and propping up Bailey; there was none for checking on the pocket flash, not when Armstrong's light served their purposes. She needed to be able to use her right hand to tilt the light to point the way, so Jack did what he could to shoulder more of Bailey's weight to enable her to do just that.

They came to a junction point. That was tricky because the murky clouds streamed into all three tunnel mouths in search of an exit. It would be easy to take the wrong branch. Jack steered Bailey to a tunnel wall and put both their backs against it and held him up in place, freeing Armstrong to search for the green arrow marking the correct tunnel.

She found it and returned, got Bailey's other arm across her shoulder, and the trio continued their onward march. It was like one of those textbook-case nightmares where life depends on fleeing deadly danger but the sleeper is slowed to a maddening tortoise pace, creeping along while swift-winged Death swoops in for the kill. But this was no dream, it was real, appallingly real.

How many junction points had they passed on their way in toward the shaft, two or three? Jack couldn't remember. No matter. All that counted was picking up one foot and putting it down, one after the other. Don't bother counting them; waste of time. Just keep going.

His ears popped and the constant roaring in his ears was replaced by intermittent bursts of sound. Rasping breath that was his own sounded like wood being sawed. The shuffling tread of his footfalls, more felt than heard, as each successive step sent tremors from his feet through bones all the way to the top of his head. Groans and inarticulate mumblings from Bailey. Maybe they were articulate but Jack couldn't make them out.

Armstrong's panting gasps were sometimes interrupted by shouted remarks that reached Jack in bits and pieces like garbled transmissions.

He thought of that hoary comedy cliché, the one where a couple of drunks hold each other up as they stagger and reel from lamppost to lamppost. That's what he, Armstrong, and Bailey would have looked like to a stranger's eyes. Not so funny when you were living it.

Another junction point. Armstrong seemed to take forever to find the green arrow marker while Jack kept Bailey on his feet. Jack told himself that that was okay, better she should take her time and get it right rather than make a mistake that would send them up a blind alley. The trouble was that Bailey's legs kept folding at the knees and he'd start sliding down the wall, forcing Jack to expend more effort to keep him upright.

It was a relief when Armstrong took her place beside Bailey, lessening some of the weight on Jack. They lurched forward, resuming their stumbling, swaying stagger along the tunnel.

Jack's hearing was returning, the roaring muting down to a continuous low murmur like surf breaking on an unseen shore. It counterpointed the sounds of their passage, the heavy breathing, gasps, and groans, the foot-dragging shuffle of their forward march.

An eternity of slogging and heaving brought them

to a third junction. Jack shook his head, stifling a groan. It wasn't fair to have come so far only to have to continue the ordeal. What of it? Fairness was irrelevant, only facts mattered. The fact was that they must go on.

Wasn't there some character in Greek myth whose punishment for offending the gods was something like this? Only he was condemned to roll a rock up and down hills for all time. Jack had it better than him, he told himself. At least he didn't have to climb any hills.

Pick them up and put them down. Jack couldn't help resenting Frith and Sanchez. They must know what had happened. Where were they? Why hadn't they come to help?

Never mind about that. Just keep moving.

The airborne murk was starting to thin out as it streamed ahead. It was like a river made up of many currents of different hues, some light, some dark, all of them intertwining and writhing, coming together and splitting apart on their journey to the same destination.

There was light ahead, a pale glow shimmering off in the dim distance. The tunnel brightened to a kind of ashen sooty dusk. A pair of figures were outlined at the far end of the milky, smoke-strewn brightness.

It took a minute for Jack to realize that the duo was Frith and Sanchez and the glow was, literally, the light at the end of the tunnel.

Armstrong called out to them, a wordless cry. She was answered by a series of flat muffled cracks from outside. Jack's hearing had recovered to the point where he was able to recognize them as gunfire.

Frith and Sanchez turned at the sound of her voice. They crouched sheltering behind the tunnel's rock walls, pointing their weapons at the gap in the wooden barrier. Smoke and dust poured steadily out through the opening. A large number of holes in the barrier let in beams of sunlight. Bullet holes.

More flat cracks sounded from outside, punching fresh holes through the boards and ricocheting off rock walls.

Frith said, "Get down! We're under attack!"

Jack heard that. He got down. So did Armstrong and Bailey. All three of them more or less collapsed at the same time, tumbling to the tunnel floor. Which was just as well. It was safer down there. For the moment.

Frith gave the trio a rundown on the situation: "Holtz said, 'That's funny.' That's all, just 'That's funny.' That's the last message we received from him on the headset. He didn't respond after that. He must've noticed something wrong but too late to do anything about it. There was no sound of a shot being fired. We found out why later.

"The blast came a few minutes later. A cloud of smoke and dust came out of the tunnel. It got so thick in here that we couldn't breathe so Sanchez and I got out. We went out on the ledge. That smoke saved our lives. It caused the shooter up top to miss his shot. Or shots. We don't know how many he fired before he tagged Sanchez."

Sanchez glanced over his shoulder at Jack, Armstrong, and Bailey where they sat on the tunnel floor with their backs to the wall. His face and clothes were blackened with dirt and soot, just like the rest of the group. He grinned, said, "I got hit in the back and knocked down but my Kevlar vest saved me from worse. Gave me a hell of a jolt, though."

Frith went on, "Some falling rocks almost hit me. The shooter must have knocked them over the edge while he was angling for a better shot. I looked up and saw him. He was leaning way over trying to get a bead on me. He made a nice fat target. I got him first. He fell off. You can see his body sprawled out on one of the ledges down there. But don't try. Stick your head out and his playmates will try to shoot it off."

Anne Armstrong said, "How many are there?"

"About ten I'd say, at least to start with. They popped up in the rocks at the bottom of the hill right after the shooter fell. I guess they'd been there for a while but the first we knew about it was when they opened fire. I don't mind telling you that it got pretty hot out on that ledge! We ducked back in here for cover. It's hard to breathe with all this crap in the air but it beats not breathing at all."

Sanchez said, "We got two of them, so that leaves about eight, give or take a corpse."

Jack was checking his pistol to make sure that it was undamaged by the blast. It seemed to be working fine. He was eager to put it into action.

Frith said, "That first shooter had a silenced rifle, of course. That's why we didn't hear anything when Holtz was shot or when he was using Sanchez for target practice. The others down below don't give a good damn how much noise they make. Why not? Nobody around to hear them."

Bailey sat slumped against the wall, hugging his middle. His chin rested on top of his chest. He raised his head a little, said, "The one up top . . . How—how'd he get there?" His voice was a harsh croak.

Frith said, "He must've been up there all the time. He sure as hell didn't drive or walk up, Holtz would have seen him coming from a mile off."

Jack said, "That's why Holtz had to go first. The Zealots probably had a man in place the whole time serving as a spotter. There's plenty of places on the hilltop to hide out. He was probably watching us the whole time we were searching the site."

Frith nodded. "That's how I read it. He must've sent for reinforcements when we found the bus."

Bailey said, "Our radios don't work in the canyon. Why his?"

Anne Armstrong said, "Probably because it's not a radio. A satellite phone could do it."

Bailey said, "That's a good one. He's got a sat-phone and we don't. He can call for help but we can't. Those CTU budget cuts will be the death of us yet. What a joke—a sick joke." He laughed without mirth, his laughter a harsh crow's caw. His face contorted with pain; he bit down on his lip to keep from crying out until the spasm passed.

Sanchez said, "Write a letter to your congressman to complain."

Bailey forced a weak grin. "I would . . . if I thought he could read."

Frith said, "We didn't know what happened to you three. Thought the blast might have got you. Glad you made it back in one piece."

Jack said, "Somebody—most likely the shooter who got Holtz—tossed a bundle of TNT down the shaft to cover up the evidence."

Sanchez said, "What evidence?"

"A mass grave at the bottom of the pit. We found the missing Zealots. There had to have been twenty bodies there, maybe more."

Sanchez frowned, puzzled. "Then who are the guys shooting at us now?"

"That's the big question."

Bailey said, "Why don't you go ask 'em, Sanchez?"

Frith lay in a prone firing position on the tunnel floor, pointing his rifle downhill. The figure of an armed man darted out from behind a boulder and ran toward the slope. Frith squeezed the trigger. The figure fell sprawling and lay motionless on a piece of open ground. Frith put another round in him to make sure. He said, "Got one!"

An instant later the dead man's teammates loosed a fusillade at the tunnel mouth. The shooters were scattered in a loose arc among a jumble of boulders and slabs at the bottom of the hill. Some were armed with rifles and others with machine gun pistols of the Mac–10 variety. They had a lot of firepower.

Frith and Sanchez wriggled backward, covering behind rock ribs and outcroppings. Rounds ventilated the remnants of the plank barrier. The real danger came from ricochets that bounced off the inside of the tunnel. The shooters didn't have the proper range and the rounds angled away into the tunnel leaving the defenders unharmed.

The death of one of their own provoked a prolonged outburst. The racketing rattle of assault rifles and machine pistols on autofire sounded like a street crew of jackhammer operators at work.

The shooting subsided, falling silent except for an occasional potshot. Frith and Sanchez bellied back into position and scanned the slope. Frith was on the east side of the tunnel mouth, Sanchez the west. A flicker of motion in the corner of his right eye caught Sanchez's attention and he swung the gun muzzle toward it but held his fire.

He said, "One of them's working his way up the west ridge. He took cover before I could get a bead on him."

More shots popped from below. Frith said, "They use that covering fire to change position, move in and up. A couple of shooters are higher up the slope now."

Jack noticed an M–4 standing propped up against the wall near Sanchez. It was Bailey's weapon, the one he'd left behind before going on the tunnel probe. The ammo pouch stood beside it. "That M–4 functional?"

Frith said, "Should be."

Jack said, "Let's get some more firepower into play."

Bailey rested a clawlike hand on Jack's shoulder. He said, "You take it. I'm not much good now—all busted up inside."

"Hang on. We'll get you to a medic."

"Sure." Bailey smiled with his lips.

Jack low-crawled across the tunnel floor to the other side. He sat with his back to the wall with legs extended. He slung the ammo pouch over his shoulder, picked up the M–4, and examined it. It checked out okay. He said, "What's the plan?"

Anne Armstrong said, "We can't just sit here and try to wait them out. It'll be a long time before help arrives. Central doesn't know we're in danger. We've been relatively safe so far because the attackers are too far down to do much damage. The angle of their line of fire is too steep. But if they get higher up on the slope and flank us they'll be in a position to shoot us to pieces with the ricochets. If we retreat deeper into the tunnel to avoid it, they'll be able to come even closer."

Frith said, "They know it. They use each burst of covering fire to climb the ledges."

Sanchez said, "They've definitely got a couple of guys on the west ridge. I see 'em moving but they take cover before I can get a shot at 'em."

Jack said, "Another thing. Sooner or later the forensics team from CTU/DENV will be arriving here. We can't let them come unsuspecting into a massacre."

Armstrong said, "What do you suggest?"

"It's been my experience that the aggressor usually has the advantage. We need to regain the initiative. Let's make a breakout."

"I agree."

Frith said, "I'm always in favor of taking the fight to the other guy. But what about Bailey?"

Bailey's harsh laugh sounded, followed by a coughing fit. Blood flecks splattered his mouth and chin. A half minute passed before he was able to speak. "Forget about me. I'm excess baggage. If we stay put, I'm sunk anyway. If you make a break I've got a chance. We all do."

Silence fell. A short-lived silence that was quickly broken by a ragged series of shots from below. Sanchez squeezed off a quick burst at a figure breaking cover on the west ridge but missed. The figure ducked down behind a rockpile that was a bit higher up.

Bailey looked Jack in the face, then Armstrong. He said, "Like I said before we went in the tunnel,

I'm expendable. More now than ever. These are the cold, hard facts so don't argue. Leave me with an extra pistol and some clips. If any of those bastards make it this far, I'll give them a warm welcome.

"Don't delay. The longer you wait the less your chances get."

He was right and they knew it. Armstrong said, "It might already be too late if they've got people on the hilltop. They might be there if the shooter who got Holtz and the dynamiter are two different people."

Jack said, "We'll just have to risk it. Otherwise they will get some shooters up there for sure and have us caught in a high-low crossfire that'll kill any chance of a breakout."

Frith said, "This being pinned down works both ways. They've got us holed up here but Sanchez and I did the same thing to them. None of this bunch has been able to circle around to the east. I tagged the one who tried."

Sanchez said, "There's plenty of cover we can use on the ledges. Woodpiles, fallen rocks, tumble-down shacks, all kinds of crap."

Jack said, "Best use it while we can, before they do."

It was decided. All that remained were the tactics. Jack and Armstrong took quick turns scanning the slope, noting strong points and weak links. A stack of old timbers stood on the ledge a stone's throw east of the tunnel mouth. The next stepped tier below this ledge featured a rusted ore bucket, a steel-wheeled hopper the size of a compact car. It lay on its side on the west side of the terrace.

A quick plan of assault was made, finalized. Jack and Sanchez would make for the ore car, Armstrong and Frith for the timber stack. Jack and Sanchez had M–4s; Frith had the M–16, and Armstrong armed herself with a second pistol, Frith's sidearm, in addition to the one she was carrying. The thinking was that the M–16's capacity for shooting at long range and close quarters would compensate for the lesser firepower of the pistols. Bailey had his own pistol and Sanchez's. He and Armstrong equipped themselves with pocketfuls of spare clips.

Jack said, "Something else we've got working for us. They think all they've got to buck is two guns, Frith and Sanchez. They don't know about Anne and me. That gives us an element of surprise plus added firepower."

Frith said, "When do we go?"

"After their next burst of covering fire. I'll go first."

Armstrong and Frith dragged Bailey to the cover of the east side of the tunnel mouth near the entrance. Bailey's face was dead white where it showed between the soot and grime streaking his face. He grinned through gritted teeth, gave them the thumbs-up sign.

Frith and Sanchez loosed a few rounds down the slope to stir up the opposition. The enemy returned fire in earnest, burning off another sizzling fusillade. Shooters popped up from behind rocks and out of ditches to sling lead at the tunnel, betraying their location by doing so. They had advanced a lot higher uphill; the nearest were only two ledges below. A pair scaling the west ridge were nearly level with the ledge below the tunnel.

Some laid down covering fire while others worked their way farther up toward their objective. The shooting fell off once the climbers took cover.

Jack readied to make his move. The bomb blast

and the tortuous trek back from the shaft had taken their toll on him, but his innate vitality and peak physical condition had helped restore some of his energies. So did the prospect of immediate action.

Frith and Sanchez opened fire, Frith selecting the nearest shooters on the eastern half of the slope, Sanchez focusing on the pair on the west ridge. Their targets had already gone to cover and there was next to no chance of hitting them. The purpose of shooting at them was to keep them pinned down so they couldn't fire at Jack when he made his breakout.

Frith said, "Go!"

Jack jumped out of the hole in the barrier, bent almost double as he angled west across the ledge with the M–4 in his hands. His appearance took the enemy by surprise. He reached the point on the ledge above the ore cart on the next terrace down before somebody took a shot at him. It missed.

Others recovered their wits and began popping away. Shots cracked, rounds whizzing through empty air around Jack to bury themselves in the hillside.

The slope to the terrace below declined at about a thirty-degree angle. Jack jumped off the ledge feet-first, throwing himself over the side. He slid down the hillside like a runner sliding into home base in a race to keep from being tagged out. It was a long slide. He set off a mini-landslide of falling rocks and dirt during the descent.

The ore cart lay on its side with its open hopper facing the slope. It was orange-brown with rust but the sides of the hopper were several inches thick and its base was about twelve inches thick, not including the undercarriage with its trucks and sets of grooved wheels.

One of the duo on the west ridge was so provoked by Jack's ploy that he rose up from behind a rock to point a rifle at him to line up a shot. Sanchez had been waiting for just such an opportunity and squeezed off a three-round burst, chopping the rifleman before he could fire.

Jack's feet hit the ledge below and then he went into a roll, a shoulder roll that took him across the terrace toward the shelter of the ore car. Lines of lead zigzagged the slope behind him, kicking up dust and cutting down small bushes and scraggly dwarf trees growing out of the hillside.

He scrambled into the hopper, thinking for an instant that it was the kind of shady retreat that a rattlesnake might prefer. If that was the case it would be too bad for the rattlers. He rolled to a halt, his shoulder slamming into the now-vertical bottom of the hopper. Happily the car was unoccupied by any other life form than himself.

Jack pulled in his feet and hands, curling up inside the hopper so that no part of him was showing. The ore car vibrated with a metallic clangor as slugs began smashing into its underside. Wheels, trucks, and undercarriage proved a formidable shield, the rounds flattening themselves into lead smears against the cart.

Shooting from below burst out with renewed intensity but a different target. Jack knew that that meant that Anne Armstrong was making her break. She was lightly armed and would be relying on the covering fire laid down by Jack, Frith, and Sanchez.

Sanchez had the surviving shooter on the west ridge covered so Jack didn't have to overly concern himself with that direction. He peeked around the east side of the ore car seeking targets. A shooter on the next ledge down huddled behind a stone wall three feet high, all that remained of a long-gone building. He had a machine pistol in each hand and was streaming lead at Armstrong as she dashed for the timber stack. A regular Two Gun Kid, thought Jack. Two Guns was pretty well covered and Jack's chances of scoring on him were slim.

A rifleman came into view much farther down near the bottom of the slope, springing up from behind a rock slab, exposing himself from the waist up. Jack triggered a short burst at him. The downhill angle was tricky and Jack's rounds passed harmlessly over the rifleman's head. It threw a scare into him and he ducked down out of sight behind the slab before Jack could correct his aim for a second try. But it stopped him from shooting at Armstrong for the moment.

Two Guns seemed to take that as a personal affront and turned his attention toward Jack. He squatted behind the woodpile, gun hands resting on top of it as he turned to squirt bursts of lead at Jack, alternating between one machine pistol and the other. He had maximum firepower and minimum accuracy. The rounds flattened themselves against the ore car, sounding like someone was tap-dancing against it.

Two Guns's change of position put him in Jack's line of fire. His head was raised above the woodpile so he could see what he was shooting at. Jack squeezed off a triple burst that blew apart the other's skull above the eyebrows.

Armstrong staggered, breaking stride. Had she been hit? She stumbled forward, falling behind the timber stack, dropping out of sight.

How many of the enemy were left? Frith had estimated ten to start with. He and Sanchez had each bagged one before Jack and the others emerged from the tunnel. Frith had since tagged another at the bottom of the hill, Sanchez had gotten one of the duo on the west ridge, and Jack had just neutralized Two Guns.

That made five. Frith's estimate might have been off because Jack thought that there were more than five shooters still in play, maybe six or even seven. It was hard to tell for sure because they moved around a lot while rarely showing themselves for more than a brief blur of motion and a burst of gunfire.

Say six shooters remained. Six versus five CTU members. Three of the CTU team had heavy firepower, the other two had pistols. Pistols were for close quarters combat, not much good in this kind of firefight. Jack was a crack marksman with a handgun but he knew their limitations in such an encounter. There was also doubt whether Bailey would be effective at any range. He'd looked weak, shaky, on the verge of passing out. The bomb blast had inflicted serious damage on him, maybe internal injuries, maybe a concussion, maybe both. He needed medical attention as soon as possible.

Jack didn't know if Anne Armstrong had been tagged or not. There was no sign of her behind the timber stack but then there wouldn't be whether she'd been hit or not. The smart way to play it was to keep the foe guessing until the optimal moment for intervention.

Three CTU shooters versus six, maybe seven of the enemy. Not bad odds. Jack meant to do what he could to improve them.

Now Sanchez showed himself at the west side of

the tunnel mouth. He immediately ducked back in, taking cover. The attackers opened fire, shooting at where he'd been. Jack scanned the landscape. He thought there were seven shooters left.

The shooting stopped almost as soon as it started as the foe realized that Sanchez's ploy had only been a feint, a ruse to draw their fire to force them to reveal their position. A knot of two or three of them were clustered on the ledge below Jack's, behind a massive old boiler that nestled in a collapsed framework of thick-beamed trestles and cross braces. The cylindrical boiler lay on its side. It was fifteen feet long and six feet wide. It and its shattered frame provided plenty of cover.

Sanchez's move had exposed their presence but failed to lure them out from behind their cover. But the gambit was a double-feint. Frith ducked out of the eastern side of the tunnel a few beats after the shooting stopped. He ran for the timber stack.

Pistol fire cracked from behind the stack. Armstrong had made it and was still in the game, firing steadily to help cover Frith. A succession of shots popped as she emptied one magazine, almost immediately following it up with another volley from her other pistol.

Gunfire blazed from three places around the boiler, tearing up the hillside, trying to intercept Frith before he reached cover. That was the heaviest concentration of firepower. Triggermen opened up from three other separate spots on the slope.

A seventh man was on the west ridge. He took advantage of Sanchez's momentary absence to step out from behind his rock and train his weapon on the back of the running Frith.

Jack was ready for him. His burst cut the other down before he could fire. The shooter staggered backward, bumped into a boulder, and pitched forward headfirst. He looked like he was taking a bow. He kept on going, rolling and tumbling down the ridge. The ridge was steeper than the Silvertop bluff and he picked up a fair amount of speed on his way down, arms and legs flailing until he hit an outcropping and bounced off, falling straight down to land in a heap at the foot of the ridge. He was motionless after that.

One down, six to go. Jack withdrew into the ore car's protective shell an instant before drawing heavy fire from the attackers. The ore car shuddered, raining a shower of rusty flakes down on Jack. But it held, impervious and bulletproof.

The crack of an M–16 told him that Frith had reached the timber stack and was responding in kind. Bullets spanged against the boiler and splintered timbers, quelling the onslaught from the three gunmen sheltering behind it. Armstrong's pistol chimed in, cracking away as she fired.

Sanchez's M–4 barked, adding its voice to the chorus. The other three shooters spread out among the rockfalls east of the boiler returned fire.

Sanchez would be making his move next. His firepower joined to Jack's would make a potent and lethal anchor for the western half of the planned crossfire. Frith's M–16 backed by Armstrong's pistols would supply the eastern component. Together they could begin clearing the slope of the rest of the enemy.

Shouting sounded from below. Jack couldn't make out what it was but it sounded like someone giving orders to the others, perhaps to unleash a counter-strike of their own.

He squirmed around in the hopper, changing position to cover the boiler and points east. He was shaggy with fallen rust flakes from head to toe. They dusted him like a coating of orange snowflakes. He ejected an empty clip and inserted a fresh one in the M–4.

The three shooters among the rocks concentrated their firepower on the timber stack. Those beams had the dimensions of railroad ties and there was a waist-high cube of them. The rounds could chip away at them but Frith and Armstrong were safe behind them, though their weapons were stilled for the moment while they took cover.

One of the shooters behind the boiler fired an assault rifle at Jack, snapping shots at him each time he stuck his head out from behind the ore car looking for a target of opportunity. A second shooter was trading bursts with Sanchez. The time was not yet right for Sanchez to make his move.

There was a lull in the gunfire directed at Jack. He'd been peeping out from behind the side of the hopper looking for a shot. He now changed tactics, unexpectedly popping up from behind the top of the overturned car.

He sprang up just in time to see a third shooter who'd been sheltering behind the boiler do the same. The other was a big man with a platinum-blond crew cut and clean-shaven face wielding an assault rifle with a tubular attachment underslung to the bottom of the barrel.

Jack knew it for a grenade launcher. He swung his gun muzzle toward its wielder but the man with the platinum hair fired first, instantly dropping out of sight behind the boiler.

The grenade launcher went off with a thump, a hollow crumping sound. It was immediately followed by a burst fired at Jack by the shooter behind the boiler who'd previously been busy trying to nail Jack.

Jack had seen the shooter take aim at the same time that the man with the platinum hair ducked. Jack dropped behind the hopper, a hot round smacking the hillside behind him.

The grenade described a tight lobbing arc, hitting the slope between the tunnel mouth and the timber stack. It bounced off, falling like ripe fruit on the ledge. It detonated not with an explosive blast but with a juicy wet splat like a fat pumpkin dropped from a height to smash apart on hard ground.

Masses of green fog erupted from it, blossoming, expanding into a monstrous cloud that squatted and heaved across the upper ledge.

The cloud was the color of mint mouthwash, a harshly unnatural green that was shot through with myriads of tiny iridescent yellow-green particles. The cloud seemed almost as much liquid as gas, like the smoke that comes boiling off dry ice.

The green fog that Lobo had told of, the toxic cloud that fell on Red Notch. Jack shouted, "Poison gas! Run! *Run!*"

He was up and running as he shouted. He didn't have to worry about the enemy because they were running, too, fleeing down the slope and onto the flat for all they were worth. He couldn't run downhill because they would get him. He couldn't go up because that's where the green cloud was massed.

He ran across the ledge toward the western ridge. He ran all-out, sprinting, legs pumping. The landscape zoomed past him. There was nothing wrong with his hearing now, the huffing of his lungs, the creaking of his gear and the pounding of his footfalls all reverberating in his ears.

Jack could hear the green cloud, too. It made a hissing sound suggestive of the effervescence of a freshly opened bottle of pop.

He did not look back but he couldn't help looking up. The western arm of the cloud raced along with him, lazily uncurling itself to overspread the ledge above. Streamers and tendrils extended from its underside, slithering off the rim of the ledge and reaching downward.

The viscous, semi-liquid nature of the stuff worked in Jack's favor. It drifted down the hillside but slowly, lazily, its buoyancy keeping it afloat. It rolled across the upper ledge but took its own sweet time doing so, sometimes pausing to curl in on itself and thrust upward to climb the hillside, only to resume its inexorable westward thrust.

Jack's ledge ran out and then there was the steeper slope of the western ridge. Jack jumped on to it and began scaling it toward the top. He now heard only the beating of his own heart pounding in his eardrums. His heaving lungs burned, his limbs felt heavy, leaden.

The footing was treacherous and he fought to keep from slipping. He grabbed the trunks of small bushes growing on the ridge and used them to pull himself up. He scrabbled at rock outcroppings to haul himself higher.

He could see the ridgetop. A gauzy green tendril

brushed the back of his hand. He jerked it away, his flesh tingling from the contact.

Jack kept moving solely by instinct. The summit was a dozen feet away—but the green cloud was already there. A thin curtain of it shimmered above him. He held his breath and scrambled upward on his hands and knees.

Green mist enveloped him, its touch like cobwebs against his bare flesh. His tortured lungs could withstand no more; he gasped for breath. The mist was cool and damp, he could taste it in his nostrils. Its scent was part medicinal, part chemical.

Jack Bauer threw himself over the ridgeline and down the other side. The far side was steeper than the near one. It was covered with weeds and a layer of short, dry, colorless grass. He tumbled downward, falling, sliding, rolling, the world pinwheeling around him.

. . . .

THE FOLLOWING TAKES PLACE
BETWEEN THE HOURS OF
2 P.M. AND 3 P.M.
MOUNTAIN DAYLIGHT TIME

. . . .

Pine Ridge, Colorado

Jack Bauer wanted to put as much distance as possible between himself and the green cloud. He didn't fight the fall, he went with it. It was no straight drop, of course; no man could have survived that. It was a skittering, sliding tumble that he helped along as much as possible down a fifty-degree-angled, weed-and brush-covered slope. His descent slowed at times, not often, but sometimes, and when it did, he did what he could to speed up the process, scrambling and rolling, anything to keep moving downward.

He had no time to think during that frantic downhill slide. He was too busy trying to keep from breaking his neck or anything else. Extensive martial arts training in judo had trained him in handling rough, violent falls but this was a marathon ordeal.

Jack reacted by reflex and instinct, dodging rock outcroppings and darting toward open, weedy spaces. Everything zipped by him in a blur that was punctuated by sudden, jarring shocks and the flailing of thorny bushes as he tore through them. He took a brutal pounding.

The downgrade began evening out, becoming less steep, slowing his plunge in the process. He slammed to a halt on a level piece of ground.

He lay on his back, gasping, panting. His head swam. His motion had stopped but the world kept moving, wheeling past him in a dizzying whirl. He shut his eyes for a few beats, and when he opened them the world had caught up with him and stopped moving, too.

Jack felt like he'd been worked over from head to toe. His heart hammered, his pulse raced. Above was blue sky and a yellow dancing sun. He took several deep breaths. His ribs ached but nothing felt broken. They were particularly tender on his left side where his gun in its shoulder holster had banged against them.

He still had his pistol. That was something. The M–4 was long gone. He couldn't remember if he'd had it with him when he went over the ridgetop or if he'd dropped it before then. The ammo pouch with its extra clips for the weapon was still with him, its strap tight against his neck as though trying to choke him. He got his fingers under the strap and tugged it to give himself some breathing room.

There was a chemical taste in his mouth and the back of his throat. The realization of it gave him a surging jolt of adrenaline that washed away the last of his stunned confusion and brought his awareness into sharp focus.

The green cloud!

Jack sat up, the action tormenting his aching body and forcing a groan from him. He'd been exposed to the gas externally and internally; externally where it had touched his skin and internally from the whiff of it he'd breathed before he escaped it.

Had he escaped it? He looked up and to the east, scanning the ridge. Its summit was several hundred feet above him, part of it obscured by the scalloped edge of green cloud. The cloud had crept a few dozen yards down the near side of the slope but its progress was arrested as though it had snagged itself on the jagged crest.

The stuff was heavier than air but not much. Its viscous quality had kept all but its westernmost arm penned on the far side of the ridge. The still air of high noon had since been replaced a slight breeze blowing out of the west that buffeted the cloud, pushing it back. The gas was thinning out, too, dispersing itself into the upper air.

Jack quickly calculated the icy equations of survival. His depended on the nature of the unknown substance to which he'd been exposed.

Was it poison gas or a nerve agent? Lethal gas had to be inhaled to do its work, while a nerve agent could kill on contact with the skin. Modern varieties of either could kill by exposure to a single microscopic particle, but he'd both breathed and been touched by the green gas. He was still alive, though, the prime factor in his high-speed mental calculus.

The bodies he'd seen in the mine shaft bore the marks of death not by gas but by violence. Some had been shot, some had had their throats cut, others had bloody, broken bodies. Corpses don't bleed.

Lobo had said that the Zealots at Red Notch had been exposed to the green cloud. One could deduce from that that its purpose was not to kill. What was its purpose?

Most CW gases are invisible, odorless, and tasteless. The green gas was none of these. It was something outside Jack's experience of chemical weapons. Its high visibility, taste, and smell suggested that at least part of its purpose was to terrify, as the mustard gas of World War I had panicked troops into abandoning their trenches and retreating when they saw its characteristic yellow cloud approaching their position. Mustard gas was an irritant, not necessarily fatal, doing its work by attacking the eyes, the tender membranes of the nose and throat and the lungs of its victims. Tear gas, a milder variant on the same principle, is often used for crowd control.

Jack was experiencing none of the symptoms of an airborne irritant. The green gas was not an irritant, then. What was it?

A nonlethal weapon for crowd control? It was unlike anything he'd ever heard of in the arsenals of the military or law enforcement agencies of any nation in the world. A nauseant? He didn't feel sick. Knockout gas? He was wide awake. His limited exposure might have cut down the gas's effects in either of these two cases. The stuff could be slow-acting, by nature or by dosage, its effects delayed while it continued working on his system.

The chain of reasoning flashed lightninglike through Jack's mind. He wasn't just sitting there while he puzzled it out, either. He'd been in action from the start, on his feet and moving.

He'd landed on the east bank of a shallow creek

that ran north-south along the center of the bottom of a valley. Both banks were thatched with thick, dark green grass, perhaps because of their proximity to the water. The greenery stood in contrast to the short, dry, yellow-brown turf that matted the rest of the valley.

The west bank stood at the bottom of a long, low slope that stretched for a hundred yards or so before rising into a high, rounded hill. The hill was taller but less steep and jagged than the one Jack had descended. It was dotted with stands of timber, unlike the opposite side with its scant sprinkling of low, scraggly brush. The far hill was crowned with an abundance of the shaggy blue-green foliage of pine trees.

The hilltop provided the only real cover in the valley. It was a place where Jack could hide and shelter if he reached it before the green gas took effect, whatever that might be. He had little doubt that hostiles would come looking for him. The Silvertop strike force was unlikely to leave any surviving witnesses to the raid. And that was the optimistic view, assuming as it did that Jack would survive the green gas.

He was alive now and would continue to act on that premise unless and until circumstance proved otherwise.

The bank was a few feet above the creek bed. He hopped down off it, raising a splash in the shallow water. A scattering of silver droplets fell back to the surface in what seemed to be slow motion.

Jack started across the creek, stepping carefully to avoid slipping on the smooth, rounded stones lining its bottom. Water milled around his ankles, rising to slop over his boot tops in mid-stream.

He clambered up the side of the muddy west

bank and began jogging across a long stretch of open ground that rose only a few degrees on its way toward the base of the hill. The green grass of the bank quickly yielded to short, dry, yellow-brown turf. It felt springy under his feet.

He angled across the tilted flat instead of crossing it directly, making for a spot at the bottom of the hill that was in line with a clump of trees higher on the slope. He wanted to make use of what minimal cover was available as soon as possible.

These first trees were about twenty yards above the bottom of the hill. Jack climbed to them. They were skinny pines about fifteen feet tall with a few sparse, forlorn-looking boughs. The trunks at their thickest were the width of a thin man's leg. Jack grabbed one to help pull himself up.

The wood writhed in his grip.

Jack pulled his hand back, recoiling. He thought for an instant he'd grabbed a snake that was curled around the trunk and had wriggled away at his touch. He looked at the tree he'd grabbed and the ground surrounding it. He saw no snake. He circled the tree carefully, looking at its far side and the ground at its base.

No snake.

He held out his hand palm-up, the one that had done the grabbing, and looked at it. It was the hand of a stranger.

Perhaps he'd never looked at it properly before. He stared at it. It seemed to swell and grow, then to dwindle and shrink.

A fascinating phenomenon. He continued to watch it. The hand continued to expand and contract in size. He realized that the cycle of expansion and contraction was in synchronization with the beating of his heart. It was an awesome revelation.

Awe turned into anxiety. He must be crazy to waste time staring at his hand when he should be climbing the hill as fast as he could!

Jack turned his face toward the slope and readied himself to continue. He examined the ground ahead to make sure there was no snake there. It came up clean and he strode briskly forward, mounting the hillside at a quick pace. He made a point of not looking at his hands as he climbed.

He was one-third of the way up the hill when he realized his error. He'd planned to use the trees for cover and here he was walking out in the middle of the open where anybody could see him!

He shook his head at his own carelessness, changing course toward the right and another clump of trees. They had some waist-high bushes at their bases. He hurried toward them but slowed as he neared them, just in case they harbored snakes.

There was a snake! He stopped short. No, it was only a dead tree branch.

Jack stood still but the hillside kept moving. Solid ground seemed to flow like water racing uphill and away from him. Earthquake!

They didn't have earthquakes in Colorado, did they? He blinked and the illusion vanished. The earth was solid and motionless beneath his feet.

Jack made the conceptual breakthrough: the *illusion* vanished. That's all it was, an illusion. Unreal, like the other phenomena that had been bedeviling him throughout the climb.

It was all in his head and the reason it was in his head was because the green gas had put it there. The green gas was a hallucinogen.

The breakthrough was thrilling and alarming. Thrilling because it gave him a handle on the weird things that were happening to him. Alarming because of its implications.

His awareness snapped into focus with an almost physical lurch. He was Jack Bauer and he was experiencing the effects of exposure to a hallucinogenic gas. An airborne psychedelic whose effects were something like LSD only stronger.

His training as an agent had included advanced courses in resisting hard interrogations. Drugs were frequently used to break a subject's will and the trainees had been dosed with a variety of psycho-chemicals to strengthen their resistance and give them a sampling of the techniques that might be used against them in the event of being taken alive by the enemy.

Now that Jack knew what was happening to him he could fight it. No, that was wrong. The drug had him in its sway and its effects could not be willed away, no more than a swimmer in the sea could will away a giant wave that was about to come crashing down on him.

He couldn't fight it but he could surf it, ride that wave out until it had spent itself and washed him safely up on shore.

He looked back the way he came, across the valley to the ridge bordering Silvertop. The sky above it was blue, free of any taint of the green.

The green was in his head now. He had to stay on top of the wave, maintaining his sense of self and purpose, stay flexible and adapt to whatever came his way until the drug worked its way out of his system.

The creek wound its way through the valley bottom like a giant snake, sunlight glistening on its surface in countless myriad swirls.

All illusion, the trick of a drugged mind.

Jack pointed himself toward the hilltop and resumed his climb. It was not unlike escaping the tunnel after the dynamite blast. You took one step forward and then another and kept on doing it until you reached your goal.

The weird physical and visual effects were Alice-in-Wonderland trimmings on bedrock reality. A rock was still a rock and a tree was still a tree, even if the rocks were made of jelly and the trees were swaying, with their branches wriggling in snaky motion.

The ground leveled out as he crested the summit of the hill. He was on a plateau, a wooded flat that spread out for miles in a sprawling pine forest. These were real pines, tall and towering with thick trunks and abundant foliage.

The pine scent was heady, intoxicating. The edge of the forest was a solid wall but when Jack approached it the trees spread apart in a maze of paths and trails. Not manmade trails but game trails.

He entered the woods. They were filled with pools of cool shadow and hot sunlit glades that alternated in a checkerboard pattern if one had the wit to see it. They were never silent but quick with life and motion: birds flitting, pine cones dropping, boughs creaking.

Jack followed a trail into the depths of the forest. It wound through the trees, around mossy boulders, down into hollows carpeted with dead pine needles and up into rises that broke into columns of sunlight shafting through spaces in the canopy of trees. It was a place of mystery and enchantment where time lost all meaning. . .

Somewhere, somewhen, somehow the scene began to stabilize and come back into focus. The initial, overpowering rush of the drug, a physical onslaught of raw sensation that sent Jack reeling among the big trees, reached its peak. The wave crested, broke, and ebbed.

The trail went up a low rise and into a clearing, a broad grassy open area about fifty feet in diameter that was enclosed by a thicket of trees.

Jack slipped through a wall of foliage to enter the glade. The grass was emerald-green, and above the treetops stood a circle of blue sky. It was an idyllic nook, like a woodland scene depicted in an illustration for a children's storybook.

He was well into the clearing before he realized he was not alone. There was a purposeful rustling motion in the bushes at the glade's opposite end. Rustling and scratching.

This did not come as a total surprise. He'd been aware for some time of noises of movement in the woods around him, but they'd been following in his wake. These noises came from the opposite direction, though: in front of him.

He'd felt more bemused than fearful ever since the drug's physical rush had lessened, and he felt no anxiety now as he moved to one side to investigate the source of the disturbance.

He saw through a gap in the brush what first looked like a huge black dog. It stood on all fours, as tall at the shoulder as a pony and weighing between three hundred and four hundred pounds. Incredible beast!

It wasn't a dog, though, it was a bear. A bear with rounded ears and a muzzle-shaped face and fur so brown it was almost black. It was tearing at a fallen log with its front paws, clawing away rotted and pulpy wood to get at the grubs and insects that infested it.

A mini version of the bear, a cub, stood nearby watching its parent take apart the log. The adult lifted a front paw swarming with insects to its snout, licking them off with broad swipes of its tongue and swallowing them down.

It could have been a scene from a TV nature special, a charming vignette of animal life in the wilderness.

A twig snapped somewhere behind Jack, sounding loud in the sudden stillness. The big bear froze. The cub was the first to notice Jack. It made a cute bawling cry.

The big bear turned its gaze toward Jack. It growled. The growl was low, muttered, and reverberant. It touched something in Jack that must have been hardwired into the human brain since caveman days, triggering a sense of full-body fear.

The bear growled again, snarling, baring gleaming yellow-white fangs all curved and dripping fat gobbets of saliva. Its fur stood on end, electric with sudden menace and aggression. It lunged forward, charging.

Jack jumped to one side at the same instant that a gunshot sounded, detonating in the glade like a thunderclap.

The bear changed course on a dime, swerving to

meet this newly perceived threat. It whisked past Jack toward the other side of the glade.

Two men stood there, crouched in postures of fear and stupefaction. One was a broad-shouldered hulk with a platinum-blond crew cut. The other was short and round-faced with a stubbly beard, dark eyes, and a slack-jawed, gaping mouth. The latter held a leveled rifle with smoke curling from its muzzle.

The image of the duo was engraved on Jack's brain with the clarity of a photograph. He could see the platinum-haired man's cold blue eyes and the jagged scar that split his left eyebrow. He could see the short man's dark eyes bulging like black olives stuck in the sweaty white pudding of his fear-ridden face. He realized the bullet had been meant for him but had missed because of his sudden lunge to avoid the charging bear.

The bear went for the short man. He fired again but too late; the bear was on him and he was bowled over backward, the gunshot zipping harmlessly through the trees.

The bear knocked him to his back on the ground and tore at him with tremendous swipes of its clawed front paws, ripping him apart as it had done to the log but with much greater ease.

He screamed, "Oh Gawd, Reb, help!"

Reb, the man with platinum hair, did not help. He was too busy running at top speed in the opposite direction.

Jack came to himself again. He knew who he was, where he was, and what he had to do.

He got the hell out of there. Fast.

. . . .

**THE FOLLOWING TAKES PLACE
BETWEEN THE HOURS OF
3 P.M. AND 4 P.M.
MOUNTAIN DAYLIGHT TIME**

. . . .

Silvertop, Colorado

Some people love a mystery. Dirk Vanaheim hated
them. It was a trait he'd had since boyhood days. He
was intensely irritated by unsolved crimes, locked
room murders, unexplained disappearances, and the
like. He took them as a personal affront. He had no
belief in supernatural intervention in human events.
Every crime must have a solution, it was only lack of
information on the players and the scene that pre-
vented its solution.

This aspect of his personality had served him well
in his chosen profession in the fields of first counter-
espionage and currently counterterrorism. He had
risen to the number two post of Assistant Special
Agent in Charge of CTU/DENV. He now had the

responsibility of securing and managing the crime scene at Silvertop.

He was thin with lead-colored hair worn brushed straight back from a high forehead. It lay on his scalp like a metal skullcap. A long face featured a pair of horizontal eyebrows over deep-set eyes with dark rings around them. The ever-present fatigue-born rings had deepened during the run-up to the Sky Mount Round Table. They could only worsen as a result of his having to handle the Silvertop mess. He had the feeling that before the Sky Mount conference was done he'd look like a raccoon.

Silvertop mess? Debacle was the word for it. Five CTU agents were dead and a sixth missing. This was more than a crime scene, it was a battlefield. The forensics team from CTU/DENV had arrived to do a thorough examination of the Zealots' blue bus in Silvertop's ghost town. They had discovered a chaos of carnage on the bluff's south slope and the grounds below it. Special Investigator Anne Armstrong and three members of the tac squad, Frith, Sanchez, and Bailey, were dead. CTU/L.A.'s SAC Jack Bauer, here on temporary duty, was missing, as was tac squad member Holtz. The corpses of a half-dozen unknown assailants had been found strewn about the south face along with the CTU dead. The bodies of the unknowns had been left mutilated to thwart a quick identification.

Vanaheim was grateful that the forensics team had arrived after the battle was over and the victors had departed, otherwise the body count would have been far greater. CTU/DENV's ranks had already been decimated as it was.

Further investigation had revealed the presence of

tac squad member Holtz on top of the bluff near the team's vehicles. He'd been shot through the head by a high-powered rifle. It was a black day for CTU/DENV and for the entire unit as a whole.

CTU/DENV chief Orlando Garcia had assigned Vanaheim the task of securing the site and the situation. Vanaheim and an eight-man tac squad had raced to the site. CTU/DENV's people were already spread thin by a variety of duties connected with protecting the Round Table conference. The most recent losses had only exacerbated the problem. Vanaheim was faced with a delicate situation in controlling the site with the limited number of personnel now available for him to draw on.

CTU's original mission charter specified that one of its goals was closer cooperation and sharing intelligence with other agencies. All government agencies are traditionally turf-conscious and jealous of their prerogatives, none more so than those involved with the national security sector. The CIA/FBI rivalry is well-known. The events of 9/11 had fostered a greater sense of unity of purpose between them as well as with the Department of Homeland Security. But this mutual amity and concord had its limits.

SAC Garcia had been quite specific: "Those are CTU dead out there. This matter is going to remain in our hands until the perpetrators are found and brought to justice."

Vanaheim was not without other auxiliary support to draw on. The U.S. Army had become involved due to certain features of the Red Notch incident. Army Intelligence officers who had a close working relationship with the CIA, CTU's parent organization, had been called in to help. They were able to supply much-needed manpower required to secure and properly investigate Silvertop.

Shadow Valley had been cordoned off. Its sole entrance where the canyon opened on Dixon Cutoff was closed and guarded by an Army Military Police detachment. The MPs were dressed in civilian clothes but their weapons were Army-issue M–16s, M–4s and sidearms. The Army, too, wanted to minimize its footprint in the affair where possible. The entrance was also guarded by a covert fifty-caliber machine gun nest, a precaution prompted by the unknown enemy's use of heavy firepower. MPs in Humvees patrolled the valleys to the east and west of the canyon to contain and detain unauthorized personnel.

The Sky Mount area had been declared a no-fly zone for the duration of the conference. Now Shadow Valley and environs had been added to the restricted list. Any snoopy reporters who somehow got wind that something big was cooking at Silvertop would be unable to overfly the site to satisfy their curiosity.

The south face of the bluff swarmed with activity. Teams of forensics experts and special investigators went about their business of methodically cataloging the carnage. The criminalistics crews included CTU/DENV agents working in conjunction with their opposite numbers from the MP's Criminal Investigation Division, CID. They took photographs, diagrammed the disposition of bodies on the slopes, made plaster moulages of tire tracks left by vehicles at the scene, and collected a wide variety of evidence, all of which were properly sealed and labeled in protective envelopes. It was too early yet for the bodies to be bagged, tagged, and taken away, but that, too, would eventually be part of the process.

Vanaheim was also able to draw on the resources of the Denver field office of the ATF. They had a dog in this fight, too. ATF agents Dean and O'Hara had been among the first casualties of the Red Notch incident. Vanaheim was working closely with ATF Inspector Cullen, now also present at the site. The two were much of a type: grim, hard, sour-faced man hunters.

They were on top of the bluff, where investigatory efforts also continued. The mass casualties on the south face had absorbed the lion's share of resources, but important activities also continued on the summit. Holtz's corpse was being examined by several specialists while a second group was covering the blue bus.

A handful of persons stood clustered around the mouth of the air shaft near the collapsed shed. They included Vanaheim, Cullen, and several of their administrative aides. They stood close to the edge—but not too close. A thin film of brown dust rose steadily from the hole.

Some hardy souls had already stretched prone on the ground to peer over the rim. They'd reported that the bottom of the pit was heaped with fresh mounds of dirt and rock that bore every sign of having been brought down by an explosive blast.

Vanaheim said, "Our last report from Armstrong and her team reported that they were going to enter the mine in order to investigate the shaft to see if it'd been used as a body dump. It had to have been blown up after that to block the inquiry."

Cullen said, "The rubble will have to be cleared and the pit examined. A big job. We'll have to get a crane hoist out here. They'll need an earthmoving bucket and enough heavy duty cable to reach to the bottom. It'll have to be cleared one bucketful at a time."

"An order's already been put in for one but it'll be hours before it gets here."

"And hours more before the pit is cleared."

Vanaheim shrugged. "What can you do? That's the way of it." He knew Cullen hated delay as much as he did.

Cullen scowled. "This Prewitt character is shaping up like another Jim Jones." He was referring to the infamous leader of the People's Temple cult who'd orchestrated a mass suicide of the nine hundred believers who'd followed him to the hellhole colony of Jonestown in South America. Those who'd refused to drink the poisoned Kool-Aid that the guru had prescribed for the mass self-extinction orgy had been murdered.

Vanaheim said, "Jones mostly killed his own. Prewitt's killing mine and yours."

Cullen said, "Jones had his death squads, too. They eliminated defectors and mass-murdered a congressman and his entourage and some reporters who went down to Guyana to investigate the cult."

"Looks like Prewitt has his own death squads as well. They're no pushovers, either. They outshot my tac squad, and they were all top men."

"At least they went down fighting. My guys Dean and O'Hara never knew what hit them. For that matter, neither do I."

One of Vanaheim's aides appeared, jogging across an open space toward the pit. He spotted his chief and changed direction, coming toward him. Vanaheim turned to face him. "What's up, Murphy?"

The aide said, "Message for you from Pike's Ford, sir."

"What is it?

Murphy glanced at Cullen standing nearby. Vanaheim said, "It's all right, he's with us. Shoot."

"Sir, they've found Jack Bauer."

There was a new addition to the Pike's Ford command post complex. It was a recreational vehicle that had been turned into a mobile laboratory and clinic. Nothing in its exterior coloring, design, or identification numbers indicated that its true owner was the United States Army. Its driver and crew wore civilian garments. It had arrived at Pike's Ford a few hours earlier that afternoon.

Its forward section housed the clinic, its rear the infirmary, and its open center space served as a kind of informal office/day room. It was hooked up to a portable generator that powered its lights, air conditioner, and various appliances and equipment.

The center space held a workstation and several chairs that folded out from the side walls. It was occupied by CTU/DENV head Orlando Garcia and Dr. Fenton Norbert.

Garcia was heavyset with salt-and-pepper hair, a craggy face, thick dark eyebrows, and a neatly trimmed mustache. He said, "How soon can I see him, Doctor?"

Norbert said, "Just another couple of minutes. My nurse is finishing up the last of his treatment." He was tall and slightly built, with a few strands of dark hair combed over his shiny scalp. He wore an open white lab coat over a white shirt, tie, and trousers. He was an active duty colonel in the Army with high-level connections with military and civilian intelligence. He had a black security rating, allowing him access to all but the most stratospheric levels of top secret material.

Garcia's brown eyes were so dark that they seemed to blend in with the pupils, giving the impression of a pair of large black dots. They were intent and intense as they fastened on the medic. "He needs to be able to talk, Doctor. That's vital."

Norbert's hazel eyes, deceptively mild, did not flinch from Garcia's gaze. "He will."

"But will he be making sense?"

"Yes. I gave him a Thorazine derivative that neutralizes the effects of the drug, as well as a stimulant to counteract the sedative."

"Good. I need to know what he knows."

"As do I."

A narrow passage along the driver's side wall connected with the clinic, which was partitioned off. A door opened on the right and a nurse emerged, brown-haired, round-faced, and solidly built. She carried a clipboard with some documents attached. She was Army, too, and her security classification was almost as high as Norbert's.

She went into the center space. "All through, Doctor."

"Thank you, Nurse."

She stood to one side to let Norbert and Garcia pass, then sat down at the workstation and began processing the documents. Norbert and Garcia had to proceed single file through the passage, Norbert leading. He opened the door, and he and Garcia entered the clinic.

It was a windowless rectangular cubicle lit by overhead fluorescent lights and smelling sharply of alcohol and disinfectants. Its design maximized the available space much in RV style but with a medical slant. A foldout examining table stood lengthwise along the vehicle's passenger side wall. The rear wall had a stainless steel sink with a cabinet above it. A locked glass-fronted cabinet stood in the corner between the rear and driver's side wall. It contained rows of glass shelves stacked with medical instruments and supplies.

Jack Bauer sat on the examining table facing the door with his legs hanging over the sides. He was stripped down to his shorts. His athletic form was mottled with a variety of bruises and abrasions, the worst of which were covered with taped gauze patches. The left side of his face was still swollen where Trooper Fisk had hit him with the flat of the pistol. His face was scratched and cut in a number of places and pasted with adhesive bandages in several places. His glittering eyes were calm and clear.

The two men came in, Norbert closing the door behind them. A lock clicked into place. He and Garcia had to do some careful jockeying to avoid bumping into each other in the cramped confines.

Norbert indicated a round-seated metal stool with tubular legs in the corner between the sink and the glass-fronted cabinet. "Why don't you sit there while I attend to my patient?"

Garcia said, "I thought you were through with him."

"A doctor's work is never done." Norbert gestured toward the chair. "Please."

Garcia, wide-bodied and thick-armed, sidestepped between table and wall and seated himself on the stool. He sat leaning forward with thick forearms resting on meaty thighs. He said, "I never expected to see you again, Jack."

Jack said, "For a while I had some doubts on that score myself."

Norbert said, "How do you feel, Jack?"

"I feel fine—all things considered."

Norbert took a silvery pen flashlight and shone it into Jack's eyes. "The pupils are dilating normally. That's good. It means that the drug's effects have been neutralized."

Jack said, "What drug is that? You said you had some answers for me, Doctor."

Garcia thrust his head forward aggressively. "I've got some questions I'd like answered myself. What happened out there on Silvertop? What happened to you and why are you the only one of the team to come back alive?"

Jack's face fell. "None of the others made it?"

"Only you."

"That's a damned shame. I'm sorry."

Garcia pressed, "Time won't wait. I need answers now. The doctor can answer your questions when you're done." His manner was surly, skeptical, and suspicious. Jack didn't blame him. He'd have been the same way himself had their positions been reversed.

Jack said, "You sure you want the doctor to hear all this?"

"Dr. Norbert is U.S. Army Colonel Norbert. He's not only a medic, he's Army Intelligence. The Army is working hand in glove with CTU on this."

Jack said, "Okay."

Norbert stood leaning against the forward wall with arms folded against his chest. Garcia said,

"Just give the highlights that I can use for immediate action. You'll be fully debriefed later."

Jack summarized the team's actions on Silvertop after going into the mine. He told of finding the mass grave at the bottom of the shaft.

Garcia said, "How many did you say there were?"

Jack replied, "I'd say at least twenty, maybe more."

"How can you be sure of that?"

"I can't, not totally. It's an estimate. The killers didn't bother covering them up with too much dirt. I've seen mass killings—too many—out in the field before, in the Balkans, Darfur, Iraq . . . You know the litany. I've got the experience to make a pretty accurate guess."

Garcia looked disturbed, dubious. "But that would be pretty much all of the Red Notch cadre!"

Jack said, "Yes. I find that to be particularly significant, don't you?"

"If true. Maybe they weren't all Zealots."

Jack shrugged. "I suppose one-half of the cadre could have killed the other and then thrown in some other folks they didn't like, but that's not how I'd bet it."

Garcia demanded, "What about Prewitt? Was he one of the dead? Or Ingrid Thaler?"

"I didn't see them. But conditions at the bottom of the shaft weren't conducive to making any positive identifications."

"So either one or both could still be alive."

"It's possible. You'll know for sure when you dig them up and haul them into the light of day."

Garcia shook his head like a bull tossing its horns.

"That won't be for some considerable time. That dynamite blast brought a lot of the shaft down on top of them."

Jack said, "Which was the purpose of the exercise."

"Eh? How so?"

"To delay identification of the bodies until the Round Table is over."

Garcia challenged, "Who'd want to do that and why?"

"Who, I don't know. Why—because that delay is key to someone's plans."

"What plans?"

Jack said, "Look at the time element, that's the critical factor. The Red Notch disappearance took place early on Thursday morning the day before the start of the conference. This morning a hit team liquidates the lone witness to the disappearance and tries to do the same to Neal and me because maybe we heard something. Today a team goes out to Silvertop and finds the blue bus and a mass grave. A strike force shows up almost immediately to eliminate the evidence and its discoverers. It was so important to the plotters that the evidence be concealed that they must have left a spotter in place to sound the alert if anybody got too close. The spotter killed Holtz, blew up the shaft, and sent for the kill squad, not necessarily in that order.

"The blue bus and mass grave were found out. Killing our team and blowing up the shaft only underlined the fact that something important is hidden in that grave. It's only a matter of time before it's unearthed and exposed. How much time? A day, maybe two at the most? That's when the Round Table ends.

"I'm saying that a plot is aimed at the conference. A deadly plot that needs the facts to be concealed while Sky Mount is in session."

Garcia knitted his two fists together and leaned forward, putting his weight on his thighs while he thought it over. "It's possible. Prewitt's crowd hates the Round Table members like poison."

Jack said, "I'll tell you something else. That strike force was no motley crew of cultists turned shooters. They were professional guns."

Garcia had been looking down at the tops of his shoes. He raised his head, turning those big-bore, gun-sight eyes on Jack. "Which brings up another question: how'd you escape when no one else on the team did?"

Jack said, "A fair question and I'll give you the answer. Because I was the only one who knew what was going to happen when Reb fired the gas grenade."

"Reb?"

"The leader of the strike force. A big, humongous dude with a dyed platinum-blond crew cut."

"How come you know his name?"

"That part of the story comes later."

Dr. Norbert took out a pocket digital recorder and set it down on a countertop. "The rest of this concerns me and my part of the operation. I'm going to record it if you have no objection."

His last remark was directed at Garcia. Garcia said, "Go ahead. We're in this together."

Nobody asked Jack if he objected to being taped. He didn't and let it pass. He went on, "The grenade exploded, releasing a cloud of green gas. I knew it was dangerous because of what Lobo had said about a gang of hog-faced demons loosing a green cloud on the compound. As soon as I saw it, I knew the only chance was to get away from it."

Garcia accused, "You ran and left the others to die!"

Jack took it without flinching. He was more than a little contemptuous. "Don't be childish. You know how the game is played. Better that one should escape to tell what happened than all should die.

"The gas grenade detonated on the tunnel level where Anne and the others were. I was on the next level down where the gas hadn't reached yet. They were done for. What good would it have done for me to make a heroic last stand and throw my life away in vain? If I escaped then at least somebody would know the truth.

"By the way, there's an ore cart on the level below the tunnel that I used for cover as my shooting point. If you check it you'll find fifty or more slugs smeared across it. In case you were wondering where I was while the shooting was going on."

Garcia looked away, rubbing the lower half of his face with his hand. After a while he said, "You're right, you're right, of course. You did what you had to do, what I would have done if I'd been in the same position. It's just that I'm so damned pissed about what they did to Anne and the others!"

Jack said steadily, "How did they get it?"

"Shot in the head at point-blank range. Cold-blooded murder!"

"I'm sorry. I liked Anne, liked them all. They were good teammates, good agents."

"I've known them all for years. I'm the one who'll have to tell their families."

There was nothing to say to that. Jack went on, "The killers gave them the coup de grâce. It was as easy as shooting a sitting duck. Easier, because the duck's not drugged up. The team would have been totally out of it, helpless as babies from the green gas."

Garcia said, "The strike force did worse to their own. Blew their heads apart with shotgun blasts. No facial or dental identification there. Then they cut their hands off and took them away with them. No fingerprint ID. We don't know if they did it just to their dead or if they killed the wounded, too."

Jack said, "Delay. There it is again. Some if not all of the bodies will eventually be identified by their DNA, height, weight, and age, distinguishing body marks such as scars and tattoos, but it'll take time. Time enough for them to accomplish their purpose."

"Which is?"

"Something massive with the Round Table on the receiving end."

Dr. Norbert cleared his throat, said, "You were lucky to get out alive, Jack."

Jack nodded. "I thought the green gas was some kind of knockout gas but it's not. It's a hallucinogen. I got a whiff of it and it sent me rocketing clear out of this world for a while. Anybody that got a lungful of it would've been knocked flat, too tripped out to do anything but lie there and look at the pretty color.

"That must be what happened at Red Notch. A strike force—maybe the one at Silvertop, maybe another, I don't know—bombed the compound with gas grenades and rounded the cultists up while they were helplessly tripping out. Some might have tried to resist or been too crazed to control so they were killed there. That explains the seemingly random dispersion of bloodstains at Red Notch. I don't think they were all killed there, not enough blood, but who knows? Dead or alive, the Zealots were loaded onto the blue bus and taken to Silvertop where they were finished off. They were thrown down the shaft and covered with dirt, not to be found until after whatever is supposed to happen at Sky Mount happens. That was the plan, anyway."

Garcia said, "You're making a lot of sense for a guy that was blitzed with a psychedelic bomb not too long ago."

Jack grinned. "You should've seen me earlier, I was flying like a moon bat. Before that I made my break by going over a ridgetop and tumbled into next valley. I climbed the next hill and went into a forest."

"Pine Ridge."

"If that's what it's called. The strike force must've seen me get away because the leader and one of his sidemen came after me. I wandered around the pines in a daze, not knowing what I was doing. I didn't know Reb and his buddy were dogging me. The stuff started to wear off but I was still pretty wasted. I stumbled into a clearing and came across a mama bear and her cub. I guess it was a mama bear but I don't know for sure.

"That's where Reb and his pal found me. I didn't even know they were there. One of them stepped on a twig and broke it. Mama bear charged me and I dodged right when Reb's pal tried to shoot me in the back. He missed, but the gunshot spooked the bear into going for the shooter instead." Jack shook his head. "Frith was right."

Garcia said, "The tac squad leader? Where's he fit in with all this?"

"Earlier he said that bears were fast. He was right. That bear moved like an express train. It knocked the shooter down and ripped him up like he'd fallen into a threshing machine. He cried for help to his partner—once. Called him Reb. Reb was busy hightailing it out of there.

"I got out, too. The bear didn't bother with Reb or me. It had what it wanted and was slicing and dicing him with those wicked claws. Seeing that pretty well straightened me up and brought me to my senses. I followed Reb out of the woods. He didn't know I was there. Once he started running he never looked back. I lost sight of him but could hear him in the distance up ahead, crashing through the brush. Good thing, too. I'd lost my bearings, and without his lead I'd have had a tough time finding my way out.

"He emerged from the pine forest and went down the hill. I hung back under cover, watching him. A pickup truck was cruising the valley looking for him and picked him up. They drove south out of the valley and must have come out on Dixon Cutoff. I stuck to the cover of the tree line, making my way south along the hilltop, figuring to make my way to the highway.

"I was in the valley near the roadway when a Humvee turned in and saw me. I didn't know if it was the killers coming back to look for me or not, but when they got closer I saw they were too military to be part of the gang. Even with civvies on you can't disguise the look. I know; I was Army myself.

"They picked me up and brought me back here to Pike's Ford. The rest you know. Dr. Norbert gave me some shots that neutralized what was left of the drug in my system, and he and his nurse patched me up."

Jack turned his face to the doctor. "That's my story. Now it's your turn, Doc. You knew what that stuff was in me and had a hypodermic full of the antidote before I said a word. What's it all about? What is that green gas? And where do you and the Army come in?"

. . . .

THE FOLLOWING TAKES PLACE
BETWEEN THE HOURS OF
4 P.M. AND 5 P.M.
MOUNTAIN DAYLIGHT TIME

. . . .

Pike's Ford, Colorado

Dr. Norbert said, "The drug to which you were exposed is called BZ."

Jack said, "Never heard of it."

The medic nodded. "I'm not surprised. Few people have, and for good reason. BZ is an incredibly potent psychedelic. It's a byproduct of the LSD craze of the 1960s. BZ is like LSD on steroids. In its unadulterated form it can produce 'trips' lasting up to a week. Luckily for you, you got it in a diluted form. One that was diluted by close to forty years. I'll explain why in a moment.

"Even in the sixties with its 'anything goes' mentality, BZ never caught on with the drug-taking public. It's too strong for the most hard-core 'recreational' drug user. Which is why it was of interest to the military. The research was, in a sense, benignly motivated. The thinking was that BZ could be used as a nonlethal weapon to incapacitate enemy forces, allowing our troops to achieve a bloodless victory.

"Before judging the attempt too harshly, keep in mind the spirit of the times. It's no secret that the CIA conducted its own extensive research into the use of LSD for interrogation, hypnosis, and mind control. See the files on Project Artichoke if you're interested. The Army experimented with BZ for possible battlefield use. It was found that BZ could be delivered in the form of a gas. The drug itself was present in microscopic amounts in an inert aerosolized carrier format of highly compressed vaporous gas. The gas would be contained in artillery shells, grenades, and canisters."

Jack said dryly, "Obviously the research progressed beyond the theoretical stage."

Norbert said, "Ah, quite. The BZ experiments reached a dead end for the same reason as CIA's work with LSD as a mind-controlling drug. It doesn't work, not in that way. Psychedelics are too unpredictable in their effects on human subjects to be depended on. They work on different people in different ways, depending on the individual's psychological makeup and the setting in which the drug is administered. Some react violently, others are incapacitated. The same subject can have wildly different reactions to identical doses taken at different times.

"The hope was that enemy troops hit with a BZ bomb would be rendered pacified and incapable of resistance. The reality was that it was just as likely to transform them into a horde of raving maniacs, maniacs with guns."

Dr. Norbert tilted his head, the overhead lights reflecting off the lenses of his spectacles to render them temporarily opaque. "Apart from the practical side, there were political considerations weighing against BZ's use in combat conditions. It would have been a propaganda coup of the highest magnitude if the other side could prove that we used a psycho-chemical gas bomb in the field. That's why it was never used by either side, since the Cold War Soviets conducted similar lines of research and could have disseminated their versions of BZ bombs to their client states for use against our troops.

"The BZ research was filed under 'Project Canceled' and forgotten as the world moved on. Unfortunately a number of prototype delivery systems had already been made, including a BZ gas grenade. Grenades are used in relatively close combat conditions, so the gas incorporated a green coloring agent that made it highly visible. Our troops would have been wearing gas masks or nose filters when using the weapon; the green coloring would allow them to see where the grenades had landed on a battlefield and react accordingly in real time.

"When the project was canceled, the BZ weaponry was ordered destroyed. The vast majority of stocks were. However, a certain number escaped destruction due to bureaucratic oversight, misfiling, snafus, and just plain human error. The BZ gas grenade was produced in 1970 and a handful of crates of it have been sitting in chemical warehouse arsenals for almost forty years now.

"This year during an exhaustive inventory of existing stocks of all CWS a quantity of BZ gas grenades came to light. Their extreme age created the added danger that the container vessels, the grenades, had weakened through corrosion and might be susceptible to leakage. They were given a top priority for immediate destruction in an incinerator specifically designed to handle CWs.

"This particular facility is in Texas. Somehow, somewhere along the way, a crate of BZ weapons was stolen from the consignment. Army CID is still investigating how it was done and by whom. Whoever commissioned the theft has a very thorough and murderous organization behind them because all the suspects in the theft were eliminated early on, killed in such a way as to look like fatal accidents or suicide."

Jack said, "Well, Doc, it looks like your wandering boys have come home."

Norbert looked vaguely embarrassed. He said, "Ahem. Er, yes."

Garcia said, "We followed up on your suggestion that Red Notch be investigated for traces of CWs, Jack. The compound itself, cabins and sheds and so forth, came up clean. But bloodstains at the site tested positive for the presence of an unknown molecular complex that was subsequently identified as BZ."

Norbert said, "The BZ in the gas grenades was designed to have an extremely short life once released. Exposure to the oxygen in open air breaks down the BZ compound, rendering it inert and harmless within approximately ten minutes. When ingested by humans who've breathed the gas, traces of the compound remain for a time in the blood and tissues."

Jack stirred uneasily. "I've been exposed. Where does that leave me?"

Norbert held his hands palms out with fingers spread in a placating gesture. "Not to worry. The antidote you were given neutralized the drug's effects. The molecular remnants are inert, harmless. They'll be broken down naturally by your body processes within forty-eight to seventy-two hours."

Jack said, "So there's no danger of a recurrence, Doctor?"

"No. Absolutely not."

"Good. I'm not eager for any flashbacks of that experience."

"Remember the gas in those grenades is close to forty years old. Apparently it's lost a great deal of its potency over time. Otherwise even your minimal exposure to it would have had much more deleterious consequences."

"I'll tell you this, Doc: it still packs a hell of a punch."

Garcia said, "You might be interested to know that the hermit Lobo tested negative for the presence of BZ. He hadn't been exposed to the gas. The same applies to the bodies of ATF agents Dean and O'Hara. Whatever happened to them happened before the gas grenades were used. Their skulls showed indications of blunt force trauma. My guess is that they were taken at gunpoint, knocked out, and taken away to be disposed of later.

"If not for the BZ traces in the bloodstains, we wouldn't have known what we were dealing with. Our forensic pathologists didn't know what they were looking for but were able to identify the molecular complex by computer analysis. I never heard of BZ myself, and they had to tell me what it was. References to it in the reports we filed with headquarters were flagged at Langley and sent up a red flag on the seventh floor. They contacted Army Intelligence, who contacted me. Dr. Norbert and his staff and mobile lab arrived here a few hours ago."

Jack said, "You were unaware of the missing crate of BZ grenades?"

"I was until earlier today." Garcia's face hardened into stubborn lines and he glared out of the corner of his eye at Norbert.

Norbert said, "Naturally the Army isn't eager to advertise the loss of a dangerous psycho-chemical weapon for fear of triggering a mass panic."

"Oh, naturally."

The doctor ignored Garcia's sarcasm and said quickly, "What's important is that it has been found. Or at least a lead to it, the only one we've had since it went missing. We'll be working closely with CTU to locate the rest of it."

Jack said, "Did your investigators turn up any links between Prewitt's group and the stolen BZ grenades?"

"Frankly our investigation hit a blank wall. But the Zealots never surfaced in any of it, not a hint. If it had, we'd have been all over them."

"How does a crackpot cult turn up in the middle of a plot involving death squads and exotic psycho-chemical weapons?"

Garcia shrugged massive shoulders. "You tell me."

Jack said, "I hope to do just that." He hopped down off the examining table, reached for his clothes, which were hanging on a wall hook, and pulled on his pants.

Garcia stood up, nearly overturning the metal stool. "What do you think you're doing, Jack?"

"Putting on my pants."

"I can see that. But what have you got in mind?"

"I'm going back to work. I've got things to do."

Garcia shook his head. "Oh no. You're in no condition to go back on duty—"

Jack said, "What do you say, Doc? Any reason why I can't get back in harness?"

"Considering what you've been through, a few days' rest is highly advised—"

"Come on. You yourself said that the drug has been neutralized in my system and that there's no danger of a recurrence."

"That's true, but the antidote is a powerful depressant."

"And offset by the stimulant you gave me which you said counteracts the antidote's effects. So I'm good to go."

"I wouldn't put it that way."

"You don't have to. I did." Jack reached for his shirt, made a face. "Whew! I'm going to need to round up some clean clothes. Where can I get some around here?"

Garcia said, "You won't be needing them. You're not going anywhere, Agent Bauer—except maybe back to L.A. You've done your part here and more. Now let the rest of us do our jobs."

Jack said, "You won't be rid of me that easily. I bought a ticket for this ride and I'm not getting off before the last stop."

"Your last stop is right here."

Norbert edged toward the door. "I'll just step outside for a moment to give you gentlemen some privacy."

Jack said, "Stick around, Doc, this concerns you, too. You want your stolen BZ back, don't you?"

"Yes, of course."

"I'm the best chance you've got of getting it back."

Garcia scoffed, "You better sit down and take a rest. That BZ is going to your head."

Jack said, "Let's get real. If I wanted to, I could go to Chappelle. He's got enough of a legitimate stake in this mission to go to Langley for a directive to keep me on assignment here."

Garcia's nostrils flared, whites showing around his black-bore eyes. "You think so, huh?"

"I don't want to go crying to Chappelle. I'd prefer to convince you by the logic of my position."

"That'll take some doing."

"Fact: I'm the only who's seen the face of Reb the strike force leader and is still alive to put the finger on him. Whoever's behind him will know that, too. You need me around in a high-profile position if only to serve as bait. The plotters know who I am but not how much I know. They'll want to get rid of me, and to do that they'll have to tip their hand, which gives us a chance of getting a hot lead."

Norbert said thoughtfully, "He's got a point."

Garcia snorted in disgust. "You're as bad as he is!"

Jack said, "Tell me you'd do anything different if our positions were reversed and you were in my shoes." Garcia fumed silently. Jack pressed, "Go on, tell me you'd quit in the middle of a mission."

"I can't. But all that means is that we're both a pair of damned fools. Happy now?"

"I'm still in?"

"You're in."

"Great. Now where can I find some clean clothes? And my gun."

• •

THE FOLLOWING TAKES PLACE
BETWEEN THE HOURS OF
5 P.M. AND 6 P.M.
MOUNTAIN DAYLIGHT TIME

• •

Pike's Ford, Colorado

Lila Gibbs said, "Is that your Reb?"

She and Jack Bauer were occupying a cubicle in a section of one of the mobile home trailers that housed CTU/DENV's command post at Pike's Ford. They sat side by side facing a flat-screen computer monitor that was set on a countertop.

Jack was freshly showered and wore a change of clothes that had been lent to him by an agent of similar height and build who had a spare set of garments in a locker in another trailer that served as a barracks for the on-site team.

He still wore his own gun and shoulder holster. Weapon and harness both had taken a lot of punishment lately but were still operable. The same could be said of Jack. He'd forgotten that he even had a gun during his BZ-induced fugue, but it had remained in his possession throughout the experience. He told himself it was a good thing he had forgotten it during his altered state because otherwise he might have been tempted to look down the barrel to see where the bullet comes out of or done some other thing that would have gotten his head blown off permanently.

He'd repeated the now-familiar routine of test-firing the gun at the outdoor range, this time to determine that it had suffered no internal damage when he'd tumbled down the ridge. It checked out fine. So did he. His eye was sharp, his hand steady, and his aim true. The shoulder harness was scratched and sweat-stained but unbroken. He stuck with it because he was used to it and didn't want to risk breaking in a new rig whose unfamiliarity might slow down the speed of his draw. Especially since he was going back out in the field to serve as live bait.

But not yet. There was still an important task to be carried out here at Pike's Ford. That's why he was now working with Lila Gibbs.

She was an expert in the use of facial morphology software for identification purposes. Her role was like that of the old-time police sketch artist who draws a suspect's picture based on eyewitness testimony. The software was essentially a twenty-first-century update of the classic police Identi-Kit that uses a variety of facial features to create a composite image of the suspect's likeness.

Jack had described Reb to her: "He's between his mid-thirties and forty in age. Height about six-four; weight anywhere from 220 to 240 pounds. He's all pumped up like a pro wrestler or bodybuilder, even his muscles have muscles. I'd say look for heavy steroid use in the profile because nobody can get that kind of build without getting on the juice. Platinum-blond crew cut, a flattop. That hair color isn't found in nature and must have come out of a bottle. His left eyebrow is split by a diagonal scar a couple of inches long. Square-shaped face with a lot of jaw and chin. Clean-shaven. No identifying marks or scars that I could see, except for that scar over the left eye. He's a mean-looking dude, too, if that's any help."

Lila Gibbs was in her forties, matronly, with curly brown hair, green eyes, and a heart-shaped face. She worked the keyboard, inputting the specifications and searching the archives. The computer was linked to the CTU data net, itself able to draw on a multiplicity of sources among law enforcement, intelligence, the military, and other governmental agencies.

She said, "The name Reb could be a help or hindrance depending on whether or not it's a longtime alias or one that was recently assumed. If the latter, it may not be in the files or it could be a name he's taken to deliberately mislead the authorities and hide his real identity. But we'll include the alias with the first search. If it hits, so much the better, and if not, we can rule it out and proceed from there."

Her fingers deftly manipulated the keyboard, calling up the data. Somewhere in an unknown location massive CIA supercomputers processed the request, winnowing through oceans of binary zeroes and ones to find the desired droplets in the cyber sea.

There were thousands of "Rebs" in the archived United States police, military, and national files, more in the international ones. A hundred fit the general description; a dozen or so had facial scars in the vicinity of their left eye. Three of that twelve were described as having scars that split the left eyebrow.

Lila Gibbs pulled up their facial photos one at a time. Jack selected the third, said, "Try that one."

The screen was filled with a police mug shot containing two views of the suspect, one full-facial and the other a profile. Jack said, "I didn't see him in profile, just full-on."

Gibbs minimized the profile and maximized the frontal. It depicted a man with shoulder-length dark hair and a full beard; a cold-eyed, glowering thug with a scar across his left eyebrow. "Is that your Reb?"

Jack said, "Could be. It could be. It's hard to be sure with all that foliage covering the face, but definitely maybe."

"I could search for other photos of the subject but this is the most recent one. There's an easy way to get rid of that mess, though."

She worked more keys and a mouse, and after a pause the subject's image broke up only to be immediately reformatted. "This is how he'd look without the hair and beard."

Jack said, "Bingo! That's him. That's Reb."

She did some more manipulations. "Just to be sure, that's how he'd look with a crew cut."

"That's him all right."

The subject was identified as one "Weld, Gordon Stuart; aka Reb, The Rebel, Gordy, Gordo," and a number of other aliases that were mostly variations and combinations of his first and middle names.

Gordon Stuart Weld, thirty-seven, born in Atlanta, had an extensive criminal record throughout the South and Southwest. He had a high IQ, a hatred for authority, and a propensity for ultra-violence.

His early years included several stays in a state reformatory and six months' confinement in a mental hospital for stabbing a schoolmate with a penknife. His psychiatric record featured frequent use of the terms "sociopathic," "narcissistic," and "paranoid." He became heavily involved in gang activity during middle school, a pattern that would continue into his adult life. He was an avid motorcycle enthusiast, a skilled rider, and an expert mechanic.

He'd enthusiastically embraced the world and lifestyle of violent biker gangs, belonging to several such outfits in the South. His lengthy arrest record showed numerous counts of assault, illegal possession of firearms, drug dealing, and theft. He was arrested for rape several times but released when complainants refused to press charges due to intimidation by his fellow gang members.

His size, strength, and ruthlessness won him a spot as gang enforcer, dealing out beatings and brutality on a businesslike basis. He freelanced as a collector for loan sharks and a hired gun for drug dealers. He served three and a half years in a state penitentiary for manslaughter and five years in Federal prison for gunrunning. His arrest record fell off after that, largely because the witnesses to subsequent crimes were found slain or simply disappeared.

He became a member of the Hellbenders Motorcycle Club, an outlaw biker gang with chapters throughout Texas and the Southwest. He rose fast through the ranks and was a major player in the gang's rackets that included methamphetamine manufacturing and distribution, forced prostitution of topless and strip club dancers, gunrunning, extortion, and murder. He was rumored to be part of the gang's elite squad of executioners.

Weld had had a falling-out with his associates in the past year following an arrest in Texas for illegal gun dealing. The mug shots in his computer file had been taken during his booking on those charges. He turned informant to avoid a lengthy prison sentence for this second Federal term. He set up his fellow biker gang partners for a bust, at the same time absconding with the loot from the racket and dropping off law enforcement agencies' radar. He was now a wanted fugitive sought by police and the Hellbenders M.C., the latter having posted an open murder contract on his head with a fifty-thousand-dollar bounty collectable by anyone who could produce same. Literally.

Jack Bauer said, "Two Hellbenders were at the gorge today where the AFT agents were found. They must be looking for Reb. His being on the run explains the platinum hair dye job, too. It's such an obvious giveaway that it could only have been done to draw attention away from his previous appearance."

Lila Gibbs said, "He should have changed his name along with his hair color."

Jack grinned. "He never planned on any outsiders hearing it and living. I got a lucky break."

"Sometimes that's all it takes to crack a case wide open."

"Let's hope this is one of those times."

Now the CTU machinery would go to work on

Reb Weld, vacuuming up every speck of data relating to his life and habits, criminal career, known associates, friends, and enemies, anything that might be of use in tracking him down. The manhunt would begin in earnest, putting the Big Heat on Weld. Jack described Rowdy and Griff, and Lila Gibbs added the data to the search.

Somewhere in that mass of facts was the answer to the big question: what was the link between outlaw biker thug and killer Reb Weld, a stolen case of BZ gas grenades, a crank-kook cult of Zealots, and a multimillionaires' conclave at Sky Mount?

A discreet rapping on a cubicle partition wall caused Jack and Gibbs to look up from the monitor screen. The knocking had been done by a soft-faced man in his mid-twenties, a staffer at the Pike's Ford CP.

Gibbs said, "Yes, Charlie?"

Charlie said, "Excuse me, Lila. Jack Bauer?"

Jack said, "Yes?"

"There's a phone call for you."

"For me?"

"Yes, sir."

Jack rose from his chair. "Thanks, Lila. Thanks a lot."

She said, "My pleasure. I'll start our mill wheels grinding on the Rebel and friends."

"Grind them fine."

Charlie said, "This way please, sir." Jack followed the youth along the central corridor to a cubicle at the far end of the trailer. Charlie indicated a satellite phone on the counter. "It's a secured phone, sir."

"Thank you." Jack picked up the receiver and Charlie made himself absent.

"Bauer speaking."

A voice at the other end of the connection squawked, "What the hell are you trying to pull, Jack?"

There was no mistaking the strident tones of Regional Division Director Ryan Chappelle in high bad humor.

Jack sighed. "Hello, Ryan."

"Are you insubordinate or just plain neglectful?" Chappelle's voice tended to get screechy when he was angry, and it was screechy now. "You were told to report to me regularly on the Sky Mount situation. That was an order, not a request. I haven't received a single report from you since you got there, not one. I've been calling you every hour and all I keep getting is your voice mail. My messages to you to contact me have been piling up with no reply. I've had to get all my information on the scene from Garcia's people and I can only imagine what they're leaving out. Even with the minimal amount I'm getting it looks like things have gone to hell in a handbasket. What's going on out there?"

Jack knew from long experience that when Chappelle was in one of these moods there was nothing to do but wait until he paused for lack of breath. "Ryan, in the last fourteen hours I've been shot at, pistol-whipped, dynamited, ambushed, gas-bombed, and attacked by a bear. I've been too busy trying to stay alive to report back to you and for that I apologize."

There was another pause while Chappelle digested the import of Jack's words. His voice was lower and more modulated when he spoke again. "Then there is an ongoing conspiracy against the Round Table."

"That's correct, Ryan."

"Thank God for that!"

Jack couldn't help but grin wryly to himself at the heartfelt relief in Chappelle's statement. Everything was okay. Ryan Chappelle was on the record as having been proven right in his conjectures about an anti–Sky Mount plot. That would look good with the top brass at CIA headquarters in Langley, Virginia.

Jack gave Chappelle a brisk summary of the salient facts. the mass murder of the Zealot cadre, the BZ gas grenade connection, and Reb Weld's kill squad. Chappelle, once again the resolute in-charge authority that he saw himself as, said, "You can figure all that out later. Right now I've got something important for you to do. Top priority, immediate action."

"What's that, Ryan?"

"Apprehend Brad Oliver."

"Brad Oliver?"

"Confidential secretary to the great Cabot Huntington Wright himself."

"I know who he is, I've met him."

"Arrest him. My fiscal analysis team finally broke through the web of shell companies and dummy corporations to finger the mystery man who's been short selling stocks to bet on catastrophe. It's Oliver."

Jack knew better than to ask Chappelle if he was sure of the information. Chappelle would never have put it out there if he were unsure.

Chappelle's tone was confidential, intense. "This is hot stuff, Jack. I only found out about it minutes ago myself. I wanted you to have it first so we can steal a march on Garcia."

"I'm working with the man, Ryan. He's going to have to know about it."

"Of course. My people are contacting him now with the intelligence. But this way you'll be right in on the kill so he can't freeze you out and grab all the credit for himself."

"You think of everything, Ryan."

"I try. One more thing, Jack, and this is strictly for your ears only: Oliver's just the tip of the iceberg. Behind him is something a hundred times bigger. The find was serendipitous—my analysts came across it while cracking Oliver's manipulations. His short selling is the opening wedge of a far greater financial conspiracy being conducted in the world markets. It's the same pattern of betting on disaster only a quantum level higher. There could be as much as a hundred million dollars' worth of shorted stocks gambling on an imminent economic meltdown."

Jack's eyebrows lifted. A hundred million dollars! He said, "That kind of money requires a major player. A hostile nation, maybe."

Chappelle said, "We're working on it. It's top secret until we've got it nailed down for sure. For now, though, grab Oliver. Sweat him. Make him talk. I'm counting on you, Jack. You know how these things are done."

"Yes, I do."

· ·

THE FOLLOWING TAKES PLACE
BETWEEN THE HOURS OF
6 P.M. AND 7 P.M.
MOUNTAIN DAYLIGHT TIME

· ·

Sky Mount, Colorado

Long shadows fell on Masterman Way as Jack Bauer
and Ernie Sandoval drove up to the gates of Sky
Mount estate. The midsummer sun was still high
in the sky but the mountains were tall, bathing the
grounds in blue shadow. Lights winked on in the
mansion and its surroundings.

The two agents were in the Mercedes. Sandoval
was behind the wheel and Jack sat on the front passenger side. Jack had felt a sharp pang of regret and
sorrow earlier when he first realized that they were
going to be traveling in the Merc; the last time he'd
been in it, Anne Armstrong had been his partner.

The car was trailed by a dark green SUV carrying
a well-armed backup unit of four CTU action men.

No unpleasantness was expected on this visit but it was good to expect the unexpected.

Anything involving the Round Table conclave had to be handled with kid gloves. Its host and attendees comprised a significant slice of America's moneyed and powerful elite; their feathers were not to be ruffled without good cause.

This explained the security arrangements at Sky Mount. Its rich and powerful guests had reasons of their own for maximizing their personal and professional privacy. They didn't want the place swarming with FBI agents and intelligence operatives who might conceivably ferret out secrets about their businesses and private lives. Knowledge is power; no one knows that better than those at the top.

That was why security at the estate itself was being handled by the Brand Agency, a private firm known for secrecy and discretion where the ultra-rich are involved. The fact that a controlling interest in the firm was held by the Masterman Trust was a further guarantor that what happened at Sky Mount would stay at Sky Mount.

Similar thinking lay behind the national intelligence establishment's decision to keep the events and revelations of Silvertop hidden behind a wall of secrecy, a directive handed down from the highest levels in Washington, D.C. It was believed that disclosure of the truth about the Zealots' mass grave and the killer strike force would trigger a panicky mass evacuation of Sky Mount.

No real, tangible evidence that those dealings involved a plot against the Round Table had as yet been unearthed. There was nothing to be taken in hand to Cabot Huntington Wright and associates to prove to them that the gathering must be gaveled to a premature and disastrous close.

Ruining the conference without good cause would create an avalanche of bad publicity and ill-will that would bury any officials rash enough to take it on themselves to cause it to be canceled simply to be on the safe side.

People resent having their lives disrupted by a false alarm. The master and guests of Sky Mount had ways of making their displeasure felt by those who'd sounded the alert because of a fire somewhere way off in the distance when the conferees hadn't even smelled the smoke.

It was the old one about the boy who cried wolf. The wolf had better be at the door, or let the crier beware.

The BZ connection was an additional complicating factor, one that would never surface if the Army had its way, and there was no reason to expect that it wouldn't.

That was a national security nightmare and potential public relations debacle that was best kept hidden from the power brokers at Sky Mount, to say nothing of the average citizens and taxpayers who're generally kept in the dark as a matter of policy.

What they didn't know couldn't hurt all parties concerned—unless the worst happened and disaster struck. So it had better not happen.

Anything else was unthinkable.

Brad Oliver's arrest would be handled with a maximum of discretion. Jack Bauer and Ernie Sandoval would make the pinch, quietly whisking Oliver out a side door and off the premises without the guests suspecting that anything was amiss.

The CTU agents were casually but correctly attired to blend in with the surroundings. They were armed only with their guns and wore no protective bullet-proof garments. Each man was equipped with a pair of nose filters and a half-dozen slapshot ampoules containing an antidote to BZ, gear that fit comfortably in their jacket pockets and had been supplied to them earlier at Pike's Ford by Dr. Norbert.

This precaution had been taken not because of any danger that might threaten at Sky Mount but in anticipation that an attempt might be made against them in transit while they were taking Oliver to the command post.

That was also the reason for the presence of the backup unit. They would wait outside the gates while Jack and Sandoval apprehended Oliver.

No advance notice had been given to the conference's hosts or guardians to avoid Oliver's learning by accident or design of his imminent arrest.

Jack and Sandoval had to endure the tedious admittance process necessary for the uninvited to gain entry to the estate.

They could have pulled a power play by using their Federal authority to bull their way in but chose not to do so for fear of prematurely alerting Oliver or any accomplices he might have inside the estate.

Oliver's status as a wanted man was a tightly held secret known only to Chappelle, Garcia, and the two agents in the Mercedes. The backup crew knew that an arrest would be made but were unaware of the suspect's identity.

Fifteen minutes passed before someone came down from the mansion to escort the agents beyond the gate. They were met this time by Don Bass, head of the Brand Agency's presence on the estate.

The first of the conference's day-long sessions had apparently not been without its rigors for the security chief, who looked considerably more rumpled and frazzled than he had early that morning. His forehead was corrugated by worry lines, his eyes were tired, and his jowly face exhibited a glum, hangdog expression.

He summoned up a cheerful grin as he climbed into the back of the car. "Hi fellows, what's up?"

Sandoval said, "A routine visit. How goes the gathering of the high-and-mighty?"

"Hectic!" Bass settled back into the seat cushions as the Mercedes rolled through the open gate and up the long curved driveway toward the mansion.

Jack turned in his seat so he could look Bass in the face. He said, "Actually, we're here to make an arrest."

Sandoval added dryly, "A routine arrest."

Bass reacted like he'd been zapped by an electric cattle prod. He bounced upright in his seat so abruptly that the top of his head barely missed hitting the roof. "What? You're kidding!"

Jack said, "No."

Bass sat leaning forward, his thickset upper body rigidly tilted at an acute angle. "There's no such thing as a routine arrest here."

Sandoval said, "We'll try and keep it that way anyhow."

Bass said eagerly, "Who's the pigeon? Anybody I know?"

Jack said, "Brad Oliver."

Bass's broad face creased in lines of wonderment and disbelief. "Masterman's stooge? What's he done?"

"We just want to have a little chat with him."

Bass's expression took on a wise and knowing look. "Can't tell, huh? More cloak and dagger stuff. Must be something big if you boys are putting the arm on him."

Sandoval said, "Naturally we'll be relying on your discretion, Don."

"You'll have my full cooperation, of course, and the entire firm's as well."

Jack said, "We'd prefer that this be kept between the three of us. Private and confidential."

Sandoval said, ".We don't want to rile up any of the guests. Might cause them to choke on their caviar and truffles."

Bass said, "I understand completely. You call the signals and I'll play them."

"Thanks, Don, I knew we could count on you."

"You bet!" Bass was happy and excited, like a young baseball fan with a ticket to a big league game. "Boy oh boy! This is really something. I never had much use for the pussyfooting little creep, but who'd have thought that Oliver had it in him to run afoul of Uncle Sammy? This'll really knock old Huntington Wright back on his heels."

The car pulled over to the side of the main drive and rolled to a halt a few lengths short of the front entrance. Sandoval said, "The three of us will handle it, Don. Please don't mention this to your associates."

"I've been to the fair before."

Sandoval switched off the car and the trio got out. A uniformed Brand guard came hurrying over to wave them away. "Hey! You can't park here—oh, sorry Mr. Bass, I didn't know it was you."

Bass said, "That's okay, they're with me. See that nothing happens to this car."

"Yes, sir!"

Jack, Sandoval, and Bass made for the front entrance, an elaborately pillared portico. Bass said in an aside, "Once you've got your man we'll have the car brought around to the side and you can take him out that way. Makes less fuss all around."

Sandoval said, "Sounds good."

Bass strode a pace ahead of the two others, his mere presence assuring that they breezed past all potential obstacles of the Brand guard variety. There were few uniformed guards in the building, most of the indoor security being handled by plainclothes operatives with the agency's emblem on the left breast of their navy blazers.

The conference's events had ended for the day, giving the guests an hour or two to freshen up and dress for tonight's formal dinner banquet.

Knots of attendees stood lingering in the grand hall, chatting and socializing. The women were mostly beautiful and on the thin side; the men displayed a far greater variety of age, height, weight, and physical attractiveness or the lack of it.

Jack recognized a number of familiar faces from the financial pages of the news and the TV business channels. There was a California aerospace tycoon, a Seattle software titan, a maverick oil wildcatter from Texas with a big stake in alternative energy sources, a deputy assistant to the Secretary of the Treasury, and a Manhattan real estate magnate, to name a few.

He caught glimpses of them as he, Sandoval, and Bass made their way through the grand hall and down a corridor leading into the east wing. Their progress was brisk but without urgency to avoid attracting any undue attention. All the in-house personnel, guards, staffers, and service persons, moved at a similar pace; only the guests lounged, ambled, or lingered.

The trio bypassed a cordon of security guards before arriving at the grandiose anteroom outside Cabot Huntington Wright's office suite. Marion Clary still occupied her post at the reception desk, glancing up as the visitors entered and greeting them with a warm smile as she recognized them.

She said, "Good afternoon, or good evening, I should say. One loses track of the time out here."

She looked down at an open ledger on her desk, scanning the entries. A frown creased her smooth, shining forehead as she looked up with mild vexation and puzzlement. "I'm sorry, but I don't seem to have you gentlemen down in my appointment book—"

Bass interceded. "This is a special matter, Marion, one that's come up rather suddenly. It's somewhat urgent. I'll take full responsibility."

"It's all very strange to me but if you think it's important—"

"It is. Is Mr. Wright in?"

Her face showed signs of strain. "I'm afraid he's away from his office."

Jack stepped forward, a pleasant smile masking inner urgency. "Actually it's Mr. Oliver we're interested in. May we see him, please?"

Marion Clary said, "Brad Oliver? He left here some time ago."

"I'm sorry to trouble you, but do you know where he went?"

"No, I don't. But he certainly was in a hurry."

Jack and Sandoval exchanged glances, Jack wondering if he looked as crestfallen as the other did.

Marion Clary went on, "Yes, he rushed right out of here. Probably one of those little minor emergencies that always seem to come up during a conference and has to be fixed immediately if not sooner."

She reached for her desk phone. "Shall I have him paged for you?"

Jack said, "No, don't do that!" The receptionist was somewhat taken aback by his sudden burst of vehemence and he added quickly, "Thank you, but that won't be necessary."

Sandoval and Bass had already stepped off to one side for a quick, low-voiced exchange. Bass got out his handset and started talking into it.

Marion Clary fretted. "I'm quite sure I don't know what all the fuss is about."

Jack assumed a cheeriness at odds with the sinking feeling in the pit of his stomach. "Just one of those little emergencies you were talking about."

Sandoval was giving him the high sign, gesturing for Jack to join them. Jack said, "Excuse me."

He went to the others. Bass's handset fell silent as a crackling transmission ended. Bass said, "That was the gatehouse. Brad Oliver signed out and drove out of here a half hour ago. Like a bat out of hell, the guard said."

Jack was out of words for the moment. He had nothing to say. Neither did Sandoval.

Don Bass looked from one to the other. "Tough break, fellows. Looks like you missed him. Gee, if you'd just contacted me ahead of time, I could have picked him up and held him till you got here!"

· ·

THE FOLLOWING TAKES PLACE
BETWEEN THE HOURS OF
7 P.M. AND 8 P.M.
MOUNTAIN DAYLIGHT TIME

· ·

Rimrock Road, Colorado

Brad Oliver had had a short run.

Sandoval said, "This is one of those good news–bad news situations. The good news is that we don't have to tell our bosses that Oliver got away from us. The bad news is that he's dead."

Jack Bauer said, "If that is Oliver down there." The two CTU agents stood in front of the Mercedes, which was parked on the shoulder of the road about twenty-five yards away from a gaping hole in the guardrail on the east side of the roadway.

The hole was several car lengths wide. It was bracketed by the twisted ends of a severed rail section. They had corkscrew shapes and were bent back so they thrust out into the empty air over the chasm.

This ordinarily empty stretch of Rimrock Road now bustled with lively activity.

A hundred-yard length of the east lane with the hole in the rail had been blocked off at both ends by patrol cars from the county sheriff's department. The two-way, two-lane road had been turned into a one-lane, two-way road in the area where Oliver's car had gone off the cliff.

Deputies with baton flashlights stood at opposite ends of the closed lane directing traffic. Southbound vehicles were temporarily halted at the north end to allow northbound vehicles to pass the accident site, then northbound vehicles were halted at the south end to allow some of the southbound vehicles to go on their way. The direction alternated every few minutes. The stop-go system caused vehicles to collect at both ends, creating a mini traffic jam.

A complicating factor was that everybody who drove by wanted to gawk and rubberneck at the spectacle, even though there was nothing much to see except the hole in the rail. Deputies shouted at the drivers of creeping vehicles, telling them to "Keep it moving! Keep it moving!"

Jack said, "Funny how an accident can draw a crowd even out here in the middle of nowhere. Before Oliver went over the side, there probably wasn't a car coming along this way more than once every five or ten minutes. Now it looks as busy as Main Street."

Sandoval said, "If it was an accident."

"And if that's Oliver."

The sun was behind western peaks, leaving the eastern slopes thickly shadowed with purple-blue gloom. Flashing lights on top of the police cars created a kind of carnivallike atmosphere. Most of the civilian vehicles had their headlights on. Emergency flares had been placed on the pavement at both ends of the closed east lane, throwing a lurid red glow in their immediate vicinity.

The closed lane and surrounding shoulder were reserved for parked patrol cars and their complement of officers who now stood around surveying the damage—all except those handling traffic control chores.

Sandoval's CTU ID card had placated the deputies who tried to shoo away the Mercedes and its accompanying SUV with the backup crew when they first arrived at the site and pulled over at the side of the road. The backup men stood grouped around their vehicle, doing what everybody else at the scene was doing; namely looking down over the edge into the gulf below.

It was a long, long way down. Vertical cliffs alternated with angled wooded slopes, stepping down for many hundreds of feet to the bottom of a rocky chasm. A handful of small fires lit the shadowy murk at the foot of the precipice. They looked like candle flames when seen from Rimrock Road. Other lights twinkled in the same general area, the lights of police and emergency vehicles that were gathered at ground level. They had to stand off some distance away from the fires because the car had fallen where the road below did not reach.

Jack said, "We'll have to go down there and take a look at the body for ourselves, even though it may be burned beyond recognition."

Sandoval said, "There's ways of identifying a burned body."

"But not immediately. It buys time."

Sandoval raised his gaze from the chasm to look Jack in the face. "You think Oliver pulled the old switcheroo and had someone else's body thrown off the cliff in his car?"

Jack shrugged. "Who knows?"

"He didn't have much time to pull off a tricky fast one like that."

"He had time enough to evade us."

"Yeah, I don't like that angle myself. It smells of a tipoff."

A state police car rolled into view driving along the shoulder of the southbound lane. A deputy halted traffic so the newcomer could edge across the lane into the closed northbound section. It halted and two uniformed officers got out: Lieutenant Bryce Hardin and Sergeant Cole Taggart.

They crossed to a knot of deputies at the side of the road. Sandoval said, "There's your buddies from the MRT, Jack."

Jack nodded. "I'd like to have a little chat with them, see what they know about the wreck. They reported it in first, according to the radio chatter."

"Why don't I go on ahead and check out the body while you do that? It'll save us some time."

Sandoval added, "Besides, it looks like a long hike over rough ground to get to the crash site and there's no need for both of us to it. You've done enough walking for today."

Jack waved it away. "That's all right."

"Why not? I'll ride down with the backup boys and you can join me later in the Merc."

Jack thought it over. "Okay."

Sandoval said, "I'll see you down below then." He started toward the SUV, paused, and turned around to face Jack again. He said, "Um, that's all you're going to do with Hardin and Taggart, right? Just talk?"

Jack said, "Just talk."

"Because you still might be sore about last night—I wouldn't blame you if you were—and Garcia'd raise holy hell if you get physical with the MRT again."

"Don't worry about it, we're all chums now."

"I bet." Sandoval's laughter was a little shaky. "See you later."

"In a bit."

Sandoval crossed to the backup crew clustered around the SUV. They all got into the vehicle, which started up, made a K-turn, and eased into the closed section of the southbound lane. Jack absently rubbed his swollen left jaw as he watched a deputy halt the traffic flow so the SUV could exit the scene.

Hardin stood off to the side talking to some deputies. Taggart stood by himself, hands on hips as he gazed into the abyss. Jack went to him.

Taggart looked up at the sound of approaching footfalls, turned, and saw Jack. He grinned tightly, said, "Well, well." He raised his hands in an I-surrender gesture, said, "Don't shoot!"

Jack said, "Ha-ha. I've already bagged my quota for today."

Taggart's toothy grin widened. "Just joshing you. No hard feelings?"

"What's done is done." Jack kept his expression blandly noncommittal. "Here we are again at another cliffside high dive."

Taggart said, "It's only been since this morning and already it seems like old times."

"Same road, different victim."

" 'Cept the ATF boys going over was no accident. They were already dead when they were put in their car and shoved over the side."

"That's the consensus." Jack indicated the hole in the guardrail with a tilt of his head. "You think this was an accident?"

Taggart pushed back his hat brim to scratch his head. "Beats me. I didn't see it."

"I thought your MRT unit was the first to call it in."

"That's right, we did. Sharon Stallings over to Mountain Lake got the call. She's working dispatcher on the front desk. Some citizen phoned in to report that he'd seen a car go plowing off the cliff and she broadcast the alert."

Jack said, "That citizen have a name?"

Taggart shook his head. "Anonymous call, I do believe."

"Was the caller male or female?"

"I don't know, but Sharon could tell you. You know how these civilians are, they don't want to get involved. Afraid they're going to be called in as a witness and lose a lot of unpaid time in court waiting to testify. Can't say as I blame 'em much. So they phone in the tip and figure they've done their civic duty."

He looked shrewdly at Jack. "Any reason to think it wasn't an accident?"

Jack said, "Two in one day on the same road seems like more than coincidence."

"It's a dangerous road and by all accounts that boy was flying when he hit the rail. Must've been doing sixty, seventy miles an hour the way that rail is all torn up. Say, who was it, anyhow?"

"Brad Oliver."

"Never heard of him."

"He worked for one of the big shots at Sky Mount."

"Uh-oh. That'll raise a big stink. Means a whole lot more paperwork for everybody."

A second state police car entered the scene, approaching from the northbound direction. It halted beside Taggart and Hardin's car, which was parked a dozen yards north of where Jack and the sergeant were standing. The new arrival held one trooper behind the wheel and two shaggy-haired figures in the backseat. Taggart smiled slyly, said, "There's your buddy Miller Fisk."

Jack failed to rise to the bait. "Looks like he's got two prisoners."

"Looks like."

Fisk tapped the horn a few times, tooting lightly, causing Hardin to look away from the deputies with whom he was chatting. Hardin crossed to Fisk's car, approaching it on the passenger side. The passenger side window was rolled down, and Hardin rested his forearms on top of the door as he bent down and leaned forward to speak with Fisk.

Jack peered at the duo in the backseat. They were Griff and Rowdy, the two Hellbenders outlaw bikers who'd appeared earlier at the site of the ATF car wreck. They looked much the worse for wear, like they'd had a pretty hard time of it.

Hardin did more telling than listening and he didn't do much of either, engaging in a quick exchange with Fisk before straightening up and taking a step back from the car. Fisk put the car in drive

and eased away, creeping up to where a deputy stood
directing traffic.

Hardin turned, looking around. He spotted Taggart, scowling when he recognized Jack. He motioned
to Taggart, gesturing for him to come over. Taggart
said, "Oh well, back to work. See you around."

Jack said, "So long."

Taggart crossed to Hardin. They stood talking for
a brief exchange, Hardin glancing again at Jack, the
same scowl still on his face. He and Taggart turned
and went to their vehicle, Hardin getting in on the
front passenger side and Taggart on the driver's side.
The car drove away, following in Fisk's wake.

Jack crossed briskly to the Mercedes and got
behind the wheel. The keys were in the ignition
where Sandoval had left them. Jack started the car
and pointed it northbound.

He had his CTU ID ready for use in getting
through the tie-up ahead but didn't need to use it.
The deputy working traffic control duty must have
assumed that any vehicle that'd been parked in the
closed section had priority and automatically halted
the traffic flow to let the Mercedes proceed.

Jack drove on the shoulder to the right of the
northbound lane to get clear of the civilian vehicles clustered beyond the restricted area. Gravel
crunched under the tires as his car snaked its way
along the curved path until breaking through to the
open road.

He had solid blacktop under his wheels now and
he stepped on the gas, the Mercedes accelerating
smoothly with a hum of power. The state police cars
were out of sight, but this stretch of Rimrock Road

led to the Mountain Lake substation a few miles ahead, and Jack guessed that that was their destination. He'd keep going if it weren't, in the hope of picking them up later, but he thought he wouldn't have to.

He reached for the hand mic of the dashboard radio comm set to contact Central to let them know what he was doing but stopped. Earlier events had given him pause. Brad Oliver had known that he was going to be arrested, and that tip could only have come from someone in CTU, someone high up in the command structure here or in L.A.

He didn't want the MRT members to know he was tailing them, and he feared that if he gave Central the information, the troopers would know. He stopped reaching for the mic and put both hands on the wheel and concentrated on closing the distance between himself and the state police cars.

A straightaway loomed ahead and Jack used it to pass several civilian vehicles poking along in the northbound lane. They were doing the legal limit but it seemed like they were crawling along to Jack, who was in a hurry to close with his quarry.

He zoomed into the opposite lane when it was clear in order to pass a few cars and trucks ahead of him. He cut it pretty close, narrowly avoiding a southbound car by swerving back into the northbound lane. The other car honked loudly in protest at the near-collision, its blaring horn Dopplering away as he speedily left it behind.

A road sign swam up in the headlights indicating a curve ahead. Jack rode the brakes, tires yelping as he cut a curve too closely before getting back on track. The blackness of empty space beyond the guardrail yawned but the car held the road as it rounded the turn.

The road straightened out again. Jack slowed, thinking that Brad Oliver must have been driving somewhat like this when he'd made the fatal plunge.

The route passed a couple of turnoffs on the left, west side of the road that were cuts in the mountainside. The Mercedes entered a lonely stretch of empty road. An oddly shaped rock formation thrusting out above the road looked familiar to Jack, who recognized it from his previous trip to Mountain Lake.

He estimated he was halfway to the substation. A pair of red taillights winked far ahead, swerving left and disappearing as they rounded a curve.

Jack eased up on the accelerator. He didn't want to show himself if that was an MRT car. He slowed to let the other vehicle gain some distance.

He rounded the curve. A scenic lookout area bordered the road's eastern shoulder where a knob of rock jutted out from the cliffside, leaving enough space for a gravel parking area and a grassy patch studded by a boulder faced with a metal plaque tourist guide.

A pickup truck sat in the parking area facing north, its lights dark. The Mercedes zipped by it. A pair of headlights flashed their sudden bright, dazzling glare in the rear window.

The pickup truck zoomed out of the parking area and into the northbound lane with its high beams on. It was a big machine and the sound of its engine was loud as it took off after Jack in a hurry.

It ate up the distance between itself and Jack's car, quickly closing the gap. It had a high suspension and its headlights were correspondingly raised so that they seemed to shine directly into the Mercedes, flooding its interior with white-hot glare.

The road hit a series of curves, forcing Jack to slow still further. The pickup was only a length or two behind him. The Mercedes handled beautifully but the pickup's greater weight compensated for its height and Jack couldn't shake it.

The curves were long, lazy, and looping but the pace was frantic. The pickup truck bumped the back of Jack's car, jostling it. Jack had to fight to keep from losing control of the wheel as the right side tires slid on the shoulder but managed to whip the Mercedes back on to the pavement.

The pickup's front was bolstered by a piece of solid steel plate that covered it from bumper to hood. Holes were cut in the plate to allow the headlights to shine through.

The pickup lunged forward, slamming the Mercedes again, delivering a bone-jostling thump to Jack. His belly knotted at the thought that another such blow might trip the car's air bag safety device, a development that could prove fatal in this lethal game of high-speed bumper cars.

Trouble was that the pickup was doing all of the bumping and the Mercedes all of the catching. Jack could do nothing but thread the curves, riding both lanes and hoping no oncoming vehicle lay around each blind corner.

Another hit destabilized the car, causing it to weave crazily and slide sideways toward the guard-rail and the abyss. The Mercedes fishtailed as it took the curve but it took it, tires digging in and biting deep into the pavement.

The pickup nudged the car, snugging its steel-plated front against the vehicle's rear at a tilted angle. The truck lunged with a snarl of power and shoved the Mercedes sideways.

The car would have been swept off the cliff if the tilt were angled outward. But the tilt was angled inward, causing the car to slide sideways toward the rock wall on its left.

The rocks loomed up in the driver's side window, their craggy surfaces harshly lit by the intense glare of the pickup's high beams. The car rushed sideways to meet them.

There was the crump of collapsing metal and an explosion of shattered glass as the Mercedes plowed into the mountainside under the pickup truck's impetus.

A stunning impact followed, setting off a massive fireworks display inside Jack's head.

Then, blackness.

· ·

**THE FOLLOWING TAKES PLACE
BETWEEN THE HOURS OF
8 P.M. AND 9 P.M.
MOUNTAIN DAYLIGHT TIME**

· ·

Mountain Lake, Colorado

Jack Bauer's awareness flickered, sputtering like a TV set with a loose connection. Bursts of sound and vision alternated with patches of darkness.

Rough handling jarred him into wakefulness, restoring his sense of self. He could think but not move. His seat belt harness was open and he was being hauled out from behind the air bag, which had mushroomed out of the top of the steering column to fill the driver's side with a big white balloon. He was dragged across the passenger seat out the open door and dropped to the ground.

The fall jolted Jack into opening his eyes. He was bathed in white light streaked by red and blue flashes. He couldn't see their source. He lay on his side on the shoulder of the road. His field of vision encompassed two pairs of legs and feet. Both sets of feet wore cowboy boots under loose-fitting trousers. One pair had sharp-pointed toes and fancy hand-tooled leatherwork, the other was squared off at the toes and unornamented.

A square-toed boot stepped on his upright shoulder and shoved him on his back, setting off fresh fireworks in Jack's head. A body wash of aching soreness kept him from blacking out.

The boot's owner straddled him and bent down. It was Taggart. He pulled Jack's gun from the shoulder holster, said, "You won't need this." He straightened up and stepped away, tucking the gun into the top of his waistband. "Maybe I'll keep it for a souvenir."

He stood on one side of Jack. Hardin, the owner of the fancy boots, stood at the other. A third figure stood at Jack's feet. The stranger was a grotesque, short, skinny, and bowlegged. He had a bony, close-cropped scalp and wore round wire-rimmed glasses that made his orbs look like those of a popeyed frog. He wore a thin vest, a dark T-shirt decorated with an elaborate skull emblem, and skintight jeans tucked into oversized combat boots with steel toes and three-inch soles.

Red and blue lights flashed on the trio, splashing them with weird highlights and color accents. The stranger gave a start, said, "Here comes a car!"

Hardin said, "What of it? We're supposed to be here, we're cops. Wave 'em on, Cole."

"Right." Taggart walked away out of Jack's vision, his footsteps sounding on hard pavement. A car approached, its headlight beams sweeping across the scene. Its engine noise was loud as it slowed to a crawl and drew abreast; the noise lessened as the car passed and drove away.

Hardin said, "That's all there is to it, Mr. Pettibone. You're nervous in the service."

Pettibone, the third man, was restless, fidgeting. One of his legs shook, vibrating to an invisible rhythm. He said, "I ain't got all night. You, neither." His nasal voice had a Western twang with a bite as sharp as a crosscut saw. He said, "The Rebel wants things done quick!"

Hardin's expression turned ugly. "I don't take orders from Weld."

Pettibone fired back, "You both take orders from the same fellow—"

"Yeah, and you ain't him, so no more of your lip."

Taggart rejoined them. "What's the problem?"

Hardin said, "Pettibone's got ants in his pants, that's all. He's scared of Weld."

Pettibone said, "Never mind about that! You do your job and I'll do mine."

Taggart stood beside Hardin. "We're doing it."

Pettibone said, "Take him to the station." By "him" he meant Jack Bauer. "I'll get rid of the car and be by directly to pick him up and take him to Winnetou."

Taggart said, "Sure you can handle that car by yourself?"

Pettibone said, "Hell, yeah! I got me a set of chains and binders in the back of the truck. I'll hook one end up to the car's rear axle, drag it to the other side of the road, and push it off the cliff. I know what I'm doing, I used to be in the wrecking business."

Taggart laughed. "Used to be, he says."

Hardin cautioned, "No fires. We don't want to call attention to this one for a while."

Pettibone shook his head. "Ain't gonna be no fires. The engine's off so there won't be no spark to touch off any spilled gas."

Hardin said, "Get to it, then. We got things to do, too." He turned to Taggart. "You take Bauer's arms and I'll take his feet so we can carry him to the car."

Taggart said, "You would leave me the hardest part of the work."

"Rank has its privileges," Hardin said, chuckling. He stood at Jack's feet while Taggart stood at his head. Taggart hunkered down, getting his hands under Jack's arms and clasping them on top of Jack's chest. Hardin grabbed Jack's feet by the ankles, holding them together and getting them under one arm. The lawmen straightened up, lifting Jack off the ground. He choked back a groan as the movement sent new pain waves shivering through him.

The scene came into view from a different perspective. The battered Mercedes slumped against a rocky mountainside. The pickup stood near it, facing north on the shoulder to the west of the road. The MRT car stood a dozen feet away, facing south in the southbound lane and blocking it. Red and blue lights flashed in the rooftop light rack.

Hardin and Taggart hauled Jack to their car. Hardin said, "Hold him up—I'll get the door." He was breathing hard, huffing and puffing. He set Jack's feet down on the pavement. Taggart stood crouched holding up Jack's upper body while Jack's legs rested on the macadam. Hardin opened the vehicle's rear door and helped Taggart heave Jack across the backseat.

Pettibone called, "Remember, Reb wants him alive and able to talk."

Taggart said, "We'll treat him like an egg wrapped in cotton." Hardin didn't say anything, he was still trying to catch his breath. Taggart slammed the rear door shut. It was a patrol car so there were no handles on the inside back doors, and a wire cage separated the front seat from the back.

Taggart got behind the wheel and Hardin got in the front passenger seat. Hardin wheezed, "Man! I got to get in shape some of these days."

Taggart said, "You're in shape, you've been exercising those table muscles."

Hardin told the other what he could do to himself. Taggart laughed, made a K-turn into the opposite lane, pointed the vehicle north, and drove away.

Hardin said, "No emergency lights. We don't need them."

Taggart switched them off, said, "Like I told the man, it's a dangerous road."

Hardin said, "For some folks, yeah."

A few cars passed them going in the opposite direction on the way to the Mountain Lake substation. The drive took less than ten minutes, each precious second giving Jack Bauer more time to collect his wits and gather what stores of energy remained to him. He could move now even though it hurt to do so. Every heartbeat was like a giant fist squeezing him, wringing him out like a wet washrag. His head pounded and he felt sick to his stomach.

The MRT car turned right into the drive leading

to the substation. Hardin said, "Pull into the motor pool so we don't have to carry him so far."

The motor pool was a two-car garage attached to the substation. Its rollup door was open and its overhead lights burned bright. The car rolled to a halt inside one of the bays. A pair of chopped, heavy-duty Harley-Davidson motorcycles with extended front forks occupied the other bay.

Taggart switched off the headlights and engine. He and Hardin got out and went to one of the rear doors. Hardin opened it. Jack lay sprawled on his side across the backseat, legs bent at the knees. Hardin used the pointy toe of one of his boots to kick the sole of Jack's shoe. He said, "Get up."

He stepped back, unfastening the flap at the top of his sidearm so he could get at it more quickly. His hand rested on the wood-handled gun butt of the big .44. "Weld wants you alive but he didn't say nothing about putting a bullet through your kneecap and that's what I surely will do if you try any of your fancy tricks. Do you read me, mister?"

Jack said, "Yes."

"On your feet then."

Jack swung his legs, sitting up and putting his feet on the garage floor. Colored dots of light showered over him, dimming his vision. He clutched the rim of the open door with both hands to keep from falling. The dizziness passed, the scene brightening as the stream of colored dots thinned and receded.

Jack pulled himself out of the car and stood up. He lurched and staggered, putting out a hand on the rear fender to steady himself.

Taggart said, "You look a mite unsteady, Jack. Let

me give you a hand." He gripped Jack's arm above the left elbow.

A closed door stood on the left side of the garage's rear wall. Hardin backed up to it, hand resting on his gun butt, steadily eyeing Jack. He reached around behind him with his free hand, grabbing the doorknob and turning it, opening the door. The door opened outward and he had to step forward out of its way to open it fully. He backed through the doorway into the station, watching Jack all the while.

Taggart said, "Here we go," the pressure of his hand on Jack's arm urging him forward. Jack advanced with slow shuffling steps, making out that he was weaker than he was in hopes of misleading the others about his condition. He made a point of staring straight ahead, not even glancing at Taggart's sidearm holstered on the right hip or his own gun stuck into the top of Taggart's waistband on the left side.

Taggart said with great good humor, "Bet you'd like to get your hands on one of these heaters, eh, Jack?"

Hardin said, "Try it. Just try."

Jack didn't try for it. He went through the doorway into the main room of the substation. Sharon Stallings sat behind the dispatcher's front desk drinking coffee. Miller Fisk was on the other side of the space, sitting with his feet up on the squad room desk and reading a hunting magazine.

The two bikers, Griff and Rowdy, were both penned in the same single detention cell. Three steel-barred cage walls met a building wall of solid concrete blocks painted pale green like the rest of the building's interior. A metal plank bunk covered by a thin fabric pallet jutted out from the stone wall. The big biker, Rowdy, sat on the bunk with his head tilted back. The smaller one, Griff, stood leaning against the front wall of the cell. Their faces were bruised, cut, and swollen from a recent beating.

Fisk looked over the top of the magazine, eyes widening as saw Jack in the custody of Hardin and Taggart. His lips puckered in a soundless whistle. "Well, looky here! So you got him!"

Taggart said, "Yeah, we picked him up for reckless driving."

Hardin said, "Get your feet off that desk, Fisk. You're not back home in the barn now."

Fisk put his feet on the floor fast and stood up. "Sorry, Uncle Bryce—"

"That's Lieutenant Hardin to you and don't you forget it!"

"Yessir!" Fisk fastened his eyes on Jack, staring at him with abject fascination. His eyes got a glazed look in them. He licked his lips. "Yes, sir!"

Taggart guided Jack across the room to the squad room desk. He said, "You don't look so good, amigo. You better sit down." He indicated the chair that Fisk had just quit, an office chair with four roller-mounted legs. Jack sat down in it. Hardin circled around to the other side of the desk so he'd have a clear line of fire if Jack tried something. His hand was still on his gun.

Taggart took out a pair of cuffs from a leather case clipped to his belt. "Gun hand first." He circled Jack's right wrist with one of the cuffs and clamped the other one to the chair arm on that side. "Now the other. Let me have your cuffs, Fisk."

Fisk was quick to comply, his eyes glimmering and his face shining. Taggart repeated the process, this time cuffing Jack's left hand to the chair's left arm. He said, "Jack's trouble with either hand. Ain't that right, Fisk?"

Fisk colored. "Never you mind about that!"

Hardin took his hand off his gun. Taggart grinned, stepped back. "There you go, Jack. Now you don't have to worry about falling out of your chair."

Jack said sourly, "That's right neighborly of you, pardner."

Taggart laughed out loud. "That's the spirit. Keep your chin up. You know, believe it or not, I kind of like you, Jack. That's the hell of it."

Fisk said, "Well, I don't!"

Taggart rested a hip on the edge of the desk. "Tell me something, Jack, just to satisfy my own curiosity. How'd you get on to us?"

Jack looked steadily at him. "The ATF men, Dean and O'Hara. They were pros. They weren't drugged. I couldn't see the cultists sneaking up on them and catching them unawares. But the MRT, fellow cops they knew and thought could be trusted, you could have walked right up and gotten the drop on them. They didn't know the truth until it was too late."

"That's not bad figuring."

"After that it was just a matter of the way things went down. You people were always in the right place at the right time to do some damage. When I found out that your outfit reported the Oliver crash first, it all added up."

"Too bad you didn't know that we had a crash all planned and ready for you."

"Yeah, too bad. I didn't think the whole unit was dirty, either."

"For what we're getting paid, we can't afford not to be."

Hardin said, "That's enough, Cole. You're talking too much."

"Why? What difference does it make?"

Jack said, "Dead men tell no tales, eh?"

Taggart nodded. "Not this side of the grave."

Hardin made a dismissive gesture and crossed to the front desk. "Any messages for me, Sharon?"

"Yes, sir. Sheriff Mack called to remind you about that confab over to Sky Mount tonight."

"Damn! I most forgot about that." Hardin glanced at his watch. "Still got time to make it. Let's go, Cole, we got to saddle up. We got that meeting with the county boys to map out security arrangements for tomorrow's Round Table."

Taggart's laugh was a short, humorless bark. "That's a good one."

"We don't show, some folks might get the crazy idea that we thought there wouldn't be a session tomorrow."

"I see what you mean. Can't have that."

Hardin spoke to the dispatcher, "Sharon, you're in charge here while Cole and I are gone." He turned to Fisk. "You hear that, boy? Trooper Stallings is in charge, and if she gives you an order it's the same as if I did, so you hop to it and do like she says, savvy?"

"Yes, sir."

"Mr. Pettibone will be by to pick up that one," Hardin said, indicating Jack. "Don't take any chances, Sharon. Make sure his hands are cuffed behind his back when you make the transfer. I want you to supervise it personally, you hear?"

"You can count on me, Bryce."

"He's got to be able to talk and he can't be too busted up. You listening, Fisk?"

"Yes, sir. Uh, sir? How much is too much?"

"He can't look like he's been beaten half to death when he's found later. Otherwise, have your fun. I know you're going to anyway."

"Aw, Uncle Bryce, you know I wouldn't do nothing without your say-so."

"Lieutenant Hardin, boy."

"Yes, sir. Lieutenant Hardin. Sir."

Taggart went to the front desk and handed Jack's gun to the dispatcher. "Add that to your collection, Sharon."

She opened a drawer on the side of her desk and placed the gun inside. Hardin frowned, said, "That's another thing, Cole. That weapon's evidence that Bauer's been here. You can't keep it."

Taggart said, "Good point. I'll get rid of it when we get back."

"Good." Hardin fastened cold eyes on the bikers in the holding cell. "We got some more house cleaning to do when we get back. Take out all the trash."

Sharon Stallings said, "When'll you be back?"

"An hour or so, no more." He and Taggart crossed toward the garage door. Hardin went out.

Taggart paused in the doorway, turning to look back. He said, "Adios, Jack. No hard feelings—at least, not on my side. I wouldn't blame you if you had some, considering. That's your prerogative."

Hardin called to him from the garage. Taggart said, "Coming." He went into the garage, closing the door behind him. After a pause came the sound of an engine starting up and then the car driving away.

Fisk licked his lips. They were already wet and glistening. His eyes were focused and intent above a loose, sloppy smile. He made a big show of cracking his knuckles. He said to Jack, "You don't look like so much now."

Jack was silent. Fisk went on, "Where's all your smart remarks?"

Sharon Stallings rolled her eyes. "For Pete's sake, Fisk, quit jawing and get on with it."

"I'm taking my own sweet time. I'm gonna enjoy this." Fisk squared off, looming above Jack in the chair. "Uncle Bryce said not to leave you half killed. He didn't say nothing about no three-quarters, though."

He punched Jack in the face. The impact snapped Jack's head back and sent the roller-mounted chair with Jack in it wheeling backward until it crashed into a wall.

Jack's face was numb where he'd been struck but he could feel something leaking from his nostrils, and the taste of blood was copper-tangy in his mouth. Rowdy and Griff crowded the front of their cell, clutching the bars and staring. Sharon Stallings watched, chewing gum. That was the detail that stuck with Jack: her chewing gum.

Fisk ruefully eyed his big fist. "Dang, I like to've skinned a knuckle on that one!"

The smaller biker, Griff, said, "You dirty dog! You've got to have a guy tied down before you beat on him . . ."

Fisk grinned wetly, waving the other's complaint away. "Shut up, runt. You had your hands free when I gave you your whomping."

"You hit me with your gun first!"

Rowdy said, "Let me out of here and try me on, farm boy!"

Fisk said, "You already. had your turn. I'm just getting warmed up on this one."

He clouted Jack with a vicious backhand to the left side of the face. Jack saw it coming and tried to roll with it. It was a swivel chair so he was able to rotate the seat away from the blow, but even so it rocked him from head to heels. The chair toppled over, falling on its right side to the floor with a crash. Fisk giggled. "Whoops!"

Sharon Stallings stood up. She showed some animation now, spots of color burning in her cheeks. "Fisk, you better not break that chair—"

Fisk grabbed a chair arm in each hand and by main strength yanked it and the man chained to it upright. He drove a hard right into Jack's belly, burying it deep. Jack doubled up as the chair zoomed backward, crashing against the front of the cell.

Fisk crossed to Jack, grabbing the chair and spinning it around a half circle so that he stood facing Jack with his back to the cell. A thin line of spittle drooled down the corner of Fisk's mouth, wetting his chin. His hot, moist breath was on Jack's face. He launched an uppercut that collided with Jack's chin. The chair wheeled backward into the side of the squad room desk.

Sharon Stallings was outraged now. "Fisk! The desk!"

Fisk stalked Jack, closing on him, his hulking form looming larger. Griff and Rowdy stood pressed against the bars of the cell. Jack made eye contact

with Griff and tilted his head in a slight but perceptible nod. Griff blinked, eyes narrowing.

Fisk never saw the nod because he was too busy
leaning over the chair and winding up to deliver
another haymaker. Jack kicked him between the
legs.

Fisk went, "Whoof!" He doubled up and grabbed
his crotch with both hands. He wavered, swaying.
Cold sweat filmed his leaden, gasping face.

Jack got both feet on the floor and spun the swivel
seat around so that he was facing the side of the desk
with his back to Fisk. He brought his feet up, bend-
ing both legs at the knees, and pushed off from the
desk as hard as he could.

The chair with Jack in it went slamming into Fisk,
knocking him off balance. Fisk backpedaled to keep
from falling. Jack dug his heels into the floor and
kept working his legs, driving the chair into Fisk and
pushing him backward.

Fisk collided with the front of the cell. Griff and
Rowdy were ready. Rowdy thrust his right arm be-
tween the bars and hooked it around Fisk's neck.
Griff was shouting, "Get him, bro! Get him!"

Rowdy pulled back hard. He was a big man, too,
almost as big as Fisk, and with plenty of muscle. The
back of Fisk's head fetched up against the bars with
a clang that sent them ringing. Rowdy grabbed his
own right wrist with his left hand and got Fisk in a
choke hold.

Jack kept his feet working, scrabbling them on the
linoleum floor to keep slamming the top of the back
of the chair into Fisk's middle. Rowdy got a knee up
against the bars where the small of Fisk's back was.

The big biker leaned back, putting his weight into the choke hold.

Fisk's eyes were like soft-boiled eggs floating in a purple face. He had both hands up clawing at Rowdy's forearm where it circled his throat but he couldn't break the other's grip.

Griff said, "Get him, bro, get him!" He'd stopped yelling and was calling out in a breathy whisper, like a crapshooting gambler urging the dice to come through for him on a long-shot roll.

Griff grabbed the top of Fisk's gun in its hip holster. It was a .357, held down not by a flap but by a leather strap. Griff's fingers tore at the strap, loosing it.

Sharon Stallings already had her gun out. It was a .357, too. She came out from behind the front desk, angling for a clear shot. Fisk was in her way, causing her to hesitate.

Griff yanked Fisk's gun clear of the holster and leveled it at Stallings. Gunfire cannonaded as he cut loose, shooting the middle out of her. She came apart and fell down in a heap.

Griff shoved the gun's smoking snout against Fisk's side but before he could pull the trigger there was a cracking sound like a crisp breadstick being snapped in two. Only instead of a breadstick it was Fisk's neck that was being broken as Rowdy pivoted his upper body and twisted Fisk's head to an angle beyond the human design tolerance limit.

. . . .

THE FOLLOWING TAKES PLACE
BETWEEN THE HOURS OF
9 P.M. AND 10 P.M.
MOUNTAIN DAYLIGHT TIME

. . . .

Mountain Lake Substation, Colorado

Griff said, "Keep holding him up—don't drop him!"

Rowdy said, "I ain't dropping nothing." He still stood with his arm through the bars holding Fisk in a chokehold. Fisk was all dead weight now with nothing to hold him up but Rowdy. His bulging-eyed, slack-jawed head lolled at an unnatural angle.

Rowdy said, "I could do this all day."

"We ain't got all day, man."

Jack said, "You're so right."

Griff's eyes lit up. "Hey, you're still with us! Stay awake, dude. Don't pass out!"

"I won't."

Griff first checked Fisk's handcuff case on his belt because sometimes cops keep their handcuff keys there in a small compartment but the search came up empty. He now stood with his hand between the bars reaching into Fisk's right front pants pocket. He stood on tiptoes, standing sideways with the side of his face pressed against the bars for a longer reach. His face was hot and the bars were cool. He was reaching in and down. He said, "I think I got his key ring—"

Rowdy said, "Don't drop it, man."

The pocket tore at the seams as Griff closed his fingers around a chunk of loose metal and fished it out. He pulled his closed fist back to his side of the bars before opening it. A key ring lay in his palm. He said, "I ain't dropping nothing."

Rowdy sagged in relief, allowing Fisk to slump a bit lower. Griff, alarmed, said, "Whoa! Keep hold of him until I'm sure the handcuff key is on this ring."

Rowdy said, "Step on it. This slob weighs a ton."

Griff's hands shook with eagerness as he held the ring up to the light and began flipping through the keys until he came to a pair of tiny black keys that looked like something out of a child's play set. "All right! Handcuff keys if ever I saw 'em—and believe me, I've seen plenty!"

"Stop bragging. Can I let this pig loose?"

"Yeah, but don't let him fall too far in case these keys don't work and we got to check him for others."

Rowdy eased Fisk down the bars to the floor, the body folding up as though it were as boneless as a bag of dirty laundry. The corpse sprawled at the foot of the barred cell door, an inert lump.

Now the bikers could see Jack Bauer, the back of him anyway. Jack's head tilted forward, chin resting on his chest. He breathed slowly, deeply.

Griff said, "Shit! He's passed out!"

Jack raised his head. "No . . . I was just resting."

"Rest later. Fight it, man! You need to stay awake and alert. We need you. You need us. We need each other to get out of this scrape."

"You should set that to music."

Griff grinned tightly, below the eyes. "You can still joke, huh? That's good. That'll keep you going. Turn around so I can see you."

Jack used his feet to rotate the chair's swivel seat in a half circle so that he was facing the cell door. He had to step on one of Fisk's outflung arms to do so. It bothered him not a bit.

Jack's right eye was blackened and his left was swollen half-shut but he could still see out of it. His nose was bloodied and his lips were smashed and split, bleeding on the inside where they'd been cut against his teeth. He felt around with his tongue; his teeth seemed to be all there. He couldn't tell if any of them were loose or not. His jaws ached at the hinges. His ribs were bruised and his belly ached.

Griff said, "What's your name, dude?"

"Jack."

"I'm Griff and this is my buddy Rowdy."

"Hi."

Rowdy said, "Pleased to meet cha', Jack."

"Likewise."

Griff said, "You handle yourself okay, Jack. That was nice work softening up that big pig for us."

Jack glanced at Sharon Stallings, a corpse in the center of a still-expanding pool of blood, then eyed Fisk. It was the first time he'd taken a good look at Fisk dead. On him it looked good. Jack said, "You men didn't do too badly yourselves."

"Thanks. Now that we've done the mutual admiration bit let's focus on something really important, like getting out of here." Griff held a handcuff key between thumb and forefinger so it was separated from the other keys on the ring. "Wheel that chair over here so I can reach you."

Jack used his feet to propel himself on the rollers so his left side was against the bars. Fisk's body blocked his progress until Rowdy collared the corpse by the shirt at the back of its neck and dragged it to one side.

Griff knelt so he was at eye level with the chair arm. He reached through the bars with both hands, the left holding Jack's cuffed hand steady while the right fitted the key into the equally tiny slotted keyhole and turned it until something clicked.

The cuffs unlocked, Jack freeing the metal bracelet from his left wrist. The flesh was marked with angry red grooves where the cuff had bitten into it. He bent his arm at the elbow and raised his hand, flexing it to restore the circulation. Numbness was succeeded by a tingling wave of pins-and-needles sensation that momentarily took his breath away.

Griff said, "I don't know if the same key will work on another cop's cuffs but it should. It'd be a hassle for them to keep track of different sets of keys for each pair of cuffs."

Rowdy said, "If it don't work you can blast the chain loose with the .357."

Jack said, "Let's try the key first." He jockeyed the chair around so that its right side pressed against the bars. It was easier to get around now that he had one hand free.

Griff fitted the key into the lock and jiggled around

with it. "Wait a minute—wait a minute—there, I got it!" There was a click and the cuff opened, falling away from Jack's wrist.

Jack flexed both hands, clenching and unclenching his fists as the feeling returned to them. The sharp edge of it chased away the fog of haziness that shrouded his awareness and sought to pull him down into the sweet, pain-free oblivion of unconsciousness.

An oblivion that might prove permanent if indulged in, he reminded himself. Mr. Pettibone was coming.

Griff urged, "Don't fade on us now, dude. We're so close to making the breakout."

Jack said, "I'm good."

"Okay. The key to the cell is on a big ring hanging on a hook behind the front desk. You can't miss it."

Jack grabbed the cell bars with both hands and pulled himself out of the chair to his feet. He lurched, almost losing his footing but regaining it before he went over. He stood there clutching the bars. Griff's mouth was moving but the words seemed to come from the bottom of a deep well—or was it the top? They were hollow and echoing in any case, mixing with the sound of crashing surf rising in his ears that threatened to overwhelm him.

Jack stood there until the spell of weakness passed and he could make out Griff saying, "Are you okay? You okay, man?"

Jack said, "Yeah." He put his hand against the wall to steady himself as he walked step by step from the cell to the front desk. He was stiff-legged and halting at first but grew surer and more certain with each step. The front desk was on a kind of dais that nearly tripped him when he stepped up onto it but he staggered to the desk and rested both fists on the desktop and leaned forward until the pounding in his head went away.

He went behind the desk and tore open a drawer. Griff called urgently across the room, "Not there, Jack! The keys are on a hook on the wall behind you!"

Jack said, "Hey man, chill." That surprised Griff so that he shut up for a minute. Jack reached into the drawer, reaching for his gun. It lay on its side on top of a pile of hardware that included guns, knives, brass knuckles, blackjacks, and other goodies.

The gun felt good in his hand, he liked the heft and weight and balance of it. He seemed to drew strength from it, like a parched plant soaking up moisture.

He fitted the gun in his shoulder sling. It felt nice nestled down below his left arm.

The key ring was where Griff had said it would be, on a ring on a peg sticking out of a plaque mounted on the wall behind the desk. The oversized ring was a steel hoop as wide in diameter as a pie tin, and when Jack saw the key he thought that little had changed over the centuries when it came to keeping prisoners penned in cells because the key looked like it could have unlocked a medieval dungeon. It had an eight-inch-long bolt with a notched and grooved rectangle at the tip and a solid steel loop at the end.

Jack went with the key to the cell. His progress was better. He never came close to blacking out and he staggered and almost fell only once.

Griff and Rowdy eyed his approach with silent wariness. Griff had a sharp-featured face with long, narrow, slitted green eyes, a beaky nose and pointed chin. Rowdy's forehead was as wrinkled as an elephant's knee, the result of deep thought. He said, "You ain't no cop, Jack. What are you—a hit man?"

Jack realized that coming from Rowdy that was a compliment. He said, "No, I'm a secret agent." It was more complicated than that but he gave them a short version they could wrap their heads around. They didn't necessarily believe him but at least they could understand him.

He stuck the key into the cell lock. The steel loop at the end was big enough for him to fit his fingers around and use for a hand grip. He needed it, too, to turn the lock and unseal its reluctant internal mechanism. Bolts and tumblers fell into place with a thud and then the door opened.

Jack got out of the way to avoid being trampled by the two bikers in their eagerness to be free of the cell. They whooped it up. Jack figured it was best to let them get it out of their systems before he made his pitch.

Griff wasted little time on euphoria, hurrying to Sharon Stallings's corpse to pry the unfired .357 from her hand. He hefted it, saying, "Nice piece! The gun, I mean."

Jack said, "There's an open drawer in the front desk that has some of your stuff in it, I think."

Griff and Rowdy went to it, pulling the weapons out and laying them on the desk. Rowdy picked up a snub-nosed .38 special and eyed it with the tender regard of a schoolgirl for a warm puppy. "I never thought I'd see this again!" He explained, "It's got sentimental value. I took it off some plainclothes cop I beat the shit out of."

Griff brandished a commando knife the size of a

small sword. It was razor sharp with a grooved blood vein on either side. "My Arkansaw toothpick!"

Jack thought that if they didn't know it already, when they found out their bikes were in the garage they'd be like a couple of kids on Christmas morning. Now was the time to start working his pitch. He said, "Why fool around with that when you can raid the substation's armory? There's sure to be one here and the keys are probably somewhere in the desk."

Griff stopped waving the knife in the air to eye Jack with crafty calculation. "I don't get you, Jack. You look like a straight citizen but you're a stone killer. What's your angle? I mean, where do you fit in with all this anyway?"

"I told you, I'm a secret agent."

"Bullshit—"

"I'm also your key to Reb Weld."

That got them. Saying the name was like invoking the magic word. Griff and Rowdy stopped dead in their tracks, exchanging poker-faced glances. The mood in the air was delicate, hanging by a thread. Their hunting instinct was on full alert and one wrong word, one misstep could trigger a mutually slaughterous gun-down.

Griff said, too casual, "I don't believe I caught that name."

Jack said, "Now who's bullshitting? Reb Weld. A name I'm not likely to forget because he's tried to kill me several times today. I've got a feeling it means something special to you, too. You boys better stick close and make sure nothing happens to me because I'm your one way of finding the Rebel and cashing in on that fifty-thousand-dollar bounty on his head."

Griff and Rowdy stood there poised on the razor's edge not knowing which way to jump, torn between greed and suspicion. Jack worked on their greed. "I'll give you the short version. You may have heard that there's a millionaires' convention being held not far from here."

Rowdy said, "Yeah, we heard of it. Impossible not to with all the cops it draws; they've really been cramping our style."

"Reb's being paid to wreck the party. My job is to stop him. You want him, too. He betrayed your outfit and sold out his club brothers so he could skip with the proceeds on their gunrunning racket."

Griff got huffy. "That's not a job to us—it's a sacred trust."

Jack said, "Yeah, with a fifty-thousand-dollar payday. We both want Reb Weld chopped for different reasons. I know how to find him. What's more, I can square this cop-killing beef so that you'll never catch any heat for it."

"You talk big."

"I can deliver. We're all in on this double kill together. You know there's not an undercover cop in the U.S. that could tie into that kind of action and ever testify about it in court."

Rowdy said, "That's right, Griff—"

"Shut up and let me think. Who the hell are you, dude?"

Jack said, "I could show you a card that identifies me as a member of the Counter Terrorist Unit but anybody can get a fake ID. You've seen me in action, I've seen you in action. I'm not asking you to take it on faith. If I can't deliver Weld, there's two of you and one of me. You're not afraid, are you?"

Griff tsk-tsked. "That's low, Jack. No need to get insulting."

Rowdy said piously, "The 'Benders fear no man!"

Jack said, "That's what I'm counting on. We can talk about the deal while we're cracking into the armory. We're going to need some heavy firepower quick and time's running out."

Pettibone wouldn't talk. He was the stubborn type. Also maybe a little bit stupid because there was no mistaking that Jack Bauer and his two biker allies meant business.

Jack said, "The trouble is he's more afraid of Weld than he is of us."

Griff said, "I'll fix that."

"Remember he's our prime lead to finding the Rebel. We need him alive and talking."

"He'll live—unless he's got a bum ticker."

Rowdy said, "He's a speed freak. If he gets off on meth there's nothing wrong with his heart. That shit's a rocket ride."

Griff said, "You should know, bro."

"Look who's talking."

The object of their attention sat tied to a straight-backed wooden chair. Jack had decided to use a wooden one instead of a roller-mounted office chair for the simple reason that wood doesn't conduct electricity.

He was not unaware of the ironies present in the reversal of fortune that had seen him transformed in less than an hour from the subject of torture to the inflictor. This turnabout troubled him not at all, considering that it was Pettibone who'd delivered him to the tender mercies of the MRT. There was no way around the hard fact that Pettibone had to be made to talk, to spill his guts about the plot against Sky Mount. Hundreds of innocent lives and perhaps the fate of a great nation depended on it.

Pettibone had walked unaware into the lion's den less than fifteen minutes earlier. He'd arrived at the Mountain Lake substation to pick up Jack for delivery to Reb Weld. He parked the pickup truck with the steel-plated front behind the back of the building where it couldn't be seen from the road. He went through the garage door into the substation, his knowledge of the site suggesting that this was a familiar routine with him. Jack wondered how many others Hardin and his crew had handed over to Pettibone for a one-way ride.

Pettibone stepped through the door only to discover the muzzle of Jack's pistol being pressed against his skull. He froze except for his eyes, which looked like they were going to pop out of the sockets. His thick-lensed glasses magnified his already bulging orbs as they took in the dead bodies of Fisk and Stallings.

Jack said, "That's right, Mountain Lake is under new management."

A quick search relieved the captive of a gun, switchblade knife, several sets of keys, a wallet, a packet wrapped in tin foil, and some pocket litter. The wallet yielded a state driver's license issued to one Arthur Conley Pettibone. Jack couldn't tell if the license or the bearer's name or both were phony but it didn't matter now that he had possession of the man himself. The tin foil packet contained several grams of a grainy white powdery substance. Rowdy put some on his forefinger and tasted it. "Crystal meth," he said. "Pretty good shit, too."

Jack folded up the packet and pocketed it. Rowdy said, "Hey!—"

Jack said, "I need you with a clear head and a steady hand for the next couple of hours."

Rowdy started to do a slow burn. "You're taking a lot on yourself, dude."

Griff clapped him on the shoulder. "Forget it, man. Jack's right. You don't know what that shit's cut with or what it might do to you. Besides, you don't want him thinking that you're one of those shooters who gets his nerve from a noseful of crank."

Rowdy decided to let it go. "I better not catch you tweaking any, Jack."

"No worry about that."

Griff said, "You know, Jack, I think I'm starting to believe your story after all."

Jack didn't know how much the bikers believed of what he'd told them, which was nothing but the truth: that he was a counterterrorist agent on a mission to stop a plot spearheaded by Reb Weld. They did believe he could help them get Weld, and that was enough for now. That and the fact that he wasn't a cop. Griff and Rowdy hated cops, as they declared at some length and with feeling. Jack actually had been a cop, a member of the LAPD SWAT team, but he saw no reason for burdening the bikers with unnecessary details that might derail the start of a potentially productive alliance.

That's how it is in the field, you work with what's at hand. Griff and Rowdy were choirboys compared to some of the warlords and cutthroats that Jack Bauer had been forced to make use of in the devious and treacherous half world of the long war against global terrorism.

Jack said, "Talk fast, Pettibone. Who is Winnetou? Where's Reb Weld? What's the plot against the Round Table?"

Pettibone had recovered from his initial fright. His jawline and chin took on a belligerent set. He said, "I ain't gonna say a goddamned thing and that's the last you're gonna get out of me."

"At least you have the sense not to deny anything. Stay sensible and save yourself a lot of grief."

Pettibone was silent, not even bothering to shake his head. He refused to listen to reason and the clock was running out. Harsh measures were called for. A preliminary roughing up and slapping around failed to make him see the light. More extreme inflictions left him gasping and groaning with pain but unwilling to unburden himself of the relevant facts.

A nasty bit of business forced from him a choking half sob. "Reb'll kill me if I talk!"

That irked Griff. "Listen up, dipshit. Reb's on the run from me and my bro here. You're scared of him? He's scared of us. You're gonna find out why."

Now Pettibone found himself tied to a chair in the garage. His eyes looked like shelled oysters, his glasses had been taken from him earlier at the start of the session.

Fisk's patrol car was parked in the substation parking lot. Rowdy started it up, drove it into the garage, and switched it off. He popped open the hood and got back behind the wheel.

Griff held a pair of battery jumper cables that he'd found in the garage and busied himself under the hood. The jumper cables had spring-hinged, rubber-handled copper pincers at each end. He attached a pair to the twin terminals on the car battery.

He crossed to Pettibone and stood facing him, holding the latter's switchblade. He thumbed the handle stud and the blade came snicking out. It was a long, thin, sharp stiletto. Griff smiled evilly and moved closer to the man tied to the chair. Pettibone's hands were tied with rope behind the back of the chair. He sat rigid, trembling, staring off into the distance.

Griff cut off Pettibone's vest and T-shirt, leaving him bare from the waist up. Pettibone's flesh, rank and unwashed, was the dead-white of creatures that spend their lives in dark caves away from the sun. He was skinny with a prominent collarbone and his rib cage showing so clearly that each separate rib could be counted.

Griff taunted, "What'd you think, I was gonna cut you?" He pressed the handle stud and the blade retracted. He pocketed the weapon. "Maybe later."

He picked up a galvanized metal mop bucket that he'd filled with water and dashed its contents on Pettibone, soaking him above the waist. He grabbed up one of the jumper cables, squeezing the rubber-handled grip. The inside of its saw-toothed jaws were sharp and pointy, the better to clamp down on battery terminals.

Griff said, "We're gonna give your tongue a jump start to set it a-wagging." He fastened the clamp to Pettibone's chest at the right nipple. Pettibone whinnied like a horse breaking a leg. Griff waited until the shrieks died down and said, "Hurts, huh? You wanna talk?"

Pettibone shook his head no. Griff fastened the other jumper cable to Pettibone's chest over his left nipple. Pettibone howled, squirming against the ropes, drumming his booted feet on the garage floor.

Griff surveyed his handiwork with evident satisfaction. "Still won't talk? No? What a dumbass." He shook his head in disbelief. "You called the tune."

He upended the metal mop bucket and placed it over Pettibone's head. Rowdy sat in the driver's seat of the patrol car, resting his elbow on the top of the door and sticking his head out of the window, grinning.

Griff said, "Start 'er up!"

Rowdy switched on the ignition and started the car. The engine noise was loud inside the garage. Live current from the vehicle's nine-volt battery streamed through the jumper cables into Pettibone, the conductivity aided by the water that had doused him.

Pettibone looked like a white marble statue that had gone too long without a cleaning. His back was arched, his flesh rigid. Every muscle, tendon, and sinew stood out in bold relief. He spasmed like an epileptic throwing a fit, his head rattling against the inside of the metal bucket.

Rowdy gunned the motor, sending blue-gray clouds pouring from the exhaust pipe and out the open garage door. Griff studied the face of Jack Bauer, monitoring his reaction. Jack's expression was blandly neutral. He wondered what Griff expected him to do, flinch? He returned the biker's survey with a pleasant smile.

Thirty long seconds passed before Griff made a throat-cutting gesture, signaling Rowdy to switch off the engine. Silence fell like a concrete tomb lid.

Pettibone slumped, sagging against the ropes. He

panted for breath between the muffled sobs that came from beneath the bucket. Griff waited a minute until the worst of it had passed before he knocked on the bucket and said, "Ready to start singing yet?"

Pettibone was still holding out. Griff said, "Hit it, Rowdy!"

Rowdy started the car again. Pettibone convulsed as the electricity zapped him, reacting so violently that the bucket was thrown clear from his head to hit the garage ceiling. Griff said, "Wow!"

The shocking ran longer the second time than the first. Griff gave the cutoff signal and Rowdy killed the engine.

Pettibone took longer to recover the second time, too. He shivered, shuddered, sobbed, and shook. He wept and drooled. Griff cupped the other's chin and tilted his head back so he could look him in the face. He said, "How about it?"

Pettibone's gurgled response was hard to make out. Rowdy frowned, said, "What's he saying?"

Jack interpreted. "The same old song: Reb'll kill him if he talks." Griff looked up at Jack. Jack raised his eyebrows as if to say, Is that all you've got?

Griff was really steamed. He told Pettibone, "I'm through playing with you." He unbuckled Pettibone's belt and started opening his pants.

Pettibone vented a fresh round of howls but this time he'd changed his tune. "I'll talk, I'll talk!"

He did.

....

THE FOLLOWING TAKES PLACE
BETWEEN THE HOURS OF
10 P.M. AND 11 P.M.
MOUNTAIN DAYLIGHT TIME

....

Rimrock Road, Colorado

A patrol car bearing the emblem of the state police
Mobile Response Team drove south on Rimrock
Road. Hardin and Taggart were in it, Taggart driving. Taggart said, "That meeting ran long. I thought
it would never end."

Hardin nodded. "Nothing Sheriff Mack likes
better than the sound of his own voice."

" 'Cept for maybe stuffing his fat face. Too bad
that ol' tub of guts won't be at Sky Mount tonight."

Hardin was philosophical. "You can't have everything. Look at the bright side: by tomorrow Mack'll
be out on his ass, looking for a new line of work."

Taggart chuckled appreciatively. "I reckon a lot of
police bigs'll be finding themselves in that position
come sunup."

"But not us, Cole."

"No, sir."

"We're clean as a hound's tooth."

The moon was high, almost directly overhead, a three-quarter bone-white orb that seemed far distant from the mountain landscape. Moonlight reflected off the strand of empty road beyond the reach of the car's headlights; rocky crags and needlelike pinnacles were silhouetted against a purple-black sky speckled with remote points of light that were stars.

Hardin worked the hand mic, radioing the Mountain Lake dispatcher's desk. The only reply was silence. Hardin replaced the mic in its dashboard bracket and settled heavily back in his seat. "Still no answer."

Taggart said, "That don't mean nothing. They might be away from the radio, out back making the handoff, transferring the prisoner to Pettibone. Probably are."

"Kind of late for that. Pettibone should've been and gone by now."

"He might be running late, too."

"Um."

Taggart looked away from the winding ribbon of road unrolling under the headlights to glance at Hardin, the lieutenant's heavy features in profile underlit by the instrument panel's glow. "Ain't worried, are you, Bryce?"

Hardin said, "I just hope Fisk didn't do something stupid."

"Like beating Jack Bauer to death?"

"It could happen."

"Not with Sharon there to ride herd on him."

"You know what that jackass nephew of mine is like, Cole. Once he starts beating on somebody he's hard to stop."

"He likes it too much."

"And he didn't like Bauer, not even a little bit."

Taggart shrugged. "Say he got carried away and Jack is dead. So what?"

Hardin said, "Weld'll be pissed."

"Screw him. As far as I'm concerned he's just another two-bit gun punk and snottier than most."

"On that score, my friend, we're in complete agreement. Unfortunately Mr. Pettibone doesn't share that opinion. He's scared of Weld. He'll be doing plenty of pissing and moaning if Bauer's dead."

"Screw him, too. If he don't like it, tough. Anyhow, we're almost there, so we'll find out what's what soon enough."

The car swung left around a bend and came on a long straightaway. The substation's lights could be seen at the end of it. The car went to it, slowing as it neared its destination.

Taggart said, "Home, sweet home." He turned left on to the drive connecting the road to the parking lot and followed it. Hardin leaned forward in his seat. "I don't see Fisk's car—"

Taggart said, "There it is, in the motor pool."

The car halted outside the garage. Hardin eased up and sat back. He groused, "Damn it, I told that boy not to park there. Honk the horn so he'll come out and move it—"

Headlights came on, filling the car interior with white light. They belonged to the pickup truck that had been standing idling out of sight behind the station. It barreled out with a roar of power and plowed into the patrol car, broadsiding it on the driver's side.

The car wrapped itself around the truck's steel-plated front. Hardin and Taggart received a hell of a jolt, only their seat belts saving them from being tossed around the car's interior. The stunning blow knocked their hats off and left the duo breathless with heads reeling.

Taggart caught a faceful of shattered glass from the driver's side window, which had fragmented upon impact. So had that side's rear window. The windshield frame was bent and the glass frosted. Taggart pawed his face trying to clear his eyes. He shouted, "He crazy—?"

Hardin groaned, his body aching. He felt cut in half from where the seat belt harness had caught him. He raised his hands in a vain attempt to ward off the truck's glaring high beams.

The car shivered as the pickup went into reverse and pulled free of it, backing up to get some running room. The driver stomped the accelerator, and the truck leaped forward to deliver another pulverizing blow to the patrol car.

The second hit transformed the car's shape from a U to a V. The driver's side accordioned. Jagged metal imploded, swatting Taggart. He writhed screaming and thrashing, but the seat belt harness held him in place. The front seat area was diminished by half, pinning its occupants against each other and crowding them against the passenger side. The windshield was gone, the entire sheet of safety glass having popped free of its now warped and distorted frame.

The pickup reversed, shaking itself loose from the

car and rolling away from it. Hardin struggled to get free but Taggart's body pinned him against the inside of the door. Taggart wouldn't stop screaming. Hardin pounded him with clublike fists in an attempt to break free or at least silence the screaming, failing at both.

The shrieks dueted with the vroom of the pickup's engine as it made its third and final charge. It hit the car at an angle, shoving it toward the rear of the parking lot. The driver stepped on the gas, pushing the car across the asphalt into a knee-high guardrail.

The car was sandwiched between the rail and the truck. The truck kept pushing. The metal rail bowed outward into empty space, rivets popping. The truck's wheels spun, burning rubber.

There was a giddy sensation of release as the rail gave way. Several feet of ground stood between the edge of the asphalt and eternity. The car slid across them under the truck's relentless pushing and jostling.

The car's passenger side wheels ran out of ground and touched emptiness. There was a bump as the undercarriage hit the edge of the cliff and the car tilted downward. It hung there for a instant before a final nudge from the truck tipped the scales and sent it tumbling off the precipice.

Taggart had stopped screaming but Hardin didn't notice it because he was too busy screaming himself. He screamed all the way down until the car hit a rocky outcropping four or five hundred feet below.

The car bounced off it like a kicked football, sailing into the void for another thousand feet before hitting bottom.

The truck rolled backward away from the edge deeper into the parking lot and halted. Jack Bauer put it into park, unfastened his safety harness, opened the driver's side door, and slid out from behind the steering wheel. He rose, holding on to the side, standing half-in and half-out of the truck cab.

Griff and Rowdy ran out from behind the substation where they'd been hiding and watching. They thought it was a hell of a show and whooped and hollered to show their appreciation.

Jack was oblivious of them, having eyes only for the spot where the car with Hardin and Taggart had gone over the edge. He said, "Adios, amigos. No hard feelings."

He was lying.

. . . .

**THE FOLLOWING TAKES PLACE
BETWEEN THE HOURS OF
11 P.M. AND 12 A.M.
MOUNTAIN DAYLIGHT TIME**

. . . .

Camp Winnetou, Colorado

Jack Bauer made the mistake of assuming.

Pettibone had told Hardin and Taggart earlier that he'd be taking Jack to Winnetou. Jack had assumed that Winnetou was a code name for someone big, a major player in the Sky Mount strike, possibly even Reb Weld's boss. That Weld had a boss was never in doubt in Jack's mind. The Rebel could never have put an operation like this together in a million years. He lacked the brains, money, and connections. Weld was strictly a hired hand in this deal. Maybe Winnetou was the hidden hand, the shadowy mastermind behind the conspiracy.

Now Jack knew that Winnetou was not a person but a place, a onetime summer camp that had stood shuttered and abandoned for thirty years. It lay in a park just north of Sky Mount, a narrow cleft in the mid-slopes of Thunder Mountain, third and northernmost of the trinity of peaks bordering the estate, Mounts Nagaii and Zebulon being the other two.

A mass of foliage screened the entrance to the dirt road connecting the site with Masterman Way. "Screened" was the word for it because the path wasn't as overgrown as it looked when seen from the paved road. It was camouflaged behind a pair of screens eight feet on a side that were made of chicken wire strung on a wooden framework and hung with bunches of leafy branches to give the impression of a wall of unbroken brush.

They were not unlike the canvas flats that are used in theaters onstage to create the illusion of a scenic background. They were light enough to be handled by one man.

They were rolled back now, pushed out of the way to allow access to the campsite that lay hidden within the woods. It would have been easy to miss the entrance even if they hadn't been there. The trees lining both sides of the path met in an archway above it, their dark boughs interlaced to form a canopy of foliage. The path drove through them like a tunnel, a tunnel whose mouth was sheltered by the real brush hemming it in at both sides.

A pair of metal gateposts each three feet high stood set back a few feet into the passage. The chain that linked them to prevent access now lay flat on the ground. So did the sentry who'd been posted here, whose duty was to keep watch and work the screens and chain to permit the exit and entry of authorized persons.

Pettibone was authorized to engage in such comings and goings. He'd been expected tonight. The pickup truck had halted at the entrance, and the sentry had come out to move aside the camouflaged screens to allow its entry. Griff had been there lurking in the brush, and he crept up behind the sentry and clapped a hand over his mouth to stifle any outcry while he cut his throat. Griff was handy with a knife and he liked the action.

He wiped the blade clean with a handful of leaves and returned the knife to the belt sheath that hung down the side of his left hip. He ran south along the paved road for fifty yards or so before coming to the place where he'd left his bike, a break in the undergrowth where Rowdy sat waiting on his motorcycle.

The bikers kick-started their machines, powerful Harley engines coming alive with a growl of power. Their headlights were dark as they rode to the entrance of the passage.

Jack Bauer sat there behind the wheel of the pickup truck. The slab of steel plate armoring the truck's front was hardly nicked or dented, seemingly impervious to the effects of this day's labors in demolishing three cars: Brad Oliver's vehicle, Jack's CTU Mercedes, and Hardin and Taggart's patrol car. It was a real Deathmobile.

Now Jack was in the driver's seat. He wore his gun holstered under his left arm and a second sidearm in a gun belt holstered on his right hip. The latter was a big .357 that had been provided courtesy of the Mountain Lake substation's armory. A fully-loaded sawed-off twelve-gauge riot shotgun from the same source lay on the passenger seat beside him. It was secured by the seat belt harness. The left side pocket of Jack's coat held spare clips for his pistol, the right held extra shotgun shells.

Griff and Rowdy had also augmented their own firepower with arms and ammo from the armory. Rowdy had a riot shotgun wedged muzzle-down in a hard saddle bucket on the Harley's right side, its butt end nestled against the inside rail of the protective A-bar that was bolted to the top of the back of the seat to serve as a backrest.

Griff sported a pair of .357s. The weapons were in their gun belts, which he wore not at the hips but across his neck and over his shoulders with the holstered pieces nestled butt-out under his arms. The gun belts crossed over his chest and upper back, making a pair of Xs. A bandana was worn knotted across the top of his head to keep his long hair out of his face during the action. The bandana and crossed gun belts heightened his resemblance to an old-time bandito but he rode an iron horse rather than one of the flesh-and-blood variety.

Jack waited for them to join him. He'd warned them of the danger of the green gas and given each of them a slapshot ampoule containing the antidote. The ampoule was in a syrette, a mini-syringe designed for battlefield use. A person exposed to the gas must remove the hypodermic needle's protective plastic cap, jab the spike into the upper thigh, and plunge the thruster home. The needle was tough and able to go straight through pants or other garments when driven into the flesh, a vital time-saving attribute where chemical weapons were involved and every second counted. Jack found himself hoping the bikers wouldn't try it out just to see what kind of a buzz it would give them.

Jack was not alone in the truck cab. Pettibone was there, too. He sat on the floor with his hands cuffed behind him and a second set of cuffs manacling his ankles. He was so skinny that the bracelets easily encircled the bottoms of his pipestem legs. A noose was snugged around his neck, its opposite end tied to the bottom of the passenger side seat. He was left ungagged; from here on in he could make as much noise as he liked. A locker at the substation had yielded a shirt, which now clothed his upper body.

He was silent, perhaps in reaction to the session earlier when he'd spewed a torrent of words, telling about the base camp at Winnetou, its hidden entrance, sentry, and layout. He'd rattled on about Weld, BZ, and the diabolical plan set to be unleashed at zero hour. He now seemed broken but Jack was taking no chances in case Pettibone had misled him or withheld some vital piece of information. Pettibone was going along for the ride and would share in the consequences of any treachery he might have up his sleeve.

The bikers pulled up on either side of the truck cab, Griff on Jack's left and Rowdy on his right. The rumble of their Harleys chorused with the heavy throb of the pickup's powerful motor.

Jack said, "I'll go in first down the middle, you two come in after and take them on the flanks."

Griff looked up at him, impatient. "We know the plan, dude."

Rowdy said, "Let's get it on!"

Jack prodded Pettibone with his boot toe, causing him to look up. Jack said, "Any last-minute information you'd like to volunteer? Because your neck is on the line as much as anyone's."

Pettibone shook his head. Jack pressed, "Nothing you're holding back?"

Pettibone said dully, "You've got it all."

Jack called out through the open windows, "All set?" He looked right, looked left. Rowdy nodded and Griff gave him a thumbs-up.

Jack worked the stick, shifting it into gear. The truck lurched forward. He hit the high beams, filling the leafy archway with bright light. A pair of rutted tracks grooved the ground where other vehicles had been before. The passage followed a long, low incline.

Jack shifted into the next gear, moving the truck along at a moderate pace. It rode fairly smoothly on absorbent shocks and reinforced springs despite the unevenness of the path. He glanced in his rearview mirror where two bright dots appeared as the bikers switched on their machines' headlights.

Branches slapped the truck cab's roof and scratched at its sides as the vehicle lumbered up the passage between the trees. It rolled through the far end into a clearing.

The park wasn't much, just a rocky cleft floored by an acre or so of weedy flats. A handful of cabins were grouped in an inverted U shape at the opposite end of the clearing. A long, low wooden plank building stood at their center. It looked like a shoebox with a roof instead of a lid. Its long side faced the end of the path through the trees.

The cabins were dark, tumbledown shacks, but the long house was in better repair. Its windows were muted squares and oblongs of light. A handful of dark figures milled around in front of it.

Jack pointed the truck at them and headed toward them. He downshifted, slowing as he neared, tapping the horn with his palm heel several times to sound a tinny beep-beep. He stuck his hand out the window and gave what he hoped would be taken for a friendly wave.

The high beams' glare pinned a half-dozen armed men. Jack wondered which of them had taken part in the attack at Silvertop and the cold-blooded execution of the BZ-stricken CTU survivors that had followed it. His own blood was feeling pretty hot at that moment.

Some of the gang had rifles, some had guns, others both. They showed no alarm yet. The truck poked along at a few miles per hour. A couple of men raised hands to shield their eyes against the glare, others turned their heads away from it. One yelled, "Dim those beams!"

Jack switched off his lights. A sudden blackness fell, made heavier by contrast with the harsh glare that had just filled the clearing. Jack speed shifted, stomping the gas while forcing the stick through the different gears as he did so.

The men were backlit by the long house's lights, muted though they were. Jack piloted the car toward them. There were sudden outcries, angry shouts.

Somebody opened fire with an assault rifle. Guns started popping, their muzzle flares spear blades of light. A burst of autofire spanged harmlessly against the truck's steel-plated front.

Jack switched the high beams back on, bathing his opponents in glare. The truck was almost on them. One or two hardy souls stood and fired but the others started breaking for the sides and long house.

A gunman stood in front of the truck shooting at it. A round punched a hole through the windshield, exiting through the roof of the cab. The truck closed with the shooter. He threw up his arms. The truck hit him with a thud and sent him flying.

Jack manhandled the wheel, whipping it to the left. The truck slewed around in a wide curving turn. The men scattered, running in all directions. Jack steered for the nearest, chasing him down. The target ran toward a cabin with the truck at his heels.

He almost made it. The front bumper tagged him and he fell under the wheels. The truck shivered twice as if it had gone over two speed bumps.

Jack swung the wheel around hard left again to keep from hitting the cabin. The right edge of the steel plate struck a corner of it and brushed it aside. The cabin collapsed in a heap of broken logs and the truck kept on going.

The rolling thunder of the truck motor was counterpointed by the angry hornet buzzing of the two Harleys as they entered the scene. One swung left and the other right. Jack couldn't tell which was Griff and which Rowdy.

A racketing fury clouted the driver's side of the truck. Jack didn't like that so well. The machine's flanks were its weak points, the front its strong point. He wheeled it around and drove toward the shooters.

He passed Griff going in the opposite direction chasing a man down. Griff fired a couple of shots across the top of the handlebars at his quarry. Jack flashed past them and missed the outcome of the clash.

A couple of riflemen stood in the space between

two cabins on Jack's right, firing at him. He made for them, slugs ricocheting off the truck's steel plate. He threw up a hand to protect his eyes as the windshield disintegrated, spraying him with cubes of broken safety glass. His face and hand were peppered with sharp stinging fragments but not his eyes. He could see fine.

The truck kept going, plowing into the shooters with a one-two combination of thuds, the machine giving a vaguely perceptible shiver as it turned them into broken heaps. The truck rolled up an incline, a tree looming in the lights.

Jack hit the brakes, the truck balking and sliding to a stop with a crunch. The tree broke in mid-trunk where the steel plate had hit it, falling in the opposite direction.

He was after Reb Weld's kill squad, not trees. He threw the gear into reverse, the truck varooming backward and running over the same bodies again. It backed into the clearing, narrowly avoiding hitting Rowdy, who was chasing a man fleeing toward the opening of the passage. Rowdy swerved wide to clear the truck's rear bumper. He shouted something. Jack couldn't make it out but it didn't sound nice.

Griff emerged from behind a cabin near the top of the inverted U. Gunfire zipped around him. It was getting hot so he turned again, weaving between two cabins for cover.

A shotgun boomed. Jack looked in his rearview mirror. Rowdy had halted his cycle to shoot a man. His first shot missed. He stood straddling the bike, shotgun raised to his right shoulder as he swung the muzzle in line with the fugitive and fired again. His quarry went down.

The clearing was empty of fleeing figures but littered with fallen ones. The enemy's firepower was now concentrated in the long house where the remaining shooters were making a stand. They were inside covering behind wooden walls and shooting through windows and the open doorway. Four of them: three at the window and one at the door.

Jack thought that wooden plank walls wouldn't provide much protection against bullets or trucks. He glanced at Pettibone, who huddled cowering in the well under the dashboard on his side of the cab as much as the short rope around his neck allowed. Jack said, "Here we go!"

Pettibone cried, "No, no!"

Jack pointed the truck at the long house and leaned on the horn to get the bikers' attention, filling the clearing with a loud rude braying. He engaged the gear and the truck rolled forward, gathering speed.

The shooters targeted the truck as it closed in on them. Jack hunched down in his seat as low as he could get while still seeing over the top of the dashboard. Line of fire tore up the turf in front of him. The shooters got their range and poured it on into the truck. Bullets spattered the armored front racketing like the proverbial hailstorm on a tin roof.

A row of slugs stitched a cratered line of bullet holes in the cab's rear panel not far from the top of Jack's head.

The long house loomed up, filling Jack's field of vision. He steered toward the window through which a trio of shooters were blasting. The truck's left front tire was shot to pieces, causing it to tilt and veer left.

Jack battled the slide, hauling the steering wheel

hard right to compensate for the drift. It took some muscle to keep the machine on course.

The building was fronted by a foot-tall wooden boardwalk. The planks snapped and splintered under the truck's weight, sounding like they were being fed into a wood chipper. They fought the vehicle's progress, trying to slow it down. It bucked and shuddered but continued its advance. The steering wheel fought to break Jack's hold but he clutched it with both hands in a death grip.

Jack stomped the gas pedal to the floor and kept it pinned, goosing a final wild burst of shrieking RPMs out of the engine.

The wall with the window was in his way. The truck punched through it, battering two shooters crouching behind it. They greased the machine's wheels as it thrust into the long house.

The long house had a long hall. Its wooden floor collapsed under the truck. The pickup continued its forward motion, tearing up planks and beams and tossing them to either side. It slid to the middle of the space before jerking to a halt.

Rafters rained down on the truck. The wall behind it had a truck-sized hole in it. Part of it caved, bringing the front half of the roof down with it. The collapse kicked up thick clouds of dry gray dust. Heaps of debris, timbers, and tabletop-sized chunks of plaster came crashing down on the cab's roof and hood.

The middle of the front half of the roof came down but the opposite ends held, the reinforced corner beams staying upright and bearing their load. Jack thought the debris had stopped falling but then another heap came cascading down.

The overhead lights stayed on, so the power source

hadn't been cut. That was a break. Jack didn't fancy playing a deadly game of hide-and-go-kill in the dark.

The engine had stalled out. Jack unfastened his seat belt harness and grabbed the riot shotgun by the stock. His left hand gripped the door handle and pulled. The door opened but only a foot or so before stopping, jammed in place by fallen rubble.

He put his shoulder to the door and his weight behind it and tried again, forcing the door open wide enough so he could get out. He put his foot out preparatory to climbing down from the cab. A piece of plaster the size of a card table top fell from above, shattering against the top of the door.

Jack pulled back but the reflex action would have been too late to save him if he'd tried to dismount a heartbeat sooner. He ducked out the open door, dragging the shotgun across the seat with him. The pump-action weapon had a cut-down muzzle and stock, making it the length of a long baton.

An arm stuck out from under the truck. It was still attached to its dead owner. Jack was careful not to step on it, not out of squeamishness but because the footing was uncertain enough without it.

The floor was an obstacle course of holes in the floorboards and piles of rubble. Plaster dust streamed down from above by the handful, powdering him with white particles and flecks. Clouds of the stuff roiled and swirled in the hall like a fog bank rolling in. Dry fog.

Jack moved in a crouch, shotgun leveled. He tried to step carefully but lost his footing on a broken plank and sat down hard. Someone deeper in the hall squirted a burst of autofire in his direction but it missed and passed over his head. He couldn't tell where it had come from, not with the streaming, billowing bank of white particles in midair obscuring his view.

He picked up a piece of plaster and scaled it off to one side. The oldest gag in the book, but it stayed in the book because it worked. The phantom shooter opened fire at the sound of the plaster hitting the floor.

Streaking muzzle flares revealed a ghostly outline of a figure off to Jack's right. Jack loosed a shotgun blast at it, held down the trigger and pumped several more blasts at it. A scream choked off and a body hit the floor, leaving only swirling white dust where the figure had stood.

Jack thought he'd got him but he had to be sure. He advanced slowly, picking his way through the mounds of debris heaped on the floor. He held the shotgun in both hands, leveled at his waist, ready to respond to any sudden threat. The debris lessened as he moved farther away from the front wall. The plaster dust was starting to settle, the white clouds thinning and breaking up.

A dark form lay sprawled on the floor in the area where Jack had fired at his assailant. He approached it cautiously in case the other was shamming, playing possum to take Jack by surprise. He neared the body and saw there was no worry about that. This opponent wasn't coming back for another round, not with the damage the shotgun had done to him.

Footfalls scuttled through disturbed debris behind him. Jack spun, ready to cut loose. A figure jumped up and ran outside through the open doorway. He was out before Jack had a shot at him.

The fugitive ran into a blast of gunfire. A scream sounded, more gunshots, and then the sound of a body hitting the boardwalk.

Jack had no desire to be shot by his allies so he hung back to one side out of the potential line of fire offered by the doorway. "Griff! Rowdy!"

Griff called back, "That you, dude?"

"Yeah!"

"What's happening?"

"It looks clear in here but keep your guard up."

"I always do, man. I'm coming in so don't shoot."

"Don't you shoot, either."

Griff came through the doorway, a gun in each hand. He circled a tangle of broken beams, sidling close to the passenger side of the truck. He stopped short, looking down at something and muttering a stifled exclamation. Jack couldn't see what it was from where he was standing.

Griff pointed his gun downward and fired once. Jack said, "Why'd you shoot?"

Griff said, "A guy was crushed under the rear wheel. He was still alive. It was a mercy killing." He looked up, looked around. "Did we get 'em all?"

Jack said, "The ones in here? I think so, but don't take any chances. There might be one or two that we missed."

Griff scanned the scene, taking in the damages. "You really brought down the house, man."

"I did what I had to do."

"That's cool. I'm into overkill myself."

"Where's Rowdy? Did he make it?"

"Sure. He's indestructible, the big bastard."

Rowdy entered. He gave Jack a dirty look. "You almost ran me over, man!"

Jack said, "Sorry."

"Sorry don't cut it. Next time watch where you're driving."

Griff said, "Lighten up, bro. Save it for Reb."

"Where's Weld? He ain't here. I know, I checked all the bodies while I was making sure they was dead."

Jack said, "Were they?"

Rowdy smiled nastily. "When I left 'em, yeah."

Griff said, "Dude, where's the Rebel? We got us a score to settle with him."

"You and me both," Jack said. "This was his rear guard. They had to be neutralized before we can take him."

Griff smirked. ' "Neutralized.' That's a good one. Maybe you really are a secret agent, the way you talk."

Jack let that one pass. It didn't matter who or what the bikers thought he was. The way to motivate them was to keep their eyes on the prize.

He said, "Reb and his kill squad have already left, gone to Sky Mount on their mission of destruction. That's where we'll find them for the showdown: Sky Mount."

. . . .

THE FOLLOWING TAKES PLACE
BETWEEN THE HOURS OF
12 A.M. AND 1 A.M.
MOUNTAIN DAYLIGHT TIME

. . . .

Beneath Sky Mount, Colorado

Rowdy said, "Look at all the goodies!"

The enemy kill squad had used the long house as their headquarters. The long house had been a mess hall back in the days when Winnetou had been a summer camp. Two-thirds of its space made up the dining area and the remainder the kitchen.

The kitchen had been pressed into service as the killers' command center. Long tables that had once been used for food preparation were now crowded with maps, charts, and diagrams, most of them depicting various aspects of Sky Mount's mansion and grounds. A wall-mounted pantry cabinet held five silenced machine pistols and ammunition for them, the "goodies" to which Rowdy was referring.

Jack Bauer took down one of the weapons from

the cabinet pegs that held it and examined it. It was a modern-day Central European–made knockoff of the classic Ingram MAC–10 and MAC–11 submachine guns. SMGs. The lightweight piece was square, boxy, and fitted with a collapsible metal tube stock. With the stock folded down the weapon wasn't much larger or heavier than a conventional semi-automatic pistol. It was chambered for .9mm rounds.

The silencer was the size and shape of the internal cardboard roller inside a wad of paper towels, only rendered in metal.

Jack attached it to the short, snouty gun muzzle. He slapped a magazine clip into the receiver, locked and loaded the piece, and thumbed the selector switch to autofire. He pointed the weapon at a metal bucket on a countertop at the far side of the room and squeezed the trigger, letting off a three-round burst.

The silenced SMG made a quick coughing noise that sounded like the stuttering of a compressed air hose. There was no explosion of gunfire, only a whispered *phtt-phtt-phtt!*

The metal bucket danced and rattled as it was drilled three times. It bounced off the counter, hit the floor, and rolled.

Griff said, "Nice!"

Jack said, "These could come in handy." He didn't have to tell the bikers twice. They were already helping themselves to the weapons with eager avidity. Jack said, "You know how to use them?"

Griff gave him a disdainful look as if he'd just been insulted. "Are you kidding?"

Rowdy said, "I cut my teeth on these babies."

The bikers stuffed the side pockets of the denim vests bearing the Hellbenders' colors with extra clips for the SMGs. Rowdy said, indignant, "This is probably part of the same load that Reb stole from the club."

Griff said, "We'll return 'em to him with interest—the slugs, anyway. Poetic justice, I call it." He locked and loaded an SMG and pointed it at Pettibone, who stood off to one side trying to make himself inconspicuous. Pettibone's hands were still cuffed behind his back but his feet had been freed. The noose still encircled his neck, its free end of rope hanging down his front.

Pettibone yelped, recoiling. Jack said, "We need him, Griff."

Griff looked disappointed but lowered the weapon. "Well . . . maybe later."

Jack said, "Why wasn't the rear guard armed with these, Pettibone?"

"They're part of Reb's private stash—for use in the Action only."

That was Pettibone's term for the planned strike against Sky Mount: "the Action." Jack was unsure whether that was the captive's private usage or the group's general label for the strike. Not that it mattered. It meant conspiracy to commit mass murder whatever it was called.

The kitchen was equipped with a rusted metal container that looked like it had once been a cooler or food storage locker. It was eight feet long, four feet high, and three feet deep.

Rowdy test-fired his SMG by shooting at it. The machine pistol went *brrrrip!* The silencer suppressed not only the reports but the muzzle flare. Jack noted that with approval. It meant that no telltale flashes of light would betray the presence of a shooter. It worked both ways, of course. Reb Weld's hit team was armed with the pieces and would similarly benefit from the suppressors' stealth.

A horizontal line of nickel-sized holes was punched through the container's side. Streams of water leaked through them. Griff fired off a burst, further holing the container. More water came squirting out from the freshly made bullet holes.

Griff cradled the SMG, smiling affectionately down at it. "This is one sweet piece!"

Rowdy said, "Hold your fire bro, I want to see something." He crossed to the container, skirting the growing circle of water puddling on the floor from the bullet holes. He looked inside. "It's filled with ice. Maybe they used it to cool their beer."

Griff said, "Any brewskis in it?"

"Nope."

"Who gives a shit then?"

Jack was mulling over something that had been puzzling him, the presence on the long table of a handful of strips of white cloth. He picked one up. It was four inches high and about eight inches long. Its ends featured vertical strips of some Velcro-like material. They made a circular band when fastened together. He said, "What's this, Pettibone?"

Pettibone said, "I dunno."

"You're alive because you're useful. I'm getting the feeling you're not useful anymore."

"What's the difference? You're just gonna kill me anyway."

"You want it now? Fine. Hey, Griff—"

Pettibone said quickly, "Wait, wait! I just remembered what they're for. They're armbands. All the Action team is wearing them."

"It's a recognition symbol."

"Yeah. The insiders at the estate will be wearing them, too. That way there won't be any screwups if they cross paths during the Action."

Griff sidled over to Pettibone and stuck the muzzle of the silencer-equipped SMG against the underside of the other's chin, causing him to tilt his head back. Griff said, "So you 'just remembered,' huh?"

Pettibone said tightly, "I—I forgot . . ."

Jack said, "How many insiders are there?"

Pettibone said, "I don't know—" He must have seen something he didn't like in Jack's face because he blurted out, "I don't! That's Reb's business and he don't like nobody sticking their nose into it!"

Griff said, "Oh yeah? We're gonna jump into Reb's business with both feet and see how he likes that."

Pettibone gulped. He had trouble talking with Griff's weapon pressing the underside of his chin but he struggled to get his message across. "Only Reb knows who's on the inside. That's the reason for the white armbands, anybody wearing one is with us and not to be harmed."

Jack said, "You're going along, Pettibone, so whatever happens to us will happen to you first. Keeping that in mind, is there anything else you forgot to tell us?"

"That's all of it, I swear!"

"You'd better be damned sure about that."

"No, that's it, that's all!"

"Okay, you get to breathe awhile longer. Griff . . ."

Griff shouted, "Bang bang!," laughing as Pettibone flinched. He lowered the weapon to his side but kept giving Pettibone evil looks. Jack picked up one of the white cloth strips, said, "Which arm?"

Pettibone said, "Either one, it don't matter." Jack's

hesitation prompted Pettibone to add, "I ain't lying!"

Jack fixed the white cloth around his left biceps, fastening it in place with the adhesive strips. He said to the bikers, "Might as well. We can't afford to overlook anything that gives us a slight edge."

Griff and Rowdy donned the white armbands. Jack put one around Pettibone's upper arm, said, "We don't want his buddies to get the idea that everything's not going according to plan."

He emptied the shotgun shells from his right side jacket pocket, replacing them with extra clips for the SMG. Rowdy said, "You ain't bringing the scattergun?"

Jack said, "I don't know if we want shotguns blasting around explosives and gas grenades. The machine pistol's better suited for the work."

"I'm bringing both. The riot gun'll be handy in case we gotta knock down any doors."

"Use it as a last resort. We're not looking to advertise our presence."

"Better to have it and not need it than need it and not have it."

"I can't argue with that."

Rowdy grabbed some of the shotgun shells and stuffed them into his pants pockets. There were plenty of flashlights around, heavy-duty baton models. Jack helped himself to one. "We'll need these, too."

Rowdy said, "You and Griff take 'em. I'll carry the shotgun in one hand and the machine gun in the other."

Jack and Griff tried out the flashlights to make sure they worked. Griff shone the powerful beam in Pettibone's face, causing the other to squint and turn away. Griff said, "I'm watching you."

Jack said, "Let's go." He, the bikers, and their prisoner crossed to the door. Rowdy said to Griff, "We can come back for the other two machine guns later."

They all exited, the kitchen door putting them on the short, north side of the long house.

The moon was behind a mountain peak and thick darkness lay on the tiny park. Jack and Griff switched on their flashlights. Jack told Pettibone, "Lead on."

Pettibone said, "This way." He rounded the northwest corner to go behind the back of the building, closely followed by the others. A well-worn footpath ran south. The group passed the end of the building and kept on going, crossing a weedy field whose west edge was bordered by thickets of brush. Beyond them a rock wall thrust up for hundreds of feet, part of the mid-slopes of Thunder Mountain.

The path trailed south for a hundred yards leaving the Winnetou campgrounds behind. Ahead rose a rocky promontory several hundred feet high, a spur that thrust out at right angles from Thunder Mountain. The spur was Sky Mount's northern border; on its far side lay the estate. Mansion and grounds stood at the base of the spur's south face.

The spur was a rock curtain cutting off all sight and sound of the estate; not even the glow of the mansion's lights could be seen in the night sky above it. It effectually isolated Sky Mount from Winnetou, ensuring that neither the camp's hooded lights nor the sound of the gun battle earlier could be discerned by those on the estate.

The corner pocket where the spur met Thunder Mountain's east face was blanketed with inky darkness. The path began to rise slightly as it neared the base of the spur. Pettibone stumbled, almost falling.

He said, "I can't walk with my hands cuffed behind me."

Griff said, "Yeah? At least you're still upright." He prodded Pettibone with the tip of the machine pistol. "Keep moving if you want to stay that way."

Pettibone lurched forward, staggering onward. A short low rise of loose dirt and rocks now came underfoot, the talus skirting the slope's base. Their goal lay at the top of it. They paused, Jack and Griff's flashlight beams picking out their destination.

A hole gaped in the solid rock wall, a massive door or portal jutting out from it at right angles. Rowdy said, "Damn!"

Griff said, "We know that Mr. Bones here was telling the truth about this one thing, anyhow."

Jack set his SMG and flashlight down on top of a waist-high boulder and took his cell phone out of his pocket. Griff said, "What're you doing?"

Jack said, "Calling for reinforcements, if I can get through."

"You wouldn't be planning on pulling a cross, would you, dude?" Griff's voice took on that too-casual tone that Jack recognized as a harbinger of potential violence.

Jack said, "I'm standing right here, you can listen in. Like I said before, this is no game of cops and robbers, this is national security business. This is the connection that'll get us all off the hook on that Mountain Lake job."

"I was born paranoid, Jack. But you've been righteous so far so I'm willing to play out the string. Go ahead."

Jack saw that Ryan Chappelle had left him another stack of voice mail messages. His mouth took on a wry twist as he ignored them and pressed the speed dial for Orlando Garcia's personal number.

He didn't know whether the cell would work here but he thought it might because he and the Pine Ridge command post were both on the same eastern side of the mountain range, unlike Shadow Valley farther to the west where the intervening peaks had effectively blocked off the signal. His cell had a scrambler to screen against electronic eavesdroppers so the communication would be secure—if it got through.

The call was answered on the third ring. Garcia said without preamble, "I'd just about written you off." The signal was mushy but audible. "Where are you? What's—"

Jack cut across the other's words, "No time for that now. There's a strike planned against Sky Mount and I'm going to stop it if I can. Have a tac squad waiting outside the estate but don't go in before you hear from me. Otherwise you might trigger the massacre we're trying to prevent. Did you get all that?"

"Now hold on a damned minute—"

"Did you get that?"

"Yes."

"Good. If you don't hear from me by two o'clock— that's zero two hundred hours, repeat, zero two hundred hours—I didn't make it and you can start evacuating Sky Mount. You read me?"

"Yes, damn it, but—"

"Zero two hundred hours and then move. Not before."

"Wait—!"

Jack broke the connection and switched off the cell. It was the trust factor all over again. Brad Oliver had been warned in advance that he was going to be apprehended. The word could only have come from someone high up in CTU/L.A. or CTU/DENV. Was it Garcia? Jack didn't know. He wasn't going to tip his hand until he did know one way or the other. He'd told Garcia just enough to salvage the situation at Sky Mount should Jack fail to accomplish his mission but not so much that Garcia could thwart him if he turned out to be working for the other side.

He pocketed the cell and picked up his weapon and flashlight. He said, "Pettibone will go first. If there's any booby traps along the way he'll get it first."

Pettibone said, "There ain't."

"You'll go first anyway."

They went up the slope in single file, Pettibone first, followed by Jack, Griff, and Rowdy. They paused at the lip of the entrance, Jack and Griff shining their flashlights on the portal.

A flat-topped summit, about six feet wide, aproned the hole in the wall. The hole was the mouth of a tunnel that stretched deep into the spur. It had been drilled through rock and lined with poured concrete. Cool, dry air wafted out of it. The night air was already cool but the tunnel was colder.

It was dark, pitch-black, not a glimmer of light showing within. Its rounded archway was seven feet tall and five feet wide. The concrete had been poured so the floor was flat. The door, or hatch, was a massive construction of milled steel three feet thick. A pair of curved hinges of corresponding size secured it to the tunnel. The hinges emerged from slots set in the inside of the frame at the head of the portal. The hatch would fit flush with the frame when it was closed.

Its exterior was faced with rock paneling that

blended in with its surroundings. In the years—decades—that it had been in place, it had become overgrown with moss and lichens of the same type as those that clung to the natural rock walls.

The inside center of the hatch featured an oversized spoked metal wheel the size of a big-rig truck's steering wheel. Its hub was mounted on a short, squat column fitted inside a cylindrical shaft set deep in the metal mounting. It could be used to open the hatch or dog it closed. The mechanism could only be operated from the inside.

Rowdy said, "It's like a bank vault door . . ."

Griff said, "With a fifty-thousand-dollar payoff inside. And it's already open. All we got to do is take Reb's head to collect."

"And not get killed."

"Yeah, that, too."

Pettibone hung back at the threshold. Jack prodded him with the tip of the SMG, said, "Move. And quit dragging your feet. We don't want to be late for the party."

Pettibone started forward, Jack following him inside, the bikers trailing him. The concrete lining was cracked and stained but the excavation was far more stable and solidly built than that of the Silvertop mine. The mine had been damp and clammy but this tunnel was dry and dusty.

Twin flashlight beams reached around Pettibone's skeletal form to probe deep into the tunnel's vitals but not deep enough to reach its end. The floor had a slight incline with a grade of less than five degrees. The group trudged silently upward along it.

The tunnel was stark, functional, utilitarian. The outside world might as well have ceased to exist for all the effect it had here. Its influence was nil. The concrete lining had an absorbent quality that muffled ambient sound. The footfalls of the intruders were whispered rustlings on the treadmill of a seemingly endless trek.

Jack herded Pettibone along, poking him with the SMG on the ever more frequent occasions that he halted his progress. Jack read that as a good sign. It meant they were nearing their goal at the end of the tunnel, a destination Pettibone had no desire to reach.

The tunnel ceased its incline and now began to run level. The flashlight beams all at once encountered something instead of being swallowed up by nothingness. They bounced off a distant shape, an unrecognizable blur.

Jack whispered over his shoulder to the bikers, "Heads up and stand by for action." A lot of ground remained to be covered but the transit was more endurable now that the end was in sight.

Jack tilted his flashlight beam to one side. A fuzzy patch of brightness swam at the end of a long stretch. He touched the tip of the silencer to the back of Pettibone's head where it met the top of his neck, a gentle reminder of the facts of life and death.

Jack didn't know what lay at the end of the tunnel, but whatever it was, he didn't want Pettibone acting up when they got there.

There was no way to hide their approach but he hoped that the opposition would be lulled by a misreading of the situation. They were expecting Pettibone to arrive with a captive Jack Bauer in tow for delivery to Reb Weld. The two of them would surely be escorted by a couple of armed men from the rear guard.

Jack planned to take advantage of that split-second window of opportunity before the foe realized the truth.

The tunnel came to an end, opening on a rectangular chamber twenty feet deep, fifteen feet high, and fifteen feet wide. This end of the shaft was fitted with a massive hatch, twin to the one at the entrance. It opened inward and was swung back all the way on its curved hinges so that its inner face pressed against the chamber wall to the left of the portal.

The first thing Jack saw inside the chamber was a golf cart, the incongruity of its presence here adding an offbeat, surrealistic touch. It was parked at the foot of a loading platform that stood at the chamber's far end.

The platform's top was four feet above the floor. A well in the left corner held a short flight of stone stairs leading up to the platform. A couple of boxes and packing crates stood on top of the platform.

A man sat on top of one of the crates facing the tunnel. A square-edged doorway opened in the wall behind him. An electric lantern was set atop a nearby crate. Its glow seemed as cheery and welcoming as sunshine after the tunnel's dark passage.

The man was stocky and squat with short hair and a goatee. He wore dark clothing and a white band on his upper left arm. He hopped off the crate and stepped forward toward the edge of the platform as the newcomers arrived. He said, "Pettibone, what kept you— Hey!" He turned, grabbing for the SMG on top of the crate.

Jack shoved Pettibone aside and made his play. He went for a head shot in case the other was wearing a bulletproof vest under his shirt.

His weapon made a throat-clearing noise as it squirted three rounds into the sentry's face. He fired it one-handed, holding the flashlight in his other hand. The piece when fired in a short burst had a recoil that was a bit heavier than that of a .45-caliber semi-automatic pistol.

The sentry flopped rearward like he was trying to do a back dive. He bumped into the crate, upsetting but not overturning it. The SMG fell clattering to the platform but didn't go off.

Jack darted across the floor to the stairwell and took the steps two at a time. He crossed the platform to the doorway, covered to one side of it, and peeked around the edge into the space beyond.

The doorway opened into a vast, cavernous area that resembled nothing so much as an underground parking garage and was the size of an airplane hangar. The enclosure was long and low-ceilinged. It was dark except for a line of electric lanterns that had been placed at regular intervals along the center of the floor to the opposite end.

It was empty, unoccupied. Jack Bauer strained his ears listening for the sound of an alarm or hue and cry. None came.

He turned his attention back to the chamber. Griff stood crouched holding his weapon to Pettibone's head. Rowdy climbed the stairs to the top of the platform and joined Jack.

Jack said, low-voiced, "This level is clear—I think." He switched off the flashlight and set it down on a crate. He said, "Cover me."

Rowdy said, "Right." He leaned the shotgun against the wall and held the SMG in both hands.

Jack ducked low and went through the doorway

into the sprawling bunkerlike construction that lay on the other side. He dodged to the right, out of the glow of the electric lanterns lining the floor and into the welcoming gloom that hovered on either side of the illuminated central path.

Rowdy covered behind the doorway's edge and stuck the SMG outside, the tip of its silenced snout quivering like a dowsing rod in quest not of water but of human targets.

The floor was carpeted with a layer of dust several inches thick once Jack moved aside from the center space. It smothered the sound of his already light-footed tread. His movements disturbed the dust, each footfall raising puffs of the stuff. It tickled his nose, and he had to fight to keep from sneezing. That would be a hell of a note, to give himself away by sneezing!

Jack advanced, guided by the lamplight glimpsed out of the corner of his eye. The space dwarfed him with its slab-sided monolithic immensity.

His eyes grew accustomed to the dimness, allowing him to make out a line of closed doors in the wall to his right. They were tall, narrow oblongs a shade lighter than the shadows engulfing them. No lights showed behind any of those doors. The wall space between them was lined with stacked cardboard boxes furry with dust.

He went to the opposite end of the bunker. A glow brightened in the right-hand corner as he neared it, an independent light source separate from the lanterns marking out the centerline.

It revealed a stairwell. A flight of stone steps climbed to a landing, then another stairway led to a second landing. The light came from electric lanterns with hooks at the top that were hung from horizontal bars of the metal railing enclosing the open side of the stairs. A closed door was set in a wall at the second, final landing. It was outlined by light coming from the other side of the door.

Jack figured he'd come far enough by himself. No point in having allies if you didn't use them. He turned, heading back toward the antechamber. This time he did it the easy way, following the well-lit center aisle. It was a well-traveled route, judging by the lack of layered dust that pervaded the rest of the bunker.

He halted at the halfway point, motioning for the bikers to join him. They came to him, Griff hustling Pettibone along with them. Jack said, "All clear. A stairway leads to the next level. I didn't want to go past that without Pettibone as a stalking horse."

Griff looked around, his eyes glittering slits, his shoulders hunched as if anticipating a blow. He said feelingly, "What a creep joint!"

Rowdy said, "What is this dump?"

They all spoke in hushed voices. Jack said, "It's a fallout shelter for surviving an atomic war. Must've been built a half century ago."

Rowdy said, "Man, I'd rather get nuked than live in this mausoleum!"

Griff said, "Hey, did you dig that golf cart?"

"Beats walking through the tunnel."

Jack said, "It's a good way to bring supplies in, too. Like bombs and gas grenades."

They went to the far end of the bunker and stood at the bottom of the stairwell. Griff said, "What's on the other side of that door?"

Jack Bauer said, "The showdown."

• •

THE FOLLOWING TAKES PLACE
BETWEEN THE HOURS OF
1 A.M. AND 2 A.M.
MOUNTAIN DAYLIGHT TIME

• •

Sky Mount, Colorado

Reb Weld did not handle frustration well. He was an action man; he liked to be up and doing. Standing around waiting did not sit well with him. Delay irritated him, especially when it involved matters over which he had no control. He was a control freak, too. He said, "What's the stall, Al?"

Grant Graham started at the sound of Weld's voice. He was standing next to Weld, but he'd been watching Al Baranco rigging the timed detonator to the last set of explosive charges. He was so caught up by Baranco's air of methodical concentration that it came as a jolt when Weld spoke up, shattering his reverie.

Baranco labored on, doing what he'd been doing, giving no sign that he'd heard the Rebel's words.

Graham flinched, said out of the side of his mouth, "Take it easy, Reb."

Weld said, "Screw you, Graham." He spoke in a normal conversational tone, contrasting with Graham's husky prison-yard whisper. Graham had taken falls on several felony counts and spent years in Federal penitentiaries.

Talking out of the side of his mouth so only fellow inmates could hear him and prison guards couldn't had become second nature to him. He'd carried the habit with him even though he was outside the walls. Being within arm's length of enough explosives to blow him to atoms as he now was only intensified this habitual trait.

Weld said, "Get with the program and shake a leg, Al."

Graham said, "Reb, please—"

"Shut up."

Al Baranco stopped what he was doing, namely attaching a wire to one of the terminals on the timing device. The device was the size and shape of a paperback book. It had a matte black plastic casing. Its face had a digital display slot screen and a numerical keypad with some additional buttons. Twin terminals protruded from the top of the case above the readout screen, small brightly polished metal knobs with little caps that screwed on or off.

Baranco held a pair of needle-nose pliers that he was using to strip the insulation off the end of one of the wires leading to a packet of blocks of C–4 plastic explosives that had been taped together.

He paused but did not look up. He said, "It's unwise to distract a man when he's setting a bomb timer, Reb."

The mansion at Sky Mount had two underground levels that were officially in use. The one nearer to the surface held storerooms of various types. Food supplies, an extensive wine collection, glassware, table settings, and the like were only a few of the commodities that were resourced there, along with a treasure trove of paintings, statuary, antiques, and other art objects that had been removed from permanent display upstairs and put in storage on Level One.

Level Two, the subcellar, housed the vitals of the mansion, the all-important mechanisms and support systems that kept it going. Here were the banks of fuse boxes, meters, dials, and relays that monitored and controlled the countless miles of electrical wiring that made up the great house's nervous system. Here were the hydraulic pumps and pipes that kept the plumbing running smoothly everywhere from the sinks in the custodians' supply closets to the outdoor Olympic-sized swimming pool—as well as the slightly smaller indoor heated pool.

Here were the boilers and furnaces and fuel tanks that gave the mansion its heat and hot water. This last was the target of Reb Weld and his associates. Sky Mount was equipped with three fuel storage tanks, each the size of a railroad freight car and filled to the brim with heating oil. They stood lined up in a row in a sunken area at one end of the subcellar.

Each tank rested on its own cradle, an intricate webwork of cross-braced metal beams and struts that held them suspended above the floor to allow workmen access to their undersides.

Reb Weld, Graham, and Baranco were grouped alongside the tank in the middle. The other two tanks flanking it had already been rigged with explosive charges. The middle tank had been gimmicked like the other two with blocks of C–4 plastic explosives in the critical junction points that would rip their bellies open and ignite their contents into a colossal firestorm of holocaust proportions.

It was a laborious, time-consuming process. The blocks of plastic explosives and the detonators had previously been stored in the fallout shelter below, an abandoned area whose existence was known only to a few. Reb and his crew had spent the night hand-carrying the blocks up the stairwell and through a secret door near the fuel tank area.

They'd been planted on the undersides of the tanks.

All three sets of charges were separately wired to a single master detonator-timer.

This had been done to save time that would have been eaten up by fixing each load with its own individual timing device and to limit the exposure time of Weld's team in the Level Two area.

Three sets of wires fed into a trunk cable. Baranco was wiring the cable to the twin terminal posts of the master timer. It was set to go off at three o'clock in the morning, when an electric charge would pulse down the trunk cord and along the three separate sets of wires whose detonator tips would simultaneously explode all charges and blow the tanks and the great house above it to kingdom come.

Once Baranco was done wiring and setting the master timer only one final task remained: to switch on the timer on a smaller charge attached to a crate holding the remaining BZ gas grenades. They'd been placed near a ventilator intake grille at the base of a metal conduit duct air shaft. The bomb would be set last but would go off first, at 2:50 A.M., ten minutes before the oil tanks blew.

The green gas would be sucked into the ventilator intake shaft to circulate throughout every room in the mansion, spreading madness and chaos. The pandemonium would have time to reach a crescendo of artificially induced psychotic frenzy among guests and staffers alike before the bombs on the oil tanks blew. The sequence was designed to maximize the body count.

The bombs would ignite a firestorm of volcanic proportions, spewing a flaming geyser upward that would scour the underground levels before rupturing the ground floor and fountaining a white-hot inferno throughout the great house.

The devastation would be awesome, the casualties immense, and the repercussions catastrophic to the nation and the economies of the world.

Reb Weld was looking forward to it. His only regret was that he wouldn't be able to view the spectacle firsthand. Chaos and destruction were his delights. Why? Because that's the way he was made.

It wouldn't be smart to stick around and watch the show, though, much as he'd like to. Or healthy, either. Not with that crazy green gas heralding the apocalyptic hellstorm.

Baranco was the demolitions expert. That action was out of Weld's league. He had to stand by, watch, and wait while Baranco worked his black art.

It was necessary but Weld didn't have to like it. He wasn't called "the Rebel" for nothing. He resented taking a backseat to anybody, especially the so-called experts who knew more about a subject than he did.

He'd always been that way, it was his singular defining trait. That and a mean streak as wide as a sixteen-lane superhighway.

He couldn't resist needling Baranco even as the bomb man was engaged in the tricky and delicate work of rigging the last fuel tank bomb. He did it because it was risky and pushed the edge, giving him a fresh jolt of the adrenaline he so inordinately craved. He was an adrenaline addict.

He'd even considered pilfering a BZ grenade from the crated cache to take with him as a souvenir. It'd be a kick to get a taste of the gas itself and see what the head was like. The survival instinct reasserted itself, overpowering that compulsion for crazy kicks. A BZ grenade would be his ticket to the execution chamber should he be caught with it, especially after tonight.

Baranco said, "I'll get on with my work now if that's all right with you, Reb."

Sarcastic bastard! Maybe there'd be a chance to cut him down to size later when his tasks were done. But not now.

Weld said, "Go ahead, nobody's stopping you."

Baranco kept pushing it. He was a needler in his own soft-spoken way, too. "I'd appreciate a little quiet while I'm fixing this last connection. If my hand should slip . . ."

He didn't have to finish the sentence.

Weld said, "I'll be quiet as a mouse. Not a peep out of me, Al."

"Thank you very much, that will be deeply appreciated."

Baranco set the pliers down in his pocket tool case

and began unscrewing the knob at the top of the terminal, preparatory to winding the hooked end of the exposed copper wiring at the base of the post.

And then his head exploded.

Jack Bauer had been standing on the top landing of the fallout shelter stairway with one hand gripping the back of the collar of the shirt that he'd scrounged up at the Mountain Lake substation to replace the garments that Griff had cut off Pettibone. Pettibone had to look normal to deceive his accomplices, or as normal as he could look even when fully clad. Jack's other hand gripped the SMG.

Griff and Rowdy crouched a few steps below him, ready to spring into action. Rowdy had been convinced of the inadvisability of bringing along the riot gun and had stowed it aside at the bottom of the stairwell for retrieval later. The bikers were armed with SMGs and a few handguns and knives were also tucked away on their persons.

Jack said, low-voiced, urgent, "Go!" He prodded Pettibone in the kidneys with the tip of the weapon to reinforce the command.

The door opened outward onto the landing. Pettibone gripped the doorknob, turned it, and pulled it toward him. The door accessed a tiny vestibule with another door at the opposite end. That door opened on to a Level Two walkway overlooking the sunken area where the fuel tanks were located. The sunken area was five feet below floor level with sets of stairs at each corner and bordered by a waist-high rail fence.

The far door was wide open. Jack hustled Pettibone through it, following at his heels. Griff and Rowdy were a pace or two behind.

A man on the walkway was starting toward the vestibule at the same time. He was Loogan, one of Weld's men. He'd been posted to secure the exit and had heard the sound of movement behind the inner door. He was advancing on it as Pettibone, with Jack behind him, came rushing out.

Loogan fired, his silenced SMG sounding a whispered stutter as it loosed a burst into Pettibone's middle. Pettibone fell back, writhing against Jack as the slugs tore into him. His last conscious act in this world was to serve as an unwitting, unwilling human shield for Jack Bauer, catching the full measure of Loogan's triggered slugs.

Jack got his gun hand free and returned fire, stitching Loogan up the middle of the chest. Loogan dropped, his weapon clattering against the walkway. The telltale sound was lost in the vastness of the space, drowned out by the background noise of throbbing pumps and creaking pipes.

Jack eased Pettibone to the floor and stepped around him. Pettibone's popping eyes stared sightless and unblinking as he sprawled inert on the walkway.

Griff and Rowdy came barreling out of the vestibule. Jack held a finger to his lips, signaling for silence. The bikers halted, charged up, kill-ready. The walkway overlooked a long side of the sunken floor, running parallel to the long axis of the nearest tank.

Jack said in stage whisper, "I'll go down here and come on them from under the tank. You go around and pin them from opposite ends." They nodded.

Jack clambered over the guardrail and dropped catfooted to the sunken floor five feet below. Griff and Rowdy were in motion, scrambling in opposite directions, hustling toward the corners of the tank pit.

Jack slipped across the space to the first tank with shadow stealth. The rigging under the tank was a webwork of black metal beams, braces, and diagonals. The underside of the tank was held suspended in its steel cradle about four feet above the floor. He ducked under the outside rail and began moving forward in a crouch, bent almost double, picking his way through the labyrinth of the undercarriage.

He went as fast as he could but his progress seemed maddeningly slow, with time measured out in every pounding heartbeat. His whole body quivered in anticipation of a shout, a shot, or a scream that would alert his prey to the fact that they were being stalked and hunted.

The steel net let light pass through it screened through a tangle of black beams. He stepped over some, ducked under others. The swelling curve of the cylindrical tank pressed downward as he neared midpoint, forcing him to drop to hands and knees to proceed. He banged his knees, barked his shins, bruised his elbows, and bumped his head in his hurry to gain ground.

The ceiling lifted as the midpoint was left behind and the tank curved upward. The smell of fuel oil was thick in his nostrils and mouth; he could taste it. The layers of cross-bracing between him and his goal thinned, allowing him to see more of the gap between the tank he was under and the one in the middle.

Silhouetted forms flashed ahead and to the right of him. The rise and fall of voices made themselves heard over the pounding of his own pulse that throbbed in his eardrums. Jack forced himself to slow down though it was torturous to fight the overpowering urge to rush into battle. The setup was all-important and he had to be in the optimum position before cutting loose. A misstep could be fatal not only to him but to hundreds of innocent lives.

He hoped with all his being that Rowdy and Griff were taking similar pains. No outcry or outburst had sounded as yet so perhaps they were. Jack couldn't wait for them to shoot a move, though; he had to seize and keep the initiative.

The trio came into his view, grouped in the open area between the tanks and a dozen paces to his left. He crept forward, inching closer.

Reb Weld with his signature platinum-blond crew cut stood a half a head taller than his sideman, a chunky character with a brown rooster-tail haircut. They both stood watching a third man who knelt hunched over on the floor with the master timer in one hand and the exposed copper wiring of the trunk cable bundling all three detonator wires to the different sets of charges in his other hand.

Jack Bauer went down on one knee, resting the silenced muzzle of his SMG in the V made by the intersection of two cross-braces to steady his aim as he lined up the sight posts on the skull of the explosives expert. He set the selector to single shot for better accuracy and rechecked his alignment to make sure he was on target.

Weld was bickering with the demolitions man. The expert was saying sarcastically, "Thank you very much, that will be deeply appreciated."

Jack squeezed the trigger.

A single cough sounded simultaneously with the top of Al Baranco's cranium flying apart. The explosives expert's head was haloed by the corona of pink mist indicative of a brain being blown to pieces.

A perfect head shot, drilling the brain, switching off all neuro-muscular reflexes and reactions, ensuring that Baranco would cease to exist without so much as a twitch.

Things happened fast after that.

Somewhere on one of the walkways there was a startled outcry of pain, a stuttering exchange of gunfire, and a scream.

Al Baranco dropped. Reb Weld and Graham recoiled from the stinging spray of disintegrated bits of bone and brain matter that had spattered them when the slug fragmented Baranco's head above the ears.

Jack flipped the selector to autofire. Graham stood between him and Weld. Jack fired a burst that chopped Graham. Graham threw up his hands over his head and shrieked as the legs were cut out from under him.

Reb Weld was quick! He dove forward away from the gunfire, going into a roll and tumbling out of it before Graham hit the floor. He leaped to his feet and lunged sideways, gaining the cover of one end of the oil tank behind him for protection.

Jack snaked out from under the tank, standing upright in the gap between the tanks. Graham lay rolling around on the floor, beating his hands against the upper thighs of his now useless legs as if they were on fire. Jack stood over him, firing a quick burst into Graham's chest. That switched Graham off but Jack put a few more into his head to be sure.

Reb Weld was racing toward the wall at the end of the sunken floor when Griff popped up at the railing of the walkway above. Both men opened fire at the same time.

Griff missed but Weld didn't, tagging the biker

twice. Griff went over backward. Weld tossed back his head and gave a rebel yell of exaltation as he reached the wall and jumped up grabbing for the guardrail.

Jack's burst caught Weld in the back in midair. Weld fell back, crashing to the sunken floor. The SMG fell from his grip and went skittering away from him, out of his reach. Weld rose on his elbows, a bloody smear marking the floor where his back had touched it. He reached for his waistband, clawing at the butt of a gun tucked in the top of his pants.

Jack advanced on Weld, methodically spraying him with autofire. Weld flopped around as the bullets ventilated him.

He weltered in his own gore, tiger-striped with blood. He raised the back of his head off the floor, neck muscles cording and quivering from the strain of trying to see who had done him in.

Griff rose to his knees on the walkway, clutching the rail to keep from falling while he watched Weld's finish.

Jack moved so Weld could see his killer. Weld's eyes widened, then narrowed as he recognized the CTU agent he'd come face-to-face with in the clearing on Pine Ridge before fate had taken a hand by intervening in the form of a charging bear.

He mouthed the word, "You!"

Jack Bauer said, "The Hellbenders send their regards."

He delivered the coup to de grâce to Reb Weld:

A head shot.

Griff had caught two slugs, one in the right side and the other in the left shoulder. He draped his arms over the bottom rail to hold his upper body upright while he stared down at a torn and bloody carcass that used to be Reb Weld.

He held out a red hand to ward off Jack when the latter moved to help him. He managed to choke out a few sentences between gasps and stifled groans.

Griff said, "I'll make it—Rowdy must've ran into trouble—check on him . . . The big slob was never any good without me."

He added after a pause, "I'll stay here and enjoy the scenery."

Rowdy had run into trouble. He sat on the opposite walkway, back propped upright against the wall. His right arm was at his side, outstretched at the elbow, his hand wrapped around the grip of a still-smoking SMG. His midsection was a red ruin of an anatomy lesson. His left hand held his insides back from tumbling out.

Incredibly he still lived, awareness in his eyes as Jack went to him.

A body lay nearby, twisted in the angular contortions of violent death: the last member of Reb Weld's elite hit team. He lay facedown, reaching for a crate of BZ gas grenades that lay inches short of the fingertips of his clutching hand. A shiny sheet-metal, square-sided length of duct conduit piping was bolted vertically to the wall above the crate, its scooped-mouth bottom covered by a metal grille and hanging two or three feet above the top of the grenade-laden box.

It was the intake port of a ventilator air shaft. Jack Bauer could feel the suction of air currents being drawn upward into its mouth and away through the piping to be carried through the precincts of the mansion above ground.

Jack moved the crate a man's length away from the intake port. A wad of C–4 plastic explosive was wedged into the bottom of the crate, wires trailing up from it and over the side waiting for a timing device to be attached. He gingerly disengaged the tip of the detonator cord from the puttylike mass, disarming it and setting the cord a safe distance away from the crate.

He hunkered down beside Rowdy, leaning forward to catch the big biker's last words. Rowdy said, "Bad luck—he got me before I could get him. Thought I was dead . . . got a big surprise when he found out I wasn't . . ."

His tired eyes cut a glance toward the BZ crate. "Guess you found what you wanted, dude . . ."

He breathed something that Jack was barely able to make out: "Valhalla is calling—"

His last breath.

Jack Bauer defanged the plastic explosives rigged to the fuel tanks, pulling the detonator cords, gathering them up, and depositing them in a safe place on the walkway. He went to see what he could do for Griff. Griff was sitting up, holding a wadded bandana against the wound in his side and using it for a compress.

He said, "Rowdy . . . ?"

Jack said, "He got his man before he died."

Griff nodded. "He went out Hellbender style then."

"That he did. I'll get help. Don't shoot any of my people when they come down here to secure the site."

"I'll try not to."

Jack opened his mouth to say something, but before he could, Griff said, "That's a joke, man. Just pulling your chain . . . go do what you have to do, I'm okay."

Jack started to walk away. Griff called after him, "Kill 'em all!"

Jack turned, said, "I'll do my best." He moved on.

He went to a stairwell that accessed the next level. He found a morbid surprise at the foot of it. Two bodies lay there where Weld and his crew had put them, undoubtedly intending to come back and carry them topside to the surface and plant them somewhere on the grounds to be found and scapegoated in the aftermath of the horrific hellfire that turned out not to be.

They were the cadavers of Abelson Prewitt and Ingrid Thaler, the grandmaster of the cult of the Zealots and his faithful second-in-command. The bodies were cold to the touch—icy—frozen.

Another piece of the puzzle had fallen into place.

Jack Bauer loaded a fresh clip into his SMG before beginning the long, wearying climb upstairs to the surface.

Don Bass exited a side door in the mansion, hurrying along a flagstone path that curved through silent, nighted gardens toward the guesthouse that served as the command center for the Brand Security Agency cadre overseeing the corps of uniformed and plain-clothes guards now on duty on the graveyard shift.

Sleep and the security chief were strangers. Bass's wavy hair stood out in tufts. His eyes were red embers buried deep in hollow, purple-bruised sockets. His movements were stiff-legged, zombielike as he forced himself to scurry at quick time toward the guesthouse turned guardhouse.

A figure stood outlined in the open front doorway waiting for him. It was Larry Noone, Bass's top man and figurative right hand, the man whose urgent phone call summoning his boss had jarred Bass out of fitful light sleep and back into action on the double.

Bass was not so tired, however, that he failed to notice the white armband prominently pinned to the upper arm of Noone's navy blazer. Bass paused at the threshold, clutching the insides of the doorframe with both hands for support while he tried to catch the breath that his hasty arrival had stolen from him.

An expression of concern marked Noone's face. "Are you all right, Chief?"

Bass blustered it out, barking, "Certainly! Just a little winded, that's all. I hustled over here after I got your call. Sounded urgent. What's up?"

Noone said, "Come in and I'll tell you."

Bass marched into the front hall, turning left to follow Noone down a short corridor. The heart of the command center lay on the other side of a closed door at the passage's end, in a room that was an electronic nerve nexus of computerized consoles whose multiscreens imaged real-time feedback from the array of closed-circuit automated TV cameras that kept the mansion and estate under constant surveillance. A graveyard shift of six top operatives would be posted at the monitors, orchestrating the flexible and adaptive Brand Security defense posture.

Bass, frowning, said, "What's with the white brassard, Larry? It's unauthorized as far as I know."

Noone glanced over his shoulder, flashing an enigmatic half smile. "Change of policy."

Bass's frown deepened. He was a stickler for detail. He said, "That's news to me and I set dress code policy."

Noone paused with his hand on the doorknob. "Step right in, Chief, and it will all be explained to you." He opened the door partway, standing aside so Bass could pass him and enter.

Bass was through the doorway and a half-dozen paces inside the command center before the horror of what he saw registered on his benumbed mind.

It was the scene of a massacre. All six board operators, male and female alike, lay strewn about the room in the places where sudden death had found them. Their bullet-riddled bodies bore wounds so numerous that they could only have been inflicted by an automatic weapon. They were torn and tattered. Blood was everywhere. Walls and consoles were cratered with bullet holes.

Don Bass was struck dumb, paralyzed with shock. A timeless interval passed before he drew a shuddering breath. His heart started beating again, hammering with a wild percussive rhythm.

Somehow he managed to turn around and face Larry Noone. Bass was surprised to find that he was not surprised at all to discover his second-in-command pointing a leveled machine pistol at him. There was a certain pride that his deductive and analytical faculties had not deserted him in the fractional span of life left remaining to him to glory in their possession. Noone had to be the killer; his bland demeanor in the face of such carnage proved it.

A distant part of Bass's mind kept on working,

noting that the machine pistol was fitted with a suppressor to silence its workings. It would have to be, since it was the weapon that Noone had used to treacherously slay the comrades and coworkers who trusted him without betraying the deed to the numerous guards stationed on the estate.

Don Bass asked only a single question: "Why?"

Noone shrugged, quirking a whimsical smile. There was an oddly elfin aspect to the big man, with his too-large knowing eyes, mouth upturned at the corners, and slightly pointed chin. Don Bass realized that the person he'd worked with, played with, and with whom he'd shared a good part of his adult professional and personal life was a complete stranger to him.

Noone said, "Call it a coup d'état. Change of power. I'm in. You're out. Way out." He held the gun pointed so it would shoot Bass in the belly where it hurt the most.

He said, "Christ! You can't imagine how long I've waited for this day—this night—this moment. I'm enjoying it so much that I hate to see it end."

Noone sighed. "But all good things must come to an end. If it's any consolation to you, Chief—and I'm sure that it's not—you can go to hell knowing that in a very short time you'll have lots of company when Sky Mount and all its lovely creatures go up in flames. I only regret that you won't be here to see it."

He added, "Die hurting, Chief."

Don Bass laughed out loud, a genuine guffaw at the bizarre turns of fate and reversals of fortune that could occur to a man not in a lifetime, but in a handful of seconds. He experienced an explosion of mirth that left him grinning from ear to ear.

Larry Noone arched an eyebrow, surprised by the other's outlandish reaction at the point of death. He wasn't sure what he'd expected from Bass at the finish but it wasn't this. He shrugged it off. "Hysteria. The mind is going. This will be a blessing for you, Don."

Bass said, "Buddy, you're about to find out how right you are."

"Oh really—?"

Larry Noone didn't live long enough to find out the truth of his words. He fell forward facedown to the floor, stone dead. The back of his head had been shot away by the burst of rounds Jack Bauer put into it at point-blank range, disintegrating the rear half of his skull as if it had been scooped out and exhibiting the gooey gray matter that remained.

Jack stood slumped against the doorframe, leaning against it for support. He let his gun hand fall to his side, holding the still smoking SMG that he'd used to liquidate Larry Noone.

Jack said, "Sorry I didn't get here sooner. I saw you running out the side door of the mansion and played a hunch that I'd better follow you and see what's what."

Don Bass said, "Lucky for me that you did."

"Luck is the difference between hanging and not hanging. I know."

"You heard everything?"

"Enough." Jack Bauer glanced at a wall clock. "Five minutes to two. Time enough for you to tell your gate guards to open up and let Garcia's tac squad in."

1 2 3 4 5 6 7 8 9
10 11 12 13 14 15 16 17
18 19 20 21 22 23 **24**

. . . .

THE FOLLOWING TAKES PLACE
BETWEEN THE HOURS OF
2 A.M. AND 3 A.M.
MOUNTAIN DAYLIGHT TIME

. . . .

Sky Mount, Colorado

Ernie Sandoval said, "You wrecked the Mercedes, you SOB."

Jack Bauer said, "Get Garcia to buy a new one."

"He just might, after this one is all wrapped up."

Don Bass chimed in, "Hell, I'll buy you one."

Sandoval said, "You can't afford it."

"The Masterman Trust can. Let them pick up the tab."

Jack nodded in agreement. "That's the spirit."

The trio were walking briskly side by side down the main corridor of the mansion's east wing. Bass had a set of keys in hand that would open the anteroom doors and the door to Cabot Huntington Wright's inner sanctum, but as it turned out they weren't needed. The anteroom door was unlocked. The room was dark, but light outlined the closed door to Wright's suite of offices.

A platoon of Orlando Garcia's tac squads augmented by an equal number of Inspector Cullen's ATF agents were swarming the estate, securing the grounds, mansion, and all-important subsurface levels where the BZ grenades and plastic explosives lay, defanged for the moment but very much a potential and potent threat until the moment that agents took possession of them, and that moment was right now.

Jack Bauer's focus lay elsewhere, on the dozen quick paces it took him, Bass, and Sandoval to cross the anteroom to Wright's private door. His hand was on the knob, and to his surprise it turned freely and he opened the door and stormed in, the other two at his heels.

Jack said, "You left your door unlocked, Mr. Wright. Careless of you."

Cabot Huntington Wright was at the opposite end of the room, standing behind his desk, stuffing folders of documents into a briefcase that stood open on his desktop. He froze at the trio's entrance, lifting his gaze from what he was doing to the intruders who'd had the audacity to invade his domain.

He looked away first, oddly abashed to be taken in such a manner. His hands were hidden behind the lid of his attaché case, which stood upright.

Jack's hand flashed inside his jacket, coming into view with a pistol that he held pointed at Wright. Wright raised his arms in the classic hands-up position, obscuring but not hiding the white armband circling his dark-suited left arm.

Bass said, "The white brassard! That clinches it."

Jack circled around the desk, still covering Wright. Wright's hands were empty of everything but foldered documents but Jack was taking no chances. He said, "It's already clinched. It was clinched when Chappelle notified Garcia that he'd found the leaker—and the person to whom he'd leaked."

Sandoval had given Jack a quick update on the way to Wright's office. Ryan Chappelle had discovered that a member of his CTU/L.A. staff had passed the word about Brad Oliver's imminent arrest. A survey of regional division headquarters' phone logs had unearthed the culprit, one of Chappelle's top aides. The leaker had confessed when confronted but claimed he had no other motive than to curry favor with the ultra-rich and powerful Cabot Huntington Wright by giving him a friendly heads-up to prepare him for the embarrassment and disruption that would result when Wright's confidential assistant Brad Oliver was arrested by CTU agents for violating the national security.

The leaker's true motive would eventually come to light in the exhaustive investigation to which he'd be subjected. What was key was the identity not of leaker but of leakee. Chappelle tried to notify Jack Bauer to alert him to the identification but he'd been unable to reach him while Jack was otherwise engaged.

Chappelle had finally swallowed his pride and relayed the information directly to Garcia, enduring the humiliation of having to admit to a longtime rival that one of Chappelle's own was the guilty party. The facts were too vital to withhold, and Chappelle put the potentially career-damaging revelations in

Garcia's hands, oblivious of how the hierarchs on the seventh floor at Langley might put a black mark in Chappelle's record book because of the dereliction of a trusted aide.

Chappelle was a patriot, and Jack had never doubted that ultimately he would do the right thing and disseminate the information where it would do the most good. But timing is everything, and Jack was heartened that Chappelle had acted sooner rather than later—for later might have been too late.

Jack Bauer now had the guilty party in hand and there was a standard operating procedure for the way things are done no matter how big the culprit is. Jack set the process in motion.

He said, "Please stay where you are, Mr. Wright, and keep your hands up. You're about to undergo what's sure to be a novel experience in your life: being searched for a weapon."

Wright affected a wry smile. He'd never quite lost his composure from the moment the trio barged in to confront him, but he had lost some of his color, the skin blanching and paling under his deep tan. Now the pallor was starting to fade and the color was returning to his cheeks.

Jack gave him a pat-down frisk, feeling around him for a concealed weapon. Jack was taking nothing for granted; for all he knew Wright might have a weapon on his person. It was that kind of a case.

Sandoval searched Wright's briefcase while Jack searched Wright. Wright said, "Don't you want to search, too, Don?"

Bass shook his head. "I'm private, I don't have jurisdiction. They do. You belong to the United States government now."

Jack said, "If not for a little bit of luck it might have been the other way around." He finished his search, said, "He's clean."

Sandoval said, "Nothing in his briefcase but documents."

"I'm sure the analysts will be interested in them."

Wright said, "I'm sure. May I put my hands down now, gentlemen? I confess that the posture is becoming something of a strain."

Jack said, "Go ahead. You can sit down, too—on the other side of the desk. I don't know what kind of gimmicks you might have built into it but I don't intend to find out the hard way."

Wright smiled with seeming affability. "My, my. Paranoia must be the prime attribute of a government snoop and spy." He went around to the front of the desk and made a show of seating himself comfortably in one of the plush visitors' armchairs.

He tapped a forefinger against the side of his forehead. "My weapons are all in here."

Jack said, "Your checkbook is your weapon, and with it you damned near took over the U.S."

"By the way, am I under arrest? And if so, what are the charges?"

"Yes—Cabot Huntington Wright, you're under arrest for conspiracy to commit treason and terroristic acts against the United States of America."

Marion Clary entered at that moment. Her hair was in disarray, she was without makeup, and her attire showed signs of having been thrown on at a moment's notice. Her demeanor varied between confusion and great distress. "Mr.—Mr. Wright? What's going on here?"

Wright rose when she entered, favoring her with

a courtly little bow. "Ah Marion, right on time as always. In case you hadn't heard, I'm being arrested for crimes against the state."

Her dominant motif turned to one of outrage. White circles showed around her eyes, and her face suddenly looked strained and haggard. "Is this some kind of a grotesque joke?"

Wright said, "Grotesque it may be, but it's no joke, I fear."

Marion Clary swayed, looking as if she might faint. Don Bass rushed to her to steady her, said, "Marion, please sit down."

She turned on him, tearing her arm free of his supportive grasp. "Keep your filthy hands off of me!"

He said, "Please sit down."

She stared at him, rigid with indignation. Wright indicated the armchair beside his, said, "Marion, yes, please do."

She staggered like a sleepwalker to the chair and plopped down in it. Sandoval crossed to the office door, closed and locked it. He said, "We don't need any more interruptions."

Wright said, "Now that I've been arrested, will you read me my rights and allow me to speak to my lawyer? One of my many lawyers?"

Jack smiled tightly. "Nice try, Mr. Wright, but in cases involving acts of terrorism the normal rules are suspended and don't apply."

Wright's smile could have passed for one of genuine pleasure. "Ahhhh . . . so that's how you work it."

"That's how the system works. But never mind about that. Let's talk about how you worked it."

"You have the floor, Agent Bauer. I'm all ears."

Jack moved around to the front of the desk, resting his hip on the corner of it. He began, "I suppose in the long run it'll all come down to the question of sanity. Speaking for myself and not as a mental health professional, I believe that you are sane."

Wright looked more pleased than ever. "Thank you, sir!"

"You're an amoral sociopath but that doesn't read as insanity in my book."

Wright's mouth downturned in a little moue of displeasure. "Now now, no name calling. Surely we don't have to descend to that."

"Call it what you like. You're not the first person to see something he wants and do whatever it takes to get it no matter who gets hurt or what the consequences. You just do it on a more grandiose scale. Otherwise you're no different from the thief who knocks an old lady on the head for her social security money."

Wright nodded, putting his hands together and making a steeple out of them. "I see. At least I've graduated from amoral sociopath to mugger. That's progress, I suppose. And what is the object of my heart's desire?"

Jack took the question seriously. "The United States of America. For starters. Beyond that, who knows? Tomorrow—the world?"

"You're telling it. Please continue."

"My pleasure. In the last twenty-four hours I've had a crash course in the theory and practice of Cabot Huntington Wright as applied to the deadly arts of conspiracy, subornment, corruption, violence, terrorism, and mass murder. You might say I've had a total immersion in the dark side of Wright, the side nobody is supposed to see."

"I daresay that qualifies you as an expert, Agent Bauer."

"I daresay," Jack said dryly. "Let's get back to basics. Crime is a matter of means, motive, and opportunity. Start with motive first. You saw a way to make yourself master of the United States. By that I mean you hatched out a scheme to destabilize the economy, bring it to its knees, and take over the nation's leading corporations at fire-sale prices."

Wright nodded encouragingly, a schoolmaster listening to a prize pupil recite his lessons. "And how was I going to achieve that ambitious goal?"

"The old-fashioned way: murder. Murder and money. It all stemmed from your unique position as chairman of the board of the Masterman Trust. That and your role as director of the yearly Round Tables, a gathering of the richest and most powerful of the land under one roof. Your roof."

"Ah yes, the illustrious Round Table. My arrest will come as a great shock to them, all those dynasts and heirs and movers and shakers who've known me as a trusted friend and confidant over these too many years."

Jack quirked a smile. "They'll get over it, especially once they learn what you had planned for them—death by hallucinogenic gas and inferno."

Marion Clary leaned forward in her seat, her hands balled into fists that perched on her upper thighs. "You're insane, positively stark staring mad!"

Jack let it pass, speaking directly to Wright. "I once read that the emperor Caligula expressed the wish that all Rome had but a single head that he might strike it off with one blow."

Wright said definitively, "Caligula was a piker. Strictly small potatoes."

Jack took note of that remark. Perhaps the smooth facade was starting to crack and the real Cabot Huntington Wright emerge. "You went Caligula one better. You gathered up the people who collectively own a majority share of the real wealth in this country—stocks, bonds, real estate, the corporations that keep the wheels turning—and planned to murder them all in their beds and loot their assets at the same time.

"Stealing what isn't yours is the motive. The means were two-fold, financial and homicidal. The financial aspect is your territory, and I'll outline it quickly for the record. You've been betting a hundred million dollars on the swift, sudden downfall of the national economy. You're the spider at the center of a global web of misdirection and deceit. Using an arsenal of financial gimmickry such as dummy and shell corporations, third-party transactions, and the like, you've been short selling an astronomical amount of stock. I'm no financial wizard but I know what that means. My boss Ryan Chappelle is a wizard with the numbers and he explained it to me.

"You bet a fortune that the bottom will fall out of the U.S. economy. If you win, your short selling of stocks will reap you many fortunes. The economy is already so shaky, all it needs is one good push to send the house of cards tumbling down. You decided to supply that push."

Wright harrumphed. "In all fairness, you'll have to admit that the economy is doing an outstanding job of bringing itself down."

"Yeah, but you wanted to take a chainsaw to it. Mass murder is the push. That's where the Round Table comes in. All the heads and majority stockholders of the biggest corporations gathered in one place. Their sudden, violent deaths would deal the economy a body blow, triggering a financial panic that would make the Crash of 1929 look like a one-day selloff in the market. Stocks would plunge to a fraction of their worth. Universal bankruptcy, mass insolvency. And there you'd be with a mountain of money reaped from your short-selling gamble that the economy would suffer such a catastrophic loss—no gamble, but a sure thing.

"With all that cash in hand you could acquire a controlling interest in every corporation in every sector of the economy worth owning: utilities, insurance, energy, health care providers, software, manufacturing, you name it. The whole enchilada. And you'd have it all. Overnight you'd become the uncrowned king of the United States—king by fact if not by law or title. Master of a financial empire that no king, emperor, or mogul even dreamed of."

Wright was unflappable. "A not unworthy ambition, if I say so myself. In all due modesty."

Jack challenged, "Why be modest? Caligula was a piker—so you said. He would have given his eyeteeth to have an axe like the one you created, designed to lop off the heads of all those friends and confidants who've trusted you over the years."

"Do tell."

"An axe made not of finely honed steel sharpened to a razor's edge but of people. Bad people. As choice a crew of thieves, sadists, and killers as ever labored for the hidden puppet master pulling their strings.

People like Brad Oliver, who handled some of the financial aspects of your dirty work."

Wright pulled a long face and looked sad. "Ah yes, poor Brad. Such a tragic death, so untimely a loss to one of the brightest rising stars in the fiscal galaxy."

Jack snorted his derision. "I bet. What happened to Brad? Did he get greedy seeing all those vast sums he was in the process of making for you and decide to feather his own nest? Your super-scheme for shorting was slick and stealthy but his pint-sized version to invest a few million of his own on the coming apocalypse was rushed and clumsy. His junior league manipulations showed up on Chappelle's radar screens because that's just what Ryan was looking for, smelly investments made in a hurry on the basis of foreknowledge of imminent catastrophe. Once Chappelle gets a whiff of something like that, he keeps digging into the numbers until he finds out the real score. Oliver's heavy-handed shorting is what put CTU on to the plot against Sky Mount in the first place."

Wright couldn't have been cooler. "Brad's one overriding fault, and I say to you what I would not hesitate to declare under oath in any court in the land, his great sin was avarice. Greed, pure and simple. He overreached himself and paid the price."

Jack countered, "Thanks to you he did. When you found out that his arrest was imminent you greased the skids out from under him, virtually literally. You tipped him off that we were coming to apprehend him, knowing that he would do what he did: take it on the run. Only before you went to him you made sure that one of your hatchetmen had arranged for Mr. Pettibone and his Deathmobile to be outside the gates waiting for him. When Brad tried to make his getaway, Pettibone ran him off the road on a thousand-foot drop to his death. Exit Brad."

Wright made a face. He was really enjoying himself now. "Dear me! Did I do all that? I'm afraid you'll have some difficulty proving that in court, Agent Bauer."

"Don't be so sure. Look at Marion Clary. She looks like she might be remembering something she'd seen but thought nothing of at the time. Like you having a private little chat in your office here with Brad right before he went out and got smeared all over the eastern slope of Mount Zebulon?"

It was a shot in the dark, but Jack figured it was worth a try. The first mention of Oliver's name had triggered a fidgety restlessness in Marion Clary, an agitation that increased as Jack explicated the mode and manner of Oliver's death.

Cabot Huntington Wright condescended to glance at the receptionist. What he saw there compelled him to take a long second look. She openly fretted, chewing her lower lip, her expression stricken, wounded.

He said, "Marion, dear, surely you don't give any credence to this preposterous twaddle?"

She held herself so tightly that it looked like her neck cords would break. Her eyes were open, staring into space. She shook her head with short, tense movements. She said, "Believe it? Of course not! But—but you did call Brad into your office yesterday afternoon to speak with him, and when it was over he had the most dreadful look on his face and he rushed off like a crazy man and drove to his death—"

"Pure coincidence. Brad had a guilty conscience because he feared his financial chicanery was about to come to light. He ran away and had the misfortune to suffer a terrible fatal accident due to his own carelessness and innate dishonesty."

She turned hurt eyes on him. "Cabot, how can you speak so cruelly about poor Brad, who never deliberately hurt anyone in his life?"

"Honesty compels me to speak the truth." Wright tsk-tsked. "I can't believe that you'd be so credulous as to listen to the ravings of this prosecutorial young man. I'm disappointed in you Marion, very disappointed."

She wasn't listening to him. Jack wondered if she was listening to an inner voice instead. He decided to press on. "That brings us to the other edge of your double-headed axe, Mr. Wright. Oliver was the financial edge. The homicidal edge was Larry Noone.

"Noone was a driving wheel in your murder train. He was perfectly placed to do so. As a high-ranking executive of the Brand Agency, Noone had access to his own private intelligence network, one rivaling any in the public sector and less hampered by red tape. By delving into the Brand computerized files he could learn with a keystroke who was dirty, who could be corrupted and who couldn't. Bribe takers, thieves, prostitutes, deviants, strong-arm goons, and contract killers, all listed there in the files. All he had to do was call them up and dangle the baited hook of Cabot Wright's money in front of them.

"It was Noone who found and recruited Reb Weld, using him to assemble a small army of hired killers. Noone who had all the inside information on security arrangements for the Round Table, allowing Weld and friends to circumvent them. Noone who murdered the board operators in the Brand command center tonight to allow Weld and his killer elite to plant bombs and poison gas in the basement on Level Two to blow up the fuel tanks to create a raging inferno to kill hundreds of innocent men, women, and children and burn Sky Mount down to the ground!"

Wright said acidly, "Of course it's in your interest to blacken the character of poor Larry Noone, considering that you're the one who killed him. That, my dear young sir, is not a tower built on groundless speculation and absurd hypothesis but a fact!"

Marion Clary recoiled as though she'd been struck. She said in a whisper that trembled on the edge of a shriek, "Larry Noone is dead, too? My God, no!"

She covered her ears with her hands to keep from hearing any more. Cabot Wright sat back in his chair, favoring Jack with a richly supercilious smile.

Don Bass went to Marion Clary. His expression was compassionate as he gently but firmly took hold of her thin wrists and eased her hands away from her ears. He said, "Marion, you must listen to me. I've never lied to you and I'm not about to start now. As the Lord is my witness, less than an hour ago Larry Noone held me at gunpoint and was about to kill me. This man Jack Bauer saved my life, and that's the honest truth."

Ernie Sandoval had sat silent for a long while taking it all in. He now spoke up. "It's a time for truth, Marion. You can't stick your head in the sand and hope it goes away. Tell her, Jack. Tell her what Cabot Huntington Wright was going to do to destroy her beloved Sky Mount!"

That caught her attention. Her head jerked slightly to one side and her eyes took on a glazed expression. "Cabot Wright . . . destroy Sky Mount?"

Jack picked up the ball. He addressed his words to Wright, aware that Marion Clary was following them with a dreadful avidity. She could be a key witness in any future trial of Wright; her testimony could be invaluable if she could be convinced to give it freely.

Jack said, "That brings us to the third leg of our murder triangle. Remember, means, motive, and opportunity. The means was money and the people it could buy, whether it was Brad Oliver and his financial sleight-of-hand or Larry Noone and his hand-picked assortment of killers.

"The motive was money, too, money and power, with one nightmarish catastrophe that would make Cabot Huntington Wright richer and more powerful than any other man in the history of the world.

"That brings us to opportunity. Like so much else in this case, opportunity wears more than one face. I've already mentioned the opportunity of having the movers and shakers of the national economy conveniently gathered together under one roof to make a big, fat target. But there's another face to that opportunity, one that is and could only be known to a select handful of persons, and you, Mr. Wright, are the most select of that select few."

"You flatter me, Agent Bauer."

"No I don't, not really. I'm just telling the plain truth the way the facts add up. The fact is that there is one secret that you are in a prime possession to know. It's the old story of the Trojan horse: the enemy was already in the citadel, hidden where no one would ever suspect them. With the Greeks and the Trojans it's a wooden horse. With you and Larry Noone's murder squad, it's a fallout shelter built long ago beneath Sky Mount that the world has forgotten but the few remember.

"A fallout shelter built at the height of the nuclear jitters of the Cold War era. A bunkerlike fortress that accesses Level Two through secret doors and hidden passages. A shelter with an escape route in case Sky Mount should be bombed flat and the shelter inhabitants unable to dig themselves out from under a mountain of rubble. So the builder created himself an escape route, drilling a tunnel through and out of a rock spur of Thunder Mountain into a little high mountain valley named Winnetou.

"The escape route, like the shelter itself, was a closely held secret. The creator didn't want the public to know about it. In case of a threatened atomic attack he'd be besieged by hordes of neighbors and strangers all wanting to escape annihilation by holing up in the shelter, too. That wouldn't do, so the shelter was kept secret and the escape route was hidden to look like part of the mountain so no outsiders would ever dream of its existence!

"What happened then? I'm guessing here, but we'll find out the facts soon enough. The builder died, the shelter entrances and exits were sealed and forgotten, and the few others who knew the secret mostly died out. But who would be better placed to know the secret or rediscover it than the Lord High Executor of the Masterman Trust, the master of Sky Mount itself, you, Cabot Huntington Wright!"

Jack Bauer waited for Wright to respond but it was Marion Clary who reacted first. She stood up suddenly, the light of a massive revelation seizing her with an irresistible force.

She blurted out, "It's true! There is an abandoned

fallout shelter hidden under Sky Mount! It was built in the nineteen-fiftics by F. X. Masterman, the last surviving heir to descend directly from old H. H. Masterman, founder of the family fortune. Francis Xavier Masterman was an eccentric with an obsession about surviving an atomic war. He spent a fortune building his shelter and escape routes. After he died the family wanted nothing more to do with F.X. and his sensational bad publicity so they capped the tunnels, sealed the hatches, pretended it wasn't there, and forgot about it.

"I know about it because I'm the archivist and knowing the history of Sky Mount is my life's work. I know it, yes—but how do you?"

Jack said seriously, "I know it, Ms. Clary, because I've been there. Just tonight I took the grand tour of it to keep a gang of murder-happy psychos from using it to blow up the fuel tanks and turn the mansion into an infernal holocaust! Where did I learn of it? From a sadistic killer named Pettibone who killed that nice young man Brad Oliver and who knows how many others.

"The big question is, who did he learn it from? From his boss, an even worse killer, who learned it from Larry Noone, who learned it from Cabot Huntington Wright! Unless you told Noone—"

"No," she said firmly, shaking her head. "I've always respected the family's wishes for privacy and kept the truth about the shelter a private matter and never spoken of it to any outsiders."

She was holding her body so tight that instead of turning her head she turned her entire body so she could look down at Cabot Wright and stare him in the eye. She went on, "I've never spoken of it to outsiders, but I have gone into detail about it on more than one occasion with my employer, Mr. Wright!"

Wright literally tried to wave it away, dismissing it with a flicking gesture of his hand. "Marion, you're becoming seriously overwrought. I begin to fear for your state of mind."

"You—you would have helped to destroy Sky Mount? All those innocent human lives? All those priceless art treasures?"

"You're being ridiculous, dear. Sit down and take a pill to relax before you give yourself a nervous breakdown."

Cabot Huntington Wright was beginning to show the first signs of agitation. He was restless, unable to sit still. He kept crossing and uncrossing his legs and squirming around in his seat as if unable to get comfortable.

Marion Clary ignored his advice. She did not sit down or take a pill. She stood her place, staring accusingly down at Wright.

Wright turned to the others as if unable to face her stare. "Do you see what you've done, gentlemen—and I use the term loosely—with your monstrous fabrication of lies and half truths, slurs and innuendos? You've driven this poor, simple soul nearly half mad with hysteria!"

Jack Bauer said softly, "Maybe she's starting to realize the truth of what you've done, Mr. Wright. The lies and scheming, the conniving at murder, and more: wholesale mass murder!"

Wright affected an air of extreme nonchalance bordering on indifference. He studied his carefully manicured fingernails, flicked an imaginary spot of dust from his lapel. But he was watching Jack out of the corners of his eyes.

Jack ignored Wright's smooth front and kept hammering his points home. He said, "Speaking of opportunity, that brings up one last important element in your master plan. It was a lucky fluke but you saw it lying there and picked it up for your own use. I'm referring to the presence of Abelson Prewitt and his inner circle of Zealots at the compound at Red Notch. Every conspiracy needs a fall guy, a patsy who can be blamed for the crime, and Prewitt was ripe for the taking. It's the time-honored ploy known as 'Pay the Law.' Give the authorities a ready-made scapegoat for the crime and the manhunt ends. Otherwise they'll keep on looking and possibly even stumble across the real culprits.

"Prewitt was your scapegoat. He was a crackpot cultist who hated the Round Table and all that it represents. There was no real history of violence in his background, but that was no problem. A lot of these cults go on their own way for years before reaching the breaking point and lashing out with overt acts. Prewitt's crank economic theories and overheated rhetoric made him perfect for framing.

"The plan was to lay the blame for the Sky Mount terror strike on Prewitt and his cadre. To carry that out they first had to be disposed of. The Mountain Lake MRT unit did the advance work. They'd all been suborned into working for the plot, bought and paid for. I'm guessing that Larry Noone handled that part of the operation. I wondered how the activity at Winnetou could have gone unreported until I found out a little while ago from Agent Sandoval that Hardin's MRT had the responsibility of patrolling that area and consistently gave it a clean bill of health.

"Red Notch was hit early Thursday morning. The MRT did the advance work of neutralizing O'Hara and Dean, the ATF agents monitoring the compound from the outside. Hardin and Taggart got the drop on the unsuspecting agents and put them out of the way. That left a clear field for Reb Weld's kill squad. They blitzed the compound with BZ gas grenades, the potent hallucinogenic gas incapacitating the cultists. A hermit who witnessed the assault said that it was carried out by 'hog-faced demons.' Hog-faced demons—that's what the killers in their gas masks looked like to him. He wasn't so far off the mark at that.

"The round-up of the Zealots didn't come off without a hitch. There was violence, some blood was spilled. Those bloodstains held the telltale chemical markers allowing for the identification of BZ as the chemical weapon agent. The cultists were herded onto their own bus and driven out to Silvertop in Shadow Valley to be disposed of. All but two of them were slaughtered and dumped down the air shaft of an abandoned mine, their bodies covered with dirt to make sure that they wouldn't be found too soon.

"Prewitt and his top lieutenant, Ingrid Thaler, were killed, too, but their bodies weren't dumped with the others. They were taken to the base camp at Winnetou and kept on ice for future use. I came across the ice chest that had been used to keep the corpses in cold storage at the camp but didn't know what it was for until later tonight. It wasn't until I found Prewitt and Thaler's bodies in Level Two that the significance of the ice chest became clear to me. The cadavers had been frozen to disguise the true time of their death. They were going to be planted outside the mansion to be found in the aftermath of the destruction. By then the heat of the firestorm would have warmed them up.

"Prewitt and Thaler being found dead at the scene of the crime would have clinched the case for the Zealots' responsibility for the terror strike. It would have been open and shut as far as the authorities and the public were concerned and no one need look any further into the matter. A crazy cult would have been blamed for the head shot that took down the national economy.

"Only it didn't work out that way. The strike was thwarted and now we know the real mastermind behind the plot was you, Cabot Huntington Wright!"

Wright was squirming. He'd been unable to sit still as Jack Bauer drove home his summation. He now made a visible effort to regain his self-possession.

Wright tried another tack. "Theories are all very well, Agent Bauer—in theory. But proving them in open court is another matter. Let us suppose for the sake of argument that your allegations against me are true? How do you propose to prove them?

"Brad Oliver is dead. Larry Noone is dead. Going by your theory that I used them as middlemen and cat's-paws to, how did you say it, get my dirty work done, how can you prove it? They can't testify, and by your own logic they're the only ones who could have tied me to these sordid murders and theft of Army secret weapons and legions of hired killers and whatnot. Proof. That's what you've got to have and that's what you lack."

Jack pounced on something Wright had let slip.

"I never said anything about Army secret weapons and neither did anyone else. That statement was volunteered by you and I call on everybody else in this room to witness that you said it."

Wright stifled a yawn. "Did I say it? I suppose I did. A man in my position, who meets so many four-star generals, politicians, financiers, defense contractors—yes, and intelligence professionals, Agent Bauer—is liable to hear all sorts of things."

He leaned forward, poking his finger in the air to make his point. "You might say that it was, er, just something in the air. Something in the air that made me chatter idly of Army secret weapons. I might even have heard a rumor about a cache of experimental drug gas that was inexplicably lost, stolen, or strayed somehow. These things get around. Perhaps I discussed the subject during an idle moment with Larry Noone.

"What of it? You can make nothing of that, not in any court in the land. I'm no illegal alien whose head you can throw a black hood over and transport to Guantanamo Bay to torture into signing a confession. I'm an American citizen—an extremely wealthy one, need I add? You'll find it very difficult to tie a tin can to this old dog's tail, Agent Bauer."

Jack said grimly, "You underestimate the effectiveness of the American government, Mr. Wright. An army of civil servants thinking about you every waking hour of the day and minutely examining the fine details of your public and private lives can unearth a hell of a lot of data about secrets, lies—and truth."

Wright laughed. "And you underestimate the power of my attorneys, Agent Bauer. My army of high-powered, high-priced attorneys and their inexhaustible battery of legal tactics and tricks."

He rose. "No, you've got nothing on me—nothing you can prove. Go ahead with this farce of an arrest if you like. My lawyers will have me free and on the street before dawn. Not the street, actually, that's just a manner of speaking. Shall we say, out of jail and in the penthouse?"

The unexpected happened, the unpredictable variable that no one can factor into his calculations. Jack Bauer never saw it coming and he wondered later, even if he had, would he have tried to stop it? He thought not.

But he didn't see it coming and neither did anybody else in the room, least of all Cabot Huntington Wright.

Marion Clary without warning seized up a letter opener from the top of Cabot Wright's desk and with a shrill, wordless screech buried it deep in his chest.

She cried, "It's true! True! True!" She stabbed Wright once with each cry, driving the daggerlike letter opener into his chest and neck.

Ernie Sandoval and Don Bass rushed forward to grab her and wrestle the weapon away from her even as Wright folded at the knees, sagging to the floor and sprawling across it, spilling his lifeblood into the deep pile carpet that greedily absorbed it just as it had tenderly cushioned his fall.

Red blood—not blue.

The best physicians were called, of course, but it was too late. One of the thrusts had pierced his heart, and he died within minutes of the assault.

Marion Clary, dazed by her own violence, kept repeating, "I had to do it, he had to be stopped . . . I had to do it. No one else could stop him, the monster . . . I had to do it. He had to be stopped."

She was still repeating it when a pair of white-coated orderlies came to take her away. They were very gentle with her. She would need gentleness.

Don Bass said, "I promise on my honor I will move heaven and earth to see that she never spends a day of her life in jail."

Jack Bauer said, "She won't—I promise you that."

Ernie Sandoval said, "If we had any guts we'd pin a medal on her."

Jack shook his head in wonderment. "The ways of fate are strange. Did you see what she stabbed him with?"

Don Bass said, "The letter opener?"

Jack said, "The antique letter opener that once belonged to Marshal Fouché, Napoleon's spy chief."

He stroked his chin thoughtfully. "The old king of spymasters reached out from beyond the grave on one final mission of righteous retribution!"

Sandoval said, "Amen to that, brother."

Don Bass shook his head. "You fellows are kidding yourselves. It's just coincidence, that's all. Sheer blind luck. She wanted to strike out and picked up the first thing that came to hand."

Jack Bauer laughed, a little self-consciously. "I know what I think. You can think what you want, Don. You can do that. It's still a free country.

"At least for today it is," he added. "That'll hold us till tomorrow."